CHERRY PICKED

A SUNDAY BROTHERS NOVEL

MAY ARCHER

Cover Design: Cate Ashwood
Cover Photo: Michelle Lancaster
Cover Model: Thomas James
Editing: The Amazing Sandra at One Love Editing
Alpha Reading (as well as all PnP quotes, all PnP-variation inspiration, and all the best ideas): Lucy Lennox
Beta Reading: Shay Haude, Leslie Copeland
Proofreading: Victoria Rothenberg, Lori Parks, Jodi Duggan

All the good bits are theirs, and any mistakes are my own!

PROLOGUE
HAWK

*It is a truth universally acknowledged that a reader in possession of
a good book must be in want of an interruption.*
~ Hawk Sunday, January 2016

HIDING in plain sight had always been my superpower.

"Haaaaawk?" my little sister singsonged from the living room doorway, not realizing that I was a mere two feet away from her. "Hawkins Sunday, my favorite brother in the whole entire universe? Hawk, pleeeeease? Come out, come out, wherever you are! I have the teeniest, *tiiiiiniest* little favor to ask you!" she called, clomping up the stairs.

I stuffed a Thin Mint into my mouth and grinned as I pulled the giant quilt more firmly over my head, snuggled deeper into the sofa cushions, and turned the page of my new book.

I loved my family—*truly* loved them. I would happily take a bullet for Emma, or my uncle Drew, or any of the four giant lummoxes I called my big brothers.

I delighted in helping them with their school projects and their town committees, with chores around Sunday Orchard, or, in Drew's case, with finding the keys and reading glasses he misplaced on the daily, usually somewhere on his person.

But a seventeen-and-a-half-year-old man had *needs*, damn it. Specifically, in this case, the *need* to eat this last box of Girl Scout cookies I'd been saving since a ravening horde of Sundays had descended like locusts and eaten all eleven of the other boxes I'd purchased, the *need* to not venture into the January sleety-rain combo for anything less than a life-or-death emergency, and the *need* to find out if the dastardly George Wickham would actually gain control of heroic, deliciously broody Mr. Darcy's estate after committing Darcy to Bedlam, or if the intrepid Miss Elizabeth Bennet, racing across England in a stolen phaeton, would arrive to save the love of her life before time ran out.

"Henry Hawkins Sunday! I know you're around here somewhere," Emma called again, her heavy snow boots pounding back down the stairs.

"Hey, hey. What's with the racket, sister?" Drew asked, meeting her in the hallway.

"Porter texted the family group chat that he lost his snow pants and ski gloves, and he wants to borrow Hawk's," Em said. "And Webb called 'cause he's bringing a friend over to go snowshoeing, and he says it's about time Hawk got some fresh air 'cause he's probably looking peaky. And *I* wanted to ask Hawk to take me to get ice cream at Scoops since he bought himself a car and everything now." She heaved the put-upon sigh of the unlicensed. "But he's off somewhere reading his books again."

I glanced up from said book, scowled at the inside of the blanket, and angrily shoved more cookies in my mouth. Em said the word *reading* in the same tone of voice one might say *preg-checking the cows* or *plucking the slugs from the cherry trees*.

The trouble with being in a family of lumberjacks (plus one aging hippie and a pint-sized wilderness warrior) was that all of them would rather be slathered in jelly and tied to an anthill than spend a full day indoors, so they couldn't imagine why I would.

Not long ago, I'd loved the outdoors, too; hiking had been a thing my dad and I did regularly. But the appeal of the activity had died with my dad. Shortly thereafter, I'd learned of the existence of *Pride and Prejudice* variations—not to be confused with the actual OG *Pride and Prejudice* because the original was still the best—and *voilà*. Instant love affair.

There'd been no going back for me.

But no matter how many times I tried to explain my fascination—the plots and the symbolism and the *love*—none of them seemed to get it.

"Don't need to worry about some character's love life, Hawklet. Got enough problems of my own," Webb would say with an impatient grunt.

"But it's fiction," Emma would say, wrinkling her nose. *"Why read about that stuff when the world's full of catastrophes and people who need help?"*

"You've been eating processed food again, haven't you?" Drew would sigh, like perhaps my strange affliction would subside if I'd just commit to eating more quinoa.

They all missed the point entirely. Of *course* the world was full of real troubles—earthquakes and political upheaval and pre-calculus tests I was doomed to fail; guys who were too gorgeous and wonderful to acknowledge my existence, and others who didn't want to take no for an answer; chores to do, and college to consider, and a sweet baby nephew who needed attention; and dealing with all of that while carrying the last name Sunday, which meant something when you lived in the gossipy confines of my beloved Little Pippin Hollow, a town so tiny they put *Little* in the name.

Who wouldn't want to escape into a world with a hard-won, well-deserved, guaranteed happily ever after?

And processed food is tasty, I thought as I shoved another cookie in my mouth.

"Poor kid," Drew said sadly. "He has at least three nice young men who'd love to take him out if he'd just crook a finger in their direction, but Corinne Perkins told Dottie French she'd heard from Camille—her niece, you know?—that Hawk says he's saving himself for something special."

"I say he should spend more time with his friends," Emma decided. "He's got bunches of 'em."

I rolled my eyes. Yes, I did, and I liked them a lot… but sometimes, it felt like my friends didn't always understand me any more than my family did.

Feisty but perfectly polite Elizabeth Bennet, on the other hand… Now, there was a woman who understood what it was like to have expectations on your shoulders. Elizabeth Bennet knew what it was like to have high standards for one's romantic partners. Elizabeth Bennet understood what it meant to have…

"Aha!" Emma yelled, snatching my blanket off my head triumphantly. "Gotcha!"

… really annoying *siblings*.

"Hey." I blinked innocently, shoving my cookies behind the sofa cushion before Emma could see them. "Hi. Fancy meeting you here."

"Hawkins, man." Uncle Drew shook his shaggy gray head. "What are you doing?"

"Just… you know… chilling. Pondering life. Deep philosophical questions. Like, should your lacrosse team really be selling wrapping paper for their fundraiser again, Em? Because I tried my hardest last year as the fundraising volunteer, but the Hollow is really more of a 'chuck it in a gift bag with some tissue paper' kind of place. Don't worry, I'll come up with a better idea for this year." I tapped my temple. "Best leave me to it."

"Why don't I believe you?" Emma set her hands on her narrow hips. "You think you'll find the answer in..." She grabbed my hand and turned my book over to read the title. *"Mr. Darcy's Wild Ride: A Romance Novel?"*

"Hawk." Uncle Drew narrowed his eyes and leaned closer to me. "Why do you have chocolate dust on your mouth?"

"Uh..." I licked my lips. "Well, actually..."

"And you smell like *artificial mint flavoring,*" he accused.

"Fine. Fine!" I jumped up from the couch and stood beside the sofa. "I was eating cookies and *reading,* okay? I admit it. Reading is not a crime, people! It's not a sign that I'm bored or depressed. It is not a cry for help. I'm not secretly longing to run an errand or do a chore. I do *not* want to slog through the snow to get ice cream—an activity, I might add, that runs contrary to millions of years of human evolution. I do not wish to eat quinoa. I have no desire to clomp through a snowy field, working up a sweat that will freeze to my body instantly while trying to keep up with Webb, whose legs are way, way longer than they have any right to be—"

"Er. Hawk, maybe now's not..." Drew began in a placating voice, looking over my head like he couldn't even meet my eye.

"Now is the perfect time!" I insisted.

It took a lot to get me angry, but once I was riled up, my frustrations needed to be vented entirely before I could move on.

"Look, I could be spending my days doing truly terrible things. Like... like..." I searched my brain for the worst crimes I could think of. "Shamelessly pilfering someone's precious boxes of baked goods, even though they'd taken the time to hide them in eleven different places throughout the house! Or, worse, toying with men's affections, leading them into dalliances, and then ruining their reputations forever before casting them aside."

"Hawk," Emma said, low and insistent. "You need to chill. *Now.*"

But I was beyond chill. Chill had deserted me along with my peace and quiet.

"I'm not a monster, you guys! I'm simply a man attempting to read a library book in solitude. If I could," I said passionately, "I would have a library of my own. A whole room filled with books. And a sofa. And cookies. A room whose function was specifically and solely to do my very favorite activity so that no one ever needed to look for me or wonder what I was doing because everyone would know. *Hawk is in his reading room*, you'd all say, and you'd say it respectfully, because when a whole room is dedicated to a task, suddenly we realize it's important. But for now, I do what I must. And I don't need everyone and their freaking uncle getting up in my face with their *delightful* suggestions for what I ought to be doing instead. And *yes*," I said, pausing long enough to draw a deep breath, "I'm using implied air quotes because none of your suggestions were at all remotely—"

"Uh. So. This is my family, Jack," Webb said from behind the sofa, startling the crap out of me.

Mouth still open, I whirled around, grabbing a pillow from the sofa as a makeshift shield.

There in the doorway stood the most enormous of my four giant brothers, looking amused and disapproving and a little embarrassed. Beside him stood a man—a man nearly as tall and broad as Webb—with blond-streaked hair, startlingly blue eyes that crinkled with intelligent good humor, and the most engaging smile I'd ever seen on another human being.

"*—delightful*," I finished in a whisper that came out all croaky and weak.

The man—Jack—lifted his hand in a little wave as he stepped further into the room, and for some stupid reason, my heart clacked unevenly around like a carriage on a rutted road.

I'd known I was gay for a while, but until that moment, sex had been kind of an abstract thing for me. Men were pleasant to look at and daydream about. Some, like Matthew Macfadyen in that *Pride and Prejudice* gazebo scene, made my pulse beat concerningly fast. Others, like Kyle Silverbow in my chem lab with his perfect pouty mouth, made me wonder distantly what kissing would be like and whether, if I were to mash our lips together, I'd be able to taste the grape bubble gum he always chewed.

This, though… this was different. This was *real*.

Not just a vague awareness of attraction but a bone-deep, skin-tightening need. A visceral *"Yes. This one. This man. Him."* that made my lower belly cramp with want and my fingers itch to touch.

A sexual awakening on a whoooooole other scale.

And for the first time in my Elizabeth-Bennet-loving life, I was feeling some distinct sympathy for her boy-crazy sister Lydia, because if *this* man asked me to run off with him, I'd be all, "Fuck, yes. Elope me, baby. How fast are your horses?"

Which was unfortunate, really, since the object of my newfound desire was a full-on adult of at least twenty-five years old or maybe even… *thirty*.

Still, I stood up a little straighter, wishing I was wearing something besides flannel sleep pants and a T-shirt, and ran a hand over my hair, hoping that, for once, the waves would be obedient and stop attempting to defy gravity at every turn.

"Sorry about that," Webb went on. "Jack Wyatt, this is my uncle, Drew Sunday. My sister, Emma—she's twelve. And… the ranting guy with the pillow shield is my youngest brother, Hawkins. He's seventeen."

"And a half," I whispered, still staring at Jack. No one heard me.

"I promise it's not usually quite this loud around here..." Webb said with a little chuckle.

Jack shook his head. "Heck, no. Don't apologize for Hawk. I don't have any siblings, myself, but I get pretty passionate about my peace and quiet, too." He aimed that smile in my direction—*click*—then fired off a teasing wink—*boom*—that shot directly through my heart. "That's why my mom and I moved down from Portland a couple months back."

Drew stepped forward, extending his hand. "Jack. You're the one who opened the new deli in town."

"Diner and sandwich shop, yeah," Jack agreed. "My mom suggested calling it Panini Jack's, but I'm not a hundred percent sold yet."

"How are you liking the Hollow?" Drew asked. "Big change from Maine?"

"In the best way. I already feel more at home here than I ever did there." Jack rocked back and forth on the balls of his feet. "Housing prices are affordable—I'm looking to find a fixer-upper I can really put my stamp on, you know? And everyone's been so *kind*. I've had two folks offer to cut me deals on produce for the restaurant this summer, Randy Justis from the Wing Factory brought me my favorite Girl Scout cookies, the mayor's wife came by to add my birthday to the town's Birthday Committee list, and one woman came by to measure me for a hand-knit sweater. I don't even think she said her name."

He sounded so bewildered and thrilled that I couldn't help smiling sympathetically.

"That'll be Helena Fortnum," Drew said, rubbing his chin. "She's a Hooker."

Jack blinked. "Uh. I don't know about that. This woman was older. Seventy or eighty, at least—"

"A Little Pippin Hooker," Em explained. "That's our local fiber arts group. She crochets."

"Ah." Jack nodded. "That makes more sense."

"What, um… what flavor were the cookies?" I blurted, because important facts were important.

Jack turned those blue eyes back on me. If he thought my question was seven kinds of weird, he didn't say so. "Thin Mints? I can bake my own cookies, of course, and I do, but there's something about the artificial mint flavoring, you know?"

Drew made a disapproving noise, but I nodded in complete understanding.

Webb clapped a hand on Jack's shoulder. "Jack's been so busy getting things set up he's hardly seen any of the actual sights around here, so I'm taking him out snowshoeing today. Next week, we might go for a hike if the weather cooperates. He's never seen a falcon before."

"It's a little early for falcons," I cut in. "They're usually not around much until March. But once spring comes, a whole bunch nest up on Fogg Peak. If you take the Hunter Trail to Glassy Ridge, there are nesting boxes maybe a quarter mile below the summit for the kestrels."

"Oh, that's right," Webb said. "I forgot you and Dad used to hike up there, Hawklet."

"All the time, rain or shine," I agreed. "We used to go lots of places. There's more than a hundred trails around Little Pippin Hollow, and they each look different depending on the season, but the trails up at Fogg Peak are the best. In autumn when the leaves turn, it's like being inside your own personal kaleidoscope."

Jack's smile grew until it was deep enough for a person to fall into and lose themselves forever. "Wow. That sounds amazing." He turned to Webb. "You guys'll have to show me."

"Sure thing." Webb bumped Jack's shoulder back companionably, and I felt a jolt of acute jealousy that my very straight brother did not deserve. "We'll make it a family affair. Em will come, won't you, Em? And Drew, you'll be up for it? I bet we can even get Porter—he's the fourth-oldest of the six of us —to make an appearance."

"And I'll go," I offered, clutching my pillow more tightly.

"You will?" Emma said dubiously. "But you just said—"

"*Pfft.* I know what I said." My cheeks went hot. Honestly, *siblings.* The one time they listened and remembered what I said was the one time I wished they wouldn't. "This is different. It's about welcoming Jack to town and showing him around. So."

"Hawk prefers *reading,*" Em explained apologetically. "Specifically, *Pride and Prejudice* retellings—hundreds of versions of the original, just with minor plot differences. He told me one day he wants to go to the Lake District in England so he can see Pemberley, the house where Jane Austen lived."

Wonderful. Just… terrific. She couldn't have made me sound more like a loser to this gorgeous man than if she'd said *we let him out of the attic occasionally.* I was *never* taking her for ice cream again.

"Pemberley is where Darcy, the hero of the book, lives. Not Jane Austen," I mumbled, shooting Emma a dark look she seemed impervious to. "And I'm sure Webb's friend doesn't want to hear us going on and on about this."

Emma, of course, ignored me. "Do you like reading?" she asked Jack.

Do you live in an attic, too?

"Oh yeah. Mostly thrillers. Can't remember reading *Pride and Prejudice,* though, let alone any retellings." Now Jack sounded apologetic, like he knew he was missing out, which was… kind of adorable. "If I haven't read the original, I bet the retellings wouldn't make much sense."

Despite the fact that I'd resolved to keep my mouth shut and not incriminate myself further, I couldn't let this misapprehension stand.

"Oh, no, that's not true at *all,*" I said fervently. "When you read the variations, you start to pick up on the story anyway. And it's really quite simple. Elizabeth Bennet, the main character, is one of five sisters. And when a couple of hot, rich single guys—including the swoony Mr. Darcy—come to their small town, her matchmaking mother loses her mind. And Lizzy and Darcy fall in love, but not really. He's like *omigod, her family is awful*. And she's like *omigod, why is he such an asshole?* And circumstances try to keep them apart for, like, the whole book, but there's all this unresolved sexual tension, and they keep coming back to each other, and in the end, *spoiler*, love wins out, which is so great because not all of us are gorgeous or rich, but all of us can aspire to find..." I coughed lightly, realizing everyone in the room was staring at me with various degrees of *what the fuck* in their expressions. "Anyway."

Jack alone didn't seem distressed by my geekiness. In fact, his smile went even brighter than before. "How cool! I like when people are unapologetically enthusiastic about their interests and opinions."

"Oh, then you're gonna *love* Hawk," Emma said dryly.

"Alright, leave your brother alone, Emma," Drew said—about ten damning minutes too late. "Let me find my dang keys, and I'll drive you to Scoops."

"On top of the breadbox," I called as he walked down the hall to the kitchen.

Webb wrapped an arm around Emma's shoulders. "Come help me find the snowshoes in the front closet. You were the last one to use them."

After they left, Jack and I stood in our spots, regarding each other awkwardly—or at least *I* was awkward. Jack looked incredible... which I'd bet was kind of his default state.

"Um. So." I looked around the room for anything to talk about that wasn't me being a giant nerd fully manifesting his first major crush. I spied the hint of green cardboard poking up from behind the couch cushion, seized the cookie box, and thrust it at him. "Thin Mint?"

"Whoa. This your secret stash?" Jack asked as he took one from the sleeve. "I'm honored."

I huffed. "Kinda. I have a lot of hungry brothers."

Jack inspected the cookie thoughtfully. "You know, Hawk..." he began in a fake-casual voice that wasn't remotely casual. "You don't actually have to come hiking if you don't want to. I won't take it personally. I meant what I said before. It's cool to like what you like. Don't let anyone make you feel bad about it."

"Yeah, well." I shrugged. "Easier said than done."

"Maybe, yeah. But in the future, you'll find people who appreciate you for who you are. And all the things that make you feel like you don't fit now? Those are the very things those people will fall in love with when the time is right." He popped the cookie in his mouth and made an appreciative humming noise.

Like cookies were what was important in that moment.

My stomach fluttered. Something warm and vibrant and real uncurled in my belly. And something that was not a crush—was *so much more* than a crush—flared to life.

"You think?" I asked softly.

Jack gave me another of those friendly, offhanded winks. "Guarantee it."

"Right. Well. That's..." *Going to fuel a lot of my dreams for the next little while,* I thought. "...good to know," I managed to croak out. "But I like hiking, too. Or at least I used to. Maybe... maybe I will again."

"Awesome," Jack said, like it was just that easy. "I look forward to it, then."

Uncle Drew had been right earlier. I *had* decided that when it came to sex and relationships, I was going to hold out for someone special. And maybe it was the *Darcy's Wild Ride* talking or the vast quantities of cookies I'd consumed, but for the first time, I thought maybe I'd found him.

My future, my happily ever after, was written right there, in the curve of Jack's smile, in his patient eyes, in his broad shoulders.

Jack Wyatt was my Mr. Darcy.

And if I held on—and held *out*—long enough, eventually, he'd see it, too.

CHAPTER ONE

JACK

"I have not the pleasure of understanding you."
~ Mr. Bennet

Seven Years Later

"So then Elizabeth suggests they take a walk in the garden, but any savvy reader knows that means get away from Mrs. Bennet so they can have privacy, right? But, like, this is one of the *steamy Pride and Prejudice* variations, so it actually means she wants a kiss..."

I grinned as I picked my way across some knotty roots on the trail, letting Hawk's words wash over me. We'd covered hundreds of miles together over the seven years of our friendship, through winter snowdrifts and scorching summer heat waves, but no matter where we went, there was always this—the tenor of his voice as he recapped his latest *Pride and Preju-dice* variation, the steady crunch of his feet on the path at my side.

Life in the quiet town of Little Pippin Hollow, Vermont, turned upside down and inside out with a regularity I hadn't foreseen when I'd moved here. My restaurant profits fluctuated with the weather, the tourist season, and even the latest dating gossip since nothing brought Hollowans to the table like the opportunity to meddle in their neighbors' love lives. This spring, Stanistead Road had been closed to traffic three days running for an impromptu cow orgy after O'Henry Brush failed to secure the back door of his cattle hauler, and a herd of cranky but otherwise unharmed Guernsey bulls and heifers tumbled out and proceeded to spend the next three days doing, as O'Henry called it, "what the good lord intended." And last February, my straightlaced (and, until very recently, *straight in all the ways*) best friend, Webb, had found himself married to a guy he barely knew and didn't much like, thanks to a pre-Revolutionary War–era town bylaw involving a bugle and an orchard.

Amidst all that chaos, it was nice to know that some things—like cheerful, vibrant Hawk Sunday, our close camaraderie, and our weekly hikes—remained constant and easy.

"Of course she does," I laughed. "Was Elizabeth glove-free in this adaptation? Because if so, I understand why you were dying to tell me about this one. The naked-palm touching got you all hot and bothered, didn't it?" I lowered my voice into a fake-breathless growl. "So *sexy*, Hawkins," I teased.

Hawk made a garbled sound. His foot slipped on some pine needles, and I grabbed his elbow to steady him before he impaled himself on his trekking pole.

"Whoa! You okay?" I smiled down at him. "Maybe we should have postponed our hike. You were just out hiking with the Nature Scouts yesterday, and that's a lot in this heat."

"Huh?" He stared down at my hand, and his cheeks turned cherry red beneath his freckles. "Oh. No. I'm fine. Just momentarily distracted when you said, uh… never mind." He blinked and straightened. "Thanks for the rescue."

I squeezed his arm before letting him go. "Always, Bird."

He gnawed on his lip for a long moment. "Just to say… you don't need to baby me, you know. I'm a grown man."

I couldn't help grinning. Hawk was definitely fully grown, not to mention leanly muscled from hiking and hard work. And even if I couldn't see that truth with my own eyes, I'd know it because he'd repeated it over and over again from the day he turned eighteen. There were very few things that could make Hawk unreasonable or impatient, but growing up as the smallest, quietest brother in his large, boisterous, over-protective family had given him a big-ass chip on his shoulder when it came to being coddled.

Despite knowing this, though, there was something about Hawk—his starry-eyed dreaminess, his passion for the things and people he loved—that had made me want to indulge and protect him from the day we'd met. For some reason, he didn't seem to mind it as much coming from me as he did from his brothers.

"Not babying you, Bird. Would I have you working full-time at my diner, or up on my roof helping me fix my damn chimney, or planning out our hiking routes every week if I didn't have full confidence in your abilities? I just like taking care of you. You're important to me. Nothing wrong with that, is there?"

His expression softened, even as his cheeks went redder. "No. Of course not." He turned back to the trail, wiping his palms on his shorts. "So, um… What were we talking about?"

I stifled a laugh. Hawk had never managed to stay upset for more than ten seconds as long as I'd known him. "Gloves, I think?"

"Right! Yes. Gloves. I can't remember if Elizabeth was wearing them at first. But it doesn't matter because…" He turned back to the trail and resumed his tale, and I tramped along beside him, listening once more.

The July sun was high in the sky now, making the pine-scented air thick and sticky-hot even under the tree canopy.

Maybe half a mile up the mountain, if I remembered correctly from the last time we'd hiked here, we'd pass through the tree line, and the terrain would get considerably steeper before we crested the final rise at Balderdash Peak. Two miles down the mountain, at the trailhead, I'd get back in my truck and remember all the other tasks I should be working on. There were invoices to pay at the restaurant, along with shift schedules to finalize, weekly menus to sort out, and stock to order. I needed to plan the final renovation projects on my Victorian money pit of a house. And my mom's birthday was coming up, so I needed a gift.

But in this moment, I wasn't racing to get to any of those tasks. There was no need to rush or worry. When I was out hiking with Hawk, there was nowhere else I'd rather be.

"So, when they got out to the garden, and they'd walked a fair distance to be out of view of Mr. Bennet's book room, Darcy grabbed Elizabeth's hand and turned her toward him. Then he, uh…" He swiped at a rivulet of sweat rolling down his temple, nearly knocking his eye out with his trekking pole. "He kissed the inside of her wrist."

"Oooh. And I know how much you love when Darcy takes liberties." I grinned. "Hey, let's stop for some water. Your voice is sounding all breathy, and you're wobbling. Heatstroke can really sneak up on you—"

Hawk shot me a sideways look. "No heatstroke. It's just… when I say he kissed her wrist, I don't mean he kissed her like *mwah*, Jack. I mean he… he ran his lips over her pulse and nuzzled her palm. Full-on, like… tongue-mauling her hand. And—"

"Seriously, Hawk, take this." I grabbed the water bottle I'd tucked in the side pocket of my backpack and held it out to him. "You're gasping. Heatstroke…"

Hawk took the water bottle obediently, but he didn't open it. "It's *not* heatstroke! I'm trying to explain…" He exhaled sharply. "See, things ended up getting really fraught. So fraught I thought they were going to anticipate their vows right there in the Longbourn rose garden. But they didn't. Because virginity and all, you know?"

"Yeah. They made a big deal about that stuff back then for no good reason." I rolled my eyes. "The whole concept of virginity as a social construct is weird. I mean, if you're attracted to someone and you care about them, what's the problem?"

"Right. *Right!*" The words came out in a squeak, and I was tempted to grab him by the arm to force him to stop walking and rest. "I'm so glad you agree with me about this! Because in the next chapter, they end up on this madcap carriage trip to Gretna Green in search of Lydia and Wickham, which meant they had to stay at inns along the way and pretend to be married for propriety's sake, and this author used the 'only one bed' schtick, which you know is my kryptonite, and the whole time, they're like, so perfectly suited to one another that the only thing missing is that they're not having sex, and I was ready to throw my book at the wall and scream, '*Dear god, what are you people waiting for?*' You know?"

"Uh-huh. Totally." I kept my eyes trained on the pinecones on the ground—slippery fuckers—and on Hawk's hiking boots. Hawk wasn't watching where he was walking at all now. Someone was gonna fall off the trail if he wasn't careful.

"And then it hit me that *I* was Elizabeth. Elizabeth was *me*. A-and… long story short… What I'm trying to say is…" He sucked in a deep breath and blurted desperately, "Jack, will you please pop my cherry?"

"Whaaa—*ooof!*" My boot slid out from under me, and I lurched sideways.

Hawk spun toward me in surprise, but when he moved to catch me, he caught me in the side with his trekking pole, tangling us together. Time slowed, and for a single moment, I stared into his shocked brown eyes… and then I hit him with the full weight of my body and sent the two of us tumbling into a pile of jagged pinecones just as Conrad and Greta Pilkner rounded the bend coming down the slope.

"I didn't mean... right this minute," Hawk said in a pained gasp.

Okay, maybe *I* was the one suffering from heatstroke. In fact, I had to be. Because there was no way my Hawk, with his wide, innocent eyes and sunshine smile, could possibly have said anything about—

"Cherries?" Conrad shouted in his usual overly effusive manner. "Hawkins, did you say you two were popping cherries? I thought cherry season was over this far north!"

Greta tutted and pulled at her husband's shoulder to whisper something in his ear.

"Ohhhhhh!" Conrad shouted again. "*That* kind of cherry popping." He chuckled. "Well, then. Nice weather for it, boys!"

I glanced down at Hawk. His face was ten serrano peppers on the Scoville scale, and he had pinecone scratches all up his arm. He struggled to pull his pole out from under my leg and ended up elbowing me in the jaw.

If I hadn't already felt like the whole world had tilted on its axis, that would've done it.

"Fuck, Hawk! Stay still. Stay still, dammit." I rolled, trapping his flailing limbs beneath me.

Gretta *tsk*ed as she passed us, dragging her husband further down the trail toward the parking area. "Language, Jack Wyatt! And kindly remember, this is a *public* hiking path!"

I stared after them for a few seconds, waiting for the world to come back into focus, and then Hawk squirmed beneath me—*beneath me*—which was the moment I realized that I was lying fully on top of him, the full length of my body sprawled indulgently over the full length of his.

I stared down into his honey-brown eyes, which were looking up at me with love and affection and—ah, fuck

—*want*. "Shit." I started to roll off him, but he freed his hands and grabbed at my shoulders, holding me in place while blinking rapidly.

"It's okay! Seriously, Jack, I'm fine! Could you just stay still and listen for a second?" He swallowed hard. "Look, I know maybe this is a bit of a, um… surprise? But it doesn't have to be a big deal. It's just… I hadn't intended to stay a virgin this long, and I realized that I keep *reading* about this stuff but never experiencing it, a-and I decided that I wanted to. To experience it, I mean. A-and I've been thinking for a while—kind of a long while, really—that you'd be the perfect person to experience it with. I want it to be… well, not *special*-special, exactly, but… nice. And I know you're not, like, in love with me or whatever…" He bit his lip. "Unless… I mean… Are you, by any chance?"

"What? *No!*" I gasped.

"Right!" he agreed quickly. "No, right. Of course not! *Same.* But sex doesn't have to mean a relationship or love or whatever, right? I just think, in an ideal world, my first time should be with someone I think is really *hot*—which, like, have you seen you?—and also someone I trust, and I trust you more than anyone. So." He shrugged, as much as a person trapped against a bed of pinecones could shrug, and stared up at me beseechingly. "What do you say?"

"*Erk!*" I squawked. My heart was beating in my throat so hard I couldn't get any actual words out. *Was* this heatstroke? Was I hallucinating? Was I dying?

Hawk thought I was *hot*? Hawk wanted…? With *me*?

Hawk continued as if my squawk hadn't been a clear refusal. "Maybe don't answer me now, okay? I know you probably need time to think about it and, like… plan it or whatever. I mean, not *plan* it, plan it, since obviously you know the, ah… mechanics and whatnot. I remember Peter, that smug asshole you dated for a couple weeks last year, bragging about you being a '*demon*' in bed—which, not gonna lie, left me with a whole lot of questions I'd really like you to answer. And Donny Whatshisface, the guy I saw you with at the Stag and Crowne back in March, who must've had, like, forty-seven hands, couldn't stop groping you in public and whispering all the stuff he liked you to do to him in a voice that was *not* a whisper—"

"Hawk," I groaned, my face going hotter than it had been while we were hiking, which was weird because all the blood in my body had rushed south.

"No, right, sorry. Tangent. My bad. Anyway, I was thinking we could get tested… o-or if you'd rather use condoms, I'm open to discussion—"

"Hawk," I insisted, belatedly rolling away to flop onto my back… only for him to sit up and continue talking while peering down at me.

"Okay, maybe not a *discussion*, per se," he said, more desperately than ever, "since clearly talking about this is making you more uncomfortable than Donny with the hands ever did, so you just tell me which you'd prefer, and it's all good with me! See how simple and straightforward this will be? You're basically my favorite person. And we've been friends forever—I'm helping you fix up your house, you helped me with my car when it had that timing belt issue— so, why not help me with this, too?"

"Hawk!" I sat up also, putting more distance between us, not that it did anything to dispel the images that were taking over my brain of all the ways I could "help" Hawk.

"Because you said it yourself, Jack!" Hawk shifted onto his knees, his voice openly pleading. "You said, 'if you're attracted to someone and you care about them, what's the problem?' So, like—"

"*Halt.*" I managed to bark. "Halt this now."

The edge of Hawk's mouth turned up. "Halt? What are you, a castle guard now?"

My head spun, and as it often did, my gaze focused on the

little hoop nose piercing Hawk had gotten a couple of months before. It was oddly delicate, like Hawk himself.

"I mean, please stop doing that mile-a-minute talking thing you do when you're nervous. I just need to think—er, to *recover*. From the fall. And the pinecones. And the... Pilkners. And... Wait. Are you okay? No, you're clearly not okay. Here, take my hand."

I yanked him up so quickly he nearly tumbled into me and sent us sprawling again. Thankfully, he wasn't heavy enough to knock me over the way I'd done to him a few minutes earlier.

"Now who's nervous babbling?" Hawk muttered under his breath. "Yeesh, I asked a simple question..."

Simple? Was he high?

"I'm not taking your vir—*er*... having..." I swallowed thickly around an obstacle in my throat. "With you... the sex," I hissed.

"Jack," Hawk said, soft and rebuking. "You make it sound dirty. I know for a fact that you sleep with people all the time. It's not like I'm asking you to do anything illicit—"

"Sleeping with my best friend's baby brother is plenty illicit!" I sputtered, stomping several feet back down the path before turning to stomp in the other direction. "Not to mention dangerous."

"Dangerous? Sex with me?" Hawk's nostrils flared as he tried to hide a smile, but I knew his expressions too well to doubt what he was feeling. *Amusement*, damn him. "I know I'm a lot younger than you, Jack, but I think you have the stamina to keep up, at least if Peter is to be believed—"

"Not dangerous like that! Jesus. And stop mentioning Peter. Also, my stamina is not an issue, thank you very much," I couldn't help but add before remembering that my sexual stamina was not a thing I should be discussing with Hawk *ever*. I spun around again. "But you *are* a lot younger than me. And Webb might be my best friend, but he'd still murder me and bury me in a shallow grave if I laid a hand on you. Hell, I'd be lucky to die a quick death. More likely, he'd get your brothers to help, like some kind of... fraternal vengeance posse. Webb, Knox, Porter. God, even Reed would make a trip north, and he probably has CIA torture training or some shit."

"Reed's a consultant. No one actually believes he's a spy," Hawk scoffed. He stood with his arms folded over his chest, watching me pace back and forth. "That's just something Porter jokes about. And since when do you care what people think?"

"Since I'm busy contemplating how your family will come for me in the dead of night and do things to me all because of your *simple* proposition that I tread on sacred ground!" I yelled, gesturing wildly at him. I huffed out a breath and added quietly, "And don't tell me I'm being dramatic because we both know better. When Webb tried to set me up with Knox, he all but invited himself along on the date to play chaperone, and Knox is older than Webb! With you..."

I didn't finish my sentence because I didn't have to. We both knew Webb was protective of his family by nature but could be stiflingly overprotective where Hawk was concerned. If he believed Hawk was in danger, he'd raze entire cities to the ground. It wouldn't matter that Hawk had consented to the danger. It wouldn't even matter that he had gone out in the damn woods and *propositioned* the danger.

"Well. Yes." Hawk sighed and deflated a little. "That is a consideration. I'd sort of hoped that you'd want this with me more than you'd care about that stuff," he said quietly.

Ugh. I ran a frustrated hand through my sweaty hair. I hated when he got quiet. Quiet meant sad and hurt when I'd rather die than hurt him.

"Hawk. *Bird.* I do care about you—"

"And it's kinda funny when you think about it," Hawk went on with a little shrug. "If Webb and the others really want me to be safe, they should be proud of me for choosing someone trustworthy to have sex with. I could just find some rando on a hookup app, I guess, but—"

My brain exploded into a heap of toxic sludge until I was afraid I was about to have a medical event.

"You will not lose your virginity to a random stranger from an app," I informed him. There was something dark and rough in my voice I'd never heard before. My heart continued to thunder in my neck, and I was lightheaded at the thought of this man—my precious Hawk—in the clutches of an unknown player. "Promise me, Bird. Promise me you will not do something as stupid as—"

Hawk threw up his hands in an uncharacteristic display of temper. "Whoaaa. Hold on, buddy. Did you or did you not meet Smug Peter on Hinge?"

I opened my mouth and shut it again. "Not the point."

"And everyone knows Knox and Gage were *both* on Grindr before they got their shit together and admitted they were in love. And Porter has GROWLr installed on his phone because he's got a thing for bears—"

"No." I shook my head. "Too much information. *Way* too much information—"

"So why is it okay for everyone else to have sex with strangers but not me?"

Because you are special. You are precious. You are mine…

That last one brought me up short.

Mine *to protect* was what I meant, obviously. Mine to care for until a person came along who deserved him.

Without waiting for a response—which was good, because responding was beyond my capabilities at that moment—Hawk began pacing the ground, ranting about double standards and overly protective brothers, jabbing his trekking pole into the ground at intervals to punctuate his points. Meanwhile, I slumped down on a fallen tree trunk and stared at Hawkins Sunday through brand-new eyes.

It was hard to remember a time in my life when I hadn't known Hawk Sunday, and since the first day we'd met, back when he was a geeky, passionate kid, he'd occupied a special place in my heart. We worked together. Hung out together. Remodeled together. Over the years, I'd shared more of my thoughts and fears and dreams with him than with anyone, even Webb. And though I called Webb my best friend, that was only because Hawk and I were closer than friends. More than brothers. He was my… my *Hawk*. The one and only.

And… okay, it wasn't that I'd never noticed the man was gorgeous, because I definitely had. He was beautiful like all the Sundays, but on a less-enormous scale, and with big, honey-brown eyes that gleamed like warm, liquid gold whenever he was particularly happy or sad, and silky curls that felt soft against my face when he fell asleep with his head on my shoulder while watching a movie.

And… yes, I'd be lying if I didn't admit that, once upon a time, I'd noticed his half-naked body at the lake and had a… a completely natural biological reaction to his beauty. Or that, one time this spring when Hawk had thrown back his head in laughter, a bolt of… *something*… had hit me with the force of a freight train, and I'd jerked off later at the memory of his smile.

But the idea of actually acting on that feeling? *With Hawk*? That Hawk and I would ever…

No. Nope. I had never allowed myself to contemplate that. Because… Jesus, why would I?

Finding guys to hook up with was literally the work of seconds. But if Hawk and I fucked up our friendship by turning it into a—I shuddered—full-blown *relationship*, things would go from "easy" to "complicated" in a heartbeat and could then slide right into "devastatingly, life-alteringly terrible" without any advanced warning. I'd seen it happen over and over again. That was why I limited my dating life to guys who were in it for casual fun and sex and kept those far away from my friendships.

So I was a little resentful that, now that Hawk had brought this up, suddenly I was staring at my *friend's* lips and not simply adding those lips to a mental catalog of hot images to jerk off to but actively imagining how those lips would taste. Knowing that if I kissed him right then, he'd welcome it. Wondering what he sounded like when he came.

Hawk had, without my consent, made our friendship *weird*.

It wasn't his fault, obviously. Since he'd never had sex, he didn't understand how it would change things. And he didn't have the same experiences I'd had, so he didn't understand how freaking perilous relationships could be.

It was therefore up to me to make sure things got un-weird. And stayed that way.

"…which is why I decided to ask you," Hawk continued, losing steam. He stretched his neck by leaning his head from side to side nervously. "So… please?"

I stood and faced him squarely. "No, we will not be having sex with each other. I'm more than ten years older than you. I'm your boss. Webb calls me your *honorary brother*. And… you don't understand how risky it would be. I care about you too much to complicate things unnecessarily."

Hawk's chin firmed, and his nostrils flared. My eyes went to the nose ring again. For some reason, I wanted to tweak it gently, brush the smooth skin of his nose and cheeks to see how soft it was.

I shook my head. Where had these ideas come from all of a sudden?

Stupid heatstroke.

Stupid pinecones.

Stupid *propositions*.

Stupid nosy Pilkners.

Stupid, stupid *sex*.

"You're saying having sex with me would be *unnecessarily complicated*," Hawk said in a whisper that seemed to hang in the heated air.

"Exactly. Yes."

My pulse was so loud it took me a second to realize that the light in Hawk's eyes had gone out and he'd curled around himself protectively, his trekking pole dangling from the strap on one wrist. "I see," he said softly. "Wow. This is embarrassing."

My heart dropped into my stomach. "No. It's okay. It's… look, I'm honored that you came to me. I care about you, and I *want* you to talk to me about things. But I—" I broke off, feeling like I'd dug myself into a hole. Anything else I said would only sound like an insincere platitude or, worse, encourage him to pursue this terrible idea.

"But you're rejecting me anyway," he finished for me.

"Not *rejecting*! The opposite. Hawk, you're too important—"

I wasn't sure what expression appeared on my face at that point, but whatever it was made him flash a big, fake smile that turned my stomach.

"I get it, okay? You don't need to— It's *fine*."

"Is it?" The cold chill down my spine was the opposite of fine.

"Sure. I'm disappointed, obviously. And I think your reasoning is… not great. But really, my disappointment is my own fault." He bit his lip and shook his head. "You know, I've been with guys in the past, and I've come close to devirgination lots of times, but I've always held back, like it was this big, significant act that I needed to plan out and find just the right person for." He shrugged. "But, like, if the person you think is the right person says *no*, then they're not the right person… right?"

I shook my head, panicked. "I… what?"

"Maybe there's no such thing as the right person. Maybe I

should just get it over with and do it with... well, anyone. That's why god invented hookup apps. I mean, like you said earlier, what's the big deal about virginity anyway?"

"Huh? No, when I said that thing about virginity earlier, I was talking about Regency England. I was talking about the heroines in your books. I wasn't talking about *you*—"

Hawk gave my forearm a cursory pat. "I think you were right earlier. It really *is* warm out here, and we have the town meeting tonight. I'm gonna head back. I'll see you later."

"But... Hawk?" I shouted as he picked his way back down the trail, an odd stiffness in his posture that was either due to his injuries from the pinecones or his injuries from... me. "Since when do you quit a hike before we reach the summit? And... wait, since when have you been with lots of guys before?"

He didn't respond or acknowledge me in any way. My heart pulled itself up out of my gut and flung itself down the trail after him like a stupid fucking traitor while I stood there in a strange kind of numb shock.

I'd screwed up, that much was obvious, but I had no idea what I should have done differently, and I had no clue how to fix it.

All I knew was that I'd better figure it out quickly before I lost something that had become even more precious than I'd let myself realize.

CHAPTER TWO

HAWK

"A girl likes to be crossed a little in love now and then."
~ Mr. Bennet

I WAS GOING to have to go into hiding. That's all there was
to it.

"What the heck's wrong with you, Hawkie?" Emma
asked, elbowing me down the row of chairs in the assembly
room of Little Pippin Hollow's town hall. "You've been acting
funny the whole way here."

*I propositioned Panini Jack, and all I have to show for it is
pinecone rash on my ass.*

*The guy I've been in love with for years confirmed that I'll only
ever be a little brother to him.*

A spot of casual heartbreak. No big deal.

"I'm fine," I insisted, low-key darting a glance around the
meeting space, just in case Jack happened to be looming
nearby. "Just because I'm not talking doesn't mean I'm upset,
Em. Can't a guy keep himself to himself around here?"

Emma's inelegant snort brought my attention to the crowd
around us. We were surrounded by Little Pippin Hollowans,
illustrating the very antithesis of keeping oneself to oneself.

One row ahead of us, Frieda Lower was complaining in a carrying voice, "Can you believe Norm Avery had the audacity to advise me—and I say that with sarcasm, mind—on the best way to irrigate the crop now that my squash are in? I'll thank him to mind his own danged business, and that's precisely what I told him…"

Oumar Diallo sat upright beside her, arms folded across his chest, and nodded along, but it wasn't clear from this angle whether he was agreeing with her or he'd fallen asleep with his eyes open again.

Meanwhile, Letty Hendelmann stage-whispered a warning to her neighbor Fran Driscoll. "Did you know right around daybreak when the sun is *just* peeking around the corner of your big oak tree that someone—not me, obviously, because I'd *never*—could see right into your guest room window? I'm just saying you might want to go ahead and hang those curtains Marie said you picked up at the Save-a-Ton back in January…"

"Yeah, no," my sister whispered, amused. "If you're looking to mind your own business, I think you were born in the wrong place."

I dropped into an empty seat next to my brother-in-law, Luke, who greeted me with a grin and an affectionate arm bump. Emma dropped into the seat beside me and turned her body in my direction, ready to continue her inquisition, so I turned toward Luke with a forced smile, hoping I didn't look as desperate as I felt.

"So! Luke! How's it going at your place? Tell me *all* about the sheep." I begged him with my mind not to ask about me, or Jack, or hiking, or… anything that would require me to further contemplate this debacle of a day.

"Going great. The new lambs are so cute." Luke's eyes went dreamy. "Aiden named them all after comic book characters. If you're not too busy volunteering with the Nature Scouts this week, you should come by—"

Webb set a hand on his husband's knee and leaned across his lap. "'Bout time you arrived, Hawk. Jack was asking for you earlier."

It seemed *Webb* was not picking up on my psychic message.

"Oh." I swallowed hard. "Was he?"

"He said you got hurt during your hike and he was worried." Webb's gaze tracked me up and down, looking for signs of injury.

Fortunately, the death blow to my pride and the slow bleed of my smashed-up heart didn't have visible symptoms.

Despite everything, some hopeful little corner of that mangled organ soared at the knowledge that Jack had been thinking about me—that he *cared*—before I ruthlessly caught it and dragged it back to Earth.

He cares about you like a brother. That's all.

"I'm fine," I said, a little more firmly than necessary. "Really. A few pinecone scratches. But if it had been more," I couldn't help adding, "I would have sought medical attention because I'm an experienced hiker and *an adult*. You know that, right?"

Webb's eyebrows dipped. "O-kayyy, jeez." He turned to look at Luke. "Is it just me, or is everyone snappish today? Maybe there was something in the air at Glassy Ridge. First Jack's biting my head off, now Hawk is cranky."

I tried not to roll my eyes. There was a low bar to me being "cranky." The dark underbelly of being a generally happy person was that people in my life didn't know how to process it on the rare occasions when I displayed any emotion besides cheerfulness. Other people got to be moody all the dang time.

Well, it was my turn now.

Luke ran fingers absently through Webb's hair. "Want me to teach you about common denominators again, baby? It comes in really handy sometimes."

Webb's lips twitched at the tease, and when he leaned into Luke's touch, I had to look away.

Fuck, I wanted that. For as long as I could remember, I'd wanted someone to look at me the way those two looked at each other—with heat and affection and the kind of deep satisfaction that came from knowing you were understood and unconditionally loved.

I wanted my Darcy.

Too bad my idiot heart had set itself on Jack freaking Wyatt, the most obtuse individual in all of Vermont, seven years ago.

Because what he and I had… it was so very close to that. It was the two of us sitting side by side on a rocky outcropping on a winter's day in comfortable silence, finding patterns in the clouds. It was me and him by the fire pit in his yard, grilling burgers, and planning house projects, and laughing over whether Jack should get a pet (I was heavily team *cat*; Jack was heavily team *pet rock*). It was us working together in the kitchen at the diner while I ate fifty-seven incarnations of a sandwich since Jack was devoted to his farm-to-table seasonal ingredients and adorably finicky about his recipes, and I loved that he trusted me to be his guinea pig.

I'd thought if we could just add a dash of unbridled passion, a little hint of "I can't wait to get you home, baby," maybe a dash of "you, me, clothes off, *now*," we could turn our friendship into love, just like tweaking a recipe. And that surely, if Jack accepted my proposal to do a little bit of cherry picking, he'd have seen how easy and perfect it could be.

Unnecessarily complicated. Pffft. What about a simple request to take a man's virginity was unnecessarily complicated?

Thank god I hadn't confessed my feelings on that damn mountain. If I'd told him that the crush at first sight I'd developed on him as a lonely teenager had only grown over the years until Jack had become the center of my personal solar system, I'd probably have been burned to ash by the shame of it all. As it was, I was only… heavily charred.

Emma leaned over me to speak to Webb. "Hawk claims he's fine, but when I asked him if he was heading up the Averill Union back-to-school charity drive again this year, he grunted. When I asked how his hike with the Mini Nature Scouts went yesterday, he only sighed instead of pulling out his phone and showing me cute kid pictures. I deliberately said something insulting about Timothée Chalamet, and he didn't argue. And," she said triumphantly, ticking off a fourth finger, "he ate *four* extra-long gummy worms on the drive here. He usually stops after two. He's definitely upset about something."

I elbowed her back into her own space. "Maybe Hawk's upset that you're talking about Hawk like Hawk's not sitting right here? Just a thought."

Mrs. Cleeward, whose hair was as bright red as the cinnamon hearts in her candy store, turned around eagerly. "Were those *my* gummy worms? Did you like them, Hawk? Did you know we're using your family's apples to make the apple juice concentrate for our candies now? In fact, Webb, I got your message about carrying the gummies in the Orchard shop. Mel's going to call Gage later in the week about a distribution agreement…"

I crossed my arms over my chest like Mr. Diallo, trying to block out the chatter, and wished I could learn the fine art of public sleeping.

"Hawk! You made it." A delicate fingernail poked the back of my shoulder. "I wasn't sure after I got your text."

I turned eagerly toward my friend Crys, taking in her newly dyed hot pink hair—which she'd styled in a short, messy bedhead look that could have been posted on TikTok with both punk rock and lesbian-chic hashtags—and smiled for the first time all night. Crys and I had only met when she'd moved to town and gotten a job at Panini Jack's a couple of months before, but she was removed from the busy-body nonsense, which made her a breath of fresh air and a really good confidant.

"Only because I *had* to come," I said fervently. "Evola Development Corp is set to ruin the Hollow. That takes precedence over everything else."

Webb heard me and sighed. "No one's ruining anything tonight, Hawk. We're here to listen to their design proposal and ask questions. The plans won't be finalized until next month."

This time, I didn't restrain my eye roll. No wonder I was "cranky." The town I loved was set to be manhandled by big-city real estate developers under the guise of building an upscale "woodland resort experience," and no one seemed inclined to stop it. In fact, at least half the town was ready to roll out the red carpet for their new overlords.

"We've been listening to them since February," I reminded him. "Every time these guys 'talk,' it sounds more and more like they consider it a done deal. Don't forget, I was on Mayor York's committee to review the site plans. Evola simply cannot raze acres of natural, old-growth forest to build *luxury alpine relaxation cabanas* and *deliciously decadent bespoke gustatory osterias* without having devastating impact on the local flora and fauna. Have you seen environmental impact studies of their *other* resorts? No, me neither. Because they don't exist. Which means Evola hasn't publicized them. Which means they're *bad*. As a person who's devoted himself to saving heirloom apple varietals, you should care about this, Webb. Anyone who cares about the Hollow should care about this."

Webb made a soothing, noncommittal noise—the kind you made when a child was pitching a fit—and I felt like growling. The proposed resort development project stood to bring hundreds of new tourists and their spending money to town, which meant many people, including some members of my own family, were already leaning toward approving it.

The fingernail poked me again. "I know we're here to stop the evil developers from paving paradise, Joni Mitchell…" Crys leaned closer and whispered under her breath. "But what's the deal with *you know who* and the plan to *you know what* him? Your text was extremely light on details. A single thumbs-down emoji? I need more."

I shrugged. "There's nothing more to say. I asked. He declined. The end."

Now I had to figure out how to give up the dream of my heart and move on. How to stop being in love with someone who represented the biggest and best parts of my life.

Romance novels had not prepared me for a situation where one-half of the fated mates decides the other isn't a suitable match. This seemed a regrettable oversight.

"Boo, that's not possible," Crys said firmly. "Tell me everything *you* said, and everything *he* said about what you said, and everything *you* said about what he said about what you said."

"I did exactly as you suggested. I asked him flat out. No chance for misunderstandings. And he…" I looked around to make sure no one was listening, but naturally, everyone and their brother was listening, especially mine. "He was *not* amenable," I admitted in a pained whisper. "Barely even considered it. Can we stop talking about this now?"

Crys shook her head. "No, because I'm still not buying it. The way he looks at you… He's very, *very* amenable, Hawk."

Luke leaned over and whispered. "What are we talking about?"

"Nothing. Nothing at all," I lied. "Go back to petting my brother." I turned to Crys again. "Explain what you mean."

As far as I could tell, Jack looked at me the way Jack had looked at me since the day we'd met—fondly, but apparently not the kind of fond that made him want to rip my clothes off and worship my naked flesh with his tongue. Not even fond enough to override his concerns about my family.

She leaned even closer, cupping her hand around her mouth and whispering in my ear unapologetically. "His eyes follow you constantly. If you're in the room, you're the center of his attention."

"Well, sure, but it's been that way forever. Because we're friends," I whispered glumly. "Which is part of the problem for him. He says he doesn't want to lose what we have. And he's my boss. And he's my 'honorary brother.' And he knows certain people wouldn't be okay with it." I tilted my head in Webb's direction.

To my shock, Crys's face broke out in a smile. "That's what he said, huh? Is that *everything* he said?"

"Isn't that enough? It's hopeless." He'd shut me down so entirely I had no recourse. I wasn't a fighter by nature, but I would have fought for this... if Jack had let me.

"But he didn't say he wasn't attracted to you."

I blinked. "Well... no," I said slowly, my battered heart thumping a little faster. "Not technically. But I felt like that was covered in the 'brothers' part."

"Is it, though? If he didn't find you attractive, he'd have said, 'You're not my type, Hawkins,' and been done with it. Wouldn't he?"

"I... I don't know." Maybe he'd been trying to save my feelings by not admitting that short, thin guys with muddy-brown eyes and cowlicks weren't his jam.

"I do." Crys's smile went sly, and she tapped her lip thoughtfully with one long nail. "And I'm thinking you need to make sure he's looking at you in a way that drives *brothers* out of his mind altogether."

I stared at her, open-mouthed. "But, like... how?"

"Easy. You just have to—" Crys's gaze moved over my shoulder, and she coughed lightly before sitting back in her seat. "Erm. Why don't we discuss specifics later?"

"Later? No way!" Couldn't she see I was dying here? I cut my hand through the air to make my point. "Tell me n—*ow-*

ow-ow!" I wailed as I accidentally whacked my funny bone on the back of the chair.

"Bird?" The voice from my dreams made me spin around to find Jack Wyatt leaning over the seat next to Mrs. Cleeward, watching me with a troubled expression that suggested he'd witnessed the whole thing. "You okay?"

I squeezed my eyes shut and ignored the spot of dampness in my eye caused by the pain.

Ugh. The only thing worse than confronting the person you love after they've rejected your affections is confronting him while surrounded by your busybody family after demonstrating that you are, indeed, the foolish child he believes you to be.

Elizabeth Bennet would *never*.

Jack's large palm cupped the back of my head, and it was harder than it should have been not to lean into his touch like Webb had earlier with Luke. "Look at me, Hawk. Are you alright?"

Closing my eyes didn't help when I could perfectly picture Jack's laser-beam-of-concern eyeballs boring a hole into my brain. And that was the problem, really, with fantasizing about someone for as long as I had. Two thousand days analyzing the precise meaning of each smile-crinkle beside his deep blue eyes and two thousand nights dreaming of him touching me like a lover had conspired to make me imagine things in his gaze that weren't there.

For example, that he might be open to the idea of some recreational sex with an inexperienced (but *very* eager to learn) younger man...

And that today, of all days, would be an auspicious time to approach him about it.

I sighed and opened my eyes.

"Thanks for your concern, but I'm fine, Jack. Now, sit down, okay? The meeting's starting."

But Jack didn't let go. His eyes searched mine for a beat,

his hand still warmly clasped in my hair. "Your scrapes from earlier… are those—?"

I felt like everyone was staring, so I twisted my neck and shook him off with a big, friendly smile. "Also fine! I'm totally, completely… *fine.*"

Jack dropped his hand—which was a good thing, and I did *not* immediately miss it. He gripped the back of his chair until his knuckles turned white. "Hawk. Are you sure…?"

I could tell he was asking about more than my pinecone rash now. "Oh, for god's sake. When a person says they're fine, they're fine!"

Everyone whipped their heads around to stare at me, like the sight of Hawk Sunday losing his shit was a newsworthy Hollowan event.

Which, okay, maybe it was.

"Now who's making things *unnecessarily complicated?*" I asked softly.

Jack's eyes darkened, but before he could say anything, Mayor York called the meeting to order. Everyone turned their focus to the front while he welcomed us and went over a few pieces of Hollow housekeeping before introducing the primary topic of tonight's meeting.

"As you know, we have an important vote coming up in just four short weeks. Our friends at Evola Corp made us a very generous offer back in February to purchase the land at Fogg Peak in order to build an exciting new resort that's sure to bring many more visitors to our little town. Tonight, we're going to hear from some of Evola's representatives about the design concepts for the Fogg Aerie Resort so that we as a community can come to a decision. I'd like to give a warm Hollow welcome to—"

"Fogg Aerie?" I scoffed under my breath. "It has a fancy name now?"

"Shh." Uncle Drew, ever the peacemaker, leaned across Emma. "At least they kept Jeremiah Fogg's name in it."

Hmph.

I missed the name of the man Mayor York introduced, but he made his way to the podium and gave the audience a warm, slightly nervous smile.

"He's cute," Em and Crys whispered to me, one in each ear. I shrugged both of them off.

The guy was definitely cute in a smiley, enthusiastic way, which, sadly, was not the type that set my blood on fire. His fair hair was neatly combed, his suit was perfectly pressed, his expression was innocent and earnest... all in all, exactly the sort of harmless-looking person a soulless corporation would send to a small town to convince them to part with their precious natural resources.

I sighed. I really *was* cranky.

"Good evening, folks," he said. "Thank you, Mayor York, for that nice introduction. Um. As Ernest said, I'm the environmental compliance officer for the Evola Development Corporation. We're so excited to be here in Little Pippin Hollow to work with you on creating the kind of resort development that would not only be mutually beneficial from a commercial standpoint but also an exciting opportunity to preserve and celebrate the beautiful landscape of Fogg Peak. We hope Fogg Aerie becomes the kind of destination resort that honors the values and purpose of Little Pippin Hollow, and we really, *really* appreciate your willingness to work with us to make sure this project is the best it can be."

My ears perked up. Environmental compliance officer? That was new. And he sounded like he actually cared about the things I was most concerned about.

"Change is hard. Progress can seem scary," Environmental Guy went on, looking genuinely sympathetic. "Sometimes, that means people see us as the bad guys. The outsiders coming in to destroy your town's charm and natural beauty. I promise, I'm no evil mastermind." He pressed a hand to his chest and flashed a sweet, rueful grin that made the audience chuckle.

Webb leaned forward to give me a significant look that I refused to acknowledge, and in front of me, Jack nodded his head like a bobblehead.

My stomach churned.

Jack and I had discussed the proposed resort a bunch of times since it had first been mentioned last winter. I'd never actually asked him which box he'd be checking when it came time for the vote, but every time I passionately defended Fogg Peak, he reminded me that there was "lots to consider."

I'd hoped that meant that he was actually *considering* things, but now I wasn't so sure. He complained about the "flatlanders" clogging the roads every fall during foliage season, but more tourists meant increased revenue at Panini Jack's. And while he might love hiking at Fogg Peak, he clearly wasn't going to let that love overcome his logic… which was kind of a running theme for the day.

"I'll be staying with Ms. Fortnum over at Apple of My Eye Inn for the next few weeks," Environmental Guy went on. "I urge any and all of you to stop by and see me if you have any questions or concerns about the project. We care about this town. We care about you."

Interesting. Back when the development had first been proposed, Helena Fortnum—leader of the Little Pippin Hookers, third grade teacher since the dawn of time, and the Hollow's biggest gossip—had been its most vocal protestor. She'd once staged a topless knit-in with the other Hookers, and she'd petitioned Mayor York to create a committee to study its environmental impact on the fragile ecosystems of this part of Vermont. Our group had met weekly for a while, drafting flyers and planning demonstrations, but then spring planting season had ramped up. Folks had gotten busy with their own lives and, it seemed, forgotten about the protests. If Ms. Fortnum was now hosting Evola's staff at her bed-and-breakfast, clearly saving Fogg Peak was no longer her priority.

Environmental Guy ceded the floor to a marketing director, who spewed some bullshit brochure-speak, and then to Evola's legal representative, whose sole purpose seemed to be to encourage us all to sleep by discussing zoning changes and proposed contract fine print in a monotonous voice.

Against my will, my mind wandered from the meeting, and I found my gaze tracing an errant blond curl caught on the edge of Jack's ear. My finger itched to brush it away or wrap it around my finger to feel the silky softness of it against my skin.

Give it up, Hawkins.

I closed my eyes and clenched my fists in my lap. Every single part of Jack Wyatt felt so much like home to me—the strength of his shoulders, the tiny vulnerable freckle at the base of his neck that begged for a kiss—that it was hard to remember he wasn't mine.

This infatuation with my brother's best friend, my boss, had to stop. It had reached dangerous levels if today's disastrous proposal was any indication. My stomach roiled with embarrassed nausea.

There were so many ways I could have approached my proposition better. Maybe if I'd flirted with Jack, or teased him, or simply kissed him and let things happen… fuck, anything besides confessing I was an anal virgin who'd selected him to deflower me—

He wouldn't sleep with you no matter how you asked him.

The thought was equal parts comforting and depressing.

Mr. Diallo snored loud enough that he jolted in his chair, and for a second, I tuned back in to what was happening on stage.

"…and pursuant to the agreement detailed in section 12.3, Evola agrees to replant fifty percent of the trees taken down during the clear-cutting of the Glassy Ridge area around Glassy Creek to make way for the recreation rotunda, within the time frame discussed in part B of the…"

I stood up so fast my chair ricocheted back, and Crys caught it with a startled "Jeez, boo!" that I barely heard over the roar in my brain.

"Whoa! Wait a minute. Clear-cut Glassy Ridge? Are you serious?" Everyone in the assembly room turned to stare at me again, but this time, I stared right back. Why wasn't anyone else standing up to protest? Why wasn't *every*one? "Glassy Ridge is what makes Fogg Peak so special. You can't just get rid of the trees because they're in the way!"

I tried not to let all of the emotion in my heart leak out through my words or through my eyes, but it was difficult. My father had adored Glassy Ridge. We'd spent hours hiking the trails, always ending up by the banks of Glassy Creek to fish, or swim, or just sit and breathe. "It's never the same creek twice, Hawkins," he'd say, watching the water with a little smile on his face. "Always a fresh slate, if you're looking for one."

The idea of that place gone forever? Replaced by a… a… recreation rotunda? *No.* There were some things I couldn't change, some dreams I might have to let go of, but not this. I refused.

The attorney cleared her throat, and the marketing person nudged her away from the microphone to take over. "Hey. Hi. Great question. Um. As I mentioned earlier, the plans to recreate the delights of Courchevel include a barrel sauna conclave, as well as an alpine lake swimming and spa experience. And that's why we need a recreation rotunda." He ended his nonsensible statement with a bland smile. "Thank you."

"B-but… that doesn't answer my question," I stammered. I glanced to Webb for support, but he was watching me with a frown. Luke looked confused. And Jack… he gazed at me over his shoulder with concern in his blue eyes, but he didn't say a single freaking word to help me.

Environmental Compliance Guy stood back up, shielding his eyes against the light until he could pick me out of the crowd. He smiled. "Clear-cutting sounds dramatic, I know." He rolled his eyes in the attorney's direction. "I promise, we're not proposing to take away the entire forest on the ridge, just one area. And I assure you, we will do—in fact, already *have* done—extensive environmental modeling in regard to the impact. In addition, the resort designers have integrated some of the existing trails into the layout of the area to preserve the history, as well as honor the original use of Glassy Ridge."

I hesitated. All of that sounded fine, but… clear-cutting was clear-cutting. Why use that word if it wasn't what they planned?

"*Hawk,*" Emma said low and insistently as she tugged on my hand. "Please sit. You're causing a scene."

Since when was Emma the kind of teenager who got embarrassed by people standing up for things?

"But… this is important, Em," I reminded her.

"No, you're right. It is important. Very," Environmental Guy agreed from the mic. "I'd love a chance to explain our specific plans for that part of the project in more detail if you'll stay after the meeting."

I nodded slowly. "Yeah. Okay. But I have many questions," I warned before I sat down.

"Awesome. I love questions." Environmental Guy shot me another smile, then gestured the lawyer back to the mic to resume rambling.

Jack hadn't taken his worried eyes off me. "Bird, keep an open mind, huh? Sounds like they're being really thorough. There are no bad guys here, right?" He gave me a lopsided smile.

"Yes," Webb whispered. "Listen to Jack."

I sucked in a breath through my nose and resolutely trained my eyes on the stage.

Jack's words, his very *reasonableness*, set my teeth on edge.

How dare he lecture me on keeping an open mind when he refused to? When had "*I like when people are unapologetically enthusiastic about their interests and opinions*" changed to "there are no bad guys here"? And, most importantly, if our friendship was the reason he wouldn't have sex with me... why wouldn't he support me when I needed him?

It was pretty pathetic when Environmental Guy, a tool of the enemy, took my concerns more seriously than the man I'd given my heart to.

"I'll stay with you afterward." Luke nudged my knee. "If you want."

I nodded, managing a small smile. Luke was thoughtful and smart, and his job as a schoolteacher made him good at reading people. He'd be a solid ally.

Crys's hand squeezed my shoulder from behind. "I'll stay, too. This is obviously important to you."

"Thanks," I whispered, grateful that someone had my back.

I blew out a breath and refused to meet Jack's eyes. I had no idea what to do about him, and the person I'd normally ask for advice was Jack himself, which clearly wouldn't work. So, instead, I was going to put him out of my mind as much as possible. I was going to focus on the fight to protect Little Pippin Hollow from the evil forces that threatened my beloved wilderness.

This was a fight I could actually take on. One I could win.

I needed to find Helena Fortnum and see if she could call another meeting of the Environmental Committee. Maybe I could get Uncle Drew on board—he didn't seem particularly riled about the issue just yet, but he'd been anti-establishment since the '60s, and if I could convince him to take a stand, lots of folks in town would take notice. Maybe I could drum up some support with the Nature Scout parents, too, since their kids tramped up and down those trails as part of their summer day camp.

The rest of the meeting passed in a blur as I made a mental list, and when the speeches concluded, I launched out of my seat, flashing Luke and Crys a "wait here" gesture, and ignoring Jack's efforts to get my attention.

For the first time in the history of our friendship, I felt like talking to Jack would make me feel worse instead of better. His protective concern usually made me feel cherished and strong, but today, it made me feel fragile. If the man asked if I was okay one more time, I might actually scream.

As I stalked to the front of the room, Environmental Guy's face lit up with recognition and a smile. "Hawkins Sunday, right? Someone mentioned you were the guy with all the smart questions." He beamed and offered his hand to shake. "Simon Wentworth, nice to meet you."

I took his hand in mine. "Wentworth? As in…" I shut my mouth before I embarrassed myself by mentioning any of my novels. *Not the time, Hawk.*

Simon's grin widened. "As in the character from Jane Austen's *Persuasion*? My mom's favorite. I swear that's why she married my dad. Do you know the book?"

I swallowed hard and felt my face heat. There were signs, and then there were *signs*. "Yeah. Yes. Of course. Though *Pride and Prejudice* is my favorite of hers. Do you… do you read Jane Austen?"

"Not really? I'm a complete geek when it comes to my job. I love reading articles and studies on environmental impact and protecting our wild areas. It doesn't leave much time for novels, as much as I love them. My mom says I'm missing out."

"You are," I agreed. "Novels are my favorite things…" I hardened my voice a fraction. "After Glassy Ridge. You know,

I haven't seen any environmental impact studies from Evola's recent developments outside Ithaca *or* up in Bangor. Why is that? And I didn't hear anything in your presentation about the endangered species on the Ridge. Does that mean you haven't looked into the situation?"

Simon inclined his head. "A man who's done his research," he approved. "Why am I not surprised? Hawkins, I assure you, Evola has a squeaky-clean track record. I don't think you'll find any complaints at all about Point Meduc or Morgan Falls. And our teams have spent long hours figuring out how best to mitigate the impact on all native species. But... why don't you and I trade reading recommendations, just to be sure? You can send me any information you think might be relevant, and I'll see if I can get you copies of our ongoing studies at our recent builds. If you want, I can talk you through them, too. Explain the special considerations we made for environmental factors in those cases."

"Okay. Yeah. I'd appreciate that." I rocked slightly on my feet. "You can call me Hawk. Everyone does."

"Hawk," he repeated solemnly. "Would you... that is to say..." He glanced down at his feet. "If you were interested in touring the area around the proposed resort sometime, we could do that. There are flag markers out there, and I could kind of walk you around the place? Maybe even change your mind?"

"You want to go hiking with me?" I asked, surprised.

"Only if you're interested." He gave me a shy smile. "No pressure."

I looked at Simon more closely. He seemed cute and well-spoken, and his stammering earnestness reminded me of... well, me. He might be employed by a villainous corporation, but that didn't mean he, himself, was so terrible. And I couldn't lie, after Jack's rejection, it felt pretty great to have someone pick *me* as a person they wanted to spend time with.

"That might be fun. But you're gonna be the one changing

your mind," I added quickly. "Every single tree out there is magnificent. You'll see."

Simon chuckled lightly. "I consider myself warned."

"Simon?" The lawyer from earlier looked back and forth between me and Simon disapprovingly. "We're leaving now."

"Sure. Coming." Simon pulled a business card from his pocket and handed it to me. "That's my cell and my email address. Let me know when you're free… *Hawk.*"

I nodded, tapping the card against my hand. "I will."

Simon grinned and gave me a jaunty salute before walking away.

"What was that all about?" Jack demanded from behind me.

I turned to face him, and… *Ugh.*

It was not *fair* that his face was still so gorgeous, even now that things between us were impossible. It was utterly *unjust* that my brain had somehow imprinted on him so that if anyone asked me to define a gorgeous, sexy man, I would automatically and without conscious thought describe Jack Wyatt. It was *inexcusable* that just when I most needed to keep distance between us, every cell of my body yearned for him to give me a hug and tell me that we were going to be okay.

"That was me talking to the environmental compliance officer to address my concerns about the proposed develop-ment," I said.

"Hmm." Jack's face creased in a frown. "You two seemed friendly."

I shrugged. "You told me to keep an open mind."

"Well, true." Jack folded his arms over his chest, then quickly unfolded them and stuffed his hands in his pockets. A second later, he clasped them together behind his back. "But I didn't mean…"

"Simon asked me to go hiking sometime," I cut in. "He's going to show me the layout of the proposed development, and I'll try to convince him to stop it."

"Wait, hold up. You're going *hiking*? You and..." He waved a hand in the direction of the side door, where Simon and the others had departed.

"Simon," I reminded him. "Yes. Is that a problem?"

Tell me it is, I begged silently. *Say, "No, Hawk. I am bitterly jealous, for hiking is* our *thing, and I never want you to hike with another." Say it, Jack.*

"Of course not."

"Right." I tried not to let my disappointment show. One mortifying rejection per day was my limit. "Okay, then. Good night."

I started to walk past him, but Jack stopped me with a hand on my arm. He licked his lips. "I, um... I think Simon might be interested in you. Not sure if you picked up on that. I thought that was something you should know so you could... handle it accordingly."

"Accordingly." I tilted my head to one side and studied him. Jack's cheeks were flushed beneath his perfect golden tan, like he was worried or upset or even maybe... jealous, unlikely as that seemed.

I suddenly remembered Crys's words from earlier. *Make sure he's looking at you in a way that drives brothers out of his mind altogether.* Well... what did I have to lose?

"Ohhh. You mean, maybe *he* should be the guy I have sex with. What a great idea! I'll put some lube in my backpack, just in case the opportunity arises. What would I do without you, buddy?" I gave Jack an impulsive half hug, the kind I'd given him a hundred times, and tried very, very hard not to notice the spicy, woodsy scent of his cologne.

"Wait. Hawk. That's not what I—"

"Good night!" I called over my shoulder as I made my way back to where Luke and Crys waited, adding a little shimmy to my step.

And for the second time that day—probably the second

time in my entire life—I walked away from Jack Wyatt instead of standing by his side.

Only this time, I let myself imagine he was staring at my ass as I did so.

CHAPTER THREE

JACK

Mary wished to say something very sensible, but knew not how.
~ Jane Austen

AFTER ALMOST BURNING my hand on the grill, dropping a knife on my thankfully steel-clad toes, and spilling an entire five-gallon bucket of fresh lemonade all over the kitchen, I had to put myself in time-out. Or, rather, Katey put me in one.

"Sit down, Jack," my assistant manager said, pulling a stool from under the worktop. Her smile was kind, even though her blonde ponytail was looking decidedly less perky, thanks to a long shift and my repeated mishaps. "Crys, Hawk, and I will finish cleaning and prep. You've had… kind of a hard week, haven't you?"

I sighed. Yes. Yes, I had. *Hard* in every single way.

I darted a glance across the kitchen at the cause of all that *hardness,* but Hawk was busy rolling silverware into paper napkins and avoiding my gaze. *Again.*

I rubbed my hands over my face, forgetting I'd just squeezed lemons. Some of the acidic juice got into my eye, and apparently, rubbing it frantically was the exact wrong reaction.

"Fuck!" I barked, jumping up from my seat so quickly that Katey jumped and dropped a stack of plastic cups she'd taken out of the dishwasher. "Sorry!" I dove for the cups, nearly butting heads with Crys as she bent down for the same purpose. "Sorry," I repeated.

Hawk abandoned his task and darted across the room, pushing me back onto the stool. "Stay right there, and I'll help Katey unload the dishwasher. If you come closer, someone's going to wind up needing an ambulance. I don't know where your mind is this week."

I gave him a dark look. *Didn't he, though?*

He leaned over to collect the cups with both knees straight —a maneuver that made his luscious ass pop in my direction like I'd donned a pair of 3D glasses. Had he always bent over that way? Had his jeans always been that tight? Had his ass always been that round and full and...

I closed my eyes and ground my teeth together. It had been just over a week since our hike. A week since he'd asked me to take his virginity. A week since the scales had fallen off my eyes and I'd noticed that Hawk wasn't just good-looking; he was... he was *sexy*. A week since my gaze had begun tracking him whenever he was in the room, noticing the clean, sweet scent of him and wondering what it would be like to take him up on his offer. To touch him. Undress him. Kiss him full on the mouth. Hear his small noises of submission and pleasure, and—

Fuck. I was half-hard, sitting there in my own kitchen in front of my employees.

I stood quickly and turned toward the stove, where I was prepping caramelized onions for the next day, and grabbed a dish towel so I could give the pan a quick shake. This distraction had to stop. Panini Jack's was my livelihood, for god's sake. The way I supported not only myself but my mom.

I'd told Hawk "no" for a reason. For several very good reasons.

"Behind you," Hawk warned before reaching up to place a small stack of clean pans on the metal shelf beside the stove.

There was nothing sexual about the motion. He'd done it a thousand times over the years, and so did everyone else. But today, I couldn't help but notice that Hawk's shirt rode up, exposing a line of skin at his hip where his jeans dipped as his lean arm muscles flexed beneath his T-shirt and—

"Christ on a Christmas cracker! Are you trying to set this place on fire?" Hawk nudged me out of the way as the edge of the kitchen towel I'd been using to grip the pan began smoking. He grabbed the safe end of the cloth, flung it into the steel sink behind him, and turned on the faucet. "What the hell is wrong with you?" he demanded, shooting me a glare over his shoulder.

You. You, you, you.

"Nothing," I croaked. This was the first time he'd looked at me properly in days, and I drank him in—his big brown eyes snapping with emotion, his floppy hair, his sturdy shoulders and lean muscles, his adorably snubbed nose and delicate nose ring, the tiny scar under one eye that he'd gotten when he'd fallen asleep reading an old hardback copy of *Middlemarch* and the heavy book had dropped on his face. He was so familiar, yet I couldn't help but look at him like a stranger in some ways. "I'm a little... out of it, I guess. I haven't slept well. I've had stuff on my mind."

Specifically, Hawk-related stuff.

Things between Hawk and I had been weird since our hike, and not only because the air seemed saturated with sex pheromones anytime he was around. After the town meeting, he'd avoided me—at least, as much as he could while still showing up every day for work during our busy summer season.

Oh, on the surface, he'd been a perfect employee—polite and agreeable as ever, twice as willing to work hard as anyone else I'd ever employed, with a smile for every person he encountered, always remembering that Norma Alvarez was allergic to pineapple and putting extra cherries in the kids' Shirley Temples.

But the truth lay in everything he *didn't* say. Ordinarily, Hawk and I talked daily about all kinds of things large and small. Though he could be shy and quiet with people he didn't know well, he'd never hesitated to open up to me about whatever was on his mind—hilarious town gossip, worries about his family, concerns about the resort development, gushing praise for the pancakes he'd eaten for breakfast, rants about his latest read.

He was two hundred tons of passionate feeling packed into one small body—the most intensely *alive* human I'd ever met—and like a comet, he left a trail of rainbow-hued emotions across my personal horizon whenever he came into my orbit. Our conversations were the soundtrack to my days, and my week had been much, much quieter without them.

Too quiet.

Dull.

I'd caught myself wanting to ask him questions or draw him out, but every topic seemed loaded with land mines. Talking about the Aerie development or the upcoming town decision was guaranteed to set him off. I couldn't ask him if he'd made that date to go hiking with Simon Wentworth— which, seriously, was that not the prissiest name ever?— without seeming as overprotective as Webb or, worse, jealous, which I definitely was *not*.

And meanwhile, every moment I spent with him, and even the moments I *didn't*, were now electrically charged with Hawk-sex thoughts—two things that should never be uttered in the same sentence, let alone mentally hyphenated. I thought about him while cooking, while grocery shopping, while chatting with friends and neighbors in town, while shoving myself under the cramped bathroom vanity in my money pit of a house in an effort to restore running water to the sink.

I understood that he was embarrassed and maybe a little hurt. He'd made an offer and been shot down, which was never fun, even if there were no romantic feelings involved. If anyone else had done it to him, for any less compelling reason than my own, I'd have kicked their ass.

But the longer he remained licking his wounds, the more wildly off course our relationship veered. I wanted *my* Hawk back. I wanted our simple, easy friendship.

And in that moment, as I stood watching Hawk scowl at the now-soggy kitchen towel in the sink, I decided enough was enough.

"Are we still on for our usual hike tomorrow, Hawk?" I blurted.

Across the room, Crys let out an excited little squeak that made everyone look at her. "Oh, silly me! I just saw the time! It's nearly eight. Katey, we should go now if you still want to hit Singles' Trivia Night at the Bugle."

Katey glanced down at the counter she'd been scrubbing. "Singles' Trivia Night? Tonight?"

"Honey, of course. Remember we said we'd go? *Now*?"

"Well… no. But I guess we could if you—"

"Now," Crys repeated, linking her elbow with Katey's and towing her out the back door. "We wanna get there early before all the cute singles get paired off with the smart ones. 'Night, guys!" she called over her shoulder.

Once they'd gone, the whole restaurant was silent aside from the steady *plink plink plink* of the faucet. Hawk's shoulders were stiff, and it almost seemed like he was holding his breath.

"Hawk?" I stood and edged closer, careful not to touch anything sharp or flammable or poisonous, stopping a foot away from him. "What do you say? Nothing, you know…

weird. Just you and me. Being normal. On a regular hike. Like we've always done."

Great, Jack. Nothing sounds more normal than insisting something's normal.

Hawk did the thing he always did when nervous. He stretched his neck by leaning his head from side to side. "A *regular, normal* hike?" He sounded half-amused, half-annoyed. After a pause, he shrugged. "Sure. I was planning to go hiking tomorrow anyway."

"Good." I let out a relieved breath. "Good. It's just... I missed talking to you this week. Things are so busy here. I haven't heard about your latest adventures with the Mini Scouts or if you've gone hiking with... anyone. I don't even know what you've been reading lately."

As friendship test balloons went, this seemed incredibly pathetic, but after rubbing his lips together for a second, Hawk nodded to himself and glanced over his shoulder at me. "I just finished a good book, actually. Total keeper-shelf, reread material. It's a *gay Pride and Prejudice* retelling, so it's Eli and Darcy this time. And it's spicy."

"Oh? Well, that's—"

He shut off the water and turned around, leaning back against the sink with his arms crossed over his chest, almost like a challenge. "Eli and Darcy are in a closet under the stairs at Rosings—you remember that's where bossy-as-fuck Lady Catherine lives when she's not gallivanting around trying to break the two of them up?"

I nodded. For a man who'd still never read *Pride and Prejudice*, I knew a hell of a lot about its variations.

"They're still at the part of the story where they think they know each other, but they're both super wrong, and they want each other but aren't ready to admit it. There's so much unresolved sexual tension it's practically clogging the air." He lifted an eyebrow. "You know?"

"Huh? Oh. Sure. Yeah. I can… I can imagine that," I agreed. The kitchen was stiflingly warm, but I fought the urge to tug at my collar.

"So they're in the front hall arguing—tension crackling like lightning in the air—when Lady Catherine comes looking for them. And they dislike each other, but they dislike Lady Catherine even more, so they duck into this closet without really thinking about it. Except once they're in there together… they're *committed*. No matter how uncomfortable it gets, they can't leave or make a single sound because Eli's reputation would be in tatters if they were caught. They're stuck in that tiny space with Darcy pressed up against Eli's back. Thigh to thigh. Practically cheek to cheek."

"Oh. Uh-huh." I swallowed hard, trying not to look like I was imagining Hawk and me in that position, even though I very much was. "Wow. Yeah. That sounds—"

"The problem is," he went on solemnly, "there's still that pesky sexual attraction. Even though they want it to go away. Even though they're pretending it doesn't exist."

"That's… rough." I cleared my throat. "So, anyway—"

"So when they're forced to be that tightly fitted together—rubbing up against each other with every breath, sharing the same air—they can't hide their attraction anymore. Darcy sees that Eli is hard under his breeches, and Eli notices Darcy's breathing getting fast and choppy…"

I knew *my* breath was coming faster, but I couldn't stop it. I stared into Hawk's golden-brown eyes, and I couldn't have looked away even if the roof collapsed.

"So they get naked, right there in the closet." Hawk's voice was only a whisper now. "Unbuttoning the falls of their pants, all quick and dirty, but trying to be so, so quiet, too, so that no one can hear them. Darcy ends up on his knees, rimming Eli. And Eli… he's never done that before, but it feels so good he can't help moaning. So Darcy gets to his feet, grabs Eli by the throat, and pins him against the wall—" Hawk demonstrated with a hand around his own throat. "—then kisses him to keep him quiet while he finishes him off with his big, strong hand." Hawk licked his lips like he was tasting a kiss there. "I can't decide if I'd like that or not."

My throat clicked with the effort of replying. "*Erk*" was all I managed to get out.

"Do *you* like that?" he asked, head tilted to one side like we were just making casual conversation now.

I was not feeling casual. Not in the slightest. My dick was hard as a rock, and I was in very real danger of lighting something on fire again… probably myself. *Spontaneous human combustion in Little Pippin Hollow! Film at eleven.*

"Nn-hn. Hnh?"

"Anyway." Hawk shrugged. "Yeah, fine. Hiking tomorrow."

I managed an affirmative-sounding noise.

"Good," Hawk agreed. "We'll take the Red Trail to Glassy Ridge. I have some… *frustration* that I need to work off."

He chucked the soggy, charred rag in the trash, then moved to the stove, putting away the onions and cleaning out the pan with competent efficiency while I watched, my brain still flatlining as all the blood in my body abandoned it.

When he was done, he turned to me. "You ready?"

Ready? I blinked, still thinking about closets and rimming and…

He reached up to flip the light switch on the wall, and his T-shirt rode up again, this time revealing the hot turquoise band of his underwear. I stared at the pale skin over firm muscles until it imprinted in my brain and wondered what it would feel like to run my fingertip over that smooth stretch of skin, to sneak the finger under the elastic band and follow the trail with my tongue…

"*Erk*," I said again.

Hawk rolled his eyes and strode to the back door. "Eight

a.m. tomorrow at the first pull-off leading to Fogg Peak. Maybe bring some of those oatmeal cherry cookie things, unless you have any Thin Mints left. Don't be late."

"*Nuh,*" I agreed, now thinking of *cherries* again.

If my brain-to-mouth connection had been working, I'd probably have asked him about his plans for the night and whether they included finding a random stranger on an app —or that weirdly perky Simon character—to take his virginity. Instead, all I could do was watch him walk away again.

This was getting to be a habit, and I didn't like it one bit.

THANKFULLY, my mom distracted me for the first part of the evening by grilling me on this month's business expenses so she could update the books for the diner. The Bedlington terrier she'd recently adopted had taken an unhealthy liking to my shoelaces and tried to trip me up at least three times while I chopped vegetables for our late-dinner summer salad.

"Dammit, Peony," I muttered for the tenth time. "Move out of my way."

"Aww," Mom cooed, scratching the cute little runt under the chin. "He likes you. You should have seen what a jerk he was to the UPS guy the other day."

"Attempted murder isn't the same thing as like," I grumbled. "And who decided to give the dog a name that sounds like *pee on me*? That seems incredibly short-sighted."

"It's because he's fluffy and sweet like a peony flower. Isn't that right, my angel? Yes, it is. Yes it *is*."

I grunted. "He looks like the byproduct of a sheep getting a little too friendly with a stuffed teddy bear."

"Hush. Don't listen to him, Peony. You're perfection."

The dog scurried away, probably to mount an attack on some unsuspecting throw pillows in the living room.

"What has you in a bad mood?" my mom asked idly as

she turned back to the laptop she'd set up on the kitchen island. It may have seemed like she was only listening with one ear, but I knew better.

"Bad mood? *Pssht*. I'm in a fine mood."

"Okay." She clicked a few keys on the keyboard.

"Business is going okay, right? Revenues are pretty comparable with last year. We're fully staffed for the first time in months. If things keep up, I *might* be able to put aside a little savings to update the kitchen, if my bookkeeper agrees."

"Mmhmm. I do."

"My house has a solid roof, finally. Oh, and the addition I was telling you about is almost done—the fireplace is in, and Remy Fortnum's making me some shelves that'll be perfect for the space. Exactly as I pictured."

"How nice."

"There was even a sale on socks at the Save-a-Ton, and I got a whole bunch of those wool ones I like," I said a little desperately. "So." I set my jaw. "There's no reason at all for me to be in a bad mood or even a less-than-wonderful mood. Obviously."

She nodded without looking up. "You sure you don't wanna use my blender for that, honey? It has an excellent puree function."

I looked down at the carrots I'd been chopping and discovered they'd been diced into a fine pulp. "Dammit." I walked over to scrape the mess into the sink before starting again.

"So… how's Hawk?" she asked, deliberately, carefully casual.

I nearly sliced my finger with the sharp blade before slapping the knife down on the counter and holding up my hand in surrender. "Can we not do this thing? This thing where you speak in code and act all nonchalant?"

Her eyes finally came up to meet mine, sparkling with

amusement. "Oh, I'm chalant. I'm *very* chalant. And I'm pretty darned sure something happened between the two of you. First clue was that you've been irritable and distracted this whole week. Second clue—" She pursed her lips. "—is that Hawk isn't here with you when he *never* misses a chance to visit Peony, which leads me to deduce that the problem is with him…"

"Deduce," I scoffed. "Okay, Sherlock Holmes."

"And third—" She shifted so her elbows were propped on the island, and the scuffed gold band she still wore after thirty years of widowhood glinted dully in the overhead light. "—I was at the library the other day and overheard Hawk asking Lars Yetzer if they have any copies of *Mars and Venus in the Workplace*." She sniffed. "I almost intervened to tell him Venus and Mars are irrelevant if he's having a problem with *you*, and outdated in any case, but I didn't. Because I'm not the kind of parent who tries to interfere in her son's life…" She lifted her chin a notch. "Much."

The revelation that Hawk was frustrated enough with me to seek out a book about workplace relations made my stomach hurt. "Wait, he asked for that book? Are you sure?"

She hesitated. "Well, yes. I don't know why, of course. Could be that he's trying to improve his relationship with Katey… though I thought she was pretty easygoing now that she's put away her obsession with Hawk's brother."

"She kinda had to since Webb and Luke are married now," I muttered. "But there were a few moments last spring that were a little hairy, so it could be that. Or maybe it's Crys. She can be… direct."

I wasn't sure yet about my newest employee. Crystal Hardin had moved to Little Pippin Hollow a few months ago, just when our business was picking up for the summer season. She'd already accepted a part-time job as a bartender at the Bugle when she'd come to me asking to pick up a few shifts a week at Panini Jack's. It had seemed serendipitous at the time, but then she and Hawk started getting closer to the point where I felt a little… left out.

"Nah, those two are thick as thieves," Mom corrected, reading my mind as usual. "I doubt it's anything to do with her."

"Well, it's nothing to do with me either," I said firmly, despite my fears to the contrary. "Hawk and I are *friends*. As usual. As *always*. In fact, we're going for another hike tomorrow."

"Oh, good." She gave me a soft smile, then set her laptop aside and moved around the island to grab place mats and salad bowls. "You know, at first, I wondered why you and Hawk kept going for your hikes together even when Webb and his other siblings got busy and started begging off. He's so much younger than you, so *different* from you, I wondered what you could possibly have in common." She laughed lightly.

I snipped some herbs from the pot on her windowsill and pointedly didn't look at her. "You don't wonder about that anymore?" My mom wasn't the only one who could be *chalant* as hell.

"God, no. Not for a long while. Hawk's good for you, baby. You were always so serious, even as a kid. Taking the world on your little shoulders. Part of that was my fault—"

"It was not." I whirled to face her. "You're a great mother. You always have been."

"Thank you, sweetie. I tried my best after your dad was gone, but it wasn't an easy life for either of us back in Portland, was it? Never enough hours in the day, never enough money in the bank, never enough food on the table." She set down the dishes and snuck a carrot chunk out of the salad to pop in her mouth.

"We survived," I said gruffly. "We made it through. We're settled now."

She knew I hated dwelling on those days, much less talking about them.

"We are. Thanks to your hard work." She cupped my cheek, serious now. "But at what cost? You never got to be carefree or to dream big dreams. You took on too much responsibility too soon. And that's why Hawk Sunday is so good for you." She patted my cheek, then busied herself setting our places at the island. "He reminds you that it's okay to have fun. When you're with him, you let yourself be passionate about things besides work."

"I'm passionate about plenty of other things that don't involve him," I argued. "Like… like… volunteering with the Nature Scouts when they came to the diner for a cooking demonstration. And renovating my house. And outdoorsy stuff—hiking and snowshoeing and swimming…" I faltered, realizing she was right. All of those were things Hawk and I did together.

Mom was kind enough not to point this out. "I'm glad you two are taking a break tomorrow. You'll relax a little. Have some fun. Cold front's moving in, so you'll have a nice cool breeze, too."

But it turned out that my mom was wrong, at least about this.

I did not relax. I did not have fun.

And while the weather might have cooled down some, things were hot as fuck on that mountain trail because Satan himself sent Hawk Sunday to torment me.

IT STARTED OFF WELL ENOUGH. After leaving my mom's, I'd gone home and crashed into bed, too tired after a week of sleepless nights to do any work on the house, and I'd woken up clearheaded and determined. I just had to make Hawk see that our relationship was perfect as it was. That nothing ever needed to change…

And then I'd seen Hawk walking toward me at the trailhead wearing my old Portland Red Claws hoodie.

He'd stolen the shirt so long ago I couldn't even remember the circumstances, and I'd seen him in it a million times… but it had never hit me like it did today, with a possessive thrill that made my mouth water.

The sweatshirt that had once been red was now faded to a weathered pink, and the angry lobster holding a Portland Red Claws banner was peeling from repeated washing. The edges of the cuffs were shredded and hung down over his hands, and the bottom of the garment came down so far that for a split second, I wondered if he had shorts on underneath. His shapely leg muscles led from the hem of the hoodie down to his thick wool socks and scarred hiking boots.

I couldn't think of a single thing to say, so I'd made a stupid comment about the weather, and then I'd tried not to swallow my tongue as my eyes tracked the mesmerizing movement of those legs for the first quarter mile.

"You're being awfully quiet," he said after a few minutes on the deserted, early morning trail.

I glanced up at the back of his head. "Sorry. Wool-gathering."

He let out a little huff of laughter. "No one uses that word anymore."

Hawk was right. I'd picked it up from him a while back when he'd recounted one of his *Pride and Prejudice* stories. He'd said it was *adorably antiquated.* "Guess that makes me special, then, huh? If nobody uses it but me and Mr. Darcy?"

Hawk went silent, the muscles of his back tight with tension, and I replayed my words in my head. What had I said wrong?

After a moment, he said, "Did you go to your mom's last night? How is she? How's Peony?"

"Good. She, ah… she was worried about you, actually. My mom, I mean, not the dog." *Way to be smooth and get things back on track, Jack.*

Hawk turned to face me so quickly that if he'd brought his trekking pole, we'd have wound up in the dirt again. "Worried why?"

"Well, because… uh." I scratched my head. Too late, I realized there was no good way for me to explain this without making things even more awkward. "She wondered why you weren't with me. We're kind of a package deal, you and me, right?"

The words were meant to be a joke, but Hawk didn't laugh.

"And also…" I cleared my throat. "Mom said there was a rumor in town that you're having problems with someone at work. You checked out a book at the library about workplace issues—"

"Ugh. Mr. Yetzer has no concept of librarian-patron confidentiality." Hawk set his fists on his hips and glared up at the sky. Between his oversized sweatshirt, his reddened cheeks, and his mulish expression, he should have looked like a kid… and maybe any time before last weekend, that's what I would have seen when I looked at him. I would have known exactly what to say to joke him out of his temper.

Now, stranded on this island of Want But Can't Have, caught between the safe harbor of Platonic Friendship and the chaotic waters of Super-Unplatonic Cherry Poaching, all I could see were the lean muscles of Hawk's thighs, his high cheekbones, that damn sexy nose ring.

But I noticed Hawk didn't offer any other explanation for the book.

"Is it me?" I asked stupidly. *I'm the problem, it's me.*

His jaw tightened. I could tell he was trying to decide whether or not to be honest with me.

"You can tell me anything, Bird," I softly encouraged.

"You've always been honest with me. I *expect* you to be honest with me. Even if I, ah… don't always react the way you wish I would." My face heated, but I kept going. "You know that you're one of the most important people in my life, right? So if there's a problem, you should tell me."

Hawk tilted his head and studied me for a long moment.

"No, Jack," he lied. "There's no problem."

CHAPTER FOUR

HAWK

"They walked on, without knowing in what direction. There was too much to be thought, and felt, and said, for attention to any other objects."
~ Jane Austen

I'D AGREED to this stupid hike for one reason and one reason only: today was my dad's birthday, and there was no place I'd rather spend it than on Fogg Peak, surrounded by the tall trees and shining water he'd loved. But I hadn't wanted to come alone.

Knox or Webb or even Emma would have been here in a heartbeat if I'd asked them, but something had held me back. My dad had bonded with each of us in our own unique way. My brothers, who'd all been forged in our dad's broad-shouldered, larger-than-life mold, right down to his Sunday green eyes, shared his passion for business, or the orchards, or white-water rafting, or racing ATVs through the Averys' field of silage corn at twilight. Emma had been his spitfire princess, and they'd shared a love of animals and a passion for justice.

Dad and I, though... we'd had Fogg Peak. We'd had *"Come for a walk with me, Hawkins?"* We'd had fox tracks in the winter and loon calls in the summer, swollen rivers in the spring and foliage in the autumn, and he'd made all of it magical. In his quiet way, he'd taught me that humans go through seasons, just like plants do, and sometimes needed to be dormant before they could grow. He'd taught me about animals adapting to their environments and that the very same things that made me feel so different—my shyness, my shortness, my bookishness, my plain brown eyes—were the things that made me special. He'd taught me that nothing stays the same forever—not sunsets, not trees, not people, not even the rocks under our feet—so you needed to appreciate things while they lasted and embrace change when it comes. He'd taught me that most things weren't worth fighting about but that some things, some *people*, were.

I hadn't hiked for years after he died. I'd thought the magic of the mountain had died along with him, and it would be too weird, too sad, for me to go without him. But then Jack had come into my life one cold winter's day a few years later.

Hiking with Jack was very different from hiking with Dad but every bit as magical. Our hikes had started out as group events with my siblings, but even back then, the two of us would end up hanging back or outpacing the others, off in our own little world as we shared our thoughts on everything from books and recipes and geology and bug spray to what it felt like growing up without a dad.

Our viewpoints were often different, but I'd never doubted for a minute that Jack *saw* me. That he *liked* me. That I didn't have to censor myself or project some happy, carefree version of Hawk Sunday in order to please him. That we fit together, easy as breathing.

Despite all that had happened last weekend, it had felt right to have him with me today, when I was feeling overly emotional and on edge, because Jack was my person. My constant. The North Star that my internal compass had aligned itself to long ago.

But it seemed I'd underestimated the nuclear fallout that one teeny-tiny, super-casual request for no-strings, cherry-popping sex would have on our seven years of devoted friendship and understanding because every word the man uttered today seemed to prove that Jack and I did *not* fit. Not today, anyway.

"You've always been honest with me," Jack said, his blue eyes wide and worried. "Even if I, ah… don't always react the way you wish I would. You know that you're one of the most important people in my life, right? So if there's a problem, you should tell me."

I studied his handsome face for a long moment, deliberating.

What the heck was I supposed to say to that?

Did Jack *really* want to know how I was feeling?

I'd told him about my "problem" last weekend, and look how that had turned out.

Did he want to know that I was mortified and heartsick over his rejection? Or that I'd tried so hard to give off what Crys had called a "subtle yet unmistakable fuck-me vibe" this week that I'd practically thrown out my back accidentally-on-purpose dropping things so I could bend over and show off my ass?

Did he want to know I was hurt and angry at his lack of support at the town meeting? Or that I'd gotten nowhere in my plan to thwart Evola because I'd been working too many shifts to seek out Ms. Fortnum at the Apple of My Eye, and when I'd texted her about getting our environmental group back together, she'd replied with a cryptic *"Plans have changed, sweetie. Msg u 18r. Hookers r assembling!"* as though meeting with the other octogenarians in her fiber-arts group was more important than saving Fogg Peak?

Did he want to know that my regular volunteer gig leading hikes with the Mini Nature Scouts had gotten canceled thanks to an outbreak of Norovirus, so I hadn't been able to speak to their parents, or that Uncle Drew had been so busy at Sunday Orchard he hadn't listened to a word I said when I tried to explain my concerns?

Did Jack want to know how sad and confused I was that he was suddenly treating me like all the people in my life who gave me loving, protective head-pats while ignoring my opinions?

Did he want to know that a tight, hot ball of anger and resentment had formed in my chest, making it hard to be my usual positive self? That I was getting so sick of my own attitude I'd started visiting the self-help section of the library?

Just like the other night at the town meeting, I had the creeping suspicion that talking to Jack would make me feel worse instead of better.

He wanted the security of our uncomplicated friendship back, and for today, at least, I wanted that, too. So I smushed all of those feelings into a little ball and swallowed them.

"No, Jack," I said, turning back to the trail and focusing my attention on the path. "There's no problem."

It took a solid half mile of walking—okay, *stomping*—uphill before the rhythm of my footsteps, the spicy fern scent of the air, and the pleasant strain in my lungs and muscles as we navigated the steepest switchback started to work their familiar magic on me, taking the edge off my jangled nerves. Up here, walking on mountains that had been formed eons ago, under the shelter of trees that had stood for centuries, my problems felt a bit smaller.

We passed a small clearing where summer flowers carpeted patches of virgin earth, and shards of sun cut down through the leaves to catch on delicate petals and stems.

"Purple hyssop," I said, breaking the silence at last to point out the native flower. "It's on Vermont's list of threatened plant species. I talked to Maryanne Kopra about doing a unit study with the Mini Nature Scouts about these endangered plants and how precious they are."

Jack hummed thoughtfully and paused to inhale the sweet licorice smell.

We continued along, my eyes roaming the area around us, searching for changes from the last time we'd hiked this particular trail up to the peak last summer. When planning out the hikes Jack and I took, I usually stuck to lower-elevation trails during the cooler seasons, saving the higher elevations for the summer months.

After a curve in the trail, I stopped and squatted down. "Drummond's rock cress. This one is on the endangered list, too."

"Oh, right. I recognize this one. Pretty," Jack said, admiring the white flowers.

"It is." I glanced up at him. "Hard to think that a year from now, a trendy barrel sauna might be sitting here instead of this plant, huh?"

Jack nodded, frowning in concern, but it felt like that concern was more for me and my inevitable disappointment once the resort was approved than the fate of the plants themselves.

"They really don't need to build so high up the mountain," I said stubbornly, as though we hadn't discussed this a dozen times before. "What if they kept the resort buildings clustered around the primary area of Coster's Meadow? As much as I'd hate to lose the vistas from that little valley, at least it would make more sense than clear-cutting the ridge."

"It's an *alpine* resort concept." Jack's voice was infuriatingly patient and oh-so-reasonable, as usual. "I think setting it among the trees on the ridge is sort of the point, Bird."

"Well, then, they can change the concept. That's what all these town meetings have been about, right? They're supposed to listen to us. To give us a voice. We get to have the final say. But if no one speaks up, if no one seems to care, why would they—"

Jack gripped the straps of his pack tighter. "Or maybe

people in town care about more than one thing. I keep telling you, it's not a black-and-white issue for most folks. There's a huge financial benefit to the resort. There's lots to consider."

That phrase again.

"Assuming people *are* considering things and not dismissing it for all the wrong reasons," I grumbled.

Financial security and stability were important—*of course they were!*—but it wasn't as though the survival of Jack's business depended on the resort. Panini Jack's had become a local institution, and folks lined up for a table on a weekend morning, even in the off-season.

I was trying to look at the situation maturely. To not be selfish. To tell myself it was okay to disagree and not let my hurt over Jack's rejection get all twisted up with his dismissal of my fears about Evola. To remind myself that Jack cared about me *lots* and that he'd proven it over the past seven years by treating me like an intelligent adult, by listening when I talked, by giving me a job at his diner, by asking my opinion on all the tiny details of his home renovation. But I was too emotional for this logic to really penetrate.

We walked further along the trail, passing old-growth hardwoods, familiar jagged outcrops, and the places where the other trails leading down all sides of the mountain—the Rock Cut, the Hunter, the Fox, the Shepherd, and bunches more too small to have names—converged into the Red Trail for the final push up to the Peak.

When we got to the Friendly Footbridge—the wooden structure that a century's worth of Hollowans had crossed in order to reach the highest areas of the mountain without braving the rushing current of Glassy Creek—by unspoken agreement, we stopped for a moment to lean against the railing in silence. The Creek, which could run dangerously high during the spring, was running low now, thanks to a stretch of warm, dry weather, but was still beautiful. The crystal-clear water meandering over rocks and boulders on its way downhill was hypnotic and comforting. I was already working up a sweat from the incline, but thankfully, the air was comfortably cool under the tree canopy… at least until the clear-cutting began.

"They're building this resort to lure tourists up to our unspoiled wilderness," I murmured, "and don't get the irony of how much they're spoiling it. The glory of this land is that it's self-sustaining, Jack. Every single thing impacts something else. You clear-cut the trees, there's less shade, and the water in the lake gets hotter. You dig a huge foundation, and you're disturbing the runoff patterns. The very shape of the lake changes. The fish die. Other plants take over. Now it's not an upscale resort set in unspoiled wilderness anymore; it's an overpriced motel on a piece of land that looks like a thousand other places on Earth. And by then, it's too late. It's *ruined*."

"Hawk, it's not in anyone's best interest to let it be ruined. That's why Evola has people on their team who'll be supervising—"

"Do you honestly think Evola's idea of *ruined* is the same as ours? As long as they're profiting, are they going to care that there are five—*five*—different types of bats that have been found in the Glassy cave system that are on the endangered list? Not to mention the Canadian lynx, the eastern mountain lion, and the American marten, all of which have been spotted on or around Fogg Peak in the last twenty years. All of them are endangered. *All of them*—" I cut myself off and blew out a breath. "Sorry. I'm sorry. I'm taking out my anger on you, and I don't mean to."

"It's okay," Jack soothed. "I meant what I said last week: you can talk to me about anything, whether I agree with you or not. If it makes you feel better to vent about bats, I'm all ears."

An image of Jack as a bat, squeaking out the *Erk! Erk!*

noises he made when I flustered him, dropped into my brain unbidden.

"What's funny?" he demanded as I snickered.

"Nothing. Just, the northern long-eared bat is one of the endangered bat species, and I was just kind of picturing you with…" I gestured to my own ears.

"Hawk Sunday," Jack said, mock outraged. "First, you mock me because I'm talking like Mr. Darcy. Now I've been downgraded all the way to *bat*? Remind me never to really piss you off, or you'll be comparing me to fungi."

This was so accurate I laughed out loud. "If it makes you feel better, northern long-eared bats are adorable and extremely useful. They eat insects that could decimate agricultural and timber industries. And while they mate in the fall, the females store the sperm and don't actually get pregnant until the spring. They're all about *delayed gratification*."

He rolled his eyes, but his blue gaze met mine, and when he saw me grin, his lips twitched into that familiar smile I loved. The knots in my shoulders loosened a fraction.

This is why you love Jack Wyatt, Hawkins.

Jack got my humor. He smiled when I smiled. I knew the rhythm of his strong, confident stride on the trail, the sound of his regular breathing interspersed with his periodic inhales to "enjoy the smell of the fir trees," the view of his chiseled calf muscles covered in wiry blond hair, and the clean scent of his sweat when we finally came out of the trees and into the summer sun. When things between us were calm, I was calmer, too… which was part of what had made this past week so hard.

Maybe it could be just as simple as that.

"Thank you for inviting me," I whispered after a long moment. "Thanks for being with me today."

Jack nodded without looking over at me again. Instead, he looked ahead where the view was starting to open up across the lower part of Glassy Valley. "He would have been proud of you, you know."

Of course Jack remembered what today was and what it meant to me. That part wasn't a shock. But something about those sweet words cut straight into my gut like a jagged shard of sheet metal.

I made a sound in my throat that finally made Jack's head turn sharply to me. I didn't know what he saw in my face, but it must have been terrible. His expression morphed from curiosity to horror as a sob broke its way out of me.

"*Bird.*"

I stumbled over the footbridge and dropped onto the nearest boulder at the edge of the trail before bending at the waist and covering my face with my hands. Hot tears slid fast and wet down my cheeks as my breath tried triple-timing it in and out of my lungs through horrid, racking sounds.

"Sorry!" I sobbed. "Sorry."

Part of me wanted to laugh at what a mess I was. What a ridiculous overreaction to a well-meaning comment! But part of me wanted to sob even harder because suddenly, a tidal wave of loss for my father that must have been hiding somewhere inside of me, packed tight like an emergency parachute just waiting for the moment it needed to break free and save a life, washed over me.

Jack was on his knees in front of me almost as quickly as I'd dropped to the rock. He reached out to grab me, and I fell into his arms, hiding my face in his damp neck and flooding it with my tears and snot.

"Oh, baby," he murmured. His hands were warm and strong on my back, rubbing firm circles as he held me tightly. "There's nothing to be sorry about. It's okay. You know it's okay. I'm sorry I said anything. So stupid. I shouldn't have said anything. *Fuck.*"

I shook my head, unable to explain that it wasn't his fault. Clearly, this had been waiting for any moment to break free. I let the tears come. If ever there was a safe place to let go and feel my damned feelings, it was here in this hallowed forest that had meant so much to my father. And it was here in the arms of a man I knew would be there for me no matter what I said or did.

"Okay," he said softly into my hair. "We're doing this. Yes. It's okay. Feelings are for feeling, right? Right. This is healthy. Let it out. That's it. This is good. Gonna break my heart, but that's fine. It's natural. Doesn't feel so natural. Feels like I want to take a swing at someone. Or hide in your Glassy bat caves. But yeah, this is good. Super great."

I finally calmed down enough to huff a laugh into his soggy shirt front. "You're doing that nervous babbling thing you always accuse me of. You've never been able to handle criers."

Jack pulled back and cupped my face, swiping across my wet cheeks with his thumbs. Concern marred his forehead. "No, I can't handle *you* crying. Pretty sure Webb could cry all day and I wouldn't feel like I want to vomit."

I tried not to interpret his words or his whispered "baby" to mean anything other than he had protective feelings for me. *Brotherly* feelings.

As soon as I remembered that, I forced myself to pull away from him and get myself together. I wiped my face on my own sweatshirt and took a deep, cleansing breath before reaching into my day pack for a water bottle.

"Sorry. Again," I said after a nice cold swig. "I should have known I'd get emotional today. I'm one giant mood swing this week." I poured out some of the water into my hand and used it to clean off the salty residue from my tears.

"Don't apologize," Jack said, bumping my arm. "It's okay."

A bird whistled in the trees, and I seized on the distraction. "Bicknell's thrush," I said, pointing a thumb over my shoulder. "It makes that spiraling, flute-like sound. Their entire breeding population is restricted to the northeast, which is unique to the species..." I broke off and shook my head. "Wow. An emotional meltdown *and* lecture on bird and bat mating habits. Next time, you'll be grateful when I stick to telling you about my *Pride and Prejudice* retellings, huh?"

Jack stood. "Not true. You've got a big heart, and it shows. I know your dad taught you a ton about these mountains, but it's clear you've kept up the research."

"Even more so after Evola came to town." I shrugged and put the water bottle back in my pack after another deep sip. "I love it here. I know I complain sometimes about how small the Hollow is, but I wouldn't want to live anywhere else."

He stepped closer to me before reaching out to run his fingers into the front of my hair. "You have some tangles..." His voice faded as his eyes landed on my nose ring. Sometimes I caught him staring at it, enough that I'd asked him one time if he didn't like it, but he'd sworn he liked it fine.

Now, his eyes rested there, and a little divot formed between his brows. I sucked in a breath. With his face this close, I could see slivers of green in his blue irises. I could see the slight color variation in his eyelashes, some with the faintest of blond tips.

Jack's breath hitched. His fingertip came down and traced the little hoop ring. My lower belly tightened, and my chest constricted. Green-blue slivers glanced between my nose and my eyes. The Bicknell's thrush stopped its trilling flute, and even the breeze seemed to stand still.

He's going to kiss me.

I felt the truth of it to my toes. Jack's lips parted as his gaze dropped to my mouth. Our bodies shifted closer together until the inside of one of his thighs brushed against the outside of mine. He tilted his head and moved closer.

"*Please,*" I breathed.

In that moment, I would have given *anything* for the fulfillment of all my years of wishing—they could clear-cut

Glassy Ridge, and all of Fogg Peak, and Sunday Orchard besides if it meant I could have one life-changing kiss from Jack Wyatt.

One of his large hands cupped the side of my face, holding me in place. He leaned closer—close enough that the stubble on his chin rasped softly against my jaw, and the warmth of his breath against my skin made me hyperaware of every pore and nerve ending. The warm, spicy scent of his cologne sent adrenaline rushing through my bloodstream, and my body felt like a suite of advanced surveillance technology all homed in on one delicious insurgent.

"*Jack*," I breathed, wondering how it was possible for time to move this slowly.

"Fuck," he murmured before—and I would swear this on my life—he took a deep inhale of the skin at the edge of my hairline. "I can't! I can't. Shit, Hawk. *We* can't."

He stepped back and turned around, but not before I noticed a very clear bulge in the front of his shorts that wasn't nearly as visible before.

Jack Wyatt had gotten hard for me.

Crys was right. He *did* find me attractive. I hadn't really let myself believe it, despite my attempts at being seductive. But if that wasn't the issue…

"Why can't we?" I demanded. "Is this really about my brothers? Or our age difference? What are you so freaking scared of?" My voice was angry, hurt, annoyed. I could hear it as clear as the thrush's renewed trill.

"I'm not *scared*," he insisted, keeping his back to me, and I was two seconds away from tearing into him for being a *liar* because he was clearly scared of something, when he finished with a whispered "I'm fucking terrified" that took the wind out of my sails.

The silence settled back around us, only this time, it wasn't complete. The breeze ruffled the edges of his hair, and the bird kept up his whirling song.

"Terrified of what?" I wanted to step closer, put my hand on his shirt, my face in the center of his back.

He shook his head. "I can't give you what you want, Bird. I know you. You want a fairy-tale romance. You want... true love conquering all. You want the happily ever after, and I... don't," he said simply, cratering my heart with one small word. "That's your dream, not mine."

"I told you before, Jack, we could keep it casual—"

He shook his head. "You'd want more from anyone you were with. Hell, I *want* you to want more, and I'd hope for your sake that you'd defy the odds and get it. But I... I can't give you that. So if we start down that path... then what? We'd both end up hurt and bitter. I'd lose my best employee and my closest..." He cleared his throat. "One of my closest friends."

I reached out to touch him, but before my hand made contact, he turned around and straightened his shoulders. "Not to mention—and I know you hate this, but it bears repeating, okay?—you *are* Webb's Hawklet. And if I fucked things up..." He met my eyes with the dreaded conviction he got sometimes when he falsely assumed he was right about something. "You're off-limits. *Period.* I don't want the relationship we have now to change. Ever."

I nodded slowly, reaching my absolute limit. "I understand."

Jack let out a breath and nodded. "Good. Thank y—"

"I *understand* you're a selfish jackass who thinks only of himself and what's best for him. I *understand* that you think I'm childish and silly. I *understand* you're hell-bent on insisting I'm not allowed to be an actual adult male because god forbid my family hear I might—*gasp!*—have sexual relations like they do. And don't even think about telling me my brothers aren't all out there fucking right now because we both know they are. Hell, Webb's probably got Luke in the dirt under an apple tree, Knox and Gage are christening every damn room in their new place while covered in Cecilia's organic honey from the gift shop—and don't ask me how I know about that because I don't care to relive it—while Reed's fucking his way through our nation's capital, and Porter's at Hannabury, probably bending over for one of his professors."

Jack's eyes widened, whether at my temper or my crude language, and I could almost see his thoughts beaming out of his brain. *My Hawk doesn't talk like that!* But guess what? Today, I sure as fuck did.

"For god's sake," I went on, the emotion I'd dammed up pouring out of me in torrents. "Even Drew, who's old enough to be a grandfather, reinjured his leg last week and *claimed* he hurt it gardening… like anyone who shares a roof with him didn't hear the noises coming out of his room the night before."

"God, stop!" Jack held up a hand. "I beg you. I do not want to know a damn thing about your family's sex lives—"

"Really? Then why the fuck do they get a say in *mine*?" I demanded. "If you don't want me, Jack Wyatt, that's your choice, and I accept it. But if you're honestly trying to pretend that you're doing this for *my* sake—slapping me up on a pedestal I never asked to be on, telling me I'm too pure and good to ever have something hot and sexual and *real*, pretending you know what I want better than I do—you can get on your fucking high horse and take a long canter off a very short bridge."

His jaw hung open as his startling blue eyes stared at me. I didn't wait around to hear his pitiful excuses. Instead, I lobbed one final line at him before taking off up the trail at a fast clip.

"I will lose my virginity this summer with or without you, Jack. Mark my words. It's happening whether you like it or not."

CHAPTER FIVE

JACK

"I am all astonishment."
~ Caroline Bingley

I stood stock-still, blinking at the space where Hawk had been for a long moment after he stalked off.

One part of my brain firmed its jaw and wanted to yell in Hawk's direction, *See? This is what happens when you complicate a perfectly wonderful friendship! Better now than after you'd developed romantic feelings for me.*

Another part twisted up and whimpered, *Come back! I was wrong! Give me a do-over!*

But, no lie, most of my brain was busy replaying Hawk's sweet voice gritting out the words *"something hot and sexual and real"* on an endless loop while picturing him naked, *"bending over"* and, in a bizarre new twist, covered in organic honey. My cock swelled uncomfortably in my pants, and I couldn't even pretend to be shocked about that since this was at least my twenty-fifth Hawk-based erection in the past seven days.

How the fuck had we gotten to this place?

Hawk was trying to change the rules of our friendship in the middle of the game, and I couldn't decide whether to be angry or… worried.

There was clearly something going on with him. Something weird. Something potentially dangerous. Maybe it was simply the resort development dredging up grief over his dad and causing him to lash out. Or maybe, I thought darkly, recalling a certain pink-haired employee, Hawk had been listening to the wrong people.

The crunch of Hawk's boots ahead of me on the trail was familiar enough to make it clear he was angry, even if I hadn't seen the frustration on his face when he'd made his defiant stand. But when his footsteps paused, I glanced up and found that he'd stopped right under a break in the canopy and tilted his face toward the sun.

My gut clenched. Christ, the man was beautiful—wide stance, thick calves, firm shoulders, head held high, so freaking alive—and Christ, he looked lonely.

Worry won out over anger.

"Hawk," I croaked. "Hey, wait up." I walked faster until we were pacing side by side. "Look, I'm sorry I upset you. That wasn't my intention. Not ever, but for sure not *today*. Truce, okay? Can we finish our hike together? I don't want this to come between us. You're too important to me."

Hawk closed his eyes, took a deep breath, and let it out slowly. He made a *mpfh* noise that wasn't the enthusiastic agreement I'd been hoping for, but when he started walking again, he made room for me beside him on the trail.

"Are you—?" I began tentatively.

"I was just thinking about my dad again," he cut in. "Did I ever tell you he played drums in a band when he was in high school?"

I shook my head, grateful for the seemingly random topic shift. "No. Was he good?"

"Nope," Hawk said, popping the *p*. He grinned. "He was

awful. They called him the Mangler. Uncle Drew still has a T-shirt from a batch they had made up when they played at a local festival. It says The Narwhals featuring the Mangler." He laughed, and the sound jolted my heart back into its normal rhythm. "What you said before, about him being proud of me... it really hit me because I think about that a lot. What would he think of me and what I'm doing with my life? What would he think of the plans for this place?" He gestured up the trail, toward the peak. "Would he have been more persuasive than I am? Would he have convinced people that the development was a terrible idea? It's good to remember that there was stuff he wasn't good at, too, and that he just kept trying his best."

"Bird, you're an incredible person. You—" I reached out a hand to touch his leanly muscled biceps, but Hawk side-stepped.

"I don't need comfort or a pep talk right now," he said softly. "I know there are plenty of things I'm good at. It's just..." He broke off, shaking his head.

I shoved my hands in my pockets. "You mean, are you good at the things that were important to him. Does part of him live in you. I get it."

Hawk's gaze flew to mine. "You don't talk about your dad much. About... that time."

"No. Partly that's because I was young when I lost him, and I don't remember him much. But I do sometimes wonder... I'm sure he'd *love* me if he were still alive, but would he *like* me? My mom used to talk about him playing tuba in the marching band back in high school and how good he was. Would he be disappointed I never learned an instrument and didn't get any of his musical talent?"

Hawk glanced over at me. "You did, though. You're a good singer." It was a reluctant admission, like he was throwing me a bone against his better judgment.

"I'm a passably okay singer," I corrected. "And that's less

about talent and more because I had hours of practice when I cooked at that dinner theater I told you about back in Portland. Now I can hardly cook without singing under my breath. Like Pavlov's dog."

"I like it," he said. "I mean, all of us do. Even the customers talk about it when they catch you singing."

"Well, if the Narwhals make a comeback to the stage, I'll be ready."

Hawk sputtered out a laugh, and I felt victorious. "Oh, god, no. Drew still plays guitar sometimes—mostly for Marco when he's trying to get back in his good graces after a fuck-up." He shook his head, amused. "He's not great at it either, which is kinda sweet. He does this really loud, reeeeeally off-key version of 'You Are So Beautiful,' and when he gets to the warbly high bit, Sally Ann and Black Bear start barking their heads off like he's hitting notes only dogs can hear. But Drew doesn't mind looking a little foolish, as long as it makes Marco smile. I think that's what true love is."

I snorted. "I think Marco listening to that racket and smiling anyway is what true love is." I lifted one shoulder. "Not that I know the first thing about relationship stuff."

Hawk's smile faded, and he rolled his eyes. "Maybe the only reason you don't know about *relationship stuff* is because you haven't tried *relationship stuff*, just like you weren't born knowing how to play the damn tuba."

I opened my mouth, then shut it again and shook my head. "Hawk... what's going on? I know you're upset about your dad, but it feels like you're angry at *me*. Is this about me saying no to the, uh..." I cleared my throat. "The cherry thing? Because that's not fair—"

"No," he bit out. Then a moment later, he dragged a frustrated hand through his hair and admitted, "Or, okay, a little bit yes. It's not just the turning down. I could deal with that. Probably. But your reasons for it don't make sense. My brothers? My age? You don't *do* relationships, and I'm required to want one because you say so? It feels like bullshit. And I'm talking 'Mr. Darcy telling Elizabeth he can't marry her because of her inferior connections'-level bullshit. You remember how much I hate that part of the book, right?"

"I do," I said with feeling. "But, Hawk—" I reached for him, but he sidestepped again, bunching his hands into fists, and I let my own hand drop uselessly to my side. I hadn't realized just how much we'd casually touched—and how much I'd come to expect it—until that moment.

"It's not all you, though. I'm just so angry at everything these days." He whispered the last words like he was confessing a dark crime. "I don't feel like myself."

"I've seen you angry before. You were angry the day we met, remember?" I teased gently.

"It's not the same. This... it's... I feel like I don't have control over any part of my life. All the things I love are slipping away, and I don't know how to hold them. I don't know what I can count on anymore. I'm angry at my dad for dying and for Webb treating me like a child. I'm angry that the town is all up in my library checkouts but can't muster the energy to care about the one issue I want them to care about. I'm angry that Evola wants to ruin this place and that poor, old Jeremiah Fogg didn't... I don't know... turn the land into a permanent wilderness preserve before he died a hundred years ago."

"I get it—" I began, but Hawk cut me off.

"Oh, I'm not even close to done. I'm also angry that Helena Fortnum texts like a teenager circa 2009. I'm angry that you're obviously trying so hard to listen to me, but for the first time, I don't feel like you're really *listening to me*. I'm angry at Simon Wentworth for being so freaking nice and handsome when by all rights he should be a warty, mustache-twirling evil villain. I'm angry that my brothers have fallen in love with the most amazing, wonderful men, while I can't even lose my virginity without embarrassing myself. I'm angry at people for thinking it's front-page news that I'm angry. And I'm angry at myself for *being angry* when none of it makes sense."

"Hawk—"

"No wonder you don't want to have sex with me. I have become a veritable *river of salt,* and my banks are overflowing," he said miserably.

I pressed my lips together to keep from pointing out that Simon Wentworth wasn't really all that handsome—*not the point, Jack, god*—and focused on Hawk.

Hawk had trusted me with a lot of things over the years, but this felt different. More. Like he was being vulnerable in a new way, showing a side of himself that scared him a little.

He sounded so lost and alone my arms ached to hold him as I had earlier. I wanted to whisper nonsense about everything being okay, that I would *make* it okay, that we would make it okay together because I was right beside him and I always would be. Nothing he could do or say would scare me away. No matter what else changed, he could always count on me.

But one look at him told me he wouldn't welcome any of that. Beneath his hoodie, his whole body was taut as a bowstring, like he was holding himself together by willpower alone, and the slightest touch might send him rocketing to the stratosphere. So I channeled my own frustrated helplessness into kicking a rock off a nearby drop-off—possibly imagining Simon's face on it, who's to say?—before opening my mouth.

"I hate that you're dealing with this," I said quietly. "But I'm glad you told me. I don't want you to hold back with me. Okay?"

"Yeah." He huffed out a laugh and pushed his hair up off his forehead, but he wouldn't meet my eyes. "Sure."

"I know some of the things you're angry about, like your

dad, are things you can't fix or change. But some of the others maybe you just need time to figure out. In the meantime, maybe you need an outlet. When I was younger, I had a lot of pent-up aggression—"

Hawk's eyes met mine. "Yeah? You never told me that."

I nodded. "I, uh… Grief is weird, you know? Comes up when you least expect it and sometimes in ways you don't expect. My mom hadn't finished her accounting degree yet, so she was working crazy hours, and things were kinda shitty, and I…" I shrugged. I didn't like talking about this stuff because I didn't like remembering it. "Anyway. Hitting a punching bag really helped. Have you thought about checking out that new kickboxing studio in Two Rivers?"

He huffed out a laugh, and his posture eased a bit. "Yeah, Crys had some ideas about that, too. First, she suggested jiujitsu since she's studied it herself—"

I was hesitant to agree with Crys's suggestions just on principle, but in this case, she might have a point. "Jiujitsu would be good for self-defense. In fact, you should probably get a belt or two before you pursue the hookup app idea, if that was something you were still, ah… thinking about."

It occurred to me the instant the words were out of my mouth that I probably shouldn't have brought that up again, especially now.

Hawk's glare confirmed this. "Did *you* get a belt in jiujitsu before *you* swiped right on Smug Peter or Handsy Donny?"

"Well…" I cleared my throat and lifted my chin. "In retrospect, maybe I should have."

"Uh-huh. Since I wasn't planning to post a profile on *OKSerialKillers*, I think I'll be okay."

"I just think you could forget the apps and find a nice guy in town. Someone you know. Someone who would—"

"*Bup bup bup*! You know what? I'm instituting a new friendship rule, Jack: you and I don't talk about this anymore. I tried finding a nice guy in town, but he turned me down."

He gave me a significant look. "*Twice*. And now he doesn't get to have an opinion about my dating life."

"But that's not—"

"—up for discussion," Hawk finished. "*River of salt*, remember? Change the subject."

His voice held a warning I'd be a fool to ignore, but I was still tempted. I didn't want there to be a whole area of his life he wouldn't share with me, and the idea of Hawk on a date with a stranger made my palms sweat.

But now was not the time to push that issue either. The whole point of this hike had been to get things on track, and I was driving Hawk further away.

"Fine," I agreed, mentally adding a *for now*.

He nodded once. "Thank you."

I gave him a sidelong glance, gauging his mood, searching my brain for a distraction. "Would now be a bad time to tell you there was a Jane Austen trivia question at Singles' Trivia last night?"

He whipped his head in my direction. "You were at Singles' Trivia Night?"

"What? Dude. You know I wasn't. Katey messaged to say she'd be coming in late tomorrow because she has a date tonight, and she mentioned one of the questions was about the early reference to baseball in *Northanger Abbey*. You know Katey's a pitcher for the Hollow Swingers, right? So she asked if I knew how Jane Austen would have known about baseball in the 1600s when she wrote her books—"

"1600s?" he moaned. "Please tell me you—?"

"Set her right?" I nodded. "Pfft. Obviously. Loyalty to you compelled me to. I told her that was hundreds of years before Jane's time. But I told her she had to ask you if she wanted to know the answer to her question."

"In *Northanger Abbey*, it's spelled as two words, and it refers to the game of *rounders*, which is a cousin of what we now know as baseball. Some people have tried to credit her with the name of the game, but that's been debunked. But the really salient point here…"

Hawk fell into a monologue about popular misconceptions of the Regency era, just as I'd hoped he would, and I could practically see the tension bleed out of him as we climbed to the peak.

I wanted to believe that he'd purged all of his anger and frustration, that we could go back to being Jack and Hawk in perfect harmony, that the hard part of the hike was over.

But as we sat at the top of the trail, admiring the 360-degree views of Little Pippin Hollow and the surrounding countryside while eating the cherry oatmeal cookies I'd brought, I realized I was wrong.

"We can't lose this, Jack," Hawk murmured as he chewed. "I can't lose it. All of my most special moments have been on this mountain. This place… it's part of who I am. We need to protect it by stopping the development. I wish you believed that—"

"If anyone can make it happen, you can," I agreed carefully. "That I believe."

"But you don't want me to try, do you?" he said flatly. "When all is said and done, despite everything I've said to you on the subject, despite everything at stake, you want the Aerie Resort to go forward as planned."

I opened my mouth to brush him off with my usual disclaimers, but this time, I stopped myself. Hawk felt like I was listening to him but not *really* listening to him? Well, maybe part of that was because I'd been holding back so I wouldn't upset him.

My feelings about the development were as complex as my feelings for Hawk himself. I loved this mountain. There were a million hidden worlds in every shady glen, under every fallen log, around every bend in the trail, and Hawk had pointed most of them out to me over the years. I never felt more free than when I visited here. And I wanted the place to remain untouched forever, for Hawk's sake.

But it wasn't just about what I wanted or what Hawk wanted either.

When I weighed that against the responsibility I owed to my employees who needed regular paychecks, or to my mom, who deserved to enjoy her semi-retirement in the Hollow after decades of debt and struggle back in Portland, or to the rest of the town, which badly needed new infrastructure…

"I don't want to fight with you about it, that's for sure," I hedged.

Hawk shot me a look, and I sighed. Hawk had given me honesty; the least I could do was return it.

"Yeah. I think it would be a mistake not to let the development move forward. With proper oversight, obviously."

"Because money is more important than this?" He swept a hand out over the vista.

"Because money *is* important," I said, my own patience fraying a bit. "As anyone who's ever done without could tell you."

"But you're not doing without! Panini Jack's is doing great," Hawk insisted, "just like Sunday Orchard has done fine for centuries, so why—"

"The orchard does just fine because Webb—and now Knox —work their asses off to make sure it does, just like I do with the diner. But it'd be nice not to worry, come November, if I have enough to make it through until the tourists come back." I exhaled sharply and went on in a more measured tone, "And it's not just about me, Bird. There are a lot of Hollowans who've had to turn to online sales to make money through winter. Nan and Len at the yarn shop. Mrs. Cleeward with her candy. We're doing as much as we can, supporting each other and creating our own local network. You know I'm committed to making the diner as farm-to-table as possible.

But how much business do you think Scoops does on a given day in January? Barely enough to keep Frank Bediako's lights on."

I bit my tongue against the other truths I could tell him—about nights I'd gone to bed hungry after my dad died because there simply wasn't money to pay for his medical bills *and* our rent *and* enough food for a growing teenager; about how I'd woken up in a cold sweat at least twice a week after buying the diner, worried I'd made a mistake and my mom and I would end up back in a tiny apartment again—but I'd never wanted to burden Hawk with those stories, especially now when he was dealing with his own shit.

"There are other ways," he insisted. "If folks are that worried, let's think up another business concept..."

"Sure. But I don't have any great ideas, do you? If there were another easy solution just sitting there, don't you think someone would have figured it out already? Evola is the business that's here with their wallet out, and they're saying all the right things. Hollowans don't need nebulous future ideas; they need money *now* so they can pay their rent and fund their kids' schools and keep their roads plowed in the winter. It's easy to say, 'Let's stick to our ideals,' when you're not the one paying the price for them."

He scowled. "You make it sound like I don't care about the people of this town. *No one* cares more about —"

"Of course you care about the Hollow," I agreed. "Just like I care about preserving this mountain as much as possible. That's what I mean when I say it's a complex issue. It's not black or white. We all need to be willing to compromise. But when it comes down to it... I believe the development needs to move forward. It's really the only way to achieve both objectives."

Hawk chewed on his lip for a long moment and was quiet for most of the hike back down the trail. When we got to the final half mile, he spoke up, and I could tell by his firm jaw that he'd thought himself around in circles until he'd ended right back in the angry place where he'd started.

"I understand what you're saying about the money. I know that's a very real issue. But you're letting that blind you. You talk about oversight, but it feels like I'm the only one who's bothering to look closely at this while everyone else is telling me to sit down and be quiet. Letting Evola move forward with a proposal that has the word *clear-cutting* in it isn't the right way to save the town *or* the mountain. The development needs to be stopped before it ruins this place that my dad… and lots of other people… love so much."

I tried to hide my sigh of resignation. It was clear he was going to dig in and pick this as the literal hill to figuratively die on. He was expecting *me* to rethink my position but refused to rethink his own.

"Okay, then," I gritted out.

His nostrils flared. "Don't patronize me, Jack Davidson Wyatt."

"Oh, we're middle-naming now?" I ran my tongue over my teeth. "Fine. You're spoiling for a fight, and I'm not gonna give it to you, Henry Hawkins Sunday. You can't just keep things the way they are indefinitely because you're scared that something bad could happen. That's not how life works."

"Well, I say it is."

"And I said *okay*."

Hawk lifted his jaw mulishly, and I wished I didn't notice and appreciate how gorgeous he was even when he was being a stubborn ass, but I did. It seemed I couldn't help noticing anymore, damn it.

I could tell Hawk wanted to argue until I agreed with him, but I refused.

Hawk was stuck in his own head. By his own admission, angry about everything on Earth. And with our rock-solid friendship suddenly seeming incredibly fragile, getting into a rip-roaring debate was the last thing I wanted. The town would make their decision one way or another in a few weeks, and maybe then Hawk could accept it.

"You heading home?" I asked when we reached the trail-head. "I'm planning to go back to the house and chill for the rest of the day. I think *Death Comes to Pemberley* is on tonight, and if you want to come over, we could—"

"Thanks, but I have plans."

"Oh." I stewed over this for several paces, then asked, "Date-type plans, or…?"

"Better." Hawk paused long enough to give me a wide smile. "Crys and I are throwing knives."

I nearly stumbled over my own feet and caught myself on the hood of my truck. "At each other?"

He snorted. "No! Honestly, your face right now. At a *target*. Crys knows a guy who knows a guy. He teaches courses and stuff. Should be fun. Even better than jiujitsu. Get that aggression out, like you said."

"But…" I blinked. "You're a pacifist. You hate weapons. You cringe at the sight of blood. You cried at *Hunger Games*. During the knife-throwing scene in *Divergent*, I thought you were going to vomit up the Skittles and popcorn you'd scarfed down while drooling over Theo James. In that one *Pride and Prejudice* variation, Wickham held Lizzy at knife-point, and it took two pints of mint chocolate chip to calm you down."

"Yeah, but this time, I'm the one with the knives, and that feels… different, somehow. It's called *broadening my horizons*. About time I did that in lots of ways, don't you think?" Hawk bumped his knuckles on the side of my truck twice before heading toward his own car. "See you tomorrow, boss."

I watched uneasily as Hawk got into his car and drove away. I didn't want to be Chicken Little about the situation, but I couldn't help thinking Hawk was having some kind of quarter-life crisis. Picking fights? Planning to lose his virgin-ity, possibly to a random stranger on a hookup app? Turning down a viewing of a *Pride and Prejudice*-related movie so he could go *knife throwing*?

Someone needed to keep an eye on him. Someone besides me.

Someone like… Webb.

Yes. Webb would be perfect. I mean, okay, he'd lose his shit if he heard about Hawk's cherry-popping plan, but rightly so because that plan was terrible. He'd sit Hawk down and…

I groaned. He'd probably try to put Hawk in a time-out or send him to bed without dessert like he was four instead of twenty-four. I didn't want Hawk humiliated in the name of protection. Not to mention, Webb had zero experience with gay hookup apps.

Maybe Knox would be the better big brother to approach. Knox was experienced and levelheaded. He'd lived in Boston, for goodness' sake. Surely he'd done the hookup thing dozens of times, if not hundreds. Maybe even… thousands.

I hesitated again.

Okay, possibly Knox had *too* much experience.

Gage, Knox's boyfriend, would be the best bet. Gage was Hawk's age, so he wouldn't treat Hawk like a kid. He'd used hookup apps in the past, but he was also in a committed relationship with Knox, so he'd be able to explain the difference in a way I couldn't. He'd tell Hawk to slow down and not rush things. For his own good.

I started my truck and headed for Sunday Orchard, but instead of pulling into the main driveway between the farmhouse and the barn they'd converted into a gift shop, I headed around the back and parked in front of a small orange cottage at the rear of the property.

The Pumpkin House was at least a hundred years old—maybe older than the farmhouse where the rest of the family lived—but it had sat vacant for most of the time I'd lived in the Hollow, and I'd always thought it looked a little sad.

Now, though, the cottage was full of life, with freshly painted shutters, white curtains riffling in the summer breeze, and long columns of brightly colored flowers marching up the path to the front door. In the side yard, Gage Goodman sprawled on a folding lounge chair in a pair of bright pink surf shorts and nothing else while his boyfriend mowed the lawn around him.

"Hey, Gage? Can I talk to you?" I asked above the loud buzz of the mower.

Gage opened one eye and peered at me. "Jack? Everything okay?"

"Yeah." I hesitated. "Probably."

Knox lifted his eyebrow at me from across the stretch of overgrown grass, but I shook my head and pointed at his boyfriend before taking a seat in the lawn chair next to Gage.

He reached for an iced coffee that had been hidden in the shade under his chair and took a deep slurp. "What's up?"

"Well, the thing is…" Now that Gage's dark eyes were on me, I shifted awkwardly. Hawk would not be happy if he knew I was here. I was trying to protect him, but he'd see it as me interfering or viewing him as a child when that was the *opposite* of my problem these days. "If I tell you something, will you keep it between us? And, uh, Knox, I guess?"

Gage frowned. "Okay…"

"It's Hawk…"

"*Ohhh.*" Gage sat up in his chair eagerly, lips tilted in a knowing smirk. "Oh, god, *finally.* I've been waiting months for you to open your eyes, man."

I frowned. "You've noticed what's going on with him?"

"Dude, the whole town has. Pretty sure only you and Webb have had blinders on. I think even the cows in the field know and are placing wagers with their bovine bookies about how long it would take you to catch on." He looked at me seriously. "Don't let their big eyes fool you. Those cows are criminals. Remember what happened when

O'Henry Brush's cattle got loose this spring? Tip of the iceberg, man."

"*Riiiight.*" I began to doubt whether Gage had been the correct person to approach about this after all.

"You know there's not a person in the Hollow who doesn't adore Hawk," Gage went on. "He's the heart and soul of this town. He deserves someone who appreciates all of him… I mean, I don't need to tell *you*, right?" He chuckled and slapped my leg playfully. "I am very on board for Hawk to get his happy ever after. How can I help?"

"Well." I blinked. "I was thinking he could use a non-brother friend to help him navigate the, ah… the dating scene."

Gage's smirk faded into a confused frown. "The dating scene."

"Yeah. That's what we're talking about, right? Hawk's going through something right now that's got him all twisted up, and he's decided he needs to lose his… I mean… he's decided he wants to try hookup apps."

Gage's jaw dropped, and he stared at me in blank horror.

I nodded grimly. "Thank you! At least *someone* understands how serious this is. I've tried to tell Hawk it's a terrible idea, but he won't listen. He's confused. He actually…" I hesitated, then admitted, "He actually said he wants to sleep with me."

Gage's eyes widened comically. "He told you that? Hot damn, Hawkins."

"He did. And I said no. Obviously."

"Obviously," Gage repeated faintly. Across the yard, the mower cut off. "Uh. Just so I understand… what's so obvious about you saying no?"

"I'm too old for him. He works for me. I'm friends with his brothers. And… I've never seen myself in a committed relationship. That way lies madness." I winced as Knox slid onto the lounge chair behind his boyfriend, wrapping his grass-coated arms around Gage's waist and nuzzling the back of his neck. "I mean, not madness for everyone. Not madness for you guys. Or Webb. Or... other people. But for me."

"What's going on, Goodman?" Knox mumbled into Gage's hair.

"Oh, nothing much." Gage linked his fingers with Knox's. "Jack was just telling me he can't sleep with Hawk because Hawk's much younger than him, they work together, and he doesn't see himself in a committed relationship."

"Is that right?" Knox lifted his head and fixed me with a hard, green gaze... which was when I remembered that Gage Goodman was fifteen years his junior, and they'd met when Gage came to work for Sunday Orchard.

Fuck. Maybe Porter would have been the better Sunday to discuss all of this with.

"So you told Hawk no," Gage said, calling my attention back to him. "And that was when he decided that he was going to use a hookup app."

I nodded. "And I told him he was going to make a big mistake, but he forbid me from talking about it anymore, which is why I came here. I thought *you* could discuss it with him."

Gage bit his lip. "You want *me* to talk to Hawk about hookup apps? I can do that."

"Goodman." Knox's tone held a warning, but laughter lurked just beneath it.

"What? I'm super qualified for this! Leave it to me, Jack. Hawk's a good-looking man. I'll help him create a profile and make sure he meets tons of guys who want a mutually beneficial, singularly satisfying sexual experience. Easy peasy."

"But that's not... I don't want you to... It's *dangerous*," I reminded Gage. "It's not all fun and games!"

"Ehhhh. It's mostly fun and games," Gage argued, eyes dancing. "If it's not, you've been using the wrong apps."

"He could find himself hooking up with a serial killer," I

snapped, standing up so quickly I tipped my chair over. "Or, worse, someone who just uses him for sex and breaks his heart!"

Gage finally lost control of himself and started laughing hysterically. As if this was a joke.

"Knox!" I thrust out a hand to him. "You get what I'm saying, don't you?"

Knox sighed. "You've got it bad, my friend. And I can't say I don't understand because lord knows I do." He tightened his hold on Gage. "I really do. But my brother is a grown man. If he wants to get his dick wet, that's his business. He'll survive. He'll figure out what he really wants. You both will."

"There has to be a better way. I just want him to find someone who cares about him," I said softly. "Someone who's not just trolling for a quick fuck. He needs someone who knows his favorite ice cream and will think it's cute that he sometimes drools when he sleeps. Someone who'll love the things he loves because he loves them and won't make him self-conscious about it. Someone who'll realize how fucking *lucky* they are to touch him... and who understands I'll kick their ass if they mistreat him."

I cringed. I sounded ridiculously sappy. I sounded... jealous.

Because you are, Wyatt. You don't want to want him, but you don't want anyone else to have him either.

Gage wiped the tears of laughter from his eyes and gave me a pitying look. "You can't think of anyone in town who'd feel that way about Hawk, huh?"

I looked at him blankly, and Gage rolled his eyes. "Right. Well. I'm on the case." He leaned back into Knox. "I've got a slew of eligible gay men in mind, starting with the environmental guy. And... oh! Baby, who's that bendy guy who teaches yoga at the senior center?"

"Joey Kincaid," Knox supplied. "He's an artist. Hawk might like that."

"The one who does the shibari photography?" I gasped.

"Yeah." Gage tapped his lip thoughtfully. "When I first moved to the Hollow, his profile kept popping up on Grindr. Pretty sure he lives four hundred seventy-five yards away from the diner. He could… show Hawk the ropes, so to speak. Or there's Remy Fortnum. He's a brilliant carpenter."

"Remy's a player! He's slept with almost everyone in town," I said desperately.

"So he's got excellent references, and he's good at… handling wood." Gage smiled. "See? We're off to a great start already. You came to the right place, Jack. We'll make sure to find someone who can take care of all Hawk's… needs."

My stomach roiled. I opened my mouth to argue with him but closed it when nothing came out. Instead, I nodded and muttered something that should have been thanks but came out sounding more like *never mind*. Then I slunk back to my vehicle and made my way home.

The universe wasn't finished fucking with me, though.

When I tried to lose myself in a renovation project—an addition to the house that I'd been working on by myself for weeks and couldn't wait to show Hawk—I was so distracted that I ended up cutting the power cord on my new jigsaw rather than the trim board I'd been aiming for. The huge spark it sent up caught the sawdust in my work area and burst into flames I'd had to whip my shirt off to smother.

Trying to fix something and lighting it on fire instead was a really fitting metaphor for the day.

I crawled into bed hours later, exhausted and lonelier than I'd been since I moved to the Hollow. But no matter how many times I rolled over and punched my pillow, I couldn't settle into sleep. I kept wondering where Hawk was, what he was doing, how he was feeling. I wanted him beside me. Smiling at me. Confiding in me.

I was doing the right thing, with Hawk *and* with Evola. I knew I was. So why did I feel so shitty and… bereft?

I crept out to my dark living room, fell on the couch, and turned on *Death Comes to Pemberley*, reciting Hawk's usual commentary in my head about Wickham getting what he deserved. My last conscious thought before I finally closed my eyes was *If even someone as foolish and blind as Mr. Darcy can sort his shit eventually, surely I can, too.*

But spoiler: I was no Mr. Darcy.

CHAPTER SIX

HAWK

"Angry people are not always wise."
~ Jane Austen

THE STEEL THROWING knife *thunked* loudly against the wooden target before falling to the cement floor with a clatter that made me jump.

"They should consider providing ear coverings or something," I murmured.

Crys shot me a sympathetic sideways glance. "Or you could try hitting the target occasionally, boo. It's less noisy that way."

I sighed. "I'm not sure this is the hobby for me," I admitted cautiously. "There was a pickup truck outside with an 'I-heart-weapons' bumper sticker. I'm more of an 'Introverted but willing to discuss Pemberley' kind of guy."

Jack wasn't wrong about me despising violence and weapons… even if he was an ass for pointing it out.

"Don't think of it like handling weapons. Think of it like darts," Crys said for the seventieth time in an hour.

"Yeah, I'm not sure how I led you to believe I was good at darts either."

Crys snickered, then let loose a knife that thunked into the dead center of her target. "Keep practicing," she advised.

I blinked. "You're shockingly good at this. I thought this was your first lesson, too."

"Nah. I got really good with knives when I was... you know, younger, but I haven't practiced in years." She flicked her wrist, and another knife landed so close to the first that both of them vibrated. "Turns out it's like riding a bike."

Sure. Like a very large, incredibly sharp bike.

"How'd you learn? Did your dad teach you?"

"Not exactly. But my granddad was an outdoorsman. Super into knives and shit. You should have seen the scars on his hands."

I carefully set down my last knife on the table next to me and shuddered. "That's... not as reassuring as you might think."

She picked up her final knife, flipped it in her hand, and launched it at the target. Muscles I hadn't noticed before bulged in her shoulder and biceps. "Fuck yeah! Bullseye again. Give me that other one if you're not going to throw it."

I picked my knife up again and weighed it in my grip. "I'm going to throw it! Just... give me a minute to remember the stance."

The large muscular throwing instructor—*Vinnie? Vicky?*—walked over and grabbed me by the hips, manhandling me into throwing position without waiting for permission.

Was it a little weird that I'd practically gotten to second base with this guy and I couldn't remember his name?

"Angle your hips like this. Chin up, eyes on the target." His voice sounded like it had been sanded down over time by every nicotine product on the market. "Spread 'em wider." He kicked one of my feet out to the side a few inches.

My face ignited. This guy's scent—tobacco and Old Spice —was like a knockoff version of Jack's delicious, spicy cologne, and I couldn't help but get a little hot under the collar.

"Better," Vlad—*Van? Valentine?*—approved. "You needa be able ta rock your center of gravity over your front foot." He moved his hands up to my shoulders and squared me to the target.

I tried not to imagine Jack's hands touching me that way… or how much I'd like it. I couldn't imagine a knife-throwing boner was a great idea.

As soon as he moved off to help someone in another lane, Crys elbowed me. "Bro, you should see your face. Jack would say it was eight serrano peppers on the Scoville scale."

The mention of Jack sent my blood pressure into the danger zone. "Can we not talk about *him*, please?"

I threw the knife with all my frustration, imagining it winging its way powerfully into the center of the wooden target at the end of the lane… and watched as it fell with a defeated *clink* about two feet in front of me.

Crys bit back a laugh. "Try again, Throwdini."

Instead of giving up and having no "broadened horizons" to show for my day, I asked the instructor very nicely for a new batch of knives so I could try again. And again. And again. I finally got a knife close enough to the target to wave a cheery hello before it, too, landed with a clang on the floor beside the other missed knives I'd thrown. I was striking out on all fronts today.

"That's it for me," I told Crys.

I wasn't sure I'd worked off my aggression exactly, except by making myself too tired to be angry. But if I wasn't already strong from carrying full serving trays at Panini Jack's, my arm would have been screaming in agony, and I knew more throwing would make tomorrow's workday painful.

Crys nodded absently and kept launching the sharp blades down the lane until it was time for us to gather them back up again and reset.

"I think Elizabeth Bennet would have enjoyed knife throwing," I decided. "It's kind of feisty."

"Mmm."

"I'm surprised more *Pride and Prejudice* variations don't have her trying archery like the Gwyneth Paltrow version of *Emma* had in it. I could see her doing that, too, and it was popular back then."

Crys effortlessly sank into throwing position and sent another knife toward the target. "I've used a crossbow before. It was epic."

"I just find it funny that these aristocratic people would be dressed in gowns and topcoats at a garden party and pick up a bow and arrow between bites of finger sandwiches on the lawn, you know?"

While she began throwing again, this time small handheld axes, I continued talking about Regency-era lawn games, even telling her about my earlier conversation with Jack about baseball and rounders. She was so focused on the axe-throwing she barely grunted in response.

"Sorry. I'm probably boring you," I finally said. My disappointment was hard to hide. I loved Crys, but... she was no Jack Wyatt.

"Nah. I just don't share your passion about Jane Austen. It's kind of like when my friend Sanjay shows me pictures of his cats. There are only so many times a person can ooh and ah over the same fat orange feline sleeping by the window, you know?"

I stared at her. "How could you not want to see pictures of a cat loafing in the sunshine? *Especially* a ginger cat?"

Before she could respond, my phone buzzed with an incoming text. My heart leaped a little, hoping Jack had come to his senses and wanted to apologize for being an asshat earlier, but no.

SIMON

Hey, Hawk! I wanted to tell you I read that article on the endangered bat populations you sent. Super fascinating. Maybe we could discuss it sometime? <smiley emoji><bat emoji><leaf emoji>

I sighed. Simon and I had been texting back and forth a bit all week, and he'd been… nice. Really nice. I'd spammed him with articles, beginning the day after the town meeting, and he'd read them all and promised he'd "pass them up the chain" at Evola.

I wasn't naive. I knew this was probably corporate-speak for "I deleted it after I read it," but at least I felt like he was trying to understand my position… which was more than I could say for some people.

You're welcome. Did you have a chance to get me those Point Meduc and Morgan Falls environmental studies you promised?

SIMON

I asked again. I need authorization to make them public, and my boss is on leave. <eyeroll emoji> But I haven't forgotten. They should get it to me this week and I'll pass it on. Sorry for the delay! <sad emoji><leaf emoji>

I was pretty sure this was corporate-speak, too, where "delayed until this week" meant "not gonna happen until hell freezes over," but at least he hadn't outright denied my request or fed me bullshit excuses.

Which, again, was better than certain people had done.

"What did your phone do that's got you scowling at it, boo?" Crys came up and peered over my shoulder. "Ohhhh. Looks like Simon wants to make sure your *environment* is *compliant.*" She wiggled her eyebrows suggestively. "Are you gonna *survey* his *land*?"

I felt my cheeks go hot. "I don't even know what that means," I said primly, turning the screen off. "Besides, it's not like that. Simon's just being friendly because of the project. I told you, I only pretended he was interested in me at the town meeting because it seemed to annoy Jack."

"Because Jack's jealous."

I shook my head. "He's really not. Jealous is how you feel when someone has something you can't have. Jack could have me. I've made that abundantly clear. I practically gift wrapped myself earlier today and stuck a bow on my ass, and Jack was like, 'Oooh, wow, no thank yew.' And then he went on to tell me I couldn't possibly use a hookup app without floundering my way into a date with the only person in Little Pippin Hollow on an FBI watchlist."

"Hey." Crys pointed one manicured finger at me. "Don't joke. You'd be surprised at how many people in the Hollow are on a watchlist. Small town like this is a breeding ground."

I rolled my eyes. "All we breed around here are prize-winning Holsteins and heirloom apples. You might need to lay off the *American Crime Story.*"

"Nope. Mark my words, there's something weird going on with Ronna at the gas station—like, taboo sex dungeon in her stockroom weird. And Chris, that guy I work with at the Bugle? He's either a werewolf or a mafia hitman on the run."

"Chris? The twinky kid who wears the homemade sweaters?" I boggled at her. "Are you sure you're not just annoyed that when Ernie yells, 'Hey, Chris,' you both turn around?"

"I've got finely honed instincts, boo," Crys countered, lifting her nose in the air. "Mild-mannered Chris has a wild side. Jack has alllll kinds of dirty fantasies about you, even if he wishes he didn't. And Mr. Environmental Compliance wants in your pants. Nobody with wholesome intentions uses that many emojis. Have you noticed that the leaf emoji looks exactly like the water-spurt emoji?"

Sure enough, a second later, another text came through.

SIMON

Maybe you and I could have dinner this week and I could give you the report in person? <smiley emoji><leaf emoji>

Crys read the message upside down and crowed. "See? Instincts. And now you owe me a coffee," she proclaimed, finally abandoning the sharp objects so we could make our way to Pippin Hot for iced lattes and blueberry scones.

"What do I tell Simon?" I asked once we were seated with our snacks. "He's nice, but…"

"But you don't want him, you want Jack. I know." Her mouth twisted. "Sadly, Jack's not on the menu at the moment. He's either gonna get right with himself, or he's not. And in the meantime, you go with the runner-up." She bit off the end of her scone and smiled slyly. "You could really benefit from a good fuck."

"Crys!" I glanced around the small cafe and bent closer to whisper-hiss, "You can't say *fuck* when Millicent Bowdoin and her little girl are right there! Say 'tup.' Then she won't understand you."

"*I* won't understand me." Crys sucked down the last of her drink with a loud slurp. "You're so weird, boo."

"Anyway, Simon isn't a runner-up," I informed her. "He seems very nice. We have lots in common. Under other circumstances…"

"You'd be tupping him to kingdom come?" Crys guessed. "Exactly. So why not go out to dinner with the guy? Not to make Jack jealous, because seriously, *tup Jack*, am I right? Go with the guy who wants you. The one who sends you cum-leaf emojis when you chat him up because he's adorably awkward when it comes to you."

She meant Simon, but I couldn't help remembering Jack making his strangled *erk* sound whenever I said something that flustered him.

"It's not that easy," I whispered. "You know, when Jack and I met—"

"You were seventeen and a half, he was both smoking hot and heroically friendly, and you fell head over heels instantly." She rolled her eyes good-naturedly. "I know. But that was a long time ago."

"That's how it started," I corrected. "And if that was all it had ever been... shit, Crys, I'd have gotten over him in a matter of weeks, no matter what I thought back then. But it wasn't. Instead, Jack was all in with me, in a way that hardly anyone in my life ever had been. Like..." I shook my head and stared at the table. How did I explain all that Jack had become to me?

I took a deep breath. "Okay, for example... when I was trying to decide whether to go to college, everyone in my family had opinions about what was best for me, right? But Jack was the only person who asked me what *I* wanted out of life, without judgment or coddling. Oh! And this one time, maybe four years ago? I had a bad day, and he knew I didn't want to talk, so he conveniently came up with something at his house that needed to be demolished and asked me to do *him* a favor by coming over and swinging a sledgehammer." I chuckled at the memory. "And then he *kept* having me over to help and basically let me choose all the fixtures for *his* house because he said he trusts me. Not my muscular, power-tool-savvy brothers, Crys. *Me.*"

"Ah, boo..."

"And also," I went on after taking a sip of my drink, "there was this incident that happened two winters ago now, I guess, where I caught a ride to Montpelier to meet up with a friend of a friend and see a show. Kind of a date thing, you know? And I was all excited. Except the guy never showed up. So there I was, stranded an hour and a bit away from home, embarrassed as fuck, freezing cold, no place to sleep, hardly any money, the whole deal. I called Jack, he drove two and a half hours roundtrip to get me, brought me cookies, took me back to his house to crash on his sofa so I didn't have to explain things to my family, and—this is the key part, Crys—he's never said a single word about it. Not once. Not even now, when he's determined to cockblock me and could totally turn that incident against me."

Crys sighed. "He's a good guy," she admitted.

"He is," I agreed. Then, more softly, "So good. And I guess… I mean, maybe none of that is like, 'Oh, wow, Hawk, so romantic, I can see why you're on fire for this man!' But, like… it *is* romantic, you know? To me, it is. He trusts me. He gets me. He appreciates me. He cherishes me. He's always made me feel—even when I'm spouting off the intricate details of a *Pride and Prejudice* retelling that would make anyone else fall asleep—like I'm the most interesting person in the room. He is so protective of the things and people he loves. And… he lets me take care of him, too. I know when he gets the little furrow right here—" I pointed to the spot between my eyes. "—it means he's tired and needs an excuse to leave a party. And I know he is a fucking *child* when he gets a cold. And I… I love him, Crys. All of him. Unreservedly. Even the annoying bits. Which is why he's kinda breaking my heart right now. Because I don't understand why he's so hell-bent on getting this resort pushed through or why he's refusing to take a chance on us and he's pawning me off with tissue-thin excuses like none of my feelings matter. Like *I* don't matter."

"But you didn't say any of this to him, right?"

"God, no." I shook my head. "I can't tell him I love him. I only asked for sex, and he already assumes I want us to exchange vows."

"So if he knew you actually *did* want to exchange vows—"

I snorted. "He'd probably freak out. While still simultaneously attempting to cockblock me." I rolled my eyes. "Everyone and their mother is out there having sex except me." I frowned and considered my words. "Wait, that didn't sound right—"

"Hawk Sunday!"

Ah, crap. I glanced over to see Luke's mom shaking some sugar packets at the cream-and-sugar station. *Please, god, don't let her have heard what I said.*

"Mrs. Williams! Hey. Hi. How are you today?"

"Invigorated! Sue and I just finished a marathon charity crochet Hook Up with Betty Ann and Melanie and Helena and the other Hookers. Nothing like eighteen hours of stitch and bitch, am I right? What about you? Were you out with the kids today?" Her eyes flicked past me to Crys, whose mouth was mysteriously covered in crumbs from *my* blueberry scone.

"Uh, no. The Mini Nature Scouts' summer camp is only on the weekdays. Mrs. Williams, this is Crystal Hardin. She's new in town, too, and works with me at Panini Jack's. Crys, Mrs. Williams is Luke's mom. You know, Webb's Luke."

Crys nodded and smiled. "Ah, right. Nice to meet you. I recognize you from the yarn store."

Mrs. Williams's face lit up. "You knit? How wonderful."

"No, ma'am. But I heard a pair of their handcrafted double-pointed needles make a great—"

"Sock-making tool!" I blurted, suddenly 100 percent convinced my friend was going to reveal more of her mysterious obsession with weapons. "DPNs are great for those pesky toe closures. Heh."

Both women looked at me like I'd lost my mind.

Crys looked back at Luke's mom. "—gift for people who knit charity hats for babies," she finished calmly. "And several of us at the Bugle chipped in to get some nice ones for Andrea."

I felt a bead of sweat run slowly down my temple. "Oh. Ha. Yeah. That, too." I was still pretty convinced Crys had purchased herself a pair of handcrafted old-lady shanks.

I couldn't quite imagine someone using a set of double-pointed needles to take down an enemy, but if anyone could do it, it would be Crys.

Mrs. Williams smiled back at her. "Well, nice to meet you, dear. Hawk, I'm off to see your uncle and his beau for an early dinner. Drew's making his *special* brownies." Her eyes twinkled. "Too bad Webb and Luke are... otherwise engaged."

I smiled grimly. Uncle Drew was particularly uninhibited under the influence of his special brownies, and when Webb and Luke were *otherwise engaged*, it usually meant everyone else in the farmhouse should sleep with noise-canceling head-phones. "That's... great. Just great."

"Newlyweds!" she said with satisfaction I wished I could share. "Take care."

She bustled out of the cafe, and Crys burst into giggles. "You crack me up, Hawk Sunday. *Pesky toe closures.*"

"And you stress me out," I grumbled under my breath. "Even more than thinking of my previously straight brother fucking his new husband does."

She threw back her head and laughed. "Keeping you off-balance is a gift, my friend. And it brings me joy."

I couldn't help but allow a partial grin. "It brings me something. Not sure what yet."

She leaned over and ruffled my hair. "I like you. I didn't expect to make a friend like you when I moved here."

I wanted to ask why the heck she'd moved to a small town like the Hollow if she hadn't planned to make friends, but I didn't want to seem judgy. Not when her friendly affection warmed my heart and helped mitigate my recent rejection just a little bit.

"Want to come over and watch a movie or something?" I

offered. "I heard *Death Comes to Pemberley* was on tonight, and I can make Marco's chicken salad recipe—"

"No can do," she said, standing up and chucking her empty cup into a nearby receptacle. "Got a hot date with a chick I met at the knife-throwing thing."

I stared at her. "*What?*"

"You heard me. Just because *you* are determined to overthink Simon's offer until you're old and gray doesn't mean *I'm* gonna be sleeping alone tonight." She winked. "Look, I get what you're saying about Jack. You have hashtag realfeels. But you also need relief. And you were willing to make do with a friends-with-bennies thing for Jack, right? So why not with cute Simon? Think about it, okay? See you tomorrow!"

I scrambled after her. "Wait, I need details. How the heck did you meet someone at the knife place? I was with you the whole time!"

"Ladies' room," she said with a shrug. "She said if I wanted more practice, her family has some dead trees on their property we could throw things at. Texted me her number and added a shit ton of emojis." She grinned. "In like Flynn, baby. I don't know why dudes need to make stuff so complicated."

I wrinkled my nose. "She asked you to throw things at dead trees… and that's an invitation for sex?"

"Sure. Throwing stuff around is excellent foreplay. I'm gonna score in all the ways." She reached out a fist to knuckle-bump me, but I refused and shoved my hands in my shorts pockets instead.

"Dear god. Literally *everyone* in this town is having sex except me. It's fucking *injustice*, is what it is!"

Crys's eyes narrowed, and she grabbed me by the front of my shirt. "Okay, Hawkins, I've tried being patient, but maybe you need some tough love instead, so listen up. Plenty of men in this town would love nothing more than to deflower your virgin ass, and you know it. The trouble is, you're hung up on the one guy who won't. You have an idea in your head that he's the perfect guy and you're meant to have this perfect love, but perfection is for storybooks. In real life, sometimes people need to fuck up before they figure shit out. Sometimes, their timing is off. And that's okay. Real life is *supposed* to be hard and messy. That's how you learn shit. That's why it's fun. But if you keep thinking of Jack as one of your romance heroes and wondering why he's not sticking to the script, you're gonna be miserable forever, boo. You are responsible for your own happiness. Don't wait for him to fix your life. Go out and take action. Grab what you want." She paused for a moment. "But, like, wear a seat belt and remember to bring protection. Okay?" She patted my chest gently, smoothing my shirt back into place. "Okay. Good talk. See you in the morning."

She strode across the parking lot in the direction of the room she rented in an old house on Pine Street, leaving me staring after her.

How ridiculous!

I was *not* waiting around for perfection, and I certainly didn't expect anyone to fix my life for me. I worked hard, dang it. And my life was full of family and friends and projects that needed my help. I liked it just fine!

Well…

Aside from the wanting-someone-who-refused-to-want-me-back thing. And the developers-ruining-my-town thing. And the random, uncontrolled bursts of anger. And my brothers treating me like I was a porcelain doll. And feeling like a loser because I made love to my hand so often I worried I was developing carpal tunnel syndrome while it seemed every other human in town was getting down and dirty. And—

Okay, so maybe Crys had a point.

I'd talked a good game about getting on a hookup app

and finding a date, but I hadn't actually done a damn thing about it. I'd set my sights on Jack the same way I'd focused on the target at the knife-throwing place, heaving myself at him with all my might… and in both cases, I'd fallen way short of the mark and had nothing to show for it but a bruised ego and a sore wrist.

Maybe I was frustrated Jack wouldn't join me in the fight against Evola because I'd gotten used to relying on his support and his strength. Because it was scary to think about doing it on my own.

Maybe I was so angry these days because I'd dammed up my frustrations about so many things for so long, not wanting to hurt or offend anyone, that now I was boiling over like a teakettle.

Maybe it was time to actually *make* a change instead of talking about it over and over.

Maybe I needed to take Simon up on his offer.

The next morning, after a very long and sleepless night stuck in the farmhouse with a pair of very amorous newly-weds and a pair of sixty-something lovers under the influence, I dragged myself into the shower and got myself to the diner with seconds to spare before my shift started.

I wasn't the only straggler.

Crys walked in with me, wearing the same clothes she'd worn the day before, rocking sex hair and a dewy smile. Katey was escorted in by Nate Kimstock from the auto shop, and the pair spent ten minutes standing in the doorway cooing and exchanging goofy smiles before Jack fixed Nate with a raised eyebrow and folded arms that sent him scurrying off. Even Jack was bleary-eyed, smelled vaguely of woodsmoke, and winced with every movement like he'd spent the night wrestling a wild animal.

An image of Handsy Donny appeared in my brain, and my stomach dropped. Had Jack hooked up with *him* last night after turning me down? Wouldn't *that* be the cherry on this shit sundae?

I bit back my overwhelming desire to grill him about it until I finally couldn't stand it any longer.

"Guess you didn't end up going home after our hike yesterday, huh?" I blurted, tossing a serving tray onto a rack and barely managing to avoid the swinging kitchen door.

Jack glanced up from the center island worktable. "W-what?" His gaze darted around the room guiltily.

"You look wrecked." The words came out like an accusation. "Who'd you hang out with?"

"Who?" he repeated. He licked his lips. "N-no one? Why? What have you heard?"

He couldn't have looked guiltier if he had an *L* for liar tattooed on his forehead.

My head throbbed, and my tired eyes burned. "I see. If you don't want to tell me, fine."

I turned around and slammed my way back out of the kitchen, which was significantly less satisfying with a swinging door.

"Hawk?" Crys asked softly as I grabbed a tray from the wait station. "Are you losing your mind, boo? What's going on?"

I pressed my fingers into my eyes. "What's going on is my sister was staying at a friend's last night, and Aiden was with his mom, so *each* of the couples living in my house apparently decided to perform their own reenactments of the Cocky Boys' greatest bangs at full volume. Luke and Webb were upstairs, Drew and Marco downstairs. There was no escape. The charge on a pair of noise-canceling headphones only lasts so long, Crys, and Marco has no idea how loud he is now that his hearing is going. My ancestors did not design that house with live porn in mind."

She flinched. "Oh, god."

"Yes. *Exactly*. Imagine those very words being moaned by

four different voices simultaneously like a lusty barbershop quartet." I sniffled. "I'm exhausted, and frustrated, and… I can't live like this anymore. This whole damn town is in the throes of a fiery mating frenzy, and I'm like a stack of kindling that's been drying out for almost twenty-five long years." I straightened my shoulders. "I think maybe you were right last night. I'll message Simon about… dinner."

Crys grinned. "Good for you," she said fiercely. "Sometimes things have to get worse before they get better. You'll see."

I really hoped she was right because I wasn't sure how much more "worse" I could take.

I managed to keep my shit contained through the morning rush and most of the lunch shift, too. I ignored Jack and his gorgeous smile and his traitorous sad eyes. I smiled at customers and took orders, remembering that little Bodhi Miller liked "extra cherries, Mr. Hawk" in his Shirley Temple. I volunteered to clean the bathrooms and pretended the acidic churn of hurt and longing and anger in my gut wasn't there. I even managed to stay calm when my family got seated in my section, even though Gage kept asking me random, ridiculous questions like "If you were forced to pick bondage or carpentry as a hobby, which would it be?"

But when Webb and Luke strolled in, looking like they'd tumbled naked through an entire orchard, projectile vomiting love and hope and satisfaction all over the diner, the last thread of my frayed control snapped.

I could not continue sleepwalking through my life, pretending things were okay. Everyone around me was reaching out and grabbing their happiness while I was morphing into a bitter, miserable jerk I could barely recognize in the mirror.

Enough was enough.

I slammed water glasses down on the table.

"You look like you just had sex in the orchard," I accused,

reaching my give-a-shit limit. I whirled around and found Jack standing two tables away, delivering a check to a customer. "*Everyone* in this town is having sex except me! I'm going to be a virgin until I die old and alone. I'm living with a damned cherry that will never be picked!"

I yanked off my apron and, in the sudden, pulsing silence that filled the restaurant, threw it at his feet. "I quit."

And then I turned and stormed out of Panini Jack's.

CHAPTER SEVEN

JACK

*"There are very few who have heart enough to be really in love
without encouragement."*
~ Charlotte Lucas

I STRAIGHTENED up slowly from the table where I'd been delivering Betty Ann Wolff's bill. Everyone in the restaurant was shocked into silence at Hawk's outburst, but I barely noticed anyone other than Hawk himself. His anger radiated off him so much so that he reminded me of the prickly pinecones we'd fallen into on the trail to Balderdash Peak…

Only this particular pinecone had been launched fast-pitch-style at my heart.

He shot me a glare and stormed out of the restaurant, setting the bells on the door jangling, and disappeared down the street.

What the fuck had just happened?

If I'd hoped that Hawk's outburst on the trail yesterday was a onetime thing or that his knife-throwing adventure might calm him down and get him back on track, today had shown me how naive that was. He'd been simmering all morning, and now…

Hawk Sunday didn't make big dramatic exits. He didn't lose his temper. And he most certainly didn't tell the whole world he was a virgin in search of a… devirginator.

Webb's eyes snapped to me.

I held up my hands. "I didn't do anything. I promise!"

Instead of being angry like I assumed he would be, he looked confused. "Do anything about what? What was that all about?"

The reality of the situation pressed down on me until I felt like I could barely breathe. Hawk was going to be mortified by his public display as soon as he calmed down and realized what he'd said in front of half the town.

I also remembered him saying one of the things he was angry about was that everyone was making a big deal about his anger. I figured most people were surprised and worried like I was, but I wanted to put the other Hollowans on notice just in case.

"Nothing to see here, people," I announced to the restaurant in a firm voice. "Please respect Hawk's privacy and allow him to have a bad day without spreading it around town. Understood?"

A few people nodded half-heartedly.

I looked longingly toward the front door again, my heart urging me to go after Hawk and comfort him. But the look he'd given me suggested that Hawk wouldn't find my presence comforting, and I couldn't leave the rest of my employees and my business in the middle of the lunch rush.

I picked up Hawk's apron and bolted for the kitchen. "Back to work," I snapped at Crys as I passed her.

I headed for an empty prep table in the back corner of the room and started measuring out ingredients for cinnamon rolls. I could make this recipe on autopilot, and working the dough was the perfect way to keep my hands busy while I figured out what the hell I was supposed to do now.

I should have anticipated that I wouldn't be alone for long.

"What the hell was that about?" Webb demanded, following me to the kitchen. He still looked confused and maybe a little outraged. "I've never in my life seen Hawk blow up like that, much less in public."

Since a good offense was often the best defense, I crossed my arms and glared at him. "If I recall, he was angry at you for flaunting your new, *energetic* relationship with everyone."

Webb's eyes flared, but his neck turned red with embarrassment, which was confession enough. "What the hell's that supposed to mean? And don't think for one minute that I'm going to feel guilty for loving my husband whenever and wherever he'll let me because that man is the greatest gift of my life and—"

I held up a hand to stop him. "Yes, yes. Spare me, okay? We know you got drunk and tripped into the perfect life partner. Good for you. Not all of us are lucky enough to *blow the bugle* with a handsome stranger who just so happens to be our soul mate—"

"You make it sound dirty," he muttered.

"—so forgive Hawk for having a moment of envy. He's obviously ready for a relationship, and it's not exactly easy to find one here in this tiny town."

"Like you'd know," Webb said with the hint of a grin. "You haven't been interested in finding a partner since I've known you."

I rolled my eyes. "I've dated plenty of people since moving here."

"Hardly," he scoffed. "You've had sex with people. There's a difference. I tried to set you up with Knox, and you had zero interest—"

"In dating your brother who was already in love with Gage?" I folded my arms over my chest again. "How was *that* going to work?"

"Well, I didn't know about his feelings for Gage at the time," Webb said reasonably. "But there were other guys. People who *would* be interested in a relationship—"

I shook my head. "Nooo. Nope. I do not need or want a relationship, thank you. Plucking out your beating heart and handing it to someone is a recipe for disaster. I've seen it time and time again. You struck gold with Luke, sure, but remember the debacle before that? No." I shook my head. "I have close friends who are there for me. I have my mom. I have this place, which takes up most of my time and energy." I spread my hands to encompass the whole restaurant. "That's plenty."

Webb leaned back against a wall where a laminated placard of sanitation procedures hung. "Being a workaholic isn't doing you any favors, Jack."

"A refrain I hear often enough from my mother, thank you very much. Besides, why are we talking about me? Hawk is the one who needs our help, Webb. He's having a rough time."

Webb shook his head. "I just don't know what's gotten into him lately. He's consumed with stopping the Fogg Peak development, he's spending all his time with this new server of yours, and now he's telling the entire world he's a virgin?" He peered at me for a moment. "The way he said it, he kind of made it sound like it was your fault. Are you…?"

"What? No!" I barked immediately. "No, I swear it. I haven't touched him."

"Whoa!" Webb's eyes widened. "Of course you haven't! God. I would never think that. I was gonna say, are you upset at him for taking out his anger on you? It's not cool, especially when you've gone above and beyond to bring him under your wing and be a mentor to him all these years. I apologize on his behalf. I really thought the kid was more mature than that."

Oof. I'd known that Webb was overprotective, but hearing

him talk about Hawk and our friendship that way made my heart squeeze.

"That *man* is mature as fuck," I shot back. "I don't need or want you to apologize for him. And don't make it sound like I've been doing Hawk a favor for the past seven years because that's bullshit. He's smart. And hilarious. Hardworking. Reliable. Kind—and I mean, kind down to his *bones*, Webb. I trust him more than anyone on this Earth, and I love spending time with him. And if *you* were spending time with him rather than blowing bugles and fucking people in orchards, you might get to know the adult he's become rather than assuming he's the same sweet Hawklet your family's always known—"

"Okay, hold up!" Webb raised both hands to stop my tirade. "What are you mad at *me* for? You make it sound like I'm running a one-man whorehouse in my own damn orchard. This was one time, and the only 'people' in question was my actual, legal husband."

The satisfaction contained in that one word made me snicker, despite my annoyance. "You're really getting off on that, aren't you? Calling Luke your *husband*."

"So freaking much, you have no idea." Webb's smile could not be contained.

I had *some* idea. Webb had been in a really dark place for a long while. Luke was a good man, a great husband, and a wonderful stepfather to Webb's son, Aiden. I was truly happy for all of them. But Webb had been so focused on settling down with his new little family that he'd become a little blind to anything outside of that.

I sighed and moved over to a metal stool to lower myself onto it. "Webb... You need to stop treating Hawk like a kid. Your whole family, really, but especially you. It's taking a toll on him."

Webb moved closer and took the other stool. "What's he said to you?"

"He hasn't said anything about you specifically," I hedged. "But it's come up in the context of other stuff he's dealing with." I was glad now that I hadn't told Webb about Hawk's indecent proposal, but I still wanted to find a way to get the point across. "He's a grown man with needs and opinions of his own, and you've gotta respect that."

"If he wants to be treated like an adult, he needs to act like one," Webb retorted. "Starting with talking to me about things that are bothering him instead of blowing up and causing a scene at his place of business—"

I shook my head. "Like the way he talked at the town meeting the other night? He said flat out how he felt about the Evola development, and how did you respond? Heck, how did *any* of us respond?"

Webb opened his mouth, then looked away and shut it again unhappily.

"Exactly. We shut him down and dismissed him. You know how important Fogg Peak was to your dad. It should be no surprise to any of us that it's important to Hawk, too."

He set his jaw, and his eyes met mine again. "Obsessing over something simply because our dad valued it isn't adult behavior—"

"Now you're just being an ass," I said mildly. "I seem to recall you picking a fight with the guy who became your *actual, legal husband* just a few months back because you thought you were going to lose a few feet of land in Sunday Orchard. Remember?"

Webb pursed his lips and said nothing.

"Hawk loves the Hollow, and he's proud of the Sunday heritage here the same way you are, Webb. There's nothing immature about him wanting to be a good steward of the land he feels connected to. There's nothing immature about him feeling especially raw because all this is happening right around your dad's birthday—"

"Ah, shit." Webb closed his eyes and ran a hand over his face. "I can't believe I forgot."

"Uh-huh. And there's nothing immature about Hawk wanting to have a relationship of his own either… as long as he does it, you know, safely." *Without Grindr.*

"Yeah, but still. The kid needs to understand—"

"The *man*, Webb." I paused, then added, "And for the record, Hawk's as much my friend as you are, so think carefully about how you're gonna end that sentence. I'm not letting you insult him in front of me."

Webb blinked at me, and I returned his look levelly. I had no desire to get into an argument with him—having one Sunday pissed at me was plenty, thanks—but I wasn't sure I could stand to hear Webb discussing Hawk like the man was still a moody teenager without losing my cool. If Hawk dealt with this all the time… if he thought *I* was dismissing him the way Webb did… well, maybe I understood where some of his anger was coming from.

"I'm not insulting Hawk! Jesus. He's my *brother*. The very best of us." Webb sounded horrified. "I love him."

"I know you do," I agreed. "Hawk knows it, too. And… maybe that's why he hasn't said anything to you. You and he are more alike than either of you know. He wants to protect the people he loves, too. But he does it by keeping his mouth shut when he's hurt or upset because he doesn't want to worry anyone."

Webb nodded thoughtfully. "Okay, maybe so. I still think he needs to try to understand the benefits of the development, though—"

"I agree with you, and I told him so. It's not cut and dried. Hawk gets that there's more to the issue, but I'm not sure he knows how to reconcile the financial concerns with the environmental. To be frank… I'm not sure any of us do. We're all so excited about the potential income and so worried about scaring Evola off, maybe we haven't thought enough about the environmental aspects. Maybe if we all listened as much as we talked," I said pointedly, "we could come up with a good solution. Together."

He sighed. "I see what you're saying. I guess we've all been busy with other things this year and haven't paid attention. I definitely haven't noticed the toll it's taken on Hawk."

I reached out to squeeze his shoulder. "Understandable. You were busy getting accidentally hitched. It's like a damned love fairy has infiltrated this town with how quickly you Sundays are falling these days."

"True story." Webb's face brightened. "Be careful, or the fairy will get you next."

"Oh, no. I'm not a Sunday," I murmured, though my heart kicked up an uncomfortable notch. "I think I'm safe."

"You're an honorary one." He smiled ruefully. "Seems like you've been a better brother to Hawk than I have these last few months."

I thought of Hawk's gorgeous face and the lean strength of his legs peeking out from beneath my sweatshirt. The luscious curve of his ass and the potent thrill of his laughter. His eyes gone gold with *want* and the needy catch in his voice on our last hike when he'd begged for my kiss with a whispered *"Please."*

I could say with certainty that brotherhood was not what I felt for him.

"I'm glad he has you." Webb ruffled my hair playfully and stood. "And don't worry too much about the fairy. Maybe it'll get Hawk instead. The way he's putting his personal business out there, I'd be surprised if he doesn't have several cherry-picking offers by sundown." He snorted and headed back toward the diner.

I stared at him in nauseated shock. "A-and you'd be okay with that?" I called. "With him just… just… finding some random guy, and…"

Webb turned before he reached the swinging door, grinning from ear to ear. "Jack, I was kidding! Come on. This is Hawk we're talking about. The king of romance novels. He's got standards. He's not the random hookup type."

"But—"

"And you call *me* overprotective." Webb laughed lightly. "I might have missed some changes in the ki—the *man*," he corrected, "but of all my siblings, Hawk's the one I've never worried about when it comes to dating. No matter how upset or frustrated he is, unless Mr. Darcy himself comes to Little Pippin Hollow, Hawk's not going to do anything rash."

Webb turned around and pushed his way through the swinging door while I couldn't help but scream after him in my head, *He already fucking has.*

CHAPTER EIGHT

HAWK

"I am only resolved to act in that manner, which will, in my own opinion, constitute my happiness, without reference to you, or to any person so wholly unconnected with me."
~ Elizabeth Bennet

I READ SOMEWHERE ONCE that a peacefulness follows any decision, even the wrong one. I wasn't a hundred percent sure that storming out of the diner today had been the correct way to handle things—if I let myself remember the stunned, sad look on Jack's face, my stomach hurt—but as I pulled my truck to a stop in front of the farmhouse, I decided it felt really good to be doing something instead of trying to ignore the creepy-crawly feeling under my skin that something needed to be done. It was time for action. Drastic action.

"Hawk?" Drew turned in surprise as I banged through the back door into the kitchen. He was dressed in full-on tie-dye today, from his Jerry Garcia T-shirt down to his organic cotton harem pants. "I thought you were working through lunch and then heading right to your Scout thing. I was about to leave to meet Marco and the others at the diner, but I lost my keys—"

"Check the junk drawer," I called over my shoulder, heading upstairs to shove a few pieces of clothing in my hiking backpack. "And I no longer work at Panini Jack's. I'm heading up to Glassy Ridge to protest the development."

"Protest?" Drew panted up the stairs behind me and paused in my bedroom doorway to catch his breath. "You quit your job? You *love* your job—"

"From now on, my full-time job is saving Fogg Peak from Evola, and I'm gonna stay out there until people take notice. I'm thinking I'll start a social media campaign. Lots of pictures showing the beautiful vistas and endangered species. Maybe tagging some environmental groups and celebrities." I broke off for a moment, making a mental list of which activist groups I could invite to join me in the protest, and then I shook myself. First things first. "Hey, where'd Porter put my sleeping bag? He borrowed it when he was home a few weeks ago and never gave it back."

"I thought you were *already* protesting the development. You sent all those letters last spring—"

I zipped my backpack and slung it on my shoulder, then tucked a pillow and blanket from my bed under my arm. "Uncle Drew," I said seriously, "I shouldn't have to explain to you of all people that I cannot continue to work for The Man while the brutal machinery of capitalism is set to grind the town I love into dust. You might not be fired up to protect the wild spaces on our planet from corporate greed anymore—"

"'The *Man?*'" He scowled. "You work for *Jack*. And I'm as fired up as I've ever been, whippersnapper!"

"Then you should know our letter-writing campaign wasn't enough. No one's taking this issue seriously." I headed back downstairs. "Do you know that clear-cutting often contributes to reductions in root strength and the water-holding capacity of the soil? It also reduces the area's ability to remove carbon from the atmosphere. We're basically agreeing to poison ourselves if we allow them to come in here with this project."

Drew followed me down and stood in the hall as I rifled through the front closet for equipment. "But they're not proposing to clear-cut the entire ridge. They said—"

"Why'd they say clear-cutting if they didn't mean clear-cutting, huh?" I demanded. "Have you asked yourself that? Does *anyone* else care about this land?"

Drew shook his head. "Hawk, of course I care. Christ, kiddo, I haven't used a pesticide since 1965—"

I emerged from the closet long enough to glare at him. "I. Am not. A *kid*."

Drew's eyes widened, and his mouth shut with a clack. "Okay, then," he said cautiously.

"Whenever I bring up my questions, everyone's answer seems to be 'Well, of course Evola wouldn't do that, silly Hawk!' and then they pat me on the head. But nobody can point to a part of the proposal where it says they won't do that. So what if they do it? Then everyone will be really sorry, and it'll be too late. If Dad were here, he'd..." I broke off with a headshake. "Anyway. I've gotta go. I told Maryanne I'd take her Mini Nature Scout Herd on a short hike, and I don't wanna disappoint the kiddos, but then I'm pitching my tent up there and getting to work." I stacked the camping lantern, the two-person tent, a first aid kit, and a wind-up generator on top of my blanket and pillow.

"Please take a breath." Drew put his hand on my shoulder. "I hear you, and... maybe you have a point. I just don't know that camping out there is the best way to make your stand. What about scheduling another meeting between the Environmental Committee and that Simon guy to see if Evola will change the proposal? Or contacting the town attorneys to see if they can negotiate—"

"We don't negotiate with terrorists, Uncle Drew!" I

yanked a thick fleece off the hanger and dropped that into my stack as well. The nights would be cold up there.

I heard Drew's sigh before he leaned against the front door. "See, now, *I* think talking is the best place to start. For example, why don't you talk to *me* about what's really bothering you? Because I know you, Henry Hawkins Sunday, and this is not the only bee in your bonnet."

"I'm tired of talking. Talking doesn't fix anything when the people you're talking to have no desire to change. All it does is make you more frustrated." I wasn't sure if I meant the development or Jack or both. It had all sort of blended together, despite my best efforts to keep them separated. "Aren't you the one who had that Janis Joplin quote on your wall for years that said, 'You are what you settle for'? Well, I'm tired of settling. Just imagine what would have happened if Elizabeth Bennet had settled for what everyone *said* was a good deal. She'd have ended up married to dumbass Mr. Collins and regretted it for the rest of her natural life. No, thank you."

"Honey," Drew began, but I cut him off by throwing my arms around him and giving him a hard, brief hug.

"I love you, Uncle Drew, but please trust me to know what I'm doing. I'm saying no to Mr. Collins. I'm moving forward. That's a good thing."

I remembered Elizabeth Bennet's own mantra, *"You must learn some of my philosophy. Think only of the past as its remembrance gives you pleasure."* I'd recited it to myself when I thought of my mom and how she'd left us behind when she divorced my dad years ago. I'd recited it when I thought of my dad and how much I missed him. And I'd recite it now, too.

I blew out a shaky breath. It wasn't easy to focus only on the good times, but it was better than getting mired in it.

A thought occurred to me, and I darted into Webb's office,

where Aiden kept some of his art supplies, and grabbed some poster board and markers. I needed to make some signs. "I'm going to educate Evola *and* the people of Little Pippin Hollow on the heritage and history of the land," I told Drew when I saw he'd followed me down the hall. "Maybe that will make it more personal. And maybe it'll help engage the rest of the town to join me in this protest." I tossed the markers in my bag before yanking the zipper closed again.

Drew shook his head sadly. "Man oh man. I suddenly realize how your grandma must've felt right before I hitch-hiked to the Bull Island Rock Festival."

"Pardon?"

"Nothing. Just… be safe." He drew me into a rough hug, patted me firmly on the back, then hugged me tightly again. "I love you, Hawk. And I promise you, you're not alone. Okay?"

I nodded, but seven minutes later, when I'd grabbed some snacks from the kitchen, loaded up my car, and hauled ass from Sunday Orchard to Fogg Peak, I couldn't help noticing there was no one riding shotgun.

And maybe that was a good thing. Maybe alone time was what I needed to finally make a clear plan for how to handle Evola… and the rest of my life.

I WAS SURROUNDED by a gaggle of four-and-five-year-old nature enthusiasts, bent over a thatch of Canada Milkvetch plants, when Crys found me on the mountain later that afternoon.

"These stems aren't fully grown yet. They can grow four feet tall—that's taller than you, Calliope," I told one of the kids. "See how pretty the tiny flowers are? Some people think the name is because the flowers are milk colored, but other people say it's because people used to feed it to cows to make them produce more milk. Unfortunately, it can also give them a very sick tummy."

"I had a sick tummy last week," Cosmo informed me.

"Yes, I heard about that—" I agreed.

"Mumma said it was *carnage*," my little oversharer went on. He frowned. "What's carnage, Mr. Hawk?"

"Uh… well," I began.

"Mr. Hawk, Mr. Hawk!" Grayson, one of the other Scouts, had wandered to the far side of the small clearing and was practically vibrating with excitement as he pointed at a low bush. "I know this one! We learned it last week! It's a pincushion plant!"

I straightened and walked over to him. "That's right. *Diapensia.* Nice job spotting that."

"I wanna see!" Mirabelle yelled, hip-checking Grayson aside in her enthusiasm and almost landing him in the bush.

Grayson put a restraining hand on her shoulder and gave her a solemn look. "Mira. Mr. Hawk says we needa be gentle with the plants, remember? Look but neeeeever touch."

"Oh, yeah." Mirabelle instantly sobered and gave me an apologetic look. "Sorry, Mr. Hawk."

I bit my lip and exchanged a laughing glance with Maryanne.

"You'll make naturalists of them yet, Hawk," she said softly. "Speaking of which, I talked to the parents about getting involved in your environmental group. Most of them have been too busy to make it to the town assemblies, but they're very interested in protecting this place. Maybe you could make up some informational flyers?"

I nodded, mentally adding that to my to-do list, along with creating some temporary signage to place in the parking area at the trailhead and up near the peak. "Maybe ask them to follow my new Instagram account? I already posted some pictures I had in my phone, and I'll be adding more every day."

Maryanne agreed, then began the long process of rounding up the kids for the trek back down the mountain. Each of them gave me an enthusiastic high five before they departed. "What plants are we gonna see next, Mr. Hawk?" Luna demanded.

"Purple hyssops. Who here likes purple?" Every one of them raised their hands. "Awesome. And we're also gonna learn about *bats*, so be ready."

"Sounds like fun! What do we say to Mr. Hawk, Herd?" Maryanne asked.

"Thank you, Mr. Hawk!" the kids chorused before pairing up with their buddies and heading back down the path.

"Wow. Someone's been a busy beaver," Crys said, entering the clearing as the kids were leaving. "You're really popular with the small humans, huh?"

I shrugged. "I started doing summer hikes with the Mini Scouts when Aiden was that age. I wanted to show him the mountain like my dad did with me. And then... I just kept doing it, even after he aged out. There's something about kids this age that's special. They're little sponges."

"If you say so, boo. I have zero patience." She turned and surveyed the bushes and plants around us doubtfully. "So... this is your new home away from home? It's... cute."

I snickered. "Not here. There are marked areas for camping where you can pitch a tent. Mine's a little ways up the trail." I bumped her shoulder and nodded in the direction of the peak. "You wanna come see?"

"Obviously. I didn't climb five billion miles up this craggy mountain on a mission of mercy just to turn around and head back right away. Besides, I have supplies for you." She reached around to pat her bulging backpack.

"You're the best."

It hadn't taken me long to realize that storming out

without my sleeping bag had been a mistake. The cold front that had blown in over the weekend had decided to stick around, at least at the higher elevation where I was camping. I'd rather have taken my chances with hypothermia than head back to town and deal with my family again, though, so I'd called Crys, who had a huge assortment of outdoor gear shoved in her closet, and asked for a favor.

It took about ten more minutes of hiking to reach the little camping area I'd chosen. It was set back about twenty feet from the trail for privacy and ringed with tall pines.

I swept out an arm. "Home sweet home. For the next little while, at least."

Crys pushed a clump of sweat-damp pink hair off her forehead and set down her backpack with a *clink*. "Sleeping bag," she announced, pulling out a quilted bag and unrolling it inside the tent. "And some other necessities." She removed two poly bags of dehydrated food, a wickedly sharp-looking knife, a Taser, and…

"Are those night-vision goggles?" I demanded.

"Yep. My ex-girlfriend left a bunch of shit before she moved out of our old place. She was a ten, but she was a prepper, so really she was a six, tops, if you know what I mean. Still, handy stuff, right? Also…"

She opened a different compartment and withdrew a glass bottle of vodka, some orange-pink juice, two plastic cups, and a tiny cooler of crushed ice. "Don't worry, the bottle and cups are recyclable. Couldn't exactly toast your protest with Earth-killing stuff."

After we got settled atop the sleeping bag inside the tent, she bartended us into some killer-looking cocktails, then settled in and began the interrogation I'd known was coming.

"So, boo, I've gotta ask… What the fuck was that all about at the diner?"

"It was about me not waiting anymore, obviously." I lifted my chin stubbornly. "It was about me making changes. Like we talked about. I've already gotten a bunch of stuff started on Instagram, and—"

"Hold up. I don't recall suggesting that you should announce to the entire town your..." She hesitated. "Freshie status."

"You can say virgin," I muttered. "I've decided it's nothing to be ashamed of. I'm gonna own it. In fact, I might start a Virgin Club and invite other-Chris from the Bugle to join me. We can both wear grandma-knit sweaters and proudly proclaim that our flowers have never been plucked."

"I'm not sure other-Chris would qualify for your club." Crys tapped the lip of the cup against her chin. "He's got the heart of a marauding Viking hiding beneath those glasses and granny sweaters."

I snorted. "If you say so."

"Besides, I'm not sure *you* are gonna qualify for your club much longer. Didn't you agree to consider a date with Simon the Enviro Geek?"

"Welllll," I hedged. "Sort of. I maybe typed out a message to him earlier, but I was too keyed up to send it."

"Boo. It's *because* you're so keyed up that you *need* to send it. If you de-escalate the importance of the cherry-popping moment and just let it happen with any decent guy, then maybe you'll stop stressing about it so much. Things with Jack will have more time to develop naturally... if they're going to develop."

I looked up from my drink to stare at her. "You think I'm stressing myself into rejection?"

"No," she said with a laugh. "It's just... sex doesn't have to be such a big deal. It's fun and powerful and beautiful and transcendental even, but sometimes it's more like a stress reliever. Like knife throwing... but with penises, in your case."

I choked on my drink. "Considering how badly I failed at knife throwing, that's maybe not the best comparison. But...

okay, let's say I agree with you. Simon only asked me to dinner. How would I even go about getting him to agree to no-strings sex? *Hello, Simon, I would like you to throw your penis at my target?"*

"That would do it." Crys had a mischievous sparkle in her eyes. "Then let the conversation flow naturally from there."

I set my cup down and buried my face in my hands to cool my burning cheeks. "I'm being serious. How do you ask a guy for sex?"

"Hawk." She shook her head. "You are the most precious pearl, and never change, okay? But also… do we really need to revisit the dirty probable meaning of his leaf emojis? He's already on board, and if he's gone anywhere in the Hollow today, I can guarantee he's heard exactly what's on your mind right now, too. Just let him know you're interested. He'll take it from there."

I nodded to let her know I heard her, but when I tried to picture it—*Simon's* lips on mine, *Simon's* hands on my body, the scent of *Simon's* cologne in my nose—it felt exciting but wrong. And when the two of us heard the crunch of approaching footsteps coming up the trail to the campsite and I peered out the tent in excited expectation… it wasn't Simon I was hoping to see.

But when the visitor ducked down to peek into the tent, it wasn't Jack *or* Simon who'd come to visit.

"Webb?" I blurted. "What are you doing here?"

"Bringing you a sleeping bag." He tossed the bag on the ground inside the tent on top of the one Crys had brought. "Drew said you left without yours, and he was worried. We all kind of were. Can you and I…" He coughed uncomfortably. "…talk, or whatever?"

Anyone who'd only known Webb since Luke came into his life would probably be pretty shocked to learn that the man had never been particularly comfortable with emotions. Since I tended to run on emotion the way cars ran on gasoline, that meant Webb and I hadn't deliberately sat down for a heart-to-heart since...

Well, ever.

Crys lifted an eyebrow in unspoken question, and when I nodded, she zipped her backpack and crawled out of the tent. "I'm leaving you the bottle, boo. Be good, okay? May Mother Earth keep her pet snakes safely tucked into their beds tonight." She held an imaginary phone to her ear. "Call me if you need me."

"Spotty cell reception up here," Webb and I said at the same time. I added, "I'm gonna climb to the peak every day to post pics and check email, though. I'll be in touch."

Crys waved and headed back down the trail, and Webb stood outside the tent for a moment. "Can I...?" He gestured at the spot on the sleeping bag that Crys had vacated, and I scooted all the way to the edge to make room for him, looping my arms around my knees.

Webb ducked inside, drawing up his long legs. The tent immediately seemed way, way too crowded with his lumber-jacky shoulder pushed up against mine. "So. Camping, huh?" Webb scratched at his beard with one fingertip. "I love camping."

"I'm not up here for recreation. I'm protesting. I'm strate-gizing." I shrugged. "I'm sucking in whatever remaining moments I can in case I fail and all of this goes away."

I expected an argument. An eye roll. An *Oh, Hawk, stop being dramatic!* But Webb just looked pensive.

"You seem calmer now," he ventured. "You were pretty upset at the diner earlier."

"Yeah. Being up here, talking with the Mini Nature Scouts... it cleared my mind a bit." I picked at a frayed spot in my jeans guiltily. "Look, I'm sorry I yelled at you. You didn't deserve that. Luke definitely didn't deserve it. I'll apologize to him."

He nodded. "That'd be good. Luke loves you, and he was

a little worried he'd upset you. I told him it seemed like you had something else on your mind, though." He gave me a sideways look. "Given what you mentioned about... cherries?"

I set my jaw. If Webb was expecting me to confess all my deepest feels, he was in for a long wait. None of the things I was feeling were suitable for discussion with the man who still thought I was a kid.

After a long moment, he nodded slowly again. "I see. Well, if you aren't in the mood to share, maybe I'll take a turn."

"Unnecessary," I said through my teeth. Just because I didn't want to share my feelings didn't mean I wanted to hear his. I was all too aware of Webb's opinions on most things.

"Too bad." He leaned back on one elbow, stretching his long legs so they stuck out of the tent, and took a deep breath. "You know, I waited a long time for Luke Williams—"

I immediately broke my resolution to stay silent. "I don't know how that's possible, since you were married to Amanda for years *and* didn't know you were gay *and* you didn't even like Luke at first," I said pointedly.

Webb chuckled, refusing to be baited. "Okay, you're right. I didn't know I was waiting for *Luke*-Luke. A flatlander all the way from North Carolina and a man to boot? I definitely didn't see that coming. What I meant was I waited a long time for a... a true partner. Someone who'd be all in on a relationship like I am. Someone who feels as intensely for me as I do for him. Deep down, I think I always wanted that. Tried to convince myself I had it with Amanda, and when that didn't work out, I told myself it didn't exist—"

"Yeah," I grudgingly admitted. "I hated that for you."

"So when Luke came along..." He traced his finger along the quilted seam of the sleeping bag. "It wasn't like anything I'd ever expected, so I didn't believe it was real. We can joke around about it, but it wasn't just sunshine and rainbows and drunken bugle blowing, you know? Falling in love with Luke made me question everything—who I was and what was important to me. It scared the shit out of me. You know how much I love chaos, right?"

I chuckled lightly because Webb's control freak tendencies were well-known.

"I fought it hard," he went on, his voice thick with remorse. "It *hurt*. And I ended up hurting Luke in the process."

I nodded. "But you got through it."

"We did. And thank fuck, because what was on the other side of all that chaos..." Webb shook his head wonderingly. "Shit, Hawk. I have a guy who believes in me. Who looks at me and sees *me*. All my faults, and my fears, and my annoying habits..." He darted a look at me. "Not that I have many, of course. Maybe one or two—"

"—dozen," I snickered.

Webb grinned. "At least. But Luke embraces all of it. I don't have to hide parts of myself or change myself in order for him to love me because he loves me just as I am, the same way I love him. But it's like... I also want to be the best version of myself for his sake." He bit his lip. "I dunno. I'm not great at putting this stuff into words. Maybe I'm not making sense."

"No, you are," I assured him. "That's... beautiful. I'm really glad for you. And a little envious. And I really hope you've told Luke all this, too. I bet he'd like to hear it."

"Well, of course. I tell him every single day." Webb frowned, like this should be obvious. "That's what we mean when we say *I love you*."

Oh.

Unlike Webb, I'd always believed in true love, which was a blessing and a curse. Where Webb had decided it couldn't be real and refused to acknowledge it when it was right in front of him, I'd gone looking for it in every person I met, and I'd found it with Jack… all but the kissing.

Or at least I thought I had.

But this thing Webb was describing, where he and Luke knew each other to the core and embraced it all… suddenly, I wasn't so sure I'd ever fully experienced that. Jack and I were incredibly close—closer than I'd ever been with anyone—but there were still things I held back, like how I really felt about him, because I hadn't wanted to scare him off. And I sensed there were things he held back from me, too, for whatever reason.

"Anyway, my point in telling you all this," Webb continued, "is to say you don't need to rush the cherry-popping thing. Having sex when you feel ready, because you want it, because you've found a partner who will respect and appreciate you for who you are, is just… smart. Sex is fun, but it's nothing like the feeling that comes when you're having sex with someone you love and respect and all that. It's okay to hold out for the real deal if you want to."

This seemed more like the overprotective Webb I knew. "So you're telling me you hiked up the side of a mountain and initiated a deep conversation about feelings all so you could tell me not to toss my virginity away?" I demanded, torn between annoyance and affection. "My outburst at the diner wasn't an open invitation to the men of the Hollow, you know."

"I know!" Webb sat up straight, his eyes unable to meet mine. "Jeez, Hawk. I just wanted to encourage you that whatever you're, you know, going through right now that led to that outburst, I have every faith you'll get through it, and you don't have to compromise what you want to get there. You've always been smarter than I am about emotional stuff, even when we were kids. You're so brave and strong—"

I snorted. "Yeah, right."

"I'm serious." And sure enough, when Webb looked at

me with those green eyes so like our dad's, there wasn't a trace of humor there. "You remind me of that little oak tree that grows out over the side of Mettle Falls. You know the one I mean? There's all this crashing water, like, *inches* away from it, that you look at it and can't help but think, holy shit, how could something so delicate have sprouted right there out of that craggy ground? How can it possibly flourish the way it does with all this craziness going on around it? You… you maybe even wish you could build a wall around it so nothing disturbs it. So it can be safe." He shot me a wry look. "Not because you think it's not strong or fully grown or *competent at being a tree*, but because it's special and precious and you very much don't want it to stop being exactly what it is."

"Webb," I whispered, shaking my head.

"But it turns out that while you're busy watching the water and worrying over the tree losing a few branches, the tree is just chilling there, doing its tree thing. Growing leaves. Turning colors. Holding strong, no matter how much ice gets dumped on it. Soaking up all that water and sunshine, swaying in the breeze. Making everything a little more beautiful in its own way and never doubting where it belongs. No fear of the water." He pushed at my knee. "That's you, Hawk."

I shook my head again. "Nope. No. That's sweet, Webb, and I don't want to ruin this beautiful moment, but you're, like, *super* wrong. I'm scared a lot. I'm scared of so many things every single day." Of disappointing people. Of losing what mattered most, like Fogg Peak and my family and Jack. Of being a burden. Of missing out.

"Well then, I'm even more impressed. Because if you're scared and you manage to be as loving and giving and open as you are anyway, you're even stronger than I thought. And if I've ever made you doubt that I saw you that way, I'm sorry. That's not on you—it's *me* wanting to control shit, as usual." Webb bumped his shoulder into mine. "I'll work on it, I promise."

I let my head fall on his shoulder. "Thanks, Webb. For hiking up here. For saying all that."

"Anytime. Here's what I know, Hawk: as sad or as envious or as doubtful or angry as you might feel, it's all going to come right in the end. There really *is* a happy ending out there for every single one of us. Sometimes getting there is hard fucking work. Sometimes it takes a long time. Sometimes you have to rethink things you thought you knew. But... it'll happen. Just keep doing your tree thing and trust the process. It'll come when it's meant to come. Okay?"

He squeezed my shoulder before putting his hands back in his lap and sitting quietly with me, soaking in the sounds of the trees moving in the late-day breeze.

"Want me to stay?" he asked after a while. "There's two sleeping bags now. I can try to text Luke..."

I shook my head. "Nah. Go back to your husband. I want to spend some time on my own. Think things through."

He stood up and brushed dirt and pine needles off his legs. "Okay. But you packed the radio, right?"

"Always, when I'm hiking or camping alone. And fresh batteries. And I know the proper channels," I said before he could ask.

"Pfft. I didn't doubt it for a second." He shoved his hair off his forehead. "But, you know, if by some chance you were to discover you *didn't* have fresh batteries, you might find some tucked into the bottom of that second sleeping bag."

I laughed out loud, and it unknotted something deep in my chest that made me stand and throw my arms around Webb's waist. "Thanks."

"Always." He gave me a quick hug, then hesitated before turning and walking down the trail. "If you talk to Jack, you don't need to mention that I was here, okay?"

"Jack?" I frowned. "Why would he care?"

Webb rolled his eyes. "He may have given me a little come-to-Jesus conversation earlier after you left the diner. Pointed out some truths about you being a fully grown adult. About how maybe we need to take steps to protect this land." He lifted his face to the treetops, where the last of the golden hour sunlight glinted off the shivering leaves.

"He did?" I demanded. "Are you kidding?"

Webb gave me a level look. "Don't look so surprised. I tried to smooth things over after you stormed out, and he wouldn't have it. Told me you had every reason to feel the way you feel and was ready to throw down with me if I dared to criticize you." He lifted an eyebrow. "Jack cares about you an awful lot, huh?"

"Yeah," I agreed, but the word came out sounding defeated. That Jack cared about me wasn't in doubt. He just cared about lots of other things *more*, like his friendship with Webb, and the difference in our ages, and the fact that, for no reason I could understand, he wasn't interested in a committed relationship while insisting that I needed one.

"Anyway, don't tell him I came, or he'll assume it was because of *him*." Webb winked. "He may have made some valid points, but I don't want him to get a swollen head over it. Later, Hawklet." He saluted me as he headed down the trail.

"Asshole," I called out with a laugh.

A crunch from behind me caught my attention, and when I whirled around, I saw Simon hiking down the trail from higher up on the peak. He gave me a frown. "Hawk? Were you talking to me?"

"N-no. My brother. Sorry." My face heated.

I'd literally just told Webb that I needed to be alone to have time to think—especially since Webb and Crys had just given me wildly conflicting advice—but somehow, my isolated camping area had become Grand Central Station.

"Thank goodness. I was hoping I hadn't earned the

moniker before even saying hello." Simon blew out a sigh of relief and smiled.

It was a nice smile, with even, white teeth that set off a little bit of a tan he'd acquired since the last time I'd seen him. Though he was dressed for hiking in a pair of Salomon boots and a Patagonia zip-up jacket, his hair was perfectly combed and he didn't look sweaty or tired at all. In fact, he looked like a poster model for healthy living.

"I can't imagine anyone yelling at you," I said, shifting my weight from one foot to the other awkwardly. "Were you hiking up at the peak? Was it for Evola stuff?"

He shrugged. "One of our crews brought some surveying equipment to the back side of the mountain, and I hitched a ride as far as that old, rickety footbridge over the creek—"

"Friendly Footbridge is a protected local historical site," I informed him. "JP Friendly painted *Despair of Honesty* on that bridge in 1913." I frowned. "You know motorized vehicles are prohibited except in specifically designated areas, right? Rocky Cut is way too steep, and the other trails on the north side far too narrow for anything with wheels, and you'd end up damaging vegetation. There are penalties, including imprisonment and fines of up to—"

"Whoa, hey! Do I look like the kind of person who'd violate posted signage?" Simon pressed a hand to his chest and grinned, the very picture of innocence.

"I guess not," I admitted. At the very least, he was smart enough not to confess to it if he had.

"Anyway, I brought my pack so I could head up to the summit once I was off the clock and stretch my legs a bit. Took some pictures for the website, too. I hadn't expected to run into anyone, though, especially you." He looked around my campsite. "Are you staying up here?"

"For a little while, yeah." I dragged out the sleeping bag Webb had brought and spread it out flat. "Have a seat if you'd like."

"Maybe for a minute." He sat down with a tired little groan, which made him seem immediately more human. "This area's beautiful."

"It is." I settled myself down on the other side of the sleeping bag. "Which is one of the reasons I care so much about preserving it."

He nodded but kept his mouth shut, which helped me relax even more. Had he tried arguing with me or defending Evola's position, my hackles would have stood right up.

After a moment, he said, "I really admire you. This is a brave thing you're doing. Standing up for something you believe in without being destructive or disruptive is mature and conscientious."

I stared at him, feeling a little like I'd stumbled into an alternate reality. First, my brother had called me brave, and now Simon, too? That wasn't a word I normally associated with myself, but it was pretty nice all the same.

"Thanks," I said softly. "That means a lot."

"You know, you didn't reply to my text last night. And you never did get in touch with me about hiking." Simon shot me a look under his eyelashes. "I couldn't decide if that meant you were busy today or… busy *forever*."

My face went hot, and I couldn't help thinking about potentially pornographic leaf emojis. "Not forever," I hedged.

"You're cute when you blush." Simon grinned, showing a truly impressive number of very white teeth, and I was pretty sure that made me blush harder. "I tried *Pride and Prejudice* again after you said it was your favorite. Mostly to impress you, I admit. But… are you gonna hate me if I say I didn't like it?"

I fake-gasped and clutched my imaginary pearls, but I couldn't keep up the pretense. "Kidding! Of course I won't."

"It was just…" He hesitated. "A bit unrealistic? I know it's fiction, but the author was really dismissive of the Wickham character. He was so two-dimensional. Every villain has an origin story. If there was no Loki, there'd be no Thor."

This time, my gasp was completely real. "Wickham? Are you serious? Dude. Some villains are just villains. *Period.*"

Simon let out an easy laugh. "Okay, maybe you're right. Maybe I'll give it another try." He bumped his shoulder into mine. "Or… maybe I'll let you explain it to me in person. What do you say, Hawk? Would you like to go out to dinner with me this week?"

CHAPTER NINE

JACK

"She began now to comprehend that he was exactly the man who, in disposition and talents, would most suit her."
~ Jane Austen

Usually I barely had time to breathe during the lunch rush, much less listen to town gossip, but three days after Hawk Sunday had stormed out of the diner and out of my life, it seemed like everyone was talking about the one thing I couldn't ignore if I tried.

"Who would have thought a good-looking thing like Hawkins Sunday would still be holding on to his purity like that?" Ellie Walcott said with her hand over her bosom. The gold from her stacked bangle bracelets caught the sunlight coming through the plate glass window and sparkled around her like golden confetti. "What a sweet boy."

Penny Chan wrinkled her nose. "I dunno. I heard from Van at the Bugle that Hawk actually slept with Trina Higgins in high school, and that's why she was heartbroken when her parents moved the whole family to Nebraska."

Norma Alvarez choked on her pancakes. "Hawkins and

Trina? Nonsense. The boy is gay as the day is long. All the Sunday brothers have an eye for the gentlemen. My son Tonio and his sweet boyfriend have been together nearly seventeen years, which means I have a *sense* for these things." She sniffed. "I wonder if Tonio has any single friends..."

I rolled my eyes but stopped myself from commenting as I delivered their food.

Two tables down, Emma Sunday sat with a few of her friends, idly scrolling through her phone, and didn't glance up when I approached with their hummus appetizer. "...so I told Uncle Drew I think it's pretty freaking cool. He's been up there three days so far, and I think he should make it an even forty. You know, like that character in that book who wandered in the wilderness for forty days and forty nights."

Her friend blinked at her. "You mean *the Bible*?"

"What?" Em looked up from her phone and scowled. "No, Gracie, the John Krakauer book about Alaska."

"Ohhh." Gracie thought this over. "I hope Hawk doesn't burn his cash to stay warm like that guy did. You could use it to get some new lacrosse gear. But yeah, I agree. It's cool what he's doing."

Cool? That Hawk reminded her of a book where the main character *died*?

No. No, it definitely was *not* cool that Hawk had decided to park himself on Fogg Peak, all alone, to protest the development... as I'd told Webb several times with increasing frustration.

But because I'd somehow stumbled into the alternate-universe, opposite-land version of Little Pippin Hollow where my beloved, peace-loving Hawk Sunday had become an angry protestor who lived in a tent on a mountain, Webb was treating Hawk's decision to go full-on Henry David Thoreau as a nonevent and refused to get involved.

"*He's fine, Jack,*" Webb had informed me, barely glancing up from the trees he was inspecting for insects. "*He's camping *twenty minutes from home, he has plenty of batteries, and nobody knows that mountain like he does. Weren't you the one saying it was time to stop treating him like a kid?"* He'd given me a side-long glance I didn't know how to interpret. *"If you're worried he's starving, maybe youuuu should be the one to go check on him. Bring him a panini."*

I wasn't only worried about Hawk's physical survival, though. Did anyone know if he was lonely? Or angry? Or if he'd brought enough books to read? Were my calls to him going directly to voicemail due to the lack of cell reception on the ridge or due to his lack of reception of... *me?*

I plunked the heavy plate down in front of the teenagers with a grunt.

As I walked away, I heard Em say, "I bet Jack's grumpy 'cause he's shorthanded, and summer's a busy season. I bet he'll be hiring soon since Hawk is—oh my heck, Gracie, look at this Instagram post!"

My stomach rolled over. No, I was definitely not hiring Hawk's replacement. Not now, not ever. Hawk had lost his temper due to... circumstances... but eventually, things would calm down. Or he would calm down. And then he'd be back. Talking to me. Teasing me. Making every part of my life feel *right* again.

Any minute now.

Probably.

I could not contemplate a future for me that didn't have Hawk in it.

"Katey, table twelve looks ready for their bill," I said, making my way into the kitchen to check on an order.

Katey turned away from a conversation with Tom, the line cook, a residual frown on her face. "Yeah, okay. But hey, is it alright with you if I duck out early tomorrow afternoon if that storm is still coming through like they're predicting? My dog doesn't handle big storms very well."

"Storm?" I reached for the plates Tom had lined up for me. "Who said anything about a storm?"

Katey and Tom exchanged a look.

"Boss, that's all most folks've been talking about all morning," he informed me, which was either patently false or my ears had become antennae that only tuned in to Hawk-related programming. "Big baddie with high winds and heavy rain. Remember that microburst that happened in Addison a few years ago? Weathermen say they're way more common than tornadoes. Bring your pets inside."

Katey nodded. "You should probably keep an eye on conditions and consider closing early so everyone can get home."

As I walked back out to deliver the order to my customers, my brain entered a well-organized spiral serving up varied and detailed images of a lone camper in a tent on an exposed mountain ridge getting sucked up into a weather vortex and transported violently into the afterlife.

"It's fine," I assured myself as I brought MaryPat Fishbaugh her lunch order. "No one is dying over this."

MaryPat looked up from her mushroom-and-swiss panini with a side of orzo summer salad. "Uh. Sure hope not, Jack. But everything looks real good."

I made a vague gesture of apology and turned away.

Everything did not, in fact, look real good. When the lunch rush died down and I finally had enough free time to pull out my phone and search the weather, I discovered the forecast was just as perilous as Katey and Tom had suggested. There was no way Hawk could continue to live in a tent on Glassy Ridge. Someone needed to talk him down, and since Webb wouldn't get involved, it had to be…

Crys plunked herself down on the bench across from me at the corner booth where I was supposed to be entering supply orders into my laptop. "Hey, are you posting an ad for

Hawk's job? Because Chris who works at the Bugle might be free for a couple lunch shifts a week."

I glanced up in confusion. "Don't you already work here?"

She rolled her eyes. "Not me. I mean other-Chris. The Clark Kent hottie with the glasses and the questionable fashion choices? You've met him," she assured me when I continued to stare at her blankly. "When you and Hawk were sitting at the bar watching that Maine regatta thing a few weeks back, he was the one making your drinks. No bells ringing? He was eating here the other day, when Hawk quit… really? Not a single recollection?"

"I was a little distracted that day," I reminded her.

She snorted. "Yeah. Well, once you actually notice him, you'll see he's *distractingly* gorgeous. Might be a problem."

"For whom?"

"For *you*? For anyone with eyes who's attracted to men?"

"Please," I scoffed. "I haven't dated anyone in months, and I didn't notice your friend at all. I think he'd be safe from me."

"Months? Is that so?" When she tilted her head, her pink hair flopped to one side. "Wonder why that is."

I had no time for whatever games she was attempting to play. "In any case, it doesn't matter because Hawk's coming back." I clicked the Enter button to submit the last order. "Sooner rather than later since there's a storm coming in. In fact, you should probably hike up there today. Make sure Hawk knows about it so he has time to evacuate." If my voice sounded as casual as I hoped it did, it would be a miracle.

"Please. There's no way Hawk's leaving. Did you know he's staked out signs all along the main hiking trail at the top, and he's been standing there every day educating tourists and locals about Evola's deforestation efforts? He's already got forty thousand followers on his new Instagram."

"Really?" The man was pigheaded as heck about the development, but I couldn't help the flush of pride that warmed my chest knowing my Hawk was standing up for what he believed in… and people were taking notice. "Good. He's bringing awareness to it, which will at least keep Evola on their toes. They'll have to play by the rules under that kind of public scrutiny." I shut my laptop with a *click.* "But you still need to convince him to take a break during the storm. He shouldn't be alone up there."

"A little rain won't hurt him." Crys set her chin. "If he won't come off the mountain so Simon can rail him into his mattress, Jack, he's not coming down for a summer storm."

I blinked. "His… he… what?"

"Oh, didn't Hawk tell you?" Crys's mouth twisted to one side. "No, I guess he wouldn't have had the chance, would he? Yeah, Simon asked him out. And you should see the flirty texts Simon's been sending! So many erotic emojis." She fake-gagged. "Hawk's all adorable and flustered about it, of course, but the man is *primed* for devirgination, and I think they could be really good together. They're both passionate about environmental stuff. As dudes go, they're both smoking hot. Can't you just picture them together? Plus, Hawk's in his reach-out-and-take-what-you-want era. He doesn't have time for people who make excuses. Simon's been very, very clear that Hawk is what he wants."

I opened my mouth, but a paralyzing chill went down my spine—*Can't you just picture them together?*—and I was very afraid I might vomit, so I closed it again.

"You know…" Crys tapped her lip thoughtfully with one chipped fingernail. "You might be onto something, though. Maybe Simon could go ride out the storm up there with him. You know Hawk has a thing for those books where the two characters are stuck sharing a room in a blizzard… What do you call those?"

"Forced proximity," I said in a nearly inaudible whisper.

She snapped her fingers. "That's it! And Simon probably knows tons about storm hazards since he's an environmental dude. He might even be trained in CPR, so, like, if one of them got struck by lightning, he could perform mouth-to-mouth…"

I swallowed thickly.

"Hawk told me you recommended he carry lube in his backpack just in case he and Simon got an opportunity, so we know he's prepared. That was thoughtful of you." She beamed guilelessly, and I knew I was being played by a master.

But damn if it wasn't working.

An embarrassing little choking sound gurgled out of my throat, and I coughed to hide it. "I said no such thing," I argued, knowing it was useless. "I think Hawk should wait for the right person. Someone he really wants, not someone convenient."

"And *I* think this topic is getting seriously old," she said sweetly.

My eye twitched. She wasn't wrong.

She pressed her lips together for a beat before patting my arm and preparing to stand up from the table. "At the risk of getting fired on the spot, I really think you should go up there and fuck him, Jack. Dunno what kind of bullshit ethical problem is burbling through the wild brook in your brainpan, but he wants *you*. He chose *you*. And you want him just as badly. So have at it. As William Hale Thompson once famously said, 'Fuck early and often.'"

"I think that was about voting," I called after her in a choked voice.

She waved her hand over her shoulder. "Po-tay-toe, po-tah-toe. Now, go get your man."

I leaned my elbows on the table and buried my face in my hands. Everyone in Little Pippin Hollow had lost their damned mind.

I LASTED twenty hours before I caved.

In that time, I talked to Drew, who literally laughed out loud when I suggested *he* should drag Hawk off the mountain and muttered something about how "Janis Joplin saved the day again, rest her soul."

I talked to Webb and Knox, who exchanged a look so long it seemed like they were having an entire conversation. Knox raised an eyebrow at Webb, Webb glared at him worriedly, Knox folded his arms over his chest and tilted his chin toward me, and Webb finally looked away with his jaw clenched. "We think Hawk'll be fine," Knox told me coolly. "He knows exactly when and where to seek shelter, and he knows the evacuation routes. But we appreciate your concern."

I even broke down and explained the whole situation to my mother, who scowled at me, sighed dramatically, and told the dog, "*Apparently*, certain adults need to learn the consequences of their actions the hard way, don't they, Peony?" which I thought was pretty unfeeling since she loved Hawk nearly as much as she loved me.

That morning, I'd been so desperate I'd actually considered approaching Helena Fortnum to beg for her help—the woman was quite spry for an octogenarian; surely a little hike wouldn't hurt her—when Tom had casually mentioned something about how the National Weather Service no longer recommended using the Lightning Crouch, whatever the hell that was.

"Guess if lightning strikes," Tom had continued, "you're just supposed to grin and bear it. At least Hawk isn't in a metal tent, right?"

Visions assaulted my brain of metal tent poles and trekking poles, metal cooking equipment and insulated water bottles gleefully conducting electricity all around Hawk's tent. Even the 1858 Flying Eagle penny his dad had given him that he wore on a chain around his neck for luck now seemed like a harbinger of doom.

And that was when I realized that I needed to bite the bullet and fetch the man off the mountain myself.

"Treat me like an adult, he says," I muttered at my boots as I trudged up the trail. "While childishly ignoring dangerous weather warnings. What kind of adult risks himself in a situation like this? A stupid one, that's what kind."

But concern for his well-being didn't explain my sweaty palms and jittery heart. Not when the only signs of the storm were a few intermittent raindrops. Not when there was plenty of time to convince him, pack him up, and get him safely home before the real storm arrived.

It took half the long-ass trail for me to realize that what was driving me, what was spinning me wildly to the edge of my comfort and sanity, was fear of seeing Hawk. Because I knew if I saw him... I wouldn't be able to hold myself back.

My feelings for him were so strong they felt like steel bands crushing my solar plexus. Even though I'd told him I couldn't be what he wanted, what he needed, I couldn't stop imagining being with him in exactly that way. His bright, familiar face had filled my dreams for the past two weeks when I was lucky enough to sleep, and the thought of touching his warm, naked skin filled the nights when I couldn't sleep at all.

I'd slept with him a thousand times in my mind, taking him fast and hard against the wall in the diner's storeroom... slowly and sensually in front of a crackling fire... quick and sweet in a stolen moment in the middle of the night. I wanted him so badly I couldn't think straight.

I sucked in a deep breath of the cool, humid air. The temperature was already dropping now that the sun was behind heavy clouds.

If I followed my own advice to Webb and tried treating Hawk like an adult, maybe I could accept his proposal for the two of us to sleep together without it having to mean anything more than that.

Yeah, right. As if I could get naked with him and not have it mean anything.

I'd told Hawk that *he* couldn't possibly want sex without romantic strings, but it was me—*me*—who knew we couldn't be together that way without being together *in all the ways.* And I...

I had no idea how to do that, and I didn't want to let him down. He was infinitely precious. Breaking him would break *me.*

Hawk's words from our last hike sounded in my head. *The only reason you don't know about relationship stuff is because you haven't tried relationship stuff, just like you weren't born knowing how to play the damn tuba.*

But life wasn't that easy. It *couldn't* be...

Could it?

"What the fuck are you thinking?" I muttered. "Of course it's not."

My stomach turned over again. Hawk was emotional these days. Impulsive. What if putting sex on the table between us was just another bad decision he'd made? What if he regretted it? What if giving in to what we wanted was the thing that broke our friendship apart, this time for good—

"Jack?"

My head snapped up to find Hawk standing a few yards down the trail. He looked rough and rugged from several days camping. His hair stood in sandy-brown cowlicks, and a long smear of dirt trailed over his cheek and down the front of an *Averill Union Bears* T-shirt that looked a couple of sizes too small for him.

He'd never been more gorgeous.

My heart knocked against my rib cage, my body ready to run to him, take him up in my arms, hold him tight, and kiss his fucking face off.

My mind froze my feet to the ground, and I could only stare at him, swallowing hard.

"Hi," I croaked.

"You…" Hawk licked his lips, looking wary and confused. "What are you doing here?"

Right. *Yes.* I had a purpose. I hadn't come here to gawk.

"There's a storm coming," I said.

Hawk looked up at the milky sky and the very evident, impossible-to-miss clouds that had gathered on the horizon. "Yep. Sure seems that way. And you… decided to hike in it?"

I moved closer, weighing the pros and cons of touching him just a *tiny* bit—just enough to assure myself he was alive and well and this was not, say, the beginning of a strangely conversation-heavy wet dream. Then again, touching him was *exactly* what dream-me would do, so that wouldn't clarify anything.

I fisted my hands at my sides and focused on pressing my nails into my palms. "I came to help you pack up. There's still plenty of time to get back down the mountain before… anything happens."

I wasn't sure, at that moment, which terrible outcome I was trying to avoid—the one where lightning struck and burned one of us to a crisp… or the one where I let myself have him, and *both* of us got burned.

"Oh." Hawk's confusion cleared, and he raised his chin. "You should probably go, then. I'm staying."

How was it possible for him to surprise me when he said exactly what I expected him to say?

Or maybe what surprised me was how straight and strong he stood, how confident he looked, as he said it. His eyes, which had been storm-tossed and emotionally ravaged for weeks, now glowed with certainty and determination. His lean muscles flexed as he folded his arms over his chest defiantly, and the movement made light glint off the scruff on his jaw. He looked every inch like a man who knew what he wanted… and that knowledge made my stomach flip and my cock stir.

For maybe the first time between us, *I* was the unsure one of the two of us. The one with questions and no answers. The one who was drowning in a churning sea of *want* and sinking for the third time. The one whose patience was coiled together with his longing and annoyance…

The one who lashed out.

"That's beyond foolish. What would your father say?" I demanded.

The hurtful words landed on the hard, damp ground between us in an ugly lump. Tension crackled in the air, more potent than the coming lightning. But instead of responding, Hawk sighed, and his shoulders slumped. Then he turned and disappeared up the trail to his campsite.

I had a moment to realize that his easy capitulation didn't feel much like a victory. Then, heart pounding with a combination of excitement and dread that nearly made me light-headed, I followed him.

When we arrived at his campsite, I saw only a single canvas tote bag and a stuff sack with his sleeping bag in it.

"This is all you have?" I demanded, turning in a circle like I expected other provisions to suddenly appear. "Where's your backpack? Your tent? Your protest signs?"

"Not that it's any of your business, but they're already in the cave." He grabbed the remaining items and shouldered past me back to the trail.

I blew out a breath of relief and followed him back down the trail, over the quaint little footbridge that crossed the thickest part of Glassy Creek, mentally calculating the distance back to the parking area—

A second later, my brain finished processing his words. "Wait. What cave?"

"I've shown you the caves on the north side of the moun-tain before."

"Well, yes, but…" I jogged to catch up to him.

"I moved my stuff there to ride out the storm. And, since you asked, my father would say job well done since *he's* the one who taught me all the trails on this mountain and how to seek shelter during a storm. The cave I chose doesn't have water issues or other hazards near the entrance, which would be the only reasons to avoid it."

"The only reason? How about comfort and safety? You can't tell me that this cave on a mountain is safer than your house. Hawk? Hawk!"

Hawk ignored me, and I followed him a quarter mile in moody silence to the familiar wide entrance of Kirkcaster. It was the largest cave in the Glassy system and a favorite with tourists because of its solid appearance and interesting history.

I let out a breath. At least he'd selected one with multiple entrances. It was large enough to stand up comfortably in and even large enough to fit the tent and all of his other supplies.

"You may go now," he said once we'd escaped the increasing drizzle and entered the cave. "Might as well get back to the parking area before you wind up drenched." He turned his back to me and busied himself unrolling his sleeping bag and setting up his battery-operated lantern.

I scowled, though he couldn't see me. "I'm not leaving."

Hawk didn't turn, but I saw his back stiffen. "Don't stay on my account. I'd hate for you to be in a situation where you don't feel perfectly *safe* and *comfortable*." He plumped his pillow before setting it inside the tent and said mockingly, "Save yourself, Jack."

My shoulders fell on a frustrated exhale. "Fine. Point taken. For the record, I still think it's bullshit to stage a protest by camping in the woods like you're some kind of modern-day Thoreau. And I'm talking 'Mr. Bennet-allowing-Lydia-to-trot-off-to-Brighton-with-the-soldiers'-level   bullshit.   You know just how much I hate that part, right? But I'm not leaving you to be stupid alone."

Hawk turned to face me, and for just a split second, his face softened, recognizing the echo of our recent fight. Then he turned back to the tent.

I reached for his backpack to pull out his camp stove and other cooking supplies. Getting a hot drink into both of us would help us stay warm since we couldn't build a fire inside the cave.

"You know," Hawk said without turning around, "no one said Henry David Thoreau was stupid when he went out to the woods."

I glanced up from pouring one of the water bottles I'd brought into his small kettle. "He went to the woods to live *deliberately.* Not to stop Evola from bringing necessary funding to his small Vermont town. And pretty sure Thoreau lived in a cabin, not a tent or a cold-as-fuck cave."

He settled himself on the sleeping bag just inside the tent and dug out a bag of trail mix. "He lived like twenty minutes' walk from his parents' house, but you don't hear stories about people trying to drag *him* home every time it rained."

"Twenty minutes? Hm. That's… less impressive than the Walden experience I'd imagined," I admitted. I chanced another glance in his direction. "You look good."

He paused with a handful of snack mix in his hand.

My face went hot. "I mean, you look *better.* Calmer. Than the last time I saw you. More confident, maybe."

He tossed the trail mix in his mouth and crunched thoughtfully, staring into the middle distance. "I think… there are things that have been bothering me for a while," he said slowly. "And I've been waiting for other people to wake up and notice them and come up with a plan for us to fix them, then getting progressively angrier when no one did. Crys called me on it the other night. She reminded me that if I want things to change, *I* need to change them myself. Or at least try."

I hated that working with me, talking to me, was something he needed to change, but… "I'm glad it's working."

Hawk nodded and smiled suddenly. "Can't lie, though. I'm dying for a shower and a good meal. Splashing in the creek and eating rehydrated stew is getting a little old."

"Well, I don't know if it counts as a good meal, but I brought some sandwiches from the diner if you're hungry."

Hawk looked at me intently, like he was trying to peer into my skull and read my mind. Good luck to him trying to find any clear thoughts in there. I'd been running on instinct and desperation all day.

"You came up here to drag me back to town… but also brought sandwiches? Why?"

"Seven years," I croaked.

"Huh?"

"That's how long we've been friends, right? And when we hike, I bring snacks. That's my job. That's… what I do. You decide where we're going, I make sure we get there safely. I'm kind of a creature of habit if you hadn't noticed."

He swallowed. "I noticed," he said softly.

The air felt heavy. Charged. I tried to play it off. "Besides, it's not a big deal. I didn't go to any trouble," I lied. "Just some Havarti-and-apple paninis that were left over from lunch. I can heat them up if you're hungry. They're in there." I nodded to my backpack.

Hawk reached for it at the same time I remembered—

"Wait just a second," I said, holding out a hand, but it was too late. Hawk tilted the bag, and out tumbled not only the foil-wrapped sandwiches but also two thick paperbacks.

He looked down at them, bewildered. "You brought me *What Jane Austen Ate and Charles Dickens Knew*? And *Mr. Darcy's Perfect Match*? Did you get these at the library?"

"Not exactly." I shrugged and poured cocoa into two

mugs, making sure his was equal parts cocoa and mini marshmallows.

"You *didn't* get them at the library? So, what, you just had these kicking around your house?" He laughed.

I ignored his question and handed him a mug of cocoa. "You've probably read them before. I just… I wasn't sure how long you were planning to stay up here, and I didn't know if you could charge your Kindle. I wanted to make sure you had what you needed in case you decided to be stubborn."

"Thank you," he said almost shyly. "This means a lot."

You mean a lot, I wanted to say, but I held myself back.

Instead, I nodded and busied myself with reheating the sandwiches on the camp stove because I didn't trust myself to look at him. Not when he was so damn sexy. Not when he was so damn close. Not when the rain had begun falling in earnest outside, creating the feeling that he and I were in a world of our own. Not when I'd missed him so damn much.

As I fussed with the sandwiches, he told me about his Save Fogg Peak Instagram, and I pretended I hadn't looked it up and greedily scrolled through the dozens of pictures he'd already posted.

Then I told him that the diner had been slammed since Evola's new surveying crew had landed in town two days ago, filling the Apple of My Eye Inn to capacity.

"Yeah, some of their crew has been hanging around up here, too," Hawk said. "One of 'em gave me some trouble the other day. Nothing physical," he added quickly when he saw my outraged expression. "Just telling me I didn't have a right to be here or to post signs at Glassy Ridge, like he wasn't aware that Evola didn't actually own the land and the project hadn't been approved yet. Means my protest is pretty timely."

"That's not okay. We should call someone—"

"No need. I mentioned it to Simon, and he took care of the

situation and apologized to me on behalf of the company. He's been really great about everything."

"Oh?" Once again, my *chalant*-ness left a lot to be desired. "Has… *Simon*… been up here much?"

"A couple times. He's been monitoring the surveying and touring around with some Evola bigwigs, and he's stopped by to chat. I assumed he was a tool of the enemy at first, but… he's fun to talk to and informed on the issues I care about. Wish he was a little more forthcoming with some of the reports he promised me on the environmental impact studies Evola is doing, but…" He shrugged. "He asked me to have dinner with him sometime, and I agreed."

"Oh? Have dinner so you can… talk more about the development?" I kept my gaze on the sandwiches like they might contain the secrets of the universe. "Good. Glad Simon's being helpful in a… professional capacity."

Hawk snorted like he knew exactly what jealous thoughts were running through my head, and Hawk being Hawk, he probably did.

I passed him a sandwich. "Eat," I said, rolling my eyes at myself.

Hawk didn't say anything else about Simon. As we ate, he turned the conversation to Instagram and Austen and hiking with the Scouts, I found myself forgetting about my irrational jealousy and worries for his safety and drawing a deep breath for the first time in days.

This, right here, was what I'd been craving. Seeing Hawk smile. Hearing him download all the thoughts in his brain. Knowing that he and I were so close, nothing—and no one—could ever come between us.

It was perfect.

Or at least it was until I fucked it all up again.

When I finished eating, I looked around to take stock of our supplies. My gaze landed on the stack of things he'd brought to the cave before my arrival, which were laid out on a tarp on one side of the cave. There was a large backpack mostly filled with snacks and a few dehydrated meals, a bunch of protest signs, a small cooler bag, and...

"Hawk," I said, interrupting his recitation.

"Uh..." He blinked. "Yes?"

Chill out, Jack.

Do not make this A Thing.

Do not start flinging around wild accusations.

"Why the *hell* do you have a second sleeping bag in here?"

CHAPTER TEN

HAWK

"A lady's imagination is very rapid; it jumps from admiration to love, from love to matrimony in a moment."
~ Fitzwilliam Darcy

JACK'S VOICE echoed off the walls, so loud I jumped and nearly bobbled my mug of cocoa. "What?"

"Two sleeping bags, Hawk. One." He pointed a finger at the bag I was sitting on. "And *two*." He pointed at Crys's sleeping bag, which I'd left with my other spare supplies.

"I... I... *What?*" I asked again. His words still weren't making sense.

"Is it...? Are you expecting Si—*someone* tonight?" Jack demanded, pushing to his feet. "Crys said... But I didn't think... Do you want me to leave?"

I gaped at him. We'd been getting along so well. He'd made me cocoa with so many marshmallows I was pretty sure my nose was sticky. He'd packed *books* in his backpack alongside his emergency flashlight and first aid kit because he knew that, to me, they were just as essential. He'd brought me my very favorite sandwiches—which were absolutely *not* left-overs from lunch, thank you very much, since these weren't on the summer menu, but I'd been too besotted by his thoughtfulness to call him out on his lie.

And now… this.

I crossed my arms. "My plans are none of your concern."

Jack stalked closer. His eyes narrowed with an intensity I rarely saw but which always managed to mangle my insides and weaken my knees. "Whose. Sleeping bag. Is. It?"

My heart galloped wildly. "Worried that I've organized tent orgies on Fogg Peak?" I goaded. "Wondering if I arranged some kind of thunderstorm sex fest here in Kirkcaster Cave? So what if I did? None. Of. Your. Business." Two could play at the stilted-speaking thing.

Jack's mouth opened in shock before closing with a determined clack. "Changed my mind. I'm not leaving. Whoever you have coming here will just have to deal."

"Suit yourself," I said.

I snatched up both our mugs and took them to the mouth of the cave to wash them out. Darkness filled the forest around us as the rain pounded the ground, but I didn't hear any thunder yet.

For three days, I'd thought of nothing but Jack. So many times, whether I was setting up signage on Glassy Ridge, or laughing over how many followers I'd gotten overnight when one of my posts went viral, or stargazing at night, I'd turned my head to say something to him, expecting him to be right there, as usual, ready to offer advice, or make a snarky joke, or simply share my joy.

I'd missed him so much I ached.

But this new tension between us? The protective walls we'd both thrown up and were now defending by launching angry barbs at each other's tender spots?

Yeah, no, I hadn't missed that.

I wanted to scream at him, to confront him with his odd inconsistencies. How could he care enough about me to make my favorite sandwiches, be attracted enough to me to get hard when we almost kissed, climb up a fucking mountain just to tempt me with his nearness, and act all jealous and overbearingly cockblocky, when he'd made it abundantly clear that *he* would not be having sex with me under any circumstances?

The sound of the falling water was hypnotic, and I wondered at the irony of being trapped here in a cave during a heavy rainstorm with the person I cared about most but who didn't want me the same way. Or… who wanted me but wouldn't allow himself to have me.

I'd changed my mind about forced proximity being hot. This shit was *awful.*

Even now, annoyed as I was, I could sense his presence in the cave behind me, feel his hot gaze tracking my every movement, practically hear his heart beat. My dick was half-hard just from his nearness. Being stranded in this small space with him all night was going to be torture. If he wouldn't be with me the way I wanted, I almost wished he'd leave so I could jerk off in the privacy of my own tent.

Why can't I?

When I walked back to set the mugs down near the rest of the cooking gear, I glanced over and found him watching me steadily.

"You can use my *extra* sleeping bag," I told him. "But you're sleeping out here. The tent is mine."

He blew out a breath. "Bird," he began. "I'm being ridiculous. I'm sorry—"

The affectionate nickname did things to my belly, but I hardened my heart.

"You should be. You're being an ass."

"I'm not… that is…" He sighed. "We've shared a tent a dozen times—"

"Yes we have." Nerves made my hands shake, but I played it cool. "But my plans tonight require privacy."

"Seriously?" Jack stared at me. "What plans? Reading? It

would be way warmer with both of us together. Remember that time at Joney Creek?"

"It's summertime. You'll be fine. And you can have my blanket, too." I avoided his eyes.

"But…"

"I want to have an orgasm, Jack," I said baldly. I took a breath and lifted my gaze to his. "A good one. I need it. Out here on my own, I've discovered it's the easiest way to fall asleep on the hard ground. Otherwise, I toss and turn. So. Sure. If you're okay being next to me while I do that, come on in. Join me."

Our eyes locked together for a heavy beat. Heat crackled between us, making a mockery of my comment about him needing an extra blanket.

Jack's eyes widened comically, and it seemed like his pupils followed suit. "Oh."

"Yeah. *Oh.*" I crawled through the tent opening and removed my boots, setting them outside. I removed my tube of lube from my backpack like lubing up in front of Jack Wyatt was the sort of thing I did all the time. Then I carefully zipped the tent closed. "Night, Jack. Sleep well."

The shifting sound of the nylon sleeping bag against the floor of the tent sounded louder than normal. I pulled off my clothes until I wore only my socks, boxer briefs, and T-shirt before scooting down into the chilly softness of my sleeping bag and praying it would heat up quickly.

My dick was suddenly softer than ever, impacted dramatically by stage fright. I hadn't been lying about discovering the positive effects of masturbation on my ability to sleep out here, but could I really do it with him listening in?

I shivered inside the bag and tried to get comfortable.

After a few minutes, Jack's voice came through the thin tent walls. "Are you… do you need anything?"

I huffed out a little laugh. Yes. I needed his hot, wet mouth on my cock. But that wasn't what he'd meant. "No. All good. Thanks, though."

He made a deep hum of acknowledgment, and the vibrations of the familiar masculine sound went straight to my balls. *What do you know?* He was already helping.

I'd left Jack the battery-operated lantern so he'd have light to lay out a tarp and unroll the spare sleeping bag. But that meant that I could make out his shadow through the fabric that separated us.

The man hadn't moved a single muscle. Almost like he was waiting for something.

Waiting for *me*.

I reached my hand down into my underwear and cupped myself before stroking slowly up my shaft. A sigh escaped me as I relaxed into the warming cocoon of the sleeping bag. The silky feel of the nylon slid across my bare arms and legs. Jack's breathing was rough, almost loud enough to make out over the rhythmic sound of the rain outside the cave's entrance.

"Fuck," I breathed softly as stage fright gave way and my cock hardened beneath my fingers. This wasn't just anyone listening—this was *Jack*. And knowing he was right there, hearing me touch myself, focused on me, wondering exactly what I was doing, was more exciting than I could have imagined.

There was a sudden flurry of movement and then the rustle of a sleeping bag much closer than I'd expected, as if he'd chosen to settle down right outside the tent's zipper door rather than on the other side of the open cave. The lantern shut off… and then there was only darkness.

More rustling sounded, practically next to my ear, followed by a soft curse and then the faint *plop* of fabric hitting fabric.

Jack was pulling off his own clothes.

Jack was *getting naked*.

Just inches away from me.

My dick hardened even more.

"*Unghh.*" I couldn't hold back the moan that escaped when I realized my tip was sticky wet. I used the slick to ease my strokes before remembering the lube I'd brought with me. The click of the bottle cap sounded like a shot in the near silence of the cave, and the first spurt of the lube wasn't much quieter.

Jack sucked in a breath. "What are you doing?"

"I told you what I'm doing." My voice sounded rough to my own ears, needy and unsteady. I wanted the release badly, but I also wanted to tease myself into waiting for it. I shoved down my boxers and took a deep breath.

"Now? Here?" His voice was high-pitched, incredulous.

I didn't answer. Instead, I used the deep sound of his voice to add to my fantasy that it was Jack's own furtive hand exploring me in the darkness of the tent while the storm raged outside.

"So good," I whispered, arching up into my grip. The lube made a squelching noise that was nearly obscene.

I didn't care if he could hear me—I welcomed it. He was attracted to me, and we both knew it. He could have been in here with me. Instead, he'd chosen to use ridiculous, arbitrary rules to keep us apart.

So be it. But I wasn't going to make it easy for him.

"Fuck," I groaned, kicking away the top layer of my sleeping bag until the chilly air washed over my hot skin. I moved a slick finger down my taint to my hole and toyed with my rim. Even though I was technically a virgin, I wasn't inexperienced. I loved playing with myself, which was partly why I was so desperate these days to experience the real thing.

I squirted out more lube, getting myself good and wet before stretching myself open. The sound of my lubed finger moving in and out of my tight hole was obvious to anyone paying attention…

And Jack was definitely paying attention.

"Bird," he croaked softly. "Are you… is that… *nngh.*"

His sleeping bag rustled again, and he let out a loud exhale before the telltale sound of his own fist shuttling over his cock made its way through the tent wall between us.

"Are you touching yourself, Jack?"

"Oh *god.*"

I bit my lip. "What does it feel like?" I whispered. "Is it as good as my mouth would be?"

My face ignited at my brazen question. Who the hell was I right now? Since when did I make graphic suggestions to anyone, much less the man who'd already expressed his unwillingness to go there with me?

But he's masturbating to the sound of you. And it's hot as hell.

"I've thought of your cock so many times," I confessed on a moan. "What it would look like. What it would taste like—"

Jack's breaths were coming in little pants now, like he was trying to be quiet but couldn't.

"—what it would *feel* like inside me."

"Hawk," Jack whispered. I wasn't sure he intended for me to hear him—in fact, I was almost certain he hadn't—and that only made it hotter.

"Gonna come," I ground out, feeling the tingles down my thighs and in my groin. "I can't hold back. Fuck, *fuck.*"

The sound of Jack's movements sped up as my brain filled with static. I shoved my t-shirt up to my neck and shouted out his name as my release washed over me, hitting hot and wet across my belly and chest and sending my nerves flying.

As I lay there coming down from the euphoria and feeling the night air settle across my exposed skin, I heard Jack's heavy breathing.

Had he…?

I opened my mouth to ask him, but then I closed it with a

snap. If he wanted to acknowledge what had just happened between us, that was up to him.

After a few more moments, I heard him moving around. I took the opportunity to clean myself up with a bandana from my backpack and snuggle back into my sleeping bag.

Jack didn't say a single word. Neither did I.

I lay awake for a long time, staring at the ceiling of the tent, feeling my anger rise yet again.

So this was where we drew the line, huh? A mutual masturbation session was fine, but actually seeing or touching each other was not? Was *this* the boundary that was supposed to protect our friendship? Because I was not feeling protected.

In fact, the more I thought about how fucking close he'd been, how it would have been the work of *seconds* for him to unzip that tent door and experience that orgasm *with* me, the more hurt and rejected I felt.

Jack Wyatt needed to leave… and he needed to stay gone.

CHAPTER ELEVEN

JACK

*"I cannot fix on the hour, or the spot, or the look, or the words,
which laid the foundation. It is too long ago. I was in the middle
before I knew that I had begun."*
~ Fitzwilliam Darcy

I couldn't say for sure the moment I fell for Hawk Sunday.

It might have been the first time he hummed along while I sang in the kitchen long after the diner had closed or one of the times I saw his head thrown back in the sunshine, cheeks rosy from a hike, burning with life like a candle flame.

It might have happened in the middle of an afternoon he'd spent sprawled on the rug in my mom's living room, holding a very serious conversation with her about worsted-weight yarn while Peony chewed the hem of his pants and he pretended not to notice, or the time I'd teased him about reading too much Jane Austen and he'd retaliated in true smart-ass, book-nerd fashion by answering me *only* in *Pride and Prejudice* quotes for an entire day.

Or... maybe it had grown so gradually that there was no way to say exactly when it happened, like slipping from wakefulness into a really beautiful dream.

I could tell you the moment I *realized* I'd fallen, though.

It was the first time I heard my name on Hawk Sunday's lips as he came. While he was still gasping through his orgasm, the thought popped into my head: *I am utterly and completely his. That's it. Forever. So what the fuck am I doing?*

That moment of enlightenment—me, covered in spunk and shaking from the most intense orgasm of my life, him breathing heavily in his tent just inches away—did not feel at all like the sweet, sappy, blossoming-flower transformation I'd always imagined love was for the few people lucky enough to find it. This was more like an earthquake—sudden and terrifying and inescapable, tearing down all the pretty walls I'd built to protect myself in one fell swoop.

And in the aftermath, as I lay awake, staring at the darkness and listening to the relentless rain, picking my way through the rubble in my brain felt a bit like an archaeological expedition—probably a lot like the ones where historians took a second look at some pottery shards depicting Achilles and Patroclus, and said, "I can't believe anyone thought they were *just friends.*"

Once I let myself look, my true feelings for Hawk were as obvious as gravity. They showed in the way I never wanted to be apart from him. The way I wanted to hear every single thing he had to say. They were there in the way his smile brightened my day and the way the idea of him being with anyone else—whether it was Simon or some random app hookup—made me lose all capacity for logic. It was even there in the way I hadn't dated anyone, even my usual fun-and-sex dating, in *months* and claimed it was because the men I hooked up with didn't "fit" in my life.

Of course they didn't. I already had Hawk.

I'd avoided relationships my whole life after watching my mom's heart break when we lost my dad, and every friend who'd ever been through a shit breakup or a devastating divorce had just cemented the fact in my mind: relationships were complicated, and got fucked up, and ended in disaster and heartbreak, always.

But somehow… I'd found myself smack in the middle of one anyway. And with every scared, hurtful word that fell out of my mouth, *I* was the one making it complicated. *I* was the one fucking it up. *I* was the one breaking my own heart… and Hawk's… in some misguided attempt to protect us.

Hadn't I told Hawk just the other day, during our last disastrous discussion about the Aerie Resort, that he couldn't keep things the way they were indefinitely because he was scared something bad could happen?

Maybe it was time I took my own damn advice.

After I cleaned myself off, I waited for Hawk to say something, but he remained silent as his breathing evened out.

I couldn't blame him. He'd put himself out there *twice*, and I'd shot him down. No wonder he didn't have anything to say to me. No wonder he wanted his privacy.

By the time I got up the nerve to flip on the lantern and open the tent to talk to him, he was snoring lightly with only his messy curls poking out of the top of his sleeping bag.

I sat there for a few minutes, looking at Hawk's face relaxed in sleep. He was so sexy, so beautiful, so mind-blowingly *mine* my breath froze in my lungs from the shock of it.

"I want you," I breathed, feeling my chest loosen just from admitting the words out loud, even though he wasn't awake to hear them. "More than anything."

How could I have him without disappointing him? I wasn't Fitzwilliam Darcy with ten thousand pounds a year and a giant fancy estate. I was a multi-thousandaire on a good month, struggling to save for retirement while making payroll.

I was no broody Prince Charming, capable of sitting around all day making dreamy eyes at Hawk from across a crowded room. I was a chronic workaholic and serial overthinker.

And I wasn't some noble guy with a brain full of heartfelt, sentimental words and grand gestures. I was... apple grilled cheese, snarky comments, and sweaty hikes.

I didn't know if that—*me*—was enough.

I leaned over and pressed a kiss to his curls.

"Love you," I breathed into the woodsy scent of him. "So much."

Without giving myself a chance to overthink it for once, I hauled my sleeping bag into the tent, zipped the door closed, and turned off the lantern before moving close to Hawk. We'd spent many nights sharing each other's warmth like this in his tent, and I wasn't about to stop now.

Especially when I had important things to say to him first thing in the morning.

I woke to the sound of a muffled gasp and felt my lips turn up instinctively when I remembered who I was sleeping next to... and why. My stomach was full of knots, but my heart was full of hope.

"Hey," I said, rolling over. Hawk's brown eyes were huge in the dim light coming through the cave opening and kept winging from me to the tent door and back, like he was trying to figure out how he felt about seeing me lying next to him. "Can we... talk?"

Hawk's eyes widened even more, wary now. "Talk?" he repeated, voice rough with sleep.

I reached out to push a rogue curl off his forehead with the tip of my finger. His skin was sleep-warm and soft. So touchable I wasn't sure how I'd gone this long without putting my hands on him. I let my finger trail down the side of his face, tracing the arch of his eyebrow and the curve of his cheekbone.

Hawk's whole body froze, and he squeezed his eyes shut. "Damn it all," he said mournfully.

I traced the curve of his jaw over the roughness of his beard. "What's wrong?"

He sighed and squeezed his eyes shut. "Another fucking dream," he muttered to himself. "I should have known. But this one feels so lifelike." He opened his eyes and shot me a glare. "FYI, the *real* you has a lot to answer for, Jack Wyatt. I'm losing my mind, and it's your fault."

The idea that he'd been dreaming of me the way I'd been dreaming of him warmed me. I tapped his nose ring gently. "This isn't a dream, Bird."

He swallowed. "That's exactly what you say in the dreams. And then I wake up, and *poof.*"

My heart twisted a little with the pleasure-pain of his admission. "I'm so sorry," I whispered.

He looked momentarily confused, like even in his dreams, he couldn't imagine me saying that.

"For… barging into my tent uninvited?"

"No." I moved a little closer to him and ran my fingers through his hair. "Maybe I should be, but I'm not even a little bit sorry for that. I'm sorry because I said no when you made me an incredible offer of yourself. And I'd like…" The air around us seemed more difficult to gather into my lungs properly. "I'd very much like to change my answer."

Time slowed down, and he stared at me, uncomprehending. "But you said… You *insisted*…"

"I know," I agreed. I tried to reassure him with my own expression that I meant what I was saying, but I could tell he doubted me. Hell, I still had plenty of my own doubts. But he needed to know before another day went by… "I want you," I breathed. "Very much."

"You? Want to have sex?" he blurted, finally understanding what I was saying. "With me?"

"Yes, you, Bird. Always you. *Only* you." I let out the

breath that had been sluggishly filling my lungs. "I don't just want to have sex with you. I… I care about you. I'd like… I'd like more than sex with you."

Hawk pushed himself to a sitting position and flung the sleeping bag open. His warm skin pebbled in the cooler air. "If this *is* a dream, I'm going to be so mad at you when I wake up."

I propped myself on my elbow and reached for the front of his shirt, fisting the cotton in my hand and pulling him toward me. When our lips met, I let out a cross between a whimper and a groan. He was so soft, so pliant against my mouth. The warm, sleepy smell of him surrounded me, and his beard growth scratched at my chin.

He tumbled on top of me with a surprised gasp, and I used it to my advantage, pulling him even tighter with an arm around him while holding his face with my other as we fell back together.

We kissed like neither of us had ever done it before, frantically… hungrily… *awkwardly*.

It was the hottest kiss I'd ever experienced. Hawk made noises that went straight to my dick. He wiggled on top of me, and if we hadn't been separated by my damned sleeping bag, I might have even enjoyed the press of his own cock against my leg.

We made out like preteens, kissing and kissing like it was the only move we knew. I couldn't get enough of his taste, his sweetness, his desire. He made me feel wanted and alive. Sexy and free.

When I moved my hands up under the back of his shirt, I felt the goose bumps still on his skin. "Baby, you're freezing. Get back in your sleeping bag."

He shook his head. "Can't have sex in my sleeping bag."

I leaned up to kiss him again through a wide smile. "We're not having sex in the cave, period. Not your first time. I'm drawing the line, Hawk."

"Oh my god," he whispered, staring down at me. "This really isn't a dream. In my dreams, you'd totally have gone for it."

The sleepy wonder in his expression was so adorable I laughed out loud. I felt lighter than I had in weeks.

He took a breath and sat back up, pulling his sleeping bag over to cover himself. "But Jack, how... what... why *now*?"

I sat up, too, so I could face him while I tried to get my thoughts together and explain. "All the things I said before— my concerns about Webb and your brothers and our ages— they're true and real, but they're not what was holding me back. I meant it when I said I'm not a relationship guy, Hawk. I never thought I'd want to be. I have no clue how to be what you need. I was—*am*—genuinely terrified that admitting I want you means we're going to fuck up our friendship, and I... I can't lose you."

"Jack," he said softly. "You won't. You can't—"

"No, listen. You said before that I put you on a pedestal you didn't want to be on. Remember? Well, sometimes I worry that you put me on one, too. I'm not romance hero material. I'm protective. And bossy. And not great at communicating a lot of the time. And I knew—*know*—that if we do the romance thing... I'm going to disappoint you. There's no way around it."

He tilted his head, studying me. "Okayyyy..."

"But then you left for three days. Three *tiny* days, Hawk. And I missed you so freaking much. I couldn't enjoy anything. I couldn't concentrate for shit—you should see what I did to the supply order yesterday, Jesus Christ. I couldn't stop feeling like every good part of me had quit when you did. So I came up here to get you back." I chewed on my lip. "The whole way up here, I... I pretty much *knew* how this was going to go. I knew if I saw you, spoke to you, I wasn't going to be able to hold back. But even then, I fought it. I saw your spare sleeping bag, and I…" I broke off with a head shake.

"Turned into a hurtful, cockblocky asshole?"

"I didn't turn into it," I muttered. "I've *been* that. Jealous as fuck, even as I pushed you away. And then…"

"Yeah?" Hawk encouraged.

"And then you climbed into the tent. And I was stuck out there *listening*. And I realized… that's what the rest of my life would be like if I didn't pull my head out of my ass. Me, on the outside, looking in. Barriers between us forever. *Missing you* forever. And I realized I have to at least *try* to be the man you need me to be—"

Hawk reached out and grabbed my hand, bringing it up to his mouth to kiss the back of it before setting both of our hands down in his lap. "You already are, Jack. You always have been. You could never disappoint me."

I pulled my hand away and forked it through my own hair. "See? That's what I mean, though. Of course I can, Hawk! And I will. I'm bound to let you down. To disappoint you in a major way. I'm not the guy you think I am—"

"And I think I see you more clearly than you see yourself," Hawk retorted. "Give me one example of how you'll let me down."

"Well, I…" My brain's gears clicked around heavily while I determined whether or not to reveal all the reasons why he shouldn't want me. I was like a used car salesman who couldn't help but admit the thing was a lemon. "I don't know, do I? If I knew how I'd let you down, I'd stop it." I exhaled sharply. "But for one thing, I'm a workaholic."

"You're committed to your business—a business where I work." He winced. "*Worked*, anyway. You being a conscientious employer doesn't bother me; it never has."

I huffed. "Okay, then, what about this… I still think the development should go forward *in some capacity*."

He winced. "That's… a tough one," he admitted. "But I

think I just need to know you're listening to me without dismissing me. We are always going to disagree on things. I do *not* think you're perfect or that you're always right. Spoiler, Jack Wyatt: that ship set sail about seven years ago when you told me you weren't into reading romance."

I laughed out loud. "I'm surprised you gave me any kind of chance at all after that."

Hawk bit my knuckle lightly before smoothing over it with his tongue. "Even the things about you that might be frustrating or disappointing *usually* have a good reason behind them..." He gave me a teasing look. "With the glaring exception of your unilateral decision that we, as legal, consenting, unattached adults who wanted one another, couldn't have sex. And honestly, that was part of why I was so damn frustrated about that. Your reasons didn't make any sense, and you wouldn't explain them. But you know what else?"

I shook my head, trying to ignore what his mouth was doing to my skin so I could focus on his words.

"I'm not a child, and I'm not a shrinking violet—not with you, anyway. If I think you're being a jerk, I'm gonna tell you so. If I think you're wrong, I'm going to do what I think is right. Last night, after... well, *every-thing*... I decided that I couldn't take this back-and-forth between us anymore. I was going to tell you this morning that I wanted you to leave. That I needed to put serious distance between us. And I would have done it, too," he said softly. "Even though I knew it was gonna hurt."

"Fuck," I breathed, realizing how close I'd come to losing my chance entirely.

"But then, there you were, apologizing and admitting you were wrong." He squeezed my fingers tightly. "Because you're a *good man*, Jack."

My heart looked for a way to escape his kindness. It

couldn't take these feelings. "I'm not, though. Not completely. I—"

"If I was injured, would you drop everything to come help me?" Hawk demanded.

"What? Of course I would," I snapped, not even wanting to think about such a thing. "And can we not talk about you getting hurt, please?"

He grinned. "Uh-huh. And what about if the people of Little Pippin Hollow experienced a natural disaster and yours was the only kitchen left operable in town? Would you increase prices to take advantage of the opportunity?"

My lips tightened. "You know I wouldn't, Bird. I'd feed everyone for free, even if it tanked my business. But I'm not talking about big stuff like that. I'm talking about little everyday disappointments. What if I forget to bring you flowers on Valentine's Day?"

He straightened up on his knees and shuffled forward. His grin was giving me dirty thoughts about his mouth. "I'd buy enough for both of us." He cupped my face and met my eyes. "I don't need flowers. I need *you*."

I tried not to stare at his lips. "I never do the dishes at home," I added pathetically. "For days at a time."

"I know." He leaned in and kissed me whisper-softly on the side of my face. "You're a monster."

"I leave wet towels on the floor of my bathroom."

"Mmhmm," he murmured, kissing my chin just as softly. "I'll have to institute a spanking regimen for naughty boys."

My dick roared to life. "What if I'm terrible in bed?" I breathed against his searching lips.

He let out a gasp of warm air against my mouth and pulled away. "Whoa, wait! You mean Smug Peter lied, and all this time I believed it? Dear god. You're right, Jack. This will never work. I'm sorry—"

I tickled his ribs, right in the spot I knew would make him

scream with laughter, and he squirmed as he grabbed my hand in both of his.

"Kidding! I'm kidding. If you're terrible in bed or your advanced age means your stamina is lacking—"

"Hawkins," I growled.

He giggled and kissed the edge of my mouth. "Then we'll have to watch tutorial videos online together. Lots of them. I'm willing to let you experiment on me until you can perfect your technique."

Our lips came together gently this time, less awkward and hungry but still just as intense. I pulled him into my lap and wrapped my arms around him, pulling his sleeping bag over his back to keep him warm.

"You drove me crazy last night," I finally admitted in the small space between us.

"Really?" Hawk's face burned red. "I kinda can't believe I actually went through with it."

"I couldn't stop thinking about you in here touching yourself. The sounds you made, Bird… *Jesus.*"

He held on to my shoulders. "I was so mad at you for not joining me when it was clear you decided to do the same."

I shook my head and held him tighter. "I didn't want it to happen like that. Because it wouldn't just be fucking. Not for me. Not with you."

"Because you want *more than sex* with me," he said slowly, repeating my earlier words. "Because you decided to try having a relationship?"

I let out a half laugh. "I don't know that it was a decision, exactly. Relationships are complicated. I've never been in one that went beyond sex, but I've seen enough to know they're not all sunshine and rainbows, even when they last. But last night, I realized… we kind of already *are* in one." I counted out the evidence on my fingers. "You're the most important person in my life, aside from my mom. I want you with me constantly, whether I'm at home or at work or hiking a damn mountain. And ever since you mentioned sex the first time, I'm like a horny teenager again because you..." I cupped his face and dragged my thumb over his kiss-swollen mouth. "You're the sexiest thing I've ever seen."

Hawk's blush, which had barely subsided since our conversation began, came back with intensity. "And you never noticed that—*me*—before?"

"I noticed," I admitted. "More often than I'd like to admit. But it's one thing to acknowledge that you're objectively gorgeous and sexy. It's a whole other thing to think of you being sexy *with me*. I tried not to let myself think that way until you put your offer on the table, and then... I dunno. It's kinda like one of those hidden-image pictures, where it's all dots and squiggles until you step back and shift your focus, and suddenly, you don't know how you could have missed it." I dragged my thumb over his mouth again, tugging at his bottom lip. His eyes went unfocused, and my gut cramped with need so hard I forced myself to pull away from him.

I was not fucking this man in a cave, damn it.

Not today, anyway.

"Too bad I didn't figure this out sooner. Would have saved us weeks of turmoil." I shook my head. "But now I need to know... What do *you* want, Hawk? You offered me friendship and sex, and I don't want to presume too much. I know you've got a lot of stuff going on right now." I waved a hand to encompass the tent, the mountain, his protest. "I know you're processing a lot of emotion. A lot of anger. If this isn't the right time for you to be thinking about more... okay." I shrugged. "Basically, I'm done telling you how you should feel about this. Tell me what you want from me."

Hawk hesitated. He put his hand on my chest, stroking me through my T-shirt like he needed the contact. "I want a relationship with you. *Definitely*. I just... I wish you weren't so hesitant about it, I guess. Does this make you happy?"

"Baby, there's no part of me that's *not* happy. Being with

you like this? Having all the things that I adore about you and getting to kiss you, too? Christ, I'm fucking ecstatic. It's just… I guess I'm processing through some stuff, too."

"Like…?"

I blew out a breath. Was I really going to talk about this shit? I darted a glance at Hawk, who looked hopeful but wary, and realized that for him, there wasn't much I wouldn't do.

"You know, ah… you know my dad died when I was a kid, obviously."

He frowned. "Yeah. Of course. We've talked about that."

"We've talked about some of it," I corrected. "About what it was like growing up without a father."

He nodded.

"But there are some parts of that I haven't really talked about much. Not that it's a secret, just… I don't like to dwell on it, you know? To really sit with those memories."

"Okay," he agreed cautiously. "I can see that."

I cleared my throat. "Like… I don't know if I ever told you that my parents were high school sweethearts? Mom played clarinet in the marching band, and Dad played—"

"Tuba," Hawk supplied softly. "It was fate."

I laughed. "Kinda, I guess. Mom got pregnant with me senior year, and my grandparents were *not* okay with that. My parents ended up getting married immediately and… instant family. No college, no youthful adventures. But my mom says neither of them regretted it." I shrugged. "My dad didn't have much family of his own—only his mom—and my mom's family kinda disowned her after the surprise wedding, so they were both excited to have a little family of their own. To build something better, you know?"

Hawk nodded. "That sounds like your mom. Positive attitude, always looking for the silver linings."

"Mostly, yeah. So after I came along, my dad did every job imaginable. He delivered newspapers before the sun rose—

sometimes he'd even take me along. He worked at a chemical plant during the day. My mom did data entry at night. They didn't have time to build much of a social network, but that was okay because we were tight. A unit. They relied on each other, and I relied on both of them, and it worked. We never had a lot, but we were happy." I paused. "And then he got sick."

Hawk made a wounded noise because he knew how this part of the story ended, but he didn't interrupt or offer me empty platitudes. He just clung to my hand like he wanted me to know I wasn't alone, and I felt an overwhelming rush of affection for him.

"It was pretty typical movie-of-the-week stuff, looking back," I said with an eye roll. "And a lot of it I didn't really understand until I was older. Our health insurance was the cheap kind that young, healthy people get because they don't realize they need better coverage until it's too late. There was no life insurance either—who had money to pay premiums when someone always needed new shoes? We never had a lot, but things got worse pretty quickly."

"Fuck," Hawk breathed.

"Yeah. It was a scary time. When I was young, my mom tried to shield me from the financial stuff as much as she could, but the worst part for me was... was seeing what happened to *her*. She was tired and strained all the time. Like the life had just been sucked out of her. And as an adult, I look back and think... *shit*. She lost her best friend, her lover, her partner, her anchor, her safety net... all in one fell swoop. Her happiness had been tied with his." I pressed the finger-tips of both hands together like the pointy roof of a house. "And when he was gone..." I removed one of my hands, and the other toppled. Hawk flinched, and I searched his gaze intently. "It's scary to imagine building something with someone when I know how easily I could lose it."

"I had no idea," Hawk whispered.

"How could you?" I shrugged. "It turned out okay. My mom is a *fighter*—you know that. She got public assistance for a while to keep some food on the table. They helped her find a full-time job at a place that paid for her to get her degree at night. I started working, too, when I was old enough. We paid off dad's medical bills and saved as much as we could. We only really got our feet under us financially maybe ten years ago now—"

"Ten years? So you spent most of your childhood…? God, Jack. No wonder you're a workaholic." Hawk propped his chin on the back of his hands, which were resting on my chest. "You've experienced true scarcity."

I shrugged again. "I never want my mom or me to get back in that place."

He pushed himself up until the sleeping bag fell off him. "That's why you're not fighting the development."

"Yeah." I rubbed a hand over my face. "It'd be nice to believe that no one in the Hollow has to do without, but that's not real life. The town could really use a steady influx of tourist cash—ideally in a way that doesn't destroy the beauty of the place the tourists are coming to see. I'm all for coming up with an alternate plan, for making sure there's plenty of oversight, all of that. But I don't wanna lose our chance either. And I sure as fuck am not gonna be the guy coming up with a brilliant idea that marries both needs—"

"Especially since you're a little busy trying to keep the diner afloat during the summer rush when you're missing your most dedicated employee?" Hawk smiled wryly.

"Exactly."

He nodded. "Thank you. For explaining that. For trusting me with it. I understand where you're coming from now."

"Maybe I should have explained it fully before. I just…" I blew out a breath.

Hawk shook his head. "It's okay. You don't owe me those stories, Jack. And it's my fault, too. I was so frustrated and my thoughts were so tangled I felt like you weren't listening to my very important reasons for feeling the way I did. I didn't stop to consider that you had your own reasons that were just as important."

I felt worn-out, stripped and bare, vulnerable in a way I'd never made myself before. "So… what happens next? Now that we're, you know… doing the relationship thing."

Hawk blinked at me, all innocence. "I sort of imagined we'd follow the traditional Little Pippin Hollow relationship protocol. Official meeting with Mayor York to declare our relationship intentions. Get our blood tests and star charts done. Register the date of our consummation with the town's Anniversary Committee. Do the public claiming ritual on the common—conveniently for us, the Pye Day Potluck is already happening today, so we won't need to wait for them to organize anything special. And, if we're very lucky, we'll get a commemorative scroll," he finished matter-of-factly.

I stared at him. "You're joking."

He laughed out loud. "Of course I'm joking. I mean, not about Pye Day, because that's actually today. But about the rest…"

"After what happened with Luke and Webb, you never know," I said darkly.

"True. Look, the real answer is…" Hawk shrugged helplessly. "I don't know what happens now. Don't forget, I don't have any more experience with relationships than you do. So maybe we write our own rules in a way that works for us. Okay?"

Me and Hawk, figuring things out together? "Yeah. That sounds pretty perfect."

"Good." He gave me a peck on the lips, but when I reached up to thread my hands into his hair and turn that kiss into something deeper and hotter, he pushed away with evident reluctance. "I can't. Not right now. The Environmental Committee is cobbling itself back together as of two days ago, and I promised I'd meet a few of the others up on Glassy Ridge at nine for a strategy and information session if the storm didn't mess everything up. I've gotta get ready. Besides, aren't you helping your mom bring stuff to the potluck?"

I groaned. "Yeahhhh. With everything else happening, I might have completely forgotten about that. I'll need to go call her and sort it out."

Hawk unzipped the tent so he could stand and began to pull on his warm clothes. I hated seeing his delicious form disappear under thick layers, but I wasn't about to take my eyes off him for a moment and risk missing part of the show.

"I suppose if I were to suggest that you abandon the protest for a morning and that I blow off the whole Pye Day thing, and that both of us go back to my house, take a nice, hot shower, and get naked in my bed... that wouldn't be a good *boyfriendly* thing to do?" I asked, trying out the new word. It sounded strange... and strangely *right*.

Hawk bit his lip against a smile. "It really wouldn't. You'd be run out of town if you forgot about Pye Day. And I refuse to abandon the protest. There's only two weeks to the vote, and I'm finally starting to get traction thanks to Instagram." He rolled his eyes. "Hawk Sunday talks about stopping the resort development for months and months, and everyone's all, '*That's nice, dear.*' I get forty thousand Instagram followers thanks to a post going viral, and suddenly they're all, 'Wait, there's a protest? About a resort? First I've heard of it.' I can't miss a chance to educate people during prime hiking time. Not even to have sex with the great Jack Wy—*uh.*"

I sighed and flipped the sleeping bag off myself so I could find my own clothes, and Hawk stopped talking abruptly, his eyes widening as he stared at me, laid out in my boxers and T-shirt.

"What?" I looked myself up and down, feeling my legs prickle in the cold cave air.

Hawk swallowed. "Nothing. No. Just. Uh. Realizing that if I wanted to, I could duck back into that tent and touch you right now. Kiss you. Do… lots of other things."

"So many other things," I agreed, letting my voice go rough.

Hawk turned away, and his shoulders heaved in a sigh. "Maybe a good boyfriendly thing to do would be to put some clothes on."

I snorted and sat up. "Does this mean I'm supposed to stay fully dressed until after the vote?" I demanded, stepping out of the tent so I could hop into my jeans and pull on my shirt. "Should I hide my ankles and wear gloves in case of *naked-palm touching*, lest you get distracted and ravish me in a garden, like in one of your spicy Pride and Prejudice variations?"

He stepped up close to me until our chests bumped. "Don't knock the naked-palm touching," he whispered against my lips. "I'm really seeing the appeal. In fact, I'm gonna be thinking of naked-palm touching all morning until I see you at the potluck this afternoon—"

I pulled back to look at him. "Wait… you're coming?"

He nodded. "Of course. Otherwise, *I'll* get run out of town. The Pilkners are coming up here to take over the campout protest for me, at least for tonight. Conrad said Greta keeps telling him to be more spontaneous now that they're retired, so…"

"So he decided 'Surprise, honey, I signed us up to sleep in a tent on a mountain' was a good choice?"

"Mmmhmm. And thank goodness he did because I can't wait one more night to be with you. So, here's what I propose…" He walked his fingers up my chest slowly. "I'm going to my meeting. You're going to help your mom. I'll come to the diner to help out—and that's not a euphemism," he said severely. "Then after the celebration is over, I'm going to stalk you back to your house in the nice, secluded woods, get my naked palms all over you, and beg you to take my virginity in the garden, or the bedroom, or that random room you added onto the back of the house that I'm kinda thinking maybe you could turn into a dedicated *ravishing* room... In fact, I think we should try to hit *all* the rooms. Okay?"

My head swam, and my dick moved. "Oh."

"*Oh?*" He frowned. "I am willing to consider amendments to this proposal, you know."

"No! No, no, no. I just... I didn't realize *this* was what being in a relationship would be like." I grinned. "Maybe I've been missing out."

"Yeah," he said softly. "Maybe we both have." Hawk lifted up on his toes, wrapped his arms around my waist, and kissed me. "So let's make up for lost time, okay?"

I grabbed his chin and leaned in to kiss him. "As you wish."

CHAPTER TWELVE

HAWK

"It's been many years since I had such an exemplary vegetable."
~ Mr. Collins

I CAME off the mountain feeling euphoric. Even though Jack had been gone for hours, I still felt the imprint of his lips on mine, of his hands on my hips, of his warm breath in my hair.

He wanted me.

When I pulled my car in front of the farmhouse at Sunday Orchard shortly after noon, I was so happy I felt buoyant. Like little champagne bubbles of excitement fizzed through my bloodstream. It wasn't every day a person got to experience something they'd been dreaming of for seven years and then spent two weeks thinking they would never, ever have. But today was *my* day, and I defied the universe itself to try to bring down my mood.

I have kissed Jack Wyatt—more than once—and he's agreed to pop my cherry. Jane Austen herself could not have written me a happier ending than this. Come at me, bro.

"Afternoon, everyone!" I sang as I walked through the front door.

Luke sat cross-legged on the couch surrounded by papers,

as usual—probably lesson plans, crochet patterns, or a combination of both. Webb, dressed in his usual summer uniform of cargo shorts and a Sunday Orchard T-shirt, sat slumped beside him, a cold drink in his hand. And Aiden crouched on the braided rug at their feet with our old dog, Sally Ann, and his new puppy, Black Bear.

"Uncle Hawk!" Aiden cried. "I thought you lived on a mountain now!"

"Only temporarily." I grinned. "And I had to come back for Pye Day, right?"

"Yeah! So… maybe can you help me?" he asked eagerly, all big green eyes and sandy hair. "I wanted to enter either Sally Ann or Bear into the pet show at the potluck, but neither one of 'em knows any tricks. Luke says Bear's too little to learn, and Dad says Sally Ann's too old, so I figured maybe if I tried to teach them *together*, they'd help each other."

"That's good thinking." I raised an eyebrow at my brother. "And I think you need to remind your dad that old dogs can definitely learn new tricks if you give them the right motivation. Right, Webb?"

Webb rolled his eyes and leaned into Luke's side.

"You mean, like… give 'em treats?" Aiden suggested doubtfully.

"Exactly that." I shot Luke a wink. "Wouldn't you agree, Luke?"

Luke laughed and blushed. "It definitely doesn't hurt," he agreed.

Aiden passed me on his way to the kitchen to get the dog treats, and the dogs scrambled to follow.

"Gotta go." I hooked a thumb up the stairs. "I've been dying for a shower and fresh clothes. Then I've gotta get to work and the potluck. Will I see you guys there?"

Luke nodded, and I shot them both a smile before turning toward the stairs.

"Hey, Hawk?" Webb called.

"Yeah?" I turned back.

"Everything… good?" he asked, his eyes raking me up and down.

For the first time in months, I didn't see that concerned look as Webb not trusting me to handle my own life. Instead, I saw it for what it probably always had been: love.

He would probably always worry about me, but his concern only had as much weight as I gave it. It was up to *me* whether I felt that worry as a crushing burden or a warm, comforting blanket.

"Yeah, Webb." I grinned. "Things are really good."

"Good," he grunted, slinging an arm around his husband.

As I made my way up the stairs, I wondered what Webb would think if—*when?*—he heard about me and Jack, but I wasn't going to stress about that.

Today, I had much more important and fun things to think about.

Jack Wyatt wanted me—really, this was so remarkable it bore repeating—and even the most jaded, cautious part of my brain, the part that usually insisted things were too good to be true, was barely whispering its usual warnings. Not when Jack had told me deeper truths this morning than he'd shared in seven years. Not when he'd stared at me with naked vulnerability and wanting on his face. Not when he'd shown himself in every way to be the man I'd dreamed of all these years.

And that wasn't the only area of my life that seemed to be looking up. My social media campaign had gotten attention outside of Little Pippin Hollow—another environmental influencer had shared one of my posts in her Instagram story just that morning—and somehow, the wider attention was getting me more local attention, too.

Several members of the Environmental Committee—not including Ms. Fortnum, who still seemed super cagey about the development for whatever reason—had hiked up to Glassy Ridge earlier in the week, looking to *me* like I was their leader and asking what help *I* needed to continue educating people about the risks of the development proceeding according to the current proposal.

After a long shower, where I sluiced off half a week's worth of dirt and took my time making some preparations for what I really hoped would be the best night of my life, I made my way to the farmhouse kitchen for some food since I figured I'd be too busy helping out once I got to the diner to eat anything.

Drew and Marco were seated at the long wooden table. Two glasses of iced tea and a half-empty plate of cheese and crackers sat off to the side of their double-solitaire game. Things looked intense.

"Marco, jack of diamonds on the… yeah. Oh, and right there, the three of clubs…"

Drew shot me a glare. "Hawkins Sunday, whose side are you on? No cheaty hints from the likes of you. He's already kicking my ass."

Marco grinned without taking his eyes off the cards in front of him. "Four out of four so far. His game is off ever since I sent him a link to an article about—"

"Zzt!" Drew hissed. "He doesn't need to know about that."

My ears perked up as I made my way to the fridge. These two were always trading obscure information on all kinds of inappropriate topics. "Was it the one about using Yohimbe for sexual vitality? Webb sent that to all of us, but what you might not have known is that *he* got it from Mrs. Williams, and it was a whole thing. Luke was mortified. But clearly, something's working for them."

Marco's concentration finally broke, and he threw his dark head back with laughter. Drew took the opportunity to slam as many cards down on the piles as he could before he ran out of moves.

"No," Marco said through a few final giggles. "It was about—"

"Marco Polo Vanzetti, if you ever want to see the inside of our bedroom again, you will cease and desist forthwith—"

"Genital shrinkage in old age," Marco finished before howling with laughter again. "You should have seen his face. I swear he wanted to whip out a measuring tape and make some assessments."

"You'll be lucky if I ever want to whip out anything ever again," Drew muttered, studying the game for any other potential move he could make. He called over his shoulder without looking, "There's some fresh tomatoes on the windowsill and fresh bread in the bread box if you're looking for a snack, Hawk."

"Good idea." I pulled mayo from the fridge and cut myself some thick slices of Drew's buttermilk bread.

"And if you're still looking for volunteers to help with your Environmental Committee," Drew said, "I'm ready to bust out my love beads and protest songs. I feel kinda bad that I haven't made that a priority. I support you, you know that."

"Really?" I glanced up at him. "That would be amazing. Yes, I'd love your help. Thank you, Uncle Drew."

He gave me a wink.

"So, Hawk, speaking of genitals—" Marco turned in his seat to look at me.

"Ooooh, no. *We* were not speaking of them," I reminded him, looking back down at my food. "For the record, I had no part in that conversation."

"—any luck in the cherry department? 'Cause if you're in the market, Gage heard from Drake, who heard from Van at the Bugle that he's got a new server over there who's a real looker—"

"Chris," I supplied.

"No, not her. It was a guy." Marco narrowed his eyes at me. "Thought you were gay. Not that you need to, you know, label yourself or whatever, but—"

"I am gay." I rolled my eyes. "There are two new employees at the Bugle. Crys, short for Crystal, who's my friend, and Chris, short for... I don't know what, who's a guy." I shook my head. "I don't get it—he's worked at the Bugle, like, five shifts a week for the past three months, but no one seems to know the man. It's a little creepy. When Gage moved to town, everyone in the Hollow knew his favorite kind of cheese, his top five Christmas memories, and his thoughts on the Bruins' playoff chances within the first week."

Marco shrugged. "All I know is what I heard, and what I heard is that he's a cutie pie who's real sweet and quiet. Now, Gage made it pretty clear this guy's not as hot as Knox, but then again, Knox was sitting right there, and Gage knows where his bread is buttered. A man's morally obligated to downplay the relative hotness of every other eligible man in the vicinity when the love of his life is in the room. It's one of those compromises folks make when they commit to each other."

"Wait just a minute." Drew narrowed his eyes. "The other day when we heard that Jayd Rollins' song on the radio and I asked you if he was better-looking than me..."

"Anyway, Hawk," Marco said quickly. "If you want me to get the guy's number—"

"Marco." Drew looked affronted. "Next, you'll be saying Jayd's a better guitar player than I am!"

Marco shot him a guilty look, and Drew gasped.

"Uh, thanks anyway, but I've got the situation taken care of," I said, hoping to extricate myself from an awkward conversation before it got worse.

When two pairs of eyes turned to me, cards forgotten on

the table, I realized I'd fully intricated myself into that awkward conversation instead.

"Is that so? Care to tell us who the lucky fella is?" Drew asked, acting ridiculously casual. He lowered his voice. "You can trust us to be discreet."

"'Course you can. We're the very *souls* of discretion," Marco agreed solemnly.

"Sure you are. Both of you can expect dictionaries in your Christmas stockings this year." I seasoned my tomatoes and slapped the bread together. "Because those words don't mean what you think they mean."

Marco narrowed his eyes. "Spill your tea, boy."

"No, thanks." I took a big bite of my sandwich, which, handily enough, made speech impossible.

My uncle and his partner made significant eye contact before both turned to look at me again.

"Well, *I* think you should hold out for Jack," Drew said. "He's a sweet potato, and he cares about you."

I choked on a crumb of bread. Had Drew heard about my proposition? Had Jack told Webb who told Drew? No. I couldn't imagine that scenario.

"You mean… Jack *Wyatt*?" I croaked, like the Hollow was littered with Jacks who cared about me.

Thankfully, they didn't laugh.

"Why not? All the best lovers start out as friends. Plus, Jack's a great cook, he's good at bocce, and he's handsome— nearly as handsome as your uncle, the love of my life," Marco added gamely.

Drew rolled his eyes and kicked Marco under the table. "Most importantly, Jack's whole attention is on you whenever you walk in a room. Been that way for years."

"And why wouldn't it be?" Marco demanded. "Our Hawkins is the bee's knees. The heart and soul of the Hollow."

I shook my head. I definitely wasn't that. "I'll consider it, but only since you made such a compelling argument," I told the two of them. They exchanged a smirk so self-satisfied, and I couldn't help adding, "Maybe I'll show up at his place naked tonight after the Pye Day Potluck and see what happens."

"What?" Drew exclaimed. "Hawk, honey, that might be a little too—"

"Don't worry," I soothed. "I'll tell him I have my uncles' blessings for him to consummate our relationship. I'm sure he'll be very moved." I patted Drew on the shoulder and gave Marco a wink before putting my plate in the sink and heading for the back door. "And I won't say a word to anyone about your genital shrinkage, Uncle Drew."

I left them both staring at my back, slack-jawed.

Nosy, meddling fuckers.

I couldn't possibly love them more.

IF I'D BEEN LOOKING FORWARD to flirting with Jack at work, it was only because I'd forgotten just how slammed the restaurant was this time of year. From the minute I arrived until the moment I left again a few hours later, I was run off my feet. How Jack had even been able to take time off the day before to come see me on the mountain was beyond comprehension.

There were a few times during the rush when I caught Jack's smile turned in my direction, and those moments were enough to make my heart bang against my chest like a prisoner whacking his tin cup against the cell bars, demanding to be let free. To say I was excited for tonight was to understate the truth *massively*.

But first, we had to get through the Pye Day festivities.

Crys looped her arm through mine as we walked to the

green in the middle of town. "You know most people celebrate Pi Day in March, right? Like, 3-14, the first few numbers of pi?"

"Uh-huh. But most people aren't from the Hollow. And around here, Pye Day isn't about celebrating the number or the dessert food. It's about celebrating the bush."

Her eyes flared wide. "Celebrating the... pardon?"

"The bush. The Joe-Pye weed bush that saved Celeste Dupont from falling into a well in 1909? It's a whole thing."

Crys was silent for a long moment, processing this. Eventually, she admitted, "I've never heard of that bush before, and I've sure as fuck never heard of Celeste Dupont, and yet somehow, this seems entirely appropriate. Why is that, Hawkins? Make it make sense."

"Because we have our own brand of logic here in the Hollow, and you're one of us now." I patted her shoulder comfortingly. "Don't worry. Real-world logic is overrated, and you'll hardly miss it."

Crys whimpered.

"Anyway, the bush no longer exists, nor does the well, and no one really remembers the details of the story. Now it's more like the obscure reason behind one of the town's most beloved potluck events. It's a chance to one-up your neighbor by bringing the latest TikTok-trendy dish. Think cinnamon rolls in multiple 'original' variations, nacho tables, and so many feta pasta incarnations you'll be able to pinpoint the day you became lactose intolerant. Before this day is done, you will be forced to decide whether you are a hopelessly conventional charcuterie board purist or one of those free-thinking butter-board revolutionaries, like O'Henry Brush, who's destroying America. And I haven't even mentioned the kombucha that comes out of the woodwork for this thing. Do not consume anything made by the Derwent family, and that includes their cousin Delaney Powers, unless you're ready to embark on the Hollow's version of an ayahuasca retreat."

"What are we bringing?"

I shook my head. "We don't bring anything because Drew makes enough plum ginger tarts to sink a ship, and this year, Knox is bringing barbecue corn ribs. Gage showed him one TikTok video, and the man fell down a rabbit hole."

"I didn't even know corns *had* ribs," she muttered.

"Did you say corn ribs?" Samir Moreland boomed from behind us. "Hell yeah! I love a corn rib."

I turned and smiled. "Knox has been perfecting his sauce for so long that Gage's body composition is more chili oil than water at this point. Definitely stop by his table before they're all gone." I didn't mention Knox probably had so many corn ribs I was fairly sure we'd be eating the leftovers until we died.

"What's Jack bringing?" Crys asked.

"Nothing. The potluck is for amateurs, not professionals. But his mom always brings a metric ton of flavor-infused lemonades she makes at home. The rosemary and mint one will change your life."

We approached the crowd of locals as everyone shuffled around to find the best spots for their offerings. Over the years, an unspoken hierarchy had instituted itself, and the most popular offerings were at the prime table locations to allow for easier traffic.

"Tourists are welcome to come, and lots of 'em bring their own stuff to share, but the organizing committee had to institute rules to keep out promotional displays and for-profit stuff," I explained. "One year, Big Johnson Brats came through in their Brat-Mobile and threw wieners at everyone. Naked buns and sausages all over the place. Norma Hart got so excited she had to be hospitalized."

Crys covered her mouth with her hand in horror.

"Exactly," I agreed. "The jokes write themselves. *Oooh!* You need to try Swathi Romano's Christmas in July gingerbread snowflake cookies. They're a fan favorite."

As we meandered through the maze of tables, picking up things to try here and there, my eyes scanned the crowd for Jack's tall form.

"Looking for someone?" Crys asked archly.

I coughed. "Maybe?"

"So Jack's rescue mission worked, huh?" She buffed her freshly manicured nails on her shirt. "You're welcome, bee tee dubs."

"That was your idea?"

"Weelllll, no. I can't take total credit. The man was a mess for days. Fucking up orders, talking to himself like he thought you were there, flying off the handle for no reason. Tense as a drawn bow. I just kinda… aimed him." She grinned, clasped her hands under her chin, and said in a tremulous, high-pitched voice, "*Ruh-roh, Jack! Bad storm's a-coming! Hawk will need someone to fuck him gently through it! Maybe I'll call Simon! He's got big-dick energy!*"

I rolled my eyes. "So you were the one who got him all riled and jealous. We fought about that, I'll have you know."

"Sure, sure." She waved a hand. "But you didn't *just* fight, did you? I could tell the minute you walked in the diner today. You have the look of a man who's experienced a Righteous Orgasm."

I felt my face go hot. "Yes, well. *Ahem.* The official devirgination hasn't happened yet."

"But it will?" She wiggled her eyebrows.

"Yeah. Tonight. He… he wants me, Crys," I whispered. "And not just sexually. We talked about a lot of stuff. Really connected, you know? And he has a lot of reservations and concerns, but…" I bit my lip but couldn't restrain my excited smile. "We're doing the relationship thing."

"Hell, yeah! Victory!" She punched both hands in the air before clapping me on the shoulder. "I think we need to find some of that hard-core kombucha. You gotta celebrate this moment before you two get down into the hard relationship work."

"Uh. Your idea of *work* is a little different from mine," I joked. "I'm not nervous about tonight at all. I'm not experienced in anal, but I've done my research, and I'm as prepared as possible. It might be a little uncomfortable, but—"

"Boo." Crys stopped walking and stared at me, torn between worry and amusement. "You know I'm not talking about the sex, right? I'm talking about the relationship itself. You know, the thing where two whole-ass humans, each with his own needs and fears and ambitions, figure out a way to coexist as part of something larger while not losing themselves entir—"

"Mr. Hawk, Mr. Hawk!" Grayson Fischer barreled into me, throwing his tiny arms around my waist. "I haven't seen you in four weeks!"

"Days," a woman with a long, black braid corrected rushing up behind him. "Four *days*, kiddo."

"Felt like weeks, though," I agreed, ruffling Grayson's curly hair. "It's good to see you, buddy." I gave the woman a smile. "Are you his mom? Because I've gotta say, you're doing a killer job. Grayson's great. Super passionate about nature."

"I am. Allison Ramos." She held out her hand to shake. "And really, I should be the one thanking you. Ever since you started doing your hikes with the kids, our whole family's developed a new hobby."

"Oh? That's awesome—"

"My husband and I have been following your Instagram, too. I think most of the Nature Scout parents have. Lots of us are committing to hike Fogg Peak weekly before the place is lost to history, like you said in the caption on one of your posts."

I remembered the picture she was talking about. The sky had been streaked with orange and yellow clouds during sunset the first night I'd spent up on the mountain. Vast swaths of trees covered the ridge, and a northern harrier could just be seen spreading its wings against the warm sky near the right edge of the frame.

"Wow. That's so great to hear."

"Scott and I—and Grayson—would love to help out with your protest if you need volunteers. I don't know what the end goal for the Peak is, after we get the 'no' vote on the current proposal—like, should it be turned into a preserve and not developed at all? Or just developed *differently*?—but if you're planning to present alternative proposals to Evola, Scott's brother is a sustainability consultant in Burlington, and he could help."

I stared at her blankly. Protecting Fogg Peak by getting the town to vote no to the current proposal had been my endgame, and I hadn't really thought about what exactly should happen after that. Coming up with an alternate proposal seemed incredibly complex and messy. A task I wasn't sure I was qualified to take on…

But if I didn't, who would?

"I, um… I appreciate that. I'd love his contact information."

"Sure thing. In the meantime, do you have any interest in opening up your page to other folks' pictures from the Peak?" she asked.

"Gosh, yes. Absolutely." I ran a hand through my hair. "I, uh… I feel a little bit disorganized," I admitted. "I'm usually a helper, not a… a *leader*. I'm still figuring this part out."

"Well, I think you're doing a great job so f—"

"Mom, look! This lady's got *potatoes*, and potatoes are my very, very best vegetable!" Grayson said, pulling on the hem of her T-shirt and pointing to a nearby table. "Can we get some?"

"I guess we'd better." Allison rolled her eyes but let him

pull her away. "See you later this week, Hawk. Thanks again for the inspiration!"

I lifted a hand in acknowledgment but stared after her, feeling a little confused and a lot overwhelmed.

"Going around inspiring people again, Hawkins?" a familiar, teasing voice said in my ear.

I turned to see Jack with a soft smile and eyes seemingly only for me. My heart fluttered, wild as a trapped humming-bird. "Hey. Hi. Hey."

My face ignited. "Hey," I said again as if that would erase the previous three attempts.

His smile widened. "Hey."

Crys looked back and forth between us and shook her head. "What is happening right now?"

Jack reached out and ran his fingers through the back of my hair, cupping my head and leaning in to press a kiss on my cheek. My heart beat so fast I thought I might slide to the ground in a dead—but hopefully graceful—faint. "Hey," he whispered into my skin.

"Yeah," I breathed. "Heyyyyyy."

Crys snickered. "Tell me you're in the honeymoon phase without telling me you're in the honeymoon phase," she said to no one in particular.

"Crys," Jack said dryly, his gaze flicking to her. "Enjoying your first Pye Day Potluck?"

"I'm trying to figure out my battle strategy here," she admitted. "Do I attack the savory foods first and then the sweets? Or kill off the sweets first since they're likely to go faster and I refuse to live at the mercy of anyone else's stomach?"

Jack and I exchanged an amused look.

"Machiavelli would tell you to find an ally first," I said gravely. "Divide and conquer."

Crys narrowed her eyes in thought. "Good call, boo. I see other-Chris over there. Imma force him to join an alliance with me." She nodded once, then saluted me. "See you on the other side."

"She terrifies me," Jack murmured, sliding his hand into mine and holding it firmly as we walked toward Darren Pascal's barbecue table.

"Honestly, same. But sometimes a little terror is a good thing." *Take, for example, the terror I feel at finally holding your hand in public,* I thought to myself.

Jack's smile said he knew exactly what I was thinking, though, and the answering tenderness on his face warmed my stomach way more than the single bite of Darren's smoked chicken sliders I managed to choke down.

If Jack was feeling any kind of way about the curious looks and beaming smiles people gave us as we wandered the town common, checking out the delicious food with our hands linked together, he didn't show it. And when we rocked up to Knox's table to get an order of corn ribs, Jack's hand retained a firm grasp on mine.

Gage's gaze landed on our joined hands, and he gave Jack a teasing smile. "So, I guess this means poor Joey Kincaid's not going to get another model for his shibari photography?"

"Goodman," Knox warned, shaking his head in amusement.

I shot Jack a confused glance.

"No," Jack told Gage shortly. "*Definitely* not."

"Probably best that I never talked to him, then, hmm?" Gage said happily. He gave me a wink. "Really thrilled for you two." He hip-bumped Knox. "We both are."

"The whole family is," Knox said firmly. "Or will be, once they hear about it."

Jack didn't seem quite so sure, but he simply nodded and slid his hand around my waist, like their approval of our relationship wasn't going to change his mind either way... which was possibly the hottest thing he'd ever done in a lifetime of incredibly hot things.

strolled away, his hand tightened around me, and I
help wondering what it would feel like on other
my body. What was Jack Wyatt like in bed? A *demon*
hug Peter claimed? Or gentle, the way he usually was
me? Bossy? Sweet? Aggressive? Playful? Loving?
was like a kid on Christmas morning, waiting to unwrap
present and see what I'd gotten, but in my dreams, I'd
joyed every possible incarnation of our lovemaking, and I
had no doubt the reality would be just as amazing.

"Omigod! Hawkins Sunday!" Gracie Hubbard squealed.
She waved at me eagerly before racing over.

I shot Jack a bemused look. Gracie was one of Emma's
friends, and I'd known her for a billion years, but she was six
years younger than me, and we weren't particularly close.

"Hey, Gracie," I said as she rocked to a stop in front of me.

"Hi!" She beamed. "I'm *so* happy that you made it back
safely and didn't have to, like, burn all your money or whatever." Her eyes widened. "Wait, did you?"

"Uh. What?" I glanced up at Jack, but he pressed his lips
together and shook his head.

"Never mind," she said, waving a hand. "You survived
your ordeal, and that's really all that matters." She clasped
her hands to her chest. "I told Emma you're... kind of my
hero."

"Uh. *What?*" I repeated.

Beside me, Jack's body shook with suppressed laughter.

"So, like... I know you're basically a famous environmental activist now, and you probs have, like, way important
friends and all, but can we get a selfie together? The other
Peakies will be so jealous."

"*Uhhhhhh... whaaaat?*" I said for a third time.

Jack was full-on chortling, bent over so his face was
pressed into my shoulder.

"Please?" she begged.

"Oh... kay?"

Gracie sighed happily, like I'd just made her entire day. She came up beside me, wrapped her arm around my waist, and before I had a chance to fix my face or even look at her phone camera, she snapped three quick pictures. "Thank you so much, Hawk!"

Jack straightened. "Gracie," he said, soberly enough to grab her attention. "If you're posting that pic on Instagram, please remember to use the Save Fogg Peak hashtags that Hawk's been using, okay? Amplify Hawk's message while you're doing your selfie thing."

"Oh gosh, of course," she agreed, wide-eyed. "No, like, I'm totally committed to the effort now. I'm Peaky for *life.*"

"You're...?" I frowned.

"Peaky. You know, a person who supports saving the Peak? I convinced my mom to talk to her bridge club and her bunco ladies about it," she said proudly. "Mom says they're having a joint meeting about it tomorrow at Panini Jack's—"

I looked up at Jack in surprise. "They are?"

"I let lots of organizations hold their meetings at the diner." He shrugged like it wasn't a big deal... but it was a *very* big deal to me. I knew he'd turned Helena Fortnum down when she'd tried to hand out flyers from the Environmental Committee at the diner earlier this year.

"—so, like, I was wondering if Save Fogg Peak has an official merch shop where we could buy T-shirts? Or is that something I could help out with?" Gracie asked.

Merchandise? Really?

"Y-yeah. Sure. You could definitely help out," I agreed.

"Sick! Thanks, Hawk!" With that, she ran off as abruptly as she'd come over.

"Jack?" I demanded, staring after her. "Did that just happen?"

"You mean, are the young people of the Hollow treating you like a celebrity because you had a kick-ass idea and you executed it? Yep. That definitely happened."

I turned to look at him. "Careful. You're starting to sound like you support the cause."

Jack grinned. "I support *you*. You're doing good work, Bird, and I'm proud of you… even if your happily ever after in this particular case looks a little different from mine."

"I think I've spent so long focusing on this one thing I wanted that I thought the no vote *was* the happily ever after. I forgot that the story didn't end there," I admitted. "If this development gets canceled, what kind of oversight do we want to guarantee before we consider a new one? What kind of development *would* be okay? I don't know. But I told you I'm going to meet up with Simon for dinner sometime, maybe even this week, and he promised me information on Evola's environmental monitoring of their recent build sites. That might be a good jumping-off point to start figuring things out."

"And you really *will* only be talking about the development at this dinner," Jack said in that overly casual, not-at-all-casual way of his.

I grinned. "What do you think?"

Jack raised an eyebrow. "I think… it sounds like you've got a busy week coming up, Hawkins."

"Oh yeah. I've got a campout protest to continue, alternate proposals to consider, an Instagram campaign to keep up with, an octogenarian Hooker to pin down, a job at the diner to get back to—assuming my boss still wants me—and a hike with the Mini Scouts. I'm swamped." I gave him a sideways look. "From what I saw at the diner earlier, you're gonna be run off your feet this week, too, eh?"

"No question." He darted a sideways look at me, then glanced at the rows of tables we hadn't yet visited. "How hungry are you, baby?"

I laughed. "For food? Not at all. For you, on the other hand, I have a powerful hunger."

As in, years and *years* of hunger that only Jack could satisfy.

Jack pulled me against him and pressed a brief kiss to my smiling lips, and I was so caught up in him I didn't give a single thought to who might be watching or what they might think. I wanted to shout my happiness from the rooftops.

"Let's go make the most of our night, then?" he suggested softly.

I nodded. "Lead the way."

CHAPTER THIRTEEN

JACK

"He is so excessively handsome!"
~ Mrs. Bennet

HAWK HAD BEEN to my house many times before. Hell, he'd helped me renovate almost every room in the place. But bringing him home tonight felt different.

For one, he hadn't been here in a couple of weeks, which meant there were plenty of little changes he noticed.

"I like the trim you picked," he said, pointing to the crown molding above the cabinets in the mud room.

"You picked it," I said with a soft laugh while we kicked off our shoes on the tile floor. "Remember you shared that folder of inspo pics? This was from one of those. Or... as close as I could figure, anyway."

Hawk's cheeks turned a little pink. "Really? No wonder I like it. What else have you done since I was here last? Did you decide what to do with the addition yet?"

I thought about the project I'd spent most of my nights working on. "I, uh... I have some plans." And when I thought about what those were, it seemed impossible that I'd hidden the truth of my feelings for Hawk from myself for as long as I had. "But since you suggested turning it into a dedicated ravishing room, I may have to rethink. How *does* one decorate a ravishing room?" I wondered.

"I have ideas." His eyes heated. "I may have to start a new inspiration folder."

"Can't wait. In the meantime, I did finish tiling and grouting the upstairs shower," I offered with a salacious eyebrow wiggle designed to make him laugh. "I got that rain showerhead if you wanted to take a look."

"I think I read about this in one of my books." Hawk's gaze followed his fingertips as they trailed lightly up the center of my sternum, fire-hot even through my shirt. "You plan to lure innocent little me upstairs to see your etchings and then have your wicked way with me, is that it?"

My heart rate sped up so fast I was nearly light-headed with it. My hands shook with the need to touch him. Seeing him here brought home just how much I wanted him in my life as more than my friend, more than my employee, more than my renovation partner.

"You caught me," I said roughly. "There'll be no going back after that. You'll be ruined."

He lifted his face to mine and studied me for a moment. "Promise?" he whispered.

Without another word, I grabbed his hand and led him upstairs, directly into my bedroom. Hawk let out a surprised bark of laughter as I tugged him across the threshold... and then his laughter dissolved into a moan when I pulled him against me and covered his lips with mine.

He tasted like the cool water of Glassy Creek after a long hike. Like fresh air after spending too long in a crowd. Like freedom. Like home.

I couldn't believe it was possible to crave someone so much when I'd spent so long denying to myself that I wanted him at all. I was still half-convinced—maybe more than half—that it might go bad somehow in a way I didn't know how to fix, but I could no more push him away in that moment than I could stop myself from breathing.

And when Hawk's hands fisted in my shirt, pulling me closer so that I had to wrap my arms around him to keep us both from tumbling to the ground, there was no choice to be made at all anymore. Hawk was every bit as hungry and demanding as I was.

Our mouths explored each other while the sounds we made were almost embarrassingly desperate—or maybe that was just me. It was hard to tell, and it didn't matter. All I knew was a gut-deep need for him, to hold and touch and devour him without ever letting go. Now that the lid was unlocked and flung open on this opportunity to be with him this way, I was all in.

"Hands are shaking." His words were muffled against my mouth.

"Sorry."

"No," he said, moving his mouth away from mine so he could let out a nervous laugh. Our cheeks pressed together, his stubble rubbing against mine. "Me. *My* hands are shaking. It's… I feel out of control."

It's his first time, for fuck's sake, I admonished myself. *First time being with someone this way. First time with* you. *Stop attacking his face.*

"Shit." I pulled back and cupped his face, rubbing my thumb over the tiny faded scar below his eye. "I'm sorry. I'm going too fast."

"Not too fast," he said gently, leaning forward to kiss me again. "Just… overwhelming. I want you so much, Jack. I've dreamed of this—*you*—for…" He let out a breath and dropped his eyes. "A long time."

"Is that right?" I tilted his chin back up until he met my eyes again. Anticipation filled the air between us like a living thing, throbbing and swirling and sucking up the oxygen in the room. "Then I'm really, *really* glad you're here with me now."

Hawk's mouth opened in surprise, and I couldn't help but lean forward to taste it again.

We kissed for a long time, standing just inside the door to my room still fully clothed, our mouths becoming frantic once again. My hands mapped the angular contours of his body through his clothes—his pebbled nipples, his firm stomach, the curve of his ass. His cock was already hard, straining against his zipper as he rubbed himself against my thigh, and his fingers were threaded into my hair like he was afraid if he let go, I might disappear altogether. His words from the cave this morning came back to me…

And then I wake up, and poof.

As much as I wanted Hawk—and fuck did I want him in every possible way—I also *knew* him. I knew what he wanted and needed from me tonight, and it was more than just kisses and unbridled passion. He deserved a slow, deliberate, no-holds-barred seduction. He deserved to know that while he might have dreamed of this for a long time, I wanted him just as badly.

I gentled the kiss and pulled back slightly. Hawk made a whimpering noise and clung tighter.

"Baby," I whispered against his lips. "Shhh. Let go for a second."

He made a frantic, negative sound and pushed himself harder against me.

"Bird." I grasped his jaw in both hands and held him in place. I kissed him softly, on his full lower lip and his cupid's bow, on either side of his mouth, on his stubbled chin. "It's okay. I'm not going anywhere."

"There's no need to wait!" he said breathlessly. "Please—"

"Hawk," I insisted, "do you know the first time I noticed how gorgeous you are?"

Distracted, he pulled back slightly and blinked like the

question confused him. His big, brown eyes were dilated with lust and confusion. "Uh. Yeah. Last night… or this morning, I guess. I was there, remember?"

I shook my head. "Nope. Last night was when my blinders fell away, and I realized all that I might lose if I kept trying to keep you in this tidy little friendship box in my mind. It was *not* the first time I wanted you."

He frowned, and his nose wrinkled. "So, then… two weeks ago. When I, um… when I propositioned you." He bit his lip. "When I changed things."

I shook my head, fighting a smile. "Wrong again," I said softly. "That was when I realized you might want *me*, which, yes, forced me to think about some things I'd been too afraid to let myself think about. But your cherry-popping proposition didn't change my feelings for you. They were there all along, just waiting for me to stop pushing them away."

"But then…"

I huffed out a laugh and pressed a kiss to the tiny dent between his eyebrows. "Four years ago, Hawkins. *Four*."

"No," he said flatly. "Impossible."

"So. Very. Possible," I informed him, punctuating each word with a tiny kiss to his lips. I nudged him to the overstuffed chair in the corner and pushed him down gently before kneeling in front of him. I had to find a way to distract myself, or this whole thing would be over in a minute. "You know, Webb and I bonded really quickly after I came to the Hollow because he knew what it felt like to have a business and family depend on him, right? He understood where I was in my life, my circumstances, because he was in a similar place. But you…" I shook my head and began stripping off his socks. "You understood *me*. I knew you were special from that first day. That I wanted to protect you at all costs. But you were a kid then, so I figured, 'Well, Jack, you've never had a brother. Maybe this is what it feels like.'"

"But it wasn't?" he whispered.

I shook my head. *"That was only when I first knew you,"* I said in my best Colin Firth impression. *"It has been many years since I have thought you one of the most handsome men of my acquaintance*—and by that, I mean utterly gorgeous, down to your soul, Hawk Sunday."

"Oh my god." Hawk's eyes widened, and he leaned forward in the chair with a gasp. "Oh. My. God. Is this actually happening? Did you just... did you just quote Darcy at me?"

"Maybe." I was pretty sure I'd *butchered* Darcy at him, but with Hawk, it was generally the thought that counted. I pecked him on the lips and pushed him back in his seat to resume my story. "Remember that time we went swimming at Lake Nitka a few years ago?"

"Yeah. We... um..." Hawk licked his lips, his gaze focused on my hands, which had begun massaging his feet and then the thick muscles of his calves. "We did the, ah... the zip-lining thing. Just us. It was one of the first times it was just you and me on one of our adventures."

"That's right. And you decided to take your shirt off before we climbed up the tower..." I massaged higher on his leg, my fingers delving under the hem of his shorts and sifting through the coarse hair there.

"Yeah." Hawk's voice was strangely gravelly, his neck flushed red. If I worried for a second that too much talking and confession might ruin the mood, one glance at the bulge in his shorts proved me wrong.

Hawk had always been a lover of words.

I kept my eyes locked with his while I kissed the inside of his knee. The hiss of his breath made my heart kick into a higher gear. "All of a sudden, you looked *different*. Muscles in your arms. In your shoulders. In these legs..." I ran my palms up the outside of his thighs, over those muscles that were thick and strong after covering endless miles of mountain terrain, until I could tug at the hem of his boxer briefs. "And holy shit, Hawkins, your ass. *Hngh*."

"I wanted you to notice," he admitted. "But you never... I didn't think..."

"I noticed," I told him firmly. "I pushed it down. I locked it away. But I sure as fuck noticed, Hawk. You killed me that day." I ran a finger between the stretchy fabric of his boxers and his hot skin, and he sucked in another shuddering breath. "You're killing me *now*."

I pulled my hands out of his shorts and skimmed a hand down over his sparse happy trail until I reached the button at his waist. Hawk's breath was coming in pants, his eyes soft and unfocused, and my hands were shaking worse than ever. I'd wanted this to be a seduction, but with every little gasp and each new inch of hot skin I touched, I was the one being seduced.

"Why didn't you tell me?" he moaned. "God, Jack, we could have—"

"That day, I was so keyed up I jerked off in the shower the minute I got home. I tried not to think about you. About the way the sun hit your skin when we were in the water. The way your eyes sparked. But there you were, right in the middle of my brain..."

I peeled open his shorts and reached inside to feel the hard shape of him through the damp navy blue cotton of his underwear. Both of us let out a groan.

"And just as I was about to come, Webb showed up at my house. Remember when the old warped front door was still there and refused to close properly? Well, he took that as an invitation to stomp himself right inside and up the stairs—"

The mention of his brother made Hawk groan again, this time in frustration. He closed his eyes and leaned back in the chair. "I hate you for mentioning my brother while your hand is on my dick."

I snickered but couldn't help leaning up to kiss his mouth.

"I cannot stop wanting to do this," I mumbled against his lips.

Hawk grabbed my head and kissed me back with everything he had. But this time, he was the one who pulled back.

"Finish the story," he demanded. "You know I can never leave a book in the middle."

I laughed again and sat back, pulling his shorts with me. "Webb was angry. Furious."

"Did he know? About you and the... the *looking*?" Hawk demanded. "Did he guess?"

I shook my head. "Hell no. He was mad because I'd let you get sunburned. Badly. He said he'd expected more from me as Hawk's *honorary big brother*. And he mentioned that you had to cancel a date with 'the hottest guy in Little Pippin Hollow' because I'd fucked up—"

Looking back now, I felt the faint stirrings of an old, illogical, unacknowledged jealousy.

"Noooo." Hawk covered his face in his hands, and his words came out muffled. "Webb cockblocked you and me because he thought I was upset about canceling a date with Kenner Salisbury?"

I fought a smile. "He told me how much you liked Kenner, how well you got along. That even though you were young, he thought Kenner might just be The One for you—"

Hawk groaned behind his hands.

"And I said, '*Isn't Kenner a kid? He's way too young for Hawk.*' And Webb reminded me that Kenner was actually a year older than you, which, in turn, reminded me just how young you were then—"

Hawk's hands dropped away from his face, and he looked at me without a trace of a smile. "So help me, Jack, if you tell me you're still too old for me..."

"No, baby," I said, leaning in to skim my nose along the skin of his thigh. "Couldn't walk away now even if I wanted to." I looked up, meeting his eyes. "And I don't."

He huffed. "But then—"

"At the time, though, Webb's fury was a pretty powerful red flag. It reminded me that you were into guys your own age, as you should be. That my job was to be your surrogate brother. That you wanted to find The One, and that was the opposite of what I was looking for."

"Thomas Webb Sunday is a dead man," Hawk decreed.

"Nah." I ran my fingers up the firm length in his underwear, making him suck in a breath, and pressed a kiss to the tense muscle right above his knee. "There's a big difference between me thinking you were gorgeous, *wanting* you, and actually trying something with you. Hell, I never even got as far as picturing the two of us together back then. And if I had and I'd screwed it up, you and I would never have become... *us*. I wouldn't be who I am now. I might have gone my whole life never knowing about that one *Pride and Prejudice* variation where Darcy turns into a dragon." I shook my head sadly. "What kind of life would that have been?"

Hawk snickered, then laughed out loud. He sat forward again, grabbed my face roughly, and kissed me.

"How are you so perfect?" he asked softly.

His words made my stomach flip—and not in a pleasant way. "Hawk, no one knows better than you that I am *not* perfect—"

"You won't screw this up, Jack," he said fiercely, understanding my panic before I could even articulate the reasons for myself. "You can't. I won't let you."

I leaned forward and pulled up the edge of his shirt before stripping it over his head and tossing it on the floor, revealing the lucky penny necklace that gleamed against the lean muscles of his chest. Hawk's legs wrapped around my back and pulled me closer so he could whisper in my ear.

"Thank you for telling me that, but story time is over," he said in a voice filled with need. "I was promised a ruination."

He bit my earlobe, and a shiver raced down my spine as my dick went impossibly hard instantly. "Ruin me, Jack."

I didn't need any convincing. I dragged my lips up his throat, and Hawk went boneless against me, sinking back into the chair. I kissed him deeply, running my hands over his skin, glorying in the little noises I drew from him. When I pulled back this time, I stood and dragged him with me, right into my arms.

"Come to bed, Bird," I murmured against his lips. "We've both waited long enough."

CHAPTER FOURTEEN

HAWK

"Till this moment, I never knew myself."
~ Fitzwilliam Darcy

JACK WYATT WAS FUCKING MAGIC.

I'd been looked at before—plenty of times—but no one had ever watched me with an intensity in their deep blue eyes that made me feel powerful and sexy. I'd been kissed—a few times—but never with an all-consuming hunger that left me shaking and addicted. I'd been touched before, too—once or twice—but I'd never felt like a single touch could light my whole body on fire or like I might come from the slightest brush of someone's hand on mine.

In short, being with Jack was so much more than teenage Hawkins could have dreamed of and even more than adult-me had imagined... despite my very frequent attempts to imagine it.

Jack stood by the bed and stared down at me laid out before him. He bit his lip, like I was something tasty and he wasn't sure where to bite first, and the very idea of that made my dick literally *throb* against my belly.

"Are you trying to make me come with the power of your

mind?" I demanded, the words coming out a little reedier than I'd expected. "'Cause maybe that can be round two, okay? Stop looking and start—*ohhhh*."

My command trailed off into a moan as Jack braced his knee on the bed and lifted my hand to his mouth. He pressed an open-mouthed kiss to the center of my palm, drawing hot, wet circles with his tongue, and… sweet mother of dragons, who knew palms felt like that? I was never making fun of Regency women for their gloves again because I was seriously, entirely compromised.

Jack dragged his mouth up my arm, stopping to lavish affection on my wrist and nip my elbow and *bury his face in my armpit*, making all those perfectly ordinary places suddenly feel sexy and sensitive. He kissed his way to my chest, nudging my necklace aside, and then moved back down again, licking and tugging at my nipples with his teeth. The low sounds of my need felt like shouts in the still quiet of the room.

"Take off your clothes," I begged. "Please, Jack."

I watched him peel his clothes off in record time, exposing his body in the warm, low light of a single bedside table lamp. He was everything I'd ever dreamed of in a man. Broad-shouldered and tall with a sandy-brown happy trail leading down into his underwear. His abdomen was slightly rounded from too many hours spent working as a chef, but I loved that about him. Had he carried a six-pack to match his well-muscled arms and shoulders, I might have been more intimidated by his perfection. As it was, he was perfect to me, and I couldn't get enough of him.

The scruff of his sandy beard had already done a number on my lips and chin, but I wanted more of it. I wanted that prickle scraping the tender flesh of my inner thighs, the thin skin over my hips, the sensitive spots behind my ears. Jack could mark me from the top of my head to the tips of my toes, and I'd wear the scrapes, scratches, and bruises with pride.

I wanted… *needed*… proof of this moment. Hard evidence I wasn't dreaming or hallucinating.

"Deep breath, baby," he murmured, frowning at me. "You're going to hyperventilate."

I reached out my arm and grabbed his wrist, yanking him back down until his body pressed mine into the mattress. "Want you so much," I admitted, forcing myself not to apologize to him for fucking it all up with my nervous anticipation.

He leaned in and kissed me again, his mouth owning me and holding me in place. I wrapped my legs around him to keep him from pulling away again. His cock was hard, pressing against mine through the layers of our underwear. His hips undulated until my head was swimming and my dick was leaking.

"More," I begged, moving my hands down underneath the waistband of his boxer briefs to cup his ass. I couldn't believe this was happening. That I, Hawk Sunday, could finally touch Jack Wyatt's naked butt.

But how much more could I do? What things did Jack like? Would he want me to move a finger between his cheeks? Would he like it if I got aggressive? Would *I*? As well as we knew one another in so many ways, this was new territory for both of us. It was unnerving… and incredibly exciting.

I thought—hoped—he mostly topped. I knew for sure that was what I wanted, tonight at least.

"Will you fuck me?" I asked, my nerves ramping back up. "Please?"

Jack palmed my cheek and met my eyes. "Hell yes. Are you sure?"

"So fucking sure. More than sure. And I, um…" How could I tell him I had plenty of experience with toys without making things awkward? "I… think it'll be okay?"

His expression softened, and he said with infinite patience, "It will definitely be okay, Hawk. We'll go slow."

"Er… no. Please don't go slow," I blurted. "I, um… I'm *prepared*. For this. Tonight. In the shower. Earlier."

Jack's lips twitched like he thought I was adorable, which wasn't a huge upgrade from awkward, but I'd take it. "That's good. But baby, there's more to it than that. If you're going to take me, we need to stretch—"

"I have toys," I blurted. "So many. Like… several. More penises than a man needs in a lifetime. Large ones, and jumbo ones, and vibratey ones, and one that's supposed to be kept in the freezer that caused a whole incident when Aiden decided to feed a 'Popsicle' to the dog and I pretended it was Porter's. But I have never had a *real* one, and I would very much like to."

Jack's eyes were wide as my words came to a stumbling halt, so I added a few more, just in case. "Specifically, *your* penis. Inside me. *Now*." I coughed, mortified. "Wow, that nervous babbling thing is real, huh?"

Jack threw his head back and laughed, which might have worried me, except the next second, he lurched up and fused his lips to mine.

"You," he whispered between biting kisses. "Are. The best thing. In my life."

Oh. Well. That was okay, then.

Jack's hands moved down to my hips to yank at my boxer briefs. I grabbed his shoulders to keep from flailing and did my best to inhale through my nose while he took complete possession of my mouth.

He pulled off long enough to finish stripping the last of our clothes off until I finally, *finally* got a look at his dick.

Surrounded by a nest of dark golden curls, it arced up over his lower belly. The tip was deep pink and shiny with precum. His balls hung low and brushed against his inner thighs as he moved toward me again. A strangled sound escaped my throat, and saliva filled my mouth.

When Jack's eyes met mine, I made another needy noise. Words were gone, and all that was left was stark desperation.

He took his time with me, kissing up my body again and teasing my shaft with the tip of his tongue. I vaguely wondered what would happen if I came suddenly on his face with a relieved and disappointed cry. Thankfully, he moved up and replaced his mouth with his hand, slick with lube from a bottle he'd fished from a bedside table drawer.

His hand gripped and squeezed me while his mouth whispered words of encouragement into my ear. "You're so hot like this. Beautiful... Those noises you make... Bird... Fuck. You're killing me..."

I arched up into his grip, begging for more, but instead of his slick hand moving faster on my cock, his fingers moved behind my sac to my hole. My entire body tightened in anticipation.

"Shh," he urged. "Relax, baby. That's it. So good. Spread your legs for me. Good, good... Breathe..."

Jack's fingertip slid inside of me. I clenched around it and arched my head back, silently screaming for more.

"Christ, you're tight." Jack's words sounded slurred. "So hot. Fuck, Hawk."

His slick finger moved in and out, reaching deeper and searching for just the right spot. "*J-jack*. There. Oh god. Right there."

Sweat beaded at my hairline. My entire body was locked and loaded, every cell ready to open fire on my nerves.

"So fucking sexy," Jack continued, almost talking to himself. His long frame was stretched out beside me, and his mouth searched for new patches of skin on my neck to nibble as he slowly added another finger inside me. And then another.

I sucked in a breath and tried to relax again, but it was tricky when my whole body was overloaded with sensation. Pleasure and fullness and a quick bite of pain that, strangely enough, only heightened the pleasure. My legs shook and my abs quivered from the effort of keeping my body together when it wanted to fly into a thousand pieces.

"Want you, Jack," I murmured, because those words for this man had become such a part of me that now they played on an endless loop in my brain. "Want you, want you, want you."

"You have me." He pressed a kiss to my belly button. "I'm right here with you, baby."

The urge to ask him to fuck me again sat frozen on my tongue as I realized those weren't quite the right words. This wasn't fucking—just like Jack had said it wouldn't be. This was bigger. More tender. More consuming.

"Then please." I pushed at his wrist, wordlessly telling him I needed more than fingers now. "Please."

When Jack finally moved to put on a condom, I watched with rapt attention. I didn't want to miss a moment of this experience. There was always the chance that he would rethink this—*us*—and I wanted to remember it with such clarity I could replay it over and over in my memory.

He moved between my legs and pushed my knees up toward my chest before grabbing a pillow and shoving it under my hips. When his gaze landed on my prepped hole, heat flared in his eyes.

Turning Jack on was the hottest thing I'd ever done.

I reached down to grab his thigh as he began to push against my opening. His eyes flicked to mine with a question, and I nodded, because whatever he was asking, the answer was *yes*.

He was big enough to stretch me past my comfort level. I tried to hold back the wince, but he noticed anyway. "Deep breath. That's it. Push out. Good. Oh fuck, Hawk… fuck, you're so tight. *Fuck*."

His voice lowered to a gravel-filled groan that went straight to my dick, filling it again almost painfully. I concentrated on breathing and reminded myself to trust him. He moved at glacial speed until he was finally, blessedly, inside me.

A part of me.

We both groaned together until he moved his mouth over mine and licked into my mouth. His physical possession of me was complete and overwhelming, deliciously mind-melting and body-numbing. With each slow stroke across my gland, he fired up my nerves until everything in the lower half of my body was ready to explode.

I grabbed at his back, his hips, his legs, anywhere at all I could stay connected to him while he thrust in and out of me. My eyes stayed wide open so I could take it all in—the sight of his cock disappearing into me, the clench of his stomach as he thrust, the sweat-slick sheen of his skin as he held himself under control, the cherry red of his lips from my stubble.

"Jack," I cried, arching into his thrust. "Jack, I'm so close."

I reached for my cock, but his hand got there first, stroking it in time with his body's movements until I hung right on the precipice, clinging to sanity with the tips of my fingers because I didn't want this to end…

"Come for me, Bird," Jack said, his gaze searing mine. "Fly for me."

His growled demand made an end-run around my brain. I let go—I *jumped*—and my release crashed over me with breathtaking force. "*Jaaaaack.*"

The noise he made when he came deep inside my body vibrated through me like a tuning fork, and in that moment, the two of us were perfectly, completely aligned. One being. One cataclysmic event.

His body shook on top of mine as the aftershocks of his orgasm washed through him. Somehow, his arms had made their way underneath me to hold me tightly to him, and our damp bodies stuck together from neck to groin.

I love you, I thought, but the words were stuck in my

throat. Instead of saying them, I moved my hands slowly up and down his back, carding gentle fingers through his hair and pressing soft kisses against the side of his face.

We stayed like that for a long moment—I would have stayed there forever—but Jack inhaled sharply like he was emerging from sleep and pressed a quick kiss to my lips. He grabbed the base of the condom and pulled out of me, murmuring something apologetic, then climbed off the bed to dispose of it.

I closed my eyes.

Please don't let this be awkward. If nothing else, please let him not regret—

"C'mere." I opened my eyes to see Jack's outstretched hand and soft smile. "Let me wash you off in the shower, sweetheart."

I took Jack's hand and let him help me up, then lead me into his bathroom. He'd turned the water on, I realized belatedly. The room was warm and steamy, and—

"Oh my god! You *did* get the rain showerhead. And the tile…" I stepped forward and ran my hand over the gleaming surface.

Jack wrapped his arms around me from behind. "And you thought I was just luring you up here to steal your virtue."

I leaned back into him, letting the rumble of his laughter settle my nerves. "I was hoping you were."

When we got under the jets, he pulled me in for another kiss. This time, it was lazy and sweet. His hands meandered down my bare back to my ass, where he interrupted himself halfway through a squeeze. "Shit, are you sore? I didn't even think."

"It's not my cheeks that are sore," I said, summoning a teasing smile. "I'm okay."

"You'd tell me if you weren't, right?"

I nodded. "That was… phenomenal, Jack. More than phenomenal."

"Good. Good. You know, it wasn't... I mean, I don't usually..." He cleared his throat. "Sex isn't always like that. That intense. That... meaningful. Christ, I sound like an idiot. What I'm trying to say is, I know what we did was special to you because it was your first time, but it was special to me, too."

I buried my face in his neck and squeezed my arms around him as tightly as I could. "It wasn't just special because it was my first time. It was special because it was *you*," I said softly.

He picked me up and pressed my back into the cold tile. I wrapped my legs around him to hold tight while our kiss deepened, and the hot water jets continued to pummel us from every direction.

When we finally felt the hot water running out, Jack quickly washed both of us off with soap and dried us with thick cotton towels before urging me under the covers and following me there. We naturally came together again in a close snuggle with my head on his chest, where his heart thumped reassuringly.

His fingers toyed with my hair until I was on the verge of falling asleep.

"I love you," he said softly. "More than anything."

He'd said the words to me before, always in a familial or friendship way, but this was different. This was *in love*. This was the shit Webb had been talking about up on that mountain. And for the first time, I felt like I had that, too.

So, I forced myself to be courageous. I leaned up and met Jack's eyes. "I love you, too. I have for a while."

"Is that right?" He bent his elbow up to prop his head on his hand and tweaked my nose ring. "How long?"

I grinned, propping my chin on his chest. "Well... *It came on so gradually, I hardly know when it began, but I believe it must date from my seeing...* that really sweet rainfall showerhead in your bathroom."

He laughed out loud. "Did you just misquote Elizabeth Bennet at me?" he demanded, making a little noise of satisfaction as he pulled me more firmly against his chest. "We are a matched pair, Hawk Sunday."

We are, I thought fiercely. *We really are.*

And if Jack and I lived in a movie or one of my *Pride and Prejudice* variations, this might have been the final scene, the fade to black before the credits rolled, the giant "The End" at the bottom of the page...

But real life wasn't quite that convenient.

CHAPTER FIFTEEN

JACK

"We are all fools in love."
~ Charlotte Lucas

MAKING love to Hawk Sunday was the best decision I'd ever made.

Nothing had changed, but everything had.

As I stood at the back of the kitchen at Panini Jack's a full week later, ostensibly mixing up a batch of sourdough but in reality playing a video montage in my mind of Hawk's smile, his little sighs, and the way his brown eyes remained soft and dreamy for long moments after I kissed him that first night we were together, I felt... settled. Secure in a way I hadn't expected to.

I felt *good*.

So good that it hardly mattered that Hawk and I had been like ships in the night this week, with Hawk spending most of his time up on Fogg Peak continuing his protest campout and me trying to keep up with the influx of Evola contractors and protest-tourists invading the town.

So good that when Crys had caught me singing "I'm Only Me When I'm With You," one of Hawk's favorite Taylor Swift songs, while I cooked earlier this morning, I'd laughed along with her teasing.

So good that even though Hawk and I still had a few things to sort out—namely, our conflicting opinions about the resort; my conflicting desires to take things slow for his sake and to have him officially move into my house *yesterday*; and one giant, bearded human conflict who hadn't answered my text earlier this week and would probably be showing up to the diner soon to challenge me to a duel over his brother's virtue—I could safely say that I was a relationship convert, and I was proud of myself for overcoming my fear so we could get to this place.

And that was, of course, when things started to get weird.

"Tom." Marla, one of my part-time waitresses, sidled up to my line cook, eyes brimming with excitement. "Guess who's got a date tonight."

Tom sucked his front tooth thoughtfully. "Better not be you, baby. I know you're angry I made that comment about your sister, but cheating is cheating."

"Hush. Not *me*." Marla slapped Tom's arm playfully. "I mean the Hollow's favorite romance-reading, mountain-saving activist. Hawk Sunday," she explained when Tom continued to look at her blankly. "He's got a date with Simon from Evola. Enemies to lovers, just like in one of his boo— what do you mean *shush*? I heard from…"

Tom whispered something urgent that made her dart a guilty look in my direction. "*Ohhh*. Wait, really? I mean. Ha. Can you *believe* the gossip in this town!" Marla said loudly. "And it's usually *super* wrong." She coughed. "I'm just gonna go do… things. Work things. Out there." She motioned back toward the dining room. "Okay, then."

"It's a business dinner," I told Tom. "Not a date."

"Sure, boss. Just a misunderstanding." Tom gave me a pitying look. "No matter what everyone in town is saying."

Everyone in town? "Don't be silly," I said, not sure if I was talking to him or myself. "Hawk and I are together. Everyone saw us at Pye Day."

"Well, yeah, but Hawk's still protesting, and you're still *not* protesting," Tom said reasonably. "And Hawk's only been back to work once since he, you know, gave his cherry speech and not at all since you two were holding hands that day. And Hawk and Simon are awful friendly. Makes sense how people would get confused, no?"

I scowled. *No*, it definitely did not. But I felt like arguing only made my case look weaker, so I clamped my lips together and mixed up a second batch of bread dough to keep myself from dwelling on this.

But after a third person mentioned Hawk's meeting in front of me—Milton Perry, that time, joking about how my "new beau" was "already stepping out on ya, eh, Jack?"—I could no longer deny that I was dwelling. I was dwelling *hard*.

It was not a date. Hawk and I had exchanged *I love yous*. We were together in every possible way: signed, sealed, and devirginated.

Even though he'd spent most of the week on the mountain, we'd managed to spend two of those nights together: one, where we'd been way too exhausted to do anything but make out, slow and lazy, before falling asleep in my bed, and another where I'd snuck up the mountain to join him in his tent... only to find that a whole herd of Mini Nature Scouts and their parents had shown up to pitch their own tents and join in the protest, giving us zero privacy to revisit our last sleeping bag adventure.

And maybe those hadn't been particularly fulfilling, but that was okay because Hawk and I had called and texted constantly, too—even more than usual. He'd ended every text conversation with a bat emoji, because the northern long-eared bat had become our symbol for delayed gratification, and it was a known fact that couples didn't have inside-joke emojis unless their relationship was in a good, solid place.

So, I was not going to descend into jealousy over this foolishness... But I mixed up a *third* batch of bread dough anyway and began kneading it a little too firmly.

Okay, fine, so I was a tiny bit jealous, but only because irrational feelings were irrational and this was my very first foray into a serious relationship. What I was not going to do was make my irrational reaction Hawk's problem.

I wasn't going to tell him what people around town were saying or speculate about how they'd even heard that this "date" with Simon would be happening. *Nope.*

I was not going to text Hawk in the middle of his meeting with the Environmental Committee to ask him to clarify the situation just to gain some reassurance. *Pfft.*

And I was sure as heck not gonna sit around dwelling on the fact that Simon was a good-looking man closer to Hawk's age, who shared Hawk's interests, and who Hawk had once called "cute." *Definitely, definitely not.*

I was going to be a mature adult, I thought as I pummeled the dough into submission.

Mature. As. Fuck.

But when Betty Ann Wolff walked in later in the afternoon, talking at full volume on her cell phone as she stood at the check-in counter waiting for her to-go lunch order, I decided that maturity didn't mean a man couldn't listen in when the town's second-biggest gossip began discussing his boyfriend.

"I'm telling you, Helena, I just talked to him at the Environmental Committee meeting, and our precious Hawk has gone soft. Mmmhmm. He actually said to me, point-blank, 'Well, Ms. Wolff, maybe we need to compromise. Maybe Evola could do some good things for this town. I bet Ms. Fortnum would agree.' Can you imagine? Plus, he's going out to dinner with that viper, and we all know what *dinner* is code for."

She paused for a long moment while I ducked down behind the counter—only because the kids' coloring menus needed to be organized and not at all so I could listen without skulking.

Hawk was considering a compromise? Right *now*, when the town was almost guaranteed to give him the "no" vote he'd been looking for?

Betty Ann sighed. "You're right. I s'pose Hawk's found his backbone about *some* things. And I'll grant you, he's doing good stuff with his Insta-what's-it. A little birdie told me that reporter, Genevieve York-Muller, might even come back to do a news feature on him. But you gotta remember, Simon's got more charm than any three men should have. It's like a dense fog of smarm settled over your inn since that guy came to town, and… *yup*. Hawk's too sweet for his own good. Not to mention, he boned Jack Wyatt last week, and that's enough to turn anyone's brain to banana pudding."

I scowled at her through the counter.

"Oh, yeah. Hawk can't keep a secret like some of us can," she said fondly. "That's why it was a smart move on your part not to fill him in on what the Hookers are doing. Might as well tattoo the words 'I have a cunning plan!' right on his expressive little face. I mean, look at the heart-eyes he's been giving Jack all these years." She chuckled. "Jack never seemed to notice Hawk was in love with him, but not for Hawk's lack of trying. It's amazing Hawk never got fed up and ditched him."

Wait, *what*?

What were Betty Ann, Helena, and the Hookers up to?

How ironic was it that Betty Ann was having a conversation about her excellent secret-keeping, at full volume, in a public place, with no regard to who might be listening?

And, most mind-blowing of all… Hawk had been in love with me for "all these years"?

He'd said he'd had feelings for me for a while, but *Jesus*. Here I was, needing reassurance after dealing with a single morning of Little Pippin Hollow gossip, and Hawk had held on to his feelings for years, never knowing if they'd be returned.

My man was even stronger than I'd realized, I thought with a rush of affection that swept away any lingering jealousy. And I was going to do everything in my power to deserve the love he'd given me.

"True story, bro," Ms. Wolff went on, almost echoing my thoughts. "So did you and the others go full-on Crochet Commando? *Excellent*." She accepted a bag of food Katey held out to her. "I heard Hawk and Simon are meeting at the Stag and Crowne later, so I… *Uh-huh*. Prime date location," she agreed grimly. "Oh, now that's an idea, isn't it? Tell Laura I agree with her. I wouldn't put it past him to be spreading rumors just for show. Mmm. Poor Hawk. *Someone* needs to keep eyes on the place, just to see if Simon tries to…"

The closing door cut her off as she walked outside, and I immediately popped up from the desk.

Simon tries to… *what*? What was Simon going to try to do?

And what the fuck was a Crochet Commando?

Crys brushed past me on her way to the credit card machine to run someone's card, trying to hide her to-go cup behind the bill folder as if I didn't know she single-handedly emptied my soda coffers daily. "Nothing to see here, boss."

"What do you know about Hawk's dinner tonight?" I blurted, still staring at the sidewalk where Betty Ann had disappeared.

She turned back to me in slow motion, a crinkle of confusion between her eyes. "The dinner with Simon? Is Hawk still planning to go now that you and he…?"

"Yes." I rolled my eyes. "Of course he is. Because it's a

business dinner. And because I'm confident enough in our relationship that I'm not going to be a jealous meathead." *Anymore*, I added silently. "I'm just… getting a weird feeling about it, but I'm probably being ridiculous. Carry on."

"You know…" Crys tilted her head. "Simon's super into him. I'm sure Hawk doesn't think of it as a date." She raised an eyebrow. "But does Simon?"

"Hawk will tell him—"

"Yeah. Of course," Crys agreed. "It's just… Okay, cards on the table, bossman. I was one hundred percent in favor of Hawk and Environmental Guy getting busy while he was waiting for you to pull your head out of your ass—"

"Pardon?"

"I mean, why not, right? Simon seemed nice, the two of them together could've generated enough heat to accelerate global warming, and when it was all over, Evola was gonna do what Evola was gonna do, and Simon was gonna leave town. No harm, no foul."

"Charming." I blew out a breath. "And you're telling me this *why*?"

Crys tapped a finger to her lips thoughtfully. "Because lots of things have changed around here in the past week."

"No shit. No matter what the gossips say, Hawk and I—"

"Yeah, not that," Crys said, waving a hand dismissively. "I mean the momentum of the battle has shifted in the Hollow. Public opinion about the development has turned decidedly in Hawk's favor."

"It has," I agreed slowly. And I couldn't help feeling satisfied about that either, despite my hopes for the resort, because what Hawk had accomplished in a matter of days was nothing short of miraculous. "He's fucking amazing, and people are listening. So?"

"Soooo…" She pursed her lips. "You can bet your ass *Simon* is listening."

I frowned, trying to read between the lines of what she

was saying. "And… what? You don't think Simon's a decent guy anymore? You think Hawk is in danger?" I tried to make this come out in a scoffing tone, but it was possible that my protective instincts made it sound more like a threatening growl.

"Easy, killer. Nobody's talking imminent physical danger. All I'm saying is that Simon is a cornered animal, and cornered animals are unpredictable. He could try to manipulate Hawk. Or make him an indecent proposal to trade sexual favors for business benefits. Or make it seem like they're on a 'date' so that it looks to the town like Hawk is betraying you, selling out on his protest, and falling in line with Evola…"

I opened my mouth to instinctively deny everything she said… then blinked. "Okay, way, *way* too many people in town know about this date-that's-not-a-date," I admitted. "Even in the Hollow, people don't tend to gossip about shit that hasn't happened yet."

"Mmmhmm. And if that's the case, Hawk needs someone to watch out for him. They're meeting at the…"

"Stag and Crowne," I said distractedly.

"Yep. Which happens to be a prime dating location." Crys gave me a look of wide-eyed innocence that might have fooled me… if she hadn't been using the exact same words Betty Ann had just used and hadn't been smirking while she said it.

I narrowed my eyes. "Okay, Chaotic Evil, be real. Do you actually think Hawk is in danger? Or did you overhear Betty Ann, and now you're shit-stirring just to see what happens if I show up at the Stag and Crowne and interrupt Hawk's business dinner like a chest-thumping caveman?"

She grinned. "I'm more Chaotic Neutral, to be honest. And I'm just providing you with all the data to make an informed decision. Now, table four's waiting for their receipt, and I don't want my boss to get upset, so if you'll excuse me…" She tapped the bill folder against her hand and walked off.

I stared at her back. I wanted to believe Crys was simply baiting me, but whatever else I doubted about her, she really seemed to care for Hawk. So although I tried to put it out of my head and remember that Hawk could take care of himself, I couldn't quite settle. I would have given a lot of money to have eyes on Hawk, or at least on Simon.

My phone weighed on my pocket like an anvil, just begging me to take it out and send a quick bat emoji text to the man I loved, but I knew he had an incredibly busy day planned, and I didn't want to distract him when I wasn't sure what, if anything, was going on.

I was contemplating the distracting powers of a *fourth* batch of bread when the universe did me a solid for the first time that day.

"Erm. Mr. Wyatt?" Katey said loudly from the kitchen doorway, using an overly formal tone I'd never heard from her before. "Are you free?"

I glanced up from the sourdough starter I was measuring. "Everything okay, Katey?"

She darted a glance over her shoulder and stepped fully into the kitchen, letting the door swing shut. "Yes! There are some Evola guys in suits here to see you," she whispered excitedly. "Said they have a *business proposition*. I put them at the big booth in the corner in case you want a little privacy. Hope that's okay."

I quickly washed my hands and straightened my shirt before heading out to greet them.

Katey was right—one of the men waiting in the booth was Simon himself, and the other was the marketing guy who'd spoken at the town meeting. "I'm Jack Wyatt," I said, approaching their table. "How can I help you?"

The words were polite enough, but when I gave Simon an

up-down and noted the extra care he'd put into his appearance—a *date* level of care—I couldn't help scowling.

Simon didn't seem to notice. He shot me a friendly smile. "Hi, Jack. I'm Simon Wentworth, and this is my colleague Nick Ormann, who is in charge of strategic partnerships at Evola. Do you have a few minutes to sit down with us? I know you're a very busy man."

After shaking their hands, my curiosity forced me to take a seat in the booth beside them. Nick had a large envelope in front of him, and Simon had a small laptop. "What can I help you with?"

Simon opened his laptop and clicked a few keys. "Actually, I think we might be able to help *each other*. One of the assignments our team has when we come on-site for an assessment like this is to identify local vendors we can partner with to provide a better experience for both our guests and the communities we come into with our resort concepts."

He turned the screen so I could see the marketing mock-up graphics.

"What am I looking at?" I asked, wondering if he had an idea to hire Panini Jack's to provide catering for any of the Evola meetings taking place here in town.

Nick slid the envelope toward me. "We'd like to offer Panini Jack's an exclusive contract to provide the food service at the high-mountain dining enclave."

I stared at them uncomprehending. "The... what?"

Simon pointed to his screen again. "As you can see, the resort design includes a quaint spot on top of Glassy Ridge where guests and visitors can stop to enjoy a one-of-a-kind local dining experience with world-class views. Right now, we're calling it Panini Jack's Aerie Grotto, at least internally, but we're open to ideas about that."

"Panini Jack's..." I swallowed, staring at the screen despite myself.

Sure enough, the design showed a tasteful, open-walled chalet nestled right on Glassy Ridge in a spot where Hawk and I had picnicked more than once. Its single-story expanse was surrounded by deep, wide decking featuring tables with umbrellas, comfortable chairs, and potted planters overflowing with colorful flowers. The stylized illustration even showed a few elegant patrons enjoying their fictional luncheon, and a few people stood propped behind easels on the edge of the deck, painting en plein air.

My breath caught. I didn't even know where to begin.

"I… don't understand," I said, mostly to buy myself enough time to determine how I felt about the ridiculous offer. On the one hand, I was flattered and couldn't help but wonder what it would be like to expand my business in partnership with a well-funded, high-end resort concept.

On the other… *what the actual fuck?*

It was a week before the town vote. Whether Simon knew about my relationship with Hawk or not, for him to suddenly be approaching a local vendor when he'd never mentioned such a thing before meant that he was running scared, just as Crys had said.

Simon turned the impromptu presentation over to Nick, who began explaining the details of the offer. I didn't even bother trying to make sense of his words when all I could think about was the betrayal Hawk would feel at this move by Simon and his cohort.

"Why me?" I asked, interrupting their pitch. "Why now?"

Simon clicked another few keys on his laptop and pointed to a spreadsheet complete with colorful graphs, but Nick was the one who continued the pitch. "Our team back in Boston crunched the numbers. You can see here on the first graph the overlap of the resort's target audience and Panini Jack's client demographic profile is significant. Which led us to this next assessment, which shows the profitability of our existing alpine restaurant concept menu items in comparison to your existing offerings. What this shows is the high likelihood of your existing menu dovetailing nicely with what we'd organically be searching for in this 'alpine lunch concept.'" He beamed at me.

Alpine lunch concept? Much like Hawk had at the town meeting just a couple of weeks ago, I wanted to say, *"But that doesn't answer my question."*

"Obviously, our legal department would need to have proof of some of our usual concerns," Simon went on smoothly, "such as financial stability, management organization commitments, including the plan to create a seamless expansion, and willingness to adapt your packaging to take into consideration Aerie at Fogg Peak's existing branding—" His phone buzzed on the table, and when he turned it over to check the display, his face fell. "Pardon me. I need to check this out. Nick, could you...?"

Nick took over the presentation again while Simon tapped out a message on his phone. Though I listened with half an ear to Nick's speech, most of my attention was on Simon.

"As Simon was saying..." Nick tapped another key on the computer, and the screen changed. "This is an initial proposal, not a legal offer... *yet*. We are confident from the backgrounding we did, though, that we can come to a mutually agreeable contract and move forward with a beneficial and profitable concept—"

"Just to be clear," I interrupted, "you're saying you want Panini Jack's because this is the type of restaurant concept you'd like to place in *that* particular position in the Aerie plans. Only in the *alpine* concept."

Simon set his phone down and nodded. "Exactly right, Mr. Wyatt."

Nick tapped the folder in front of me. "Inside, you'll find a summary of our proposal, as well as a list of action items we'll need your input on. In addition, you'll see Evola's partnership one-pager outlining the reasons why we find partnering with local vendors to be a mutually beneficial scheme, as well as a way to strengthen our commitment to invest back into the communities that entrust us with their land."

I nodded slowly. That part sounded fine. Excellent, really. The timing was suspect, but this was a generous mission for a company like Evola and would mean even more money for the Hollow.

"Impressive," I admitted reluctantly.

Simon seemed to relax a fraction. "Good. I'm glad you—"

"I have to ask, though…" I cut in. "There's been a lot of concern in town about the prospect of clear-cutting up on the Ridge. What will happen if the vote doesn't go through next week? If Evola has to submit a revised plan, is there a possibility for…" I consulted the paperwork. "*Panini Jack's Aerie Grotto*… to be located elsewhere on the mountain?"

Nick opened his mouth to respond, but Simon stopped him with a touch to his arm. Simon's expression hardened, though his voice remained friendly and open. "Unfortunately not. If the plans need to be changed, we will have to rescind the offer. Not because we don't value you as a partner and want your concept to be part of the resort offerings, but because the remaining acreage left for the resort footprint wouldn't allow as many dining concepts in the plan."

He closed his laptop and folded his hands over it before lowering his voice. His phone buzzed again, but this time, he ignored it. "Listen, Jack. I know you're close with a lot of people in town, and I know you're most likely going to be between a rock and a hard place in the vote next week. Nick and I *personally* understand if you need to abstain or even vote against the development. But unfortunately, our upper management won't sign off on partnering with a vendor who doesn't fully support the development." He shrugged apologetically. "They feel it shows a lack of trust, and what's a partnership without trust, am I right? I'm not saying this in any way to coerce or impact your vote, but as someone who's been in the Hollow long enough to feel a certain kinship with the people here, I wanted to give you a heads-up about what's at stake. That's not coming from Evola. That's coming from me as a *friend*. Do you understand?"

Nick frowned but kept his mouth shut, letting Simon lead the show.

Oh, I understood, alright.

I understood that Betty Ann was right when she said Simon was way more charming than any one person ought to be. I almost believed that he was genuinely worried for me *as a friend*.

And I also understood that there was absolutely no way I could vote *yes* to the proposal the town was currently considering. Not anymore.

To tell the truth, I'd already been wavering, mostly out of loyalty to Hawk. But after seeing Nick's schematic of Glassy Ridge without its thick, sheltering trees, I'd felt a tug of the same cold wrongness in my gut that Hawk must've been feeling about this project all along. And after listening to this mafia-style unconditional-support-or-else pitch, I couldn't imagine allowing Evola to come in and build so much as a tool shed unless the town was guaranteed a much higher level of oversight.

Hawk had been right all along. Our beloved wilderness area and the pristine views we all seemed to take for granted would never be the same.

Before I could open my mouth to politely decline, Simon's phone buzzed again. His face showed a flash of anger before he wiped it away and his pleasant smile was back in place. He leaned over and whispered something in Nick's ear that made Nick's forehead crinkle in concern before he caught me looking and shot me a smile meant to reassure me.

Simon reached out his hand for me to shake. "So sorry to do this, but I have to run. I'll leave you in Nick's hands for any questions you have. He's the best person to help answer them anyway. I really hope to see more of you moving forward, and I especially would love to see more of this"—he waved his hand around the restaurant—"incorporated in our resort plans. It's an exciting opportunity, and I hope you'll give it serious consideration. We'd be lucky to have you on the team."

After another genuinely friendly smile, he hurried out of the restaurant.

I could see why Hawk had started to change his mind about this guy. To ignore his own gut. It was very difficult to dislike someone who could be so charming...

But look at me, managing it anyway.

I glanced at Simon's retreating form before turning back to Nick. "I hope everything's okay. He left here in a hurry."

"Oh." Nick waved a hand dismissively. "Simon's always getting called in to take care of one thing or another. That's how it goes when you're the CEO's son-in-law."

My heart squeezed. "Simon's... married?"

"Shoot." He grimaced. "He'll kill me if he knows I was talking about his personal life. But just between us, yes, he's engaged, but Lacey can't plan the wedding until this vote is done and Simon gets back to Boston. I promise, though, Simon doesn't let personal connections impact his business decisions."

Ohhh, I highly doubted that.

Nick leaned forward and tapped my paperwork. "So... any other questions I can answer right now?"

I had about a million of them, but none of them had anything to do with the development.

Had I misunderstood Simon's motives? Had Hawk? And Crystal? And Betty Ann and Helena?

I doubted it.

Either Simon was attempting to cheat on his fiancée with Hawk, or he was manipulating Hawk the way Crys had suggested. If his fiancée's father was CEO of the company, the stakes were considerably higher for him than any of us thought.

As soon as Nick had said his goodbyes and made a final request for me to consider their offer, I tried calling Hawk on his cell phone, but he didn't answer. This wasn't wholly unexpected, since I knew Hawk planned to hike up to the peak after the Environmental Committee meeting today—another storm was forecasted to blow in overnight, not nearly as dramatic as the one from last week but bad enough that he'd suspended the campout for the evening and wanted to retrieve the protest signs he'd left at the top of the mountain —and the reception up there was terrible.

But I tried again five minutes later. And *again* five minutes after that, pacing back and forth across the mostly empty restaurant and staring at my phone, willing Hawk to pick up. The Environmental Committee meeting had finished more than an hour ago, and rain clouds were already gathering over town, giving the sky an eerie light. Why wasn't he back in cell phone range so he could prepare for his meeting with Simon?

"What'd your phone do to you, bossman?" Crys asked, coming up behind me a few minutes later.

I whirled to face her. "Crys, how sure are you that Simon is actually interested in Hawk?"

She rolled her eyes and grinned. "Seriously? This again? I'll take J-E-A-L-O-U-S for $1000, Alex."

"It's not jealousy. Simon's coworker just mentioned that he was engaged to a woman in Boston—"

Crys dropped her teasing look and became instantly more alert. "The fuck you say."

"—and I need to know, is it possible Simon's only been expressing professional interest? What are the chances that you misinterpreted what he wanted from Hawk?"

"Nonexistent," Crys said without hesitation. "He's making a play... or trying to look like he is. He stopped by

Hawk's campsite like four times. Once, he even brought Hawk a giant bag of gummy worms from Cleeward's Candies, which Hawk ended up sharing with the little kids, and I heard him say, 'I asked Marla Cleeward what kind were your favorite.' Plus, you should see his texts. They… *huh.*" Her eyes met mine and narrowed. "You know, come to think of it, I think every single text mentioned the project. It's not *what* he said; it's how he said it. But even his flirty emojis were all, like, leaves instead of water droplets. Plausible deniability." She sounded impressed and enraged at the same time. "Jack, what's going on?"

I shook my head. "I'm not sure exactly, but I don't like it." The bells on the diner door jangled, and I heard Katey greet some new customers, but I couldn't focus on work. Not now.

"You do know Hawk was never really interested in Simon, not even when he thought you weren't interested in him, right?" Crys offered.

"Yeah." For *years*, apparently, even when I'd been too blind and scared to see it. "I'm not jealous right now; I'm pissed that someone is trying to fuck things up for the man I love. And I know Hawk can take care of himself," I added, just in case she was thinking that, "but he shouldn't have to. Not while I'm around. At the very least, someone needs to warn him that he's dealing with a deceptive asshat—"

"Seems to be a lot of those around here lately," Webb grumbled sardonically from behind my shoulder.

I closed my eyes. *Of course* Webb picked that time to show up. Of course he did.

CHAPTER SIXTEEN

HAWK

"What are men to rocks and mountains?"
~ Elizabeth Bennet

My siblings had the worst timing.

I left the Environmental Committee meeting with my mind buzzing over all the things I needed to do before my dinner meeting with Simon.

I had to collect the protest signs I'd left at the Peak that morning since poster board and the soaking rain we were supposed to get tonight would not mix. I had to run by the library to pick up some flyer-printing supplies Mr. Yetzer had donated, which did a lot to mitigate my lingering annoyance with his gossipy ways. I had to run home to sort through the huge pile of laundry and camping supplies I'd dropped at the farmhouse that morning and find a more appropriate outfit for the Stag and Crowne. I needed to call Dora York to arrange a bigger room for our next meeting since my little Environmental Committee now exceeded the forty-person capacity of the small room we'd been allotted, even with several members inexplicably absent. And if I got all of that other stuff done, I *might* have time to stop by the diner just long enough to kiss the supportive and patient boyfriend I hadn't seen in thirty-three hours and make plans with him for later tonight since I was missing him like crazy and our adorable text conversations were *not* cutting it.

As I walked out to my car, I fantasized briefly about canceling my meeting, kidnapping Jack Wyatt, and taking him home to do all sorts of unspeakably delicious things to his big, naked body—probably on the front porch, at least for the first round, since I didn't have the patience to make it all the way to his bed... but I couldn't.

Support for Save Fogg Peak had grown so exponentially that if we kept our momentum going for another week or so, I was confident Little Pippin Hollow would vote a resounding *no* to the proposed development, and the Peak would be protected.

The Hawk I'd been at the town meeting a few weeks back would have rejoiced that the mountain would remain the same... but lots of things had changed in a very short time, and my dreams had changed along with them.

Last night, lying in my sleeping bag on the mountain while Jack worked the closing shift at the diner a few miles away, I'd thought a lot about the future—mine, his, *ours*, even the mountain's. I was still pretty short on specifics, but I knew one thing for certain: any happy ending where Jack's dream got sacrificed for mine wasn't *my* happy ending anymore.

Protecting the Peak by having it stand unchanged as a testament to the past was as deeply rooted in my own fears as Jack's anti-relationship bias had been rooted in his. And for us to really move forward together, I had to consciously let go of that fear like Jack had. I had to believe there was a solution where both of us would be happy. And I had to commit to doing the work to get there, even if it meant stepping out of my comfort zone and becoming a guy who knew about sustainable design.

Like Marco had told me the other day, "It's one of those

compromises folks make when they commit to each other." It turned out when the old dudes weren't measuring their genitals, they were pretty fucking wise.

Unfortunately for me, all of this wisdom meant keeping my plans with Simon tonight. I wanted the dang reports he'd been dangling over my head for weeks, and I wanted to get his thoughts on delaying the vote until Evola could come up with an amended proposal.

And *then* I would get back to the business of kidnapping my boyfriend for front-porch sex shenanigans.

Needless to say, when I got Em's text needing a favor just as I got to my car, I was not feeling receptive.

EM

Gracie says she needs your help up at Fogg Peak near the old footbridge.

I unlocked my door, sat inside, and banged my forehead gently on the steering wheel.

Help with what? I'm meeting someone for dinner and I have a billion errands to do first.

EM

IDK? She said it's important and asked me to find you, but I'm babysitting the Preswick twins at the movie theater.

Another message came in, practically on top of the last.

EM

Should she be on the mountain with a storm coming? I'm worried she... Shit! Popcorn situation. Later.

I quickly typed out a reply:

Wait! Give me Gracie's number!

But when a full minute passed with no response, I knew I'd missed my window.

I banged my head a little harder and whimpered, waving a mental goodbye to the possibility of a visit with Jack before my meeting. Then I started the car and headed to Fogg Peak.

I couldn't *not* go. Gracie was a sweet, helpful person who'd become passionate about the resort development, but her judgment was sometimes… questionable. It was equally possible that she "needed my help" making a TikTok of the gathering rain clouds by the historic footbridge and that she "needed my help" because she'd sprained her ankle, panicked, and messaged Em instead of calling 9-1-1.

If I hiked up the much steeper, craggier, and lesser-used Rock Cut Trail, I could make it to the footbridge in half the time. Then I could help Gracie—or call in appropriate help if it was an actual emergency—get her *and* my signs off the mountain before the rain began, and still make it to the meeting with Simon.

But when I got to the Rock Cut pullout, I was shocked to find I wasn't the only one there.

"Ms. Fortnum?" I demanded, pulling my car in beside her SUV and the group of Hookers assembled there. "Mrs. Williams? Is this why you weren't at the Environmental Committee meeting?" I glanced dubiously up the steep trail. "Were you… hiking?"

The Hookers exchanged a look.

"Not hiking," Mrs. Thorndyce said. "We were, ah…" She glanced at Ms. Fortnum and made a rolling hand motion.

"Having a Hooker bonding ritual," Ms. Fortnum inserted smoothly. She patted the yarn bag at her side.

"Yes," Ms. Williams agreed. "Yes, indeed. Working on some… pesky toe closures." She gave me a beaming smile. "It's been marvelously uplifting."

"Putting some good vibes into the mountain," Phillip

Vincent said with an eyebrow wiggle. "For longevity and vitality."

A woman in the back of the group snorted. "We were putting something in *something*, that's for sure."

"Oh, god." I squinted at Helena. "Please tell me you guys haven't started doing naked things on the mountain where the Mini Nature Scouts could see you."

The Hookers had been known for topless knitting in the past, but I'd never heard of them doing it outside like this. I envisioned myself on a hike with the kids, pointing out a grove of ancient trees... only for them to get an eyeful of ancient *something else.*

Gene Reddy laughed and clapped me on the shoulder. "Not this time, young Sunday. Not this time."

I blew out a breath. "Did any of you happen to see Gracie Hubbard up there?"

Helena shook her head. "No... but then again, we didn't go all the way up to the summit. We were... over by Coster's Meadow and then came the long way back around the old logging trail."

It seemed strange that they'd headed over that way where the only interesting things to see were the Evola surveyor's trailer and the town's large pumpkin patch... which, admittedly, would be in full bloom right about now.

Rather than asking them more details of their pumpkin-patch ritual—because with my luck, they'd answer—I shoved my feet into my hiking boots I'd left in the car and grabbed my spare day pack, checking to see if I had enough water and my first aid kit. I really wished I hadn't left the stuff sack containing my strong flashlight and radio at home with the rest of my camping gear.

"Awful late to be heading up now," Helena said with a frown. "And you're going alone?"

I glanced up from my pack. "I have to check on Gracie. She's out here by herself and doesn't have much hiking experience." I surveyed the thick clouds on the horizon. "Plus, I need to get my signs under cover."

She pursed her lips and studied me. "Thought you had a date with Simon tonight?"

"A date?" I wrinkled my nose in confusion. I wasn't surprised she knew about my dinner plans—somehow, Ms. Fortnum knew more about the happenings in Little Pippin Hollow than anyone—but that also meant she'd probably known Jack and I were together before *we* had. "I'm not going on a date with Simon. I don't think my boyfriend would enjoy that very much."

"See?" Mrs. Williams jabbed Ms. Fortnum's arm with her elbow. "Told you Hawk was loyal."

"To Jack? Of course I am. Simon and I are meeting for a business dinner. He promised to show me environmental studies on Evola's last couple of big projects," I explained. "Hopefully that'll help us figure out what a good compromise would be here in the Hollow. Personally, I'm thinking something smaller, further down on the mountain—"

"Compromise," Helena sighed. "Hawk Sunday. You kids today with your wacky ideas."

I rolled my eyes. "The people of the town need the financial boost from increased tourism. You run an inn—an inn where the Evola folks have been staying for months," I pointed out. "You understand the need for revenue *and* for compromise."

"Hmm." She sniffed. "If you say so. I think it's gonna take more than that. But don't worry, Hawk. We have your back. The Hookers have assembled."

She'd said that before, more than once. I couldn't help thinking that if they had my back, they'd have been at the Environmental Committee meeting instead of doing some midafternoon sex ritual, but I appreciated the thought.

I waved goodbye and headed out, concentrating on foot

placement as I covered loose, scree-covered terrain as quickly as I could.

When I got to the place where Rock Cut Trail intersected Glassy Creek Trail, I heard the low rumble of thunder in the distance. Thankfully, it wasn't raining yet, and the clouds moving in weren't particularly menacing—just enough to cool the air as I climbed higher on the mountain.

About a hundred yards before I reached the part of the trail that crossed the historic footbridge, I saw a flash of turquoise behind the tree line—not a color normally seen in nature, at least not around here.

I stopped in my tracks and opened my mouth to call Gracie's name, but she waved frantically and pressed a finger to her lips, urging me to silence.

What in the world?

At least she looked healthy—she was standing, all four limbs and head intact, waving so wildly her "Peaky4Life" T-shirt rode up to expose the high waist of her hiking shorts... shorts that were soaking wet and plastered to her body like she'd gone wading.

As I approached her, I looked cautiously around for some unseen danger that necessitated silence—an animal, maybe? There were black bears in Vermont, though not generally on the Peak—

"Shit." I let out a soft curse as Gracie grabbed my wrist and yanked me off the path into her hiding spot.

"Gracie," I hissed. "What—?"

"Shhhh. Hawk, listen," she whispered. "The Evola guys... they're d-destroying *everything*. We have to st-stop them. I have a video, and we need to p-post it all over Instagram—"

Sweet Jesus. This rescue mission really *had* been about a video?

I thought longingly of the 3.5 delightful minutes I could have had with Jack and tried to tamp down my annoyance.

"Gracie, we need to get off the mountain before the rain comes. You're shivering already—"

I unzipped my jacket and began removing my backpack so I could give it to her. It wasn't particularly warm, but it was better than nothing.

"N-no, Hawk." She glanced toward the path, then dragged me further back into the dense thicket of trees. "Evola is *here*. Right now. The surveyors were messing around, I think, bringing their equipment up *way* higher than they were supposed to, a-and… just watch the video. Please? Then we need to… you know, collect evidence or whatever before the rain washes it away. I watch the *Murder, Mystery, Makeup* videos on YouTube—"

I sighed impatiently, ready to cut her off, then stopped myself.

I fucking *hated* it when people made assumptions about my capabilities based on my age or what they thought they knew about me. I'd be livid if someone was that dismissive to Em. It would be quicker just to watch the video and *then* strong-arm her down the mountain to safety.

Besides, if she really had seen something, I could mention it to Simon at our meeting and make sure he took care of it.

"Fine. You put my jacket on, and I'll watch," I agreed.

Gracie handed me her phone and obediently took the jacket as I hit the Play icon.

The video was hard to follow at first, mostly bouncing trees while the phone was steadied, but then it zoomed in to a figure. It took me a few moments to recognize Simon Wentworth himself standing next to a muddy 4x4 vehicle—the kind that was used lower down the mountain by Evola's surveying team but absolutely prohibited this high up the trails. The vehicle had clearly taken out the historic footbridge and now lay in the debris pile half submerged in the rapidly running Glassy Creek.

"Listen," Gracie urged in a hushed voice.

In the video, Simon was holding a handheld radio, pacing behind the wrecked 4x4, and the voice that emerged from the speakers was tinny and partly covered by the rushing water but unmistakably his.

"… how the fuck does a vehicle like this wind up with two flat tires and you didn't notice? And don't give me shit about rocks, man. This is an all-terrain vehicle. It's designed to— Look, enough with the bullshit. I asked you to take out the bridge quietly, not to leave your fucking 4x4 lying in the fucking creek like a big fucking neon sign that says 'Evola was here.'"

He listened to the person on the other end for a few breaths. *"Oh, really? And how do you expect me to haul it out of here by myself in the rain? You guys need to get back up here with the pickup and tow this— What do you mean the pickup has flat tires, too? Well, what about the… Motherfucker! All of them? Then bring the heavy equipment, for god's sake, and— No, not now. Wait until full dark. Bring a whole crew if you need to. Their expenses will be paid. Everyone will be off the mountain because of the storm. If we can pull the vehicle out before morning, no one will know it was us. They'll think the bad weather took out the bridge."*

He kicked a rock on the ground and sent it pinging into the side of the 4x4.

I scrambled to make sense of what I was watching and hearing.

Gracie must have seen me struggling because she paused the video and grabbed my arm, forcing me to meet her eyes. "Hawk. Evola sent their guys up here to take down the bridge to stop people from being able to get to the top of the mountain without having to go through the creek."

"You were coming down from Glassy Ridge," I realized, glancing at the screen and judging the camera angle.

She nodded. "Taking a couple more pictures of the storm clouds rolling in. I was heading back down, and I stepped off the trail for a second to… well, to *p-pee*… and then I heard the engines and then his huge *crash*, and I was scared, so I stayed out of sight in the bushes. And then I saw *that* and t-texted Emma because I didn't know what else to do. The creek is running really high after the last few rainstorms, and I had to go maybe half a mile downhill before I found a place to cross that was sh-shallow…" She glanced down at her wet shorts and corrected herself. "Shallow-*ish*. But no one's gonna cross it going uphill while the b-bridge is out. Especially not after more rain falls tonight."

"And if they can't cross it, they can't get to the top where the best views are," I said, blowing out a breath. "And…"

"And we won't be able to p-protest up there anymore," she concluded. "Which means reaching fewer people with our message in the week before the vote."

"Damn it."

I was trying not to mourn the loss of the beloved bridge until we were back down the mountain and safe, but it was hard. If I'd thought I'd known what anger was a couple of weeks ago, it was only a pale ghost of what was rising in me now.

How fucking *dare* Simon and his minions do something like this? The betrayal of it, the injustice of having someone come in and steal a piece of the Hollow's heritage, was infuriating.

I suddenly wished I'd taken a jiujitsu class or two because I really, *really* wanted to kick someone. Namely, Simon.

Gracie was still shivering violently in my jacket, so I fished the survival blanket from the First Aid kit out of my backpack along with my water bottle. I found a fallen log for her to sit on and focused on getting her warm and hydrated. Once I wrapped the blanket around her, I met her eyes. "You're okay. You did good staying hidden." I glanced back down at her phone. "What happens next? Is Simon still up here?"

"I think so? I haven't seen him come in this direction, but he might have taken another trail. There's m-more of the video, but it's basically him talking about stuff I don't understand."

She glanced over her shoulder to make sure no one had come upon us without her notice. We were still alone. She hit the Play button again.

"Jesus Christ, I'm supposed to be on my date *right now, remember? After I spread the news around town, all it would have taken was a few blushes, a quick stolen kiss, and the two of us leaving the restaurant together, and everyone would believe Sunday was on our side."* Simon paused. *"I don't give a shit if you approve of my methods, asshole. It was working! And I was thisclose to getting Jack Wyatt to sign a contract that would have put him in the palm of my hand, too. Now I'm up here dealing with your fuckup."*

Simon argued back and forth with the other person, and when he paced away from the creek, I couldn't make out his words. But he paced back in time for Gracie's phone to pick up his next statement. *"...don't care what it costs. And no one tells Lacey or her father about this, do you understand? It never fucking happened. This project has already taken so long she's started making noises about canceling the wedding."*

"Who's Lacey?" Gracie whispered.

"I don't know," I murmured. I suddenly wondered if there was anything I *did* know about Simon Wentworth. "But I'm for damned sure going to find out. First things first, though, let's call for help—"

I pulled my phone from my pocket, but Gracie already knew what I was going to find.

"No service here," she said with a grimace. "Up the trail, closer to the creek, I was able to send Em a message, but as soon as I got a little further, it disappeared again."

"Right. Okay. I don't suppose you can make it back to your car on your own?"

She swallowed hard and glanced with wide eyes in the direction of the trail. "I could t-try? But what if I run into any Evola guys?"

"Never mind," I said, quickly making a new plan. I didn't want Gracie on the trail alone, scared and shivering as she was, with a storm coming in to make the terrain more diffi-cult. Frankly, I wasn't sure I could get her back down to my car without help if the rain picked up. "Come with me. We're going to find Simon and his *radio*, we're going to find shelter, and we're going to get someone up here to help us."

But first, I was going to get an explanation.

CHAPTER SEVENTEEN

JACK

"My courage always rises at every attempt to intimidate me."
~ Elizabeth Bennet

THERE WAS nothing quite so volatile as an angry Sunday… except, in this case, an angry Wyatt.

I'd managed to sidetrack Webb from whatever kind of glove-slapping come-to-Jesus he'd been planning when he first walked in by uttering five simple words, "I think Hawk's in trouble."

In an instant, Webb had tabled his issues with me and demanded details, so I'd filled him in on what little I knew and suspected about Simon and his scheme.

"Hawk's still not answering," Webb said for the third time in as many minutes.

"Try him again," I instructed.

The pile of papers on my desk scattered as I grabbed my keys, but I didn't stop to pick them up. I was too consumed with the need to beat Simon Wentworth into the ground and then bury his body where nothing but rabid wildlife could find it.

Did northern long-eared bats eat humans? If not, perhaps they'd make an exception.

"According to our family tracking app, Hawk's last location was the pullout for the Rock Cut Trail on the northern side of Fogg Peak, two hours ago," Webb said, checking his phone as he followed me back to the dining room. "Why would he be there instead of at the main parking area for one of the easier trails? And why isn't he calling us back?"

"I don't know," I said, responding to both questions. "He's supposed to be meeting Simon for dinner soon. He should have been back in cell range long before now. Maybe he got delayed." I waved to get Crys's attention, and she excused herself from a customer to head toward me.

"Or he's ignoring our calls," Webb finished.

"Hawk wouldn't ignore my calls," I said without thinking.

"Oh really." Webb raised an eyebrow. "And remind me why that is, exactly?"

I pretended not to hear him. "I'm leaving for the night," I told Crys. "You all set here?"

"Katey, Tom, and I will manage," Crys assured me. "Go warn Hawk."

I pulled Webb back through the kitchen and out to my truck. "Rock Cut pullout, you said?"

"Yeah. But I'm thinking we should head to the Stag and Crowne. If Hawk's running late, we could have a little chat with Simon before Hawk even gets there." His voice was the kind of angry rumble he got only when someone he loved was threatened.

I understood that growl on a fundamental level now.

"Let's head to Rock Cut first and see if his car is there, then double back to the restaurant." I hopped in the truck and started the engine, making sure Webb was inside the vehicle before jamming it into reverse. "Keep your eye on his location."

I drove through town, gritting my teeth against the urge to

speed, especially when thick raindrops began spattering the windshield. Webb remained silent, except for the periodic side-eye looks he sent me, which spoke volumes.

I glanced out my side window. Despite the rain, two little girls were riding on plastic unicorn toys in the fenced front yard of a white clapboard house. Two grown women stood under the cover of a wide front porch, watching the girls and laughing at their antics despite the mud covering both girls and the toys they were riding on.

Finally, I couldn't take the tension in the truck anymore. "Fine. You win. I'm in love with your brother," I blurted. "He's in love with me. We're together."

"No shit." He folded his arms over his chest and sat back in his seat, utterly unsurprised. "Good thing I wasn't waiting to hear it from you."

"I texted you earlier this week!"

"You texted, 'Hey, drop by the diner soon? Wanna run something by you.' That's what you say when you wanna debate the pros and cons of a riding lawn mower, Jack. Not when you're shacked up with a man's baby brother."

"Look, what did you want me to say? I know how you feel about Hawk, and I could venture a guess as to how you'd feel about Hawk ending up with *me*," I said darkly. "I wasn't gonna ask for your blessing, and I sure as fuck wasn't gonna ask your permission. Hawk's an adult—an adult who's recently been knife throwing, I might add, and who wouldn't hesitate to remind me of that fact if I *was* foolish enough to ask his big brother for permission to have a relationship with him. I prefer my essential organs to have as few holes as possible."

"You're wrong," Webb said.

I shot him a look. "I assure you, I am very averse to puncture wounds."

He rolled his eyes. "Not that, dumbass. You said you

know how I feel about you and Hawk together. Clearly, you don't."

"Huh?"

"Jesus. And they say *I'm* dense when it comes to emotions. You're my best friend, fucker. I..." Webb stretched his neck from side to side, like Hawk did when he was uncomfortable. "I love you. Why *wouldn't* I want Hawk to be with a good guy who works hard and protects people he loves? I'm just annoyed that Luke says I was the last person in town to realize you two have been 'mutually pining' for years." He smirked. "Though, gotta say, I still figured it out before you did."

I realized my jaw had dropped, and I forced it shut. "But... wait. If you feel that way, why were you pissy when you walked into the diner just now?"

"I wasn't *pissy*," he scoffed. "I'm a grown man, Jack; I don't *get* pissy. I may, however, have been... *justifiably annoyed*." He threw up his hands. "Dude, my best friend just fell in love, and he somehow managed to con the kindest, most loving human in Little Pippin Hollow into falling in love with him, too, but no one even mentioned it to me. Not a postcard. Not a telegram. Not a folded-up note shoved in my locker." His tone was joking, but the hurt in his voice was clear. "If my family wasn't solidly dialed in to the Hollowan gossip network, you and Hawk would have had seven kids before I knew anything."

"Kids?" I goggled at him for so long I missed the light change at the corner of Parrish and Stanistead, and the car behind me laid on the horn. "Whoa. No one said anything about kids."

Webb snorted. "So I take it that's a no on children, then? Have you and Hawk talked about it?"

"No. I..." I shook my head to clear it. "We've been together a week, Webb, and he's been up on a mountain most of that time."

"Hmm. So you're a *yes* on kids?"

"No! I…" I paused.

I honestly had no clue how I felt about having children. I had no desire to parent solo, that was for sure, and since I'd never intended to have a relationship, that put children squarely in the column of "Nice, But for Other People," along with luxury yachts and the ability to write poetry. Now, though, I was having to rethink all of my columns. Because I didn't *not* want children, and if Hawk wanted them…

Well, Hawk deserved the fairy tale. The happily ever after, just like Elizabeth and Darcy.

Nothing in life was guaranteed, of course. People changed. Dreams changed. Bad shit happened when you least expected it. There would *always* be things that Hawk and I disagreed about and maybe even argued over. Chaos and mess and misunderstandings. But…

I thought of those little girls, riding their muddy unicorn tricycles with joy on their faces and decided maybe the chaos *was* the fairy tale. Maybe happily ever after was just the beginning of the story.

"…I think I'm gonna have this conversation with your brother first," I told Webb firmly.

He laughed.

"But I'm sorry I didn't tell you about us sooner," I offered as we approached the Rock Cut pullout. I shoved his shoulder. "And I'm glad you're with me now."

"Me too," Webb said. He pointed at a familiar rain-soaked Toyota parked in the dirt lot. "Especially since it looks like my brother has a death wish. What was he thinking, hiking up the steepest trail on all of Fogg Peak in the rain?"

I threw my truck into Park, then reached behind me for my hiking boots and rain jacket. "If he's here instead of meeting Simon, there's gotta be a good reason."

I shrugged my jacket on and stomped my boots a few times to get the feel of them after wearing chef clogs. Thankfully, I kept my hiking gear in the back of the truck these days for impromptu visits to my boyfriend in his tent.

Webb, on the other hand, only wore running shoes and no rain gear. "Stay here," I advised, waving him back inside the truck. "There's no point in you getting drenched when I can look for him on my own, and I'll go faster without you. If I can't find him… I dunno. Maybe the timing belt in his car was acting up again and he caught a ride back to town with someone else. We'll look elsewhere."

Webb eyed me warily but eventually nodded and hopped back in the dry cabin of the truck.

I tossed him my keys. "If I'm not back in an hour, it means I found him holed up somewhere to wait out the storm. I'll stay and catch a ride with him, and you can head home."

"Or it means you got hurt," Webb pointed out.

I waved my phone. "Plenty of places to send a text up there. It might just take a while. If you still haven't heard from us an hour or so after the storm ends, send someone up. Just don't put anyone in danger."

"He says while heading up a mountain in a rainstorm." Webb huffed.

"That's different," I said with a wink before turning and making my way to the trailhead.

I hiked fast, filling my rain jacket with steam from my overly warm body until I was too hot to keep it on. I stripped it off and tied it around my waist in hopes it would continue to keep my shorts dry at the very least.

By the time I got to the spot where Rock Cut merged with the Red Trail and headed up toward the summit, my shirt stuck to me like plastic wrap, but I didn't mind. The cooling effect was worth it.

There was no sign of Hawk anywhere, but I wasn't sure what that meant. Was he even up here at all?

I'd come too far to turn back, though, so I kept going at least until I came to the footbridge that spanned Glassy

Creek… or used to. An all-terrain vehicle lay half in the creek, tangled with the broken remains of the wooden bridge.

"What the fuck?" I quickly pulled out my phone and texted Webb, but of course I didn't have service in this particular spot. Rather than fumbling around trying to find a patch of reception, I trusted that my phone would continue to try and send the message until it went through. In the meantime, I snapped several photos of the wreckage.

I could imagine only one entity responsible for putting motorized vehicles on a prohibited trail and, apparently, attempting to drive it over a narrow, wooden footbridge.

"Fucking *Evola*," I muttered aloud.

Was this what had brought Hawk to the mountain? But where the hell was he now?

I glanced across the rapidly moving water to the trail on the other side of the creek. Had he gotten stuck further up the mountain? Had he turned and taken another, easier trail back down?

Thunder rolled slowly through the sky, vibrating the ground underneath my feet and reminding me that anyone further up the mountain would need to take cover to stay safe if they knew what they were doing…

And no one, *no one* knew this mountain like my Hawk.

If he was uninjured and able, he'd take cover like he had when we…

I whipped back down the Red Trail until I reached the unmarked turnoff that led toward the caves. This was where he'd be, if he was physically able to get here. And if he wasn't… I didn't want to think about that.

Heavy drips of rain landed on my head from the trees above and slid down my face. I shoved my wet hair out of my eyes and squinted through the gloom and shadows, trying to remember exactly where the entrance to Kirkcaster was so I wouldn't accidentally pass it.

But it turned out, there was no way to miss it because the

interior of the cave was brightly lit, and a loud, familiar voice echoed through the opening.

"—Austen would be *horrified*. You don't *deserve* the name Wentworth! From now on, you'll be known around here as Simon fucking *Wickham*, for all your false charm and scammy, manipulative bullshit!" Hawk's voice softened. "Sorry for the cursing, Gracie."

I snorted, then bent over at the waist, braced my hands on my thighs right there in the rain, and took my first deep breath since seeing the wreckage at the bridge.

Wait, Gracie?

And *Simon*?

I put my celebration on hold and crept up to the mouth of the cave to peer in. A small fire crackled inside a stone ring at the edge of the cave entrance, and Em's friend Gracie sat huddled next to it, wrapped in a foil blanket. Hawk, meanwhile, paced nearby, gesturing wildly with his hands while he appeared to be *lecturing* Simon Wentworth.

"Of all the worthless, duplicitous... You're meant to be a caretaker of the environment, Simon! Instead, you've been destroying it—"

Simon Wentworth didn't look particularly charming at the moment. His light hair was a sodden mess that hung across his scowling face, his tidy clothing looked like he'd been rolling in mud puddles, and his toothpaste smile was nowhere to be seen. He sat against one wall of the cave with his arms wrapped around his bent knees, shivering.

But Hawk was okay.

Hawk was *better* than okay; he was *angry*. And angry meant alive and not gravely injured. It meant flame-bright and provocative, and gorgeous and fiercely capable, and a thousand other things that made me want to grab him and kiss him and hold him tight.

Simon sighed and laid his head on his arms. "I already agreed to your terms, Hawk. Can you stop your sanctimonious monologuing? I'm cold and tired, and I wanna go back to the inn."

"Then go!" he said, pointing in my direction without looking. "By all means. We've already made our agreement, so godspeed. I mean, an *experienced hiker* like yourself can probably get your ass down the mountain even with a sprained ankle, right?"

"Your fault I sprained it," Simon muttered. "You pushed me into the creek!"

"Oh, please. I called your name as I approached the creek, and you threw *yourself* in. You're just lucky I was too nice to leave you there."

"And then you threw a boulder at my leg—"

"It was a pebble," Hawk argued. "And only because you were trying to escape." He looked a bit guilty but lifted his chin in a defiant gesture. "And I already apologized for that. Meanwhile, *you* have not apologized for being a sneaky, underhanded, reputation-destroying liar who tried to cover up criminal trespass and destruction of public property. But sure, blame me for your misfortune. Next time I come upon a potentially unhinged person throwing a tantrum on the side of a mountain, I'll take the time to make some *soothing bird calls* to get his attention, shall I?"

Christ, I loved this man. Loved him beyond all reason and logic, exactly as he was, for all that he was, in all of his many moods. And it hit me, forcibly, that loving Hawk didn't make me vulnerable; it made both of us stronger. The man was melded into my bones permanently now, no matter what life had in store for us, and I was so fucking *glad*.

So, I did what any man in love would do when the object of his affections leaves him an opening like that.

I stepped closer to the entrance and let out my best attempt at a *soothing* Bicknell's thrush trill.

Hawk paused mid-rant and whirled toward me.

"Hey, Bird," I said, drinking in his sweet face, the face of my best friend, my partner in crime, my beloved. My soul mate. "How's it going?"

"Jack!" Hawk ran across the cave and threw himself against me, wrapping his arms around me. "Thank god," he murmured into my chest. "Oh, thank god."

I held him and inhaled the familiar scent of him, now edged in woodsmoke and the damp scent of the murky cave. "You okay?" I breathed against his ear.

Hawk nodded, his face still pressed against my wet shirt. "Better now, though."

I pulled his face back and met his eyes before kissing him tenderly and slowly.

He broke off with a happy sigh. "How are you here?"

"I came up here to warn you about Simon." My face was tight with a huge grin I couldn't hide. "Looks like I'm the last to know about a lot of things where you're concerned."

"Wha—oh." Hawk blinked, then bit his lip and blushed. "Well. Possibly." He coughed lightly. "Simon was manipulating me the whole time he was here. Worse, he was manipulating the town."

Hawk pulled me close to the fire to dry off before showing me the video of Simon ranting at the footbridge. When he got to the part about destroying Hawk's reputation in an effort to sway the town's voters, I clenched my jaw. And when Simon mentioned his offer to me, I shot the man a furious look.

"I was *never* considering your offer, asshole." To Hawk, I added, "I hope you know I wouldn't agree to something like that, Bird. I don't want financial security if it means selling my soul to get it. In fact, I don't want the resort to go forward at all anymore if it means letting guys like Simon run things. You were right, baby. Some things are more important than money."

The smile Hawk gave me was incandescent. "I didn't think for a minute that you'd agreed. But… what about a different proposal? One that will still bring tourists to the

Hollow but keeps all development off Glassy Ridge, ensures the town oversight of the development and construction of a brand-new plan, and removes Simon from the Aerie project entirely?"

"What?" I frowned. "But I thought you wanted…"

"I want a future that's better for all of us," he said softly. "You and me, and the whole town, too. I think a lower-mountain resort complex could be a good thing. Like you said, it would bring in jobs and tourism that can only help us become more financially stable. Just think what the taxes would do for the school system. And thanks to Gracie's excellent videography skills out by the creek—" He nodded at Gracie, who beamed back a proud smile. "—and a second video confession Simon gave us after we hauled his ass to the cave, that's exactly what we're going to get." He turned to Simon and raised an eyebrow. "Or else these videos will be made public to my Instagram followers. And nobody wants that, do they, Simon?"

Simon huffed out a disgusted noise.

"What? But… you're not making them public now?" I demanded.

Hawk shrugged. "The only actual crime Simon committed is colluding to destroy the bridge, which might result in him paying a few hundred dollars in fines. And there's no reason to believe Evola knows what Simon's been up to here. Simon swears he was acting alone because of the pressure he was feeling to impress his almost-father-in-law. It feels wrong to unleash social media hate on the company and open his fiancée to public ridicule when their only crime was trusting the wrong person. Instead, Simon's going to make an enormous donation to the Rebuild Friendly Footbridge fund I'm about to start; then he's heading back to Boston to tell his higher-ups at Evola that he's become a Peaky for Life." Gracie snort-giggled, and Hawk grinned. "You know, Simon, I seem to recall telling you at our first meeting that I'd change your mind about this development."

He turned toward Simon, and his grin faded when he saw that Simon was busy hopping toward the entrance of the cave.

I took a single step in his direction, but Hawk held me back with a hand on my arm. "Let him go. His crew is probably out there removing the 4x4 that's polluting our creek. If he wants to hobble back there, that's his choice. He knows we have the videos."

Simon clenched his jaw. "I'm not likely to forget. You're threatening to ruin my career—"

"You were actively attempting to ruin our mountain," Hawk shot back. "You made that choice. I just chose not to let you."

"He's going to get lost out there," I muttered.

Hawk shook his head. "I heard engines. All he has to do is hike back to the main trail, and they'll pick him up."

I moved closer to him and pulled him into my arms again, trying to ignore the wet layers of T-shirt between us. "Don't fuck with Hawk Sunday," I said softly.

"No kidding!" Gracie stood up and did a little dance. "He was sooo hard-core, Jack. Like, literal, actual *heroism*. I can't wait to post about… Oh, no! I can't post this at all, can I?"

"Not this," Hawk agreed. "But what if I made you an official collaborator on the Save Fogg Peak Instagram account? That way, you could post all the other pictures you take on your hikes or of our protests. You'd be doing me a favor."

"Seriously?" Gracie's big eyes went wide. She sniffed a little and pulled the emergency blanket around her. "This is the best day."

I met Hawk's eyes. "You think he's going to follow through on his promises?"

He nodded. "Honestly, it's the only way Evola stands a

chance at developing here. If we showed these videos to Little Pippin Hollow, they'd vote straight no on everything."

I leaned in and kissed him again. "I'm so fucking proud of you."

"Guys?" Gracie said, nudging Hawk with her elbow. "The rain has stopped. Should we make a break for it?"

Hawk let go of me and turned on his phone flashlight. "Absolutely. Lead the way."

Gracie and I did the same. Then I sent a second text to Webb, this one telling him all was well and promising to explain more later, and we set off down the Red Trail toward the main parking area, where Gracie had left her car.

It took us three times longer to get down the mountain than it normally would, and by the time we got to Gracie's beaten-up sedan, she was clearly exhausted.

"Why don't you let me drive? I can drop you off now and bring you your car tomorrow," Hawk suggested.

Gracie stood straight, her battered emergency blanket hanging off her shoulders like a queen's robe, and fixed him with a steely-eyed glare I hadn't known her capable of. "I'm not a *kid*, Hawk," she insisted. "I just helped you foil Simon's shitty plan to push this resort through. I'm capable of driving myself."

I coughed to cover my laugh, and Hawk pressed his lips together to hide his smile. "Understood," he said solemnly. "In that case, will you drop us at Rock Cut pullout before you go home?"

She grinned. "That I can do."

Once we were on the road, my phone pinged with several messages, all from Webb. The final one agreed to take my truck as long as I called him when I was safely home to tell him the story.

When Gracie dropped us off, she got out of the car to give Hawk a big hug. "Thank you for coming to help. I knew you would."

Hawk shifted awkwardly. "Of course. Peaky for life, right?" He reached out a hand to fist-bump.

"Always," she said, bumping it and jumping in for another quick hug.

As soon as she'd hopped back in her car and drove off, Hawk turned to me. The air was heavy with the leftover humidity from the rain, and the moon had risen fully, bathing the world in milky light. The scent of rain and fresh pine needles filled the air and the hush of latent drips falling from nearby trees formed a soft patter in the distance.

We stared at each other, and I'd just opened my mouth to ask if he was okay when Hawk suddenly shoved me against the hood of his car. I barely gasped in a breath before he attacked my mouth with his.

I grabbed him to keep from falling backward. He was all hands and tongue and hard dick lurching up into my inner thigh.

My hands roamed everywhere on his body without thought, shoving up his shirt and mapping the contours of his back and shoulders.

"Want you," he panted against my mouth. "So fucking much."

He yanked my rain jacket from around my waist and dropped it on the dirty ground before kneeling on it and fumbling at the waistband of my shorts. All I could do was stare down at him in the moonlight. Rock Cut was nearly impassible after the rain, and the chances of anyone driving to this out-of-the-way pullout at this time of night were infinitesimally small… but they weren't zero, which made it even more electrifying.

"*Oh, fuck,*" I moaned as he palmed my dick. "Hurry."

I yanked off my shirt and leaned over to pull his off, too. I wanted his skin. I wanted to feel him against me as much as possible.

His cold hands fished out my hot dick, causing me to hiss

at the sensation. Before I could finish making the sound, it turned into a groan of pleasure at the feel of his hot, slick tongue wrapping around my cock.

His eyes were locked on mine, liquid and hungry, and that sexy fucking hoop in his nose winked up at me from the shadows. Hawk Sunday was a fucking wet dream... *and he was on his knees for me.*

My fingers tangled in his hair as I begged myself to take it easy, to keep from shoving myself as deep into his throat as possible and taking everything from him.

Neither of us said a word. The only sounds were the faint slurps from his lips and tongue and my heavy, broken breathing. The raindrops in the trees continued their irregular patter, and the cool, damp air of the summer night curled around us.

I couldn't stand not kissing him. Even though his mouth felt amazing on me, I yanked him up and crushed his mouth to mine, kissing him again and again, tasting myself on his tongue, and wanting to imprint those mingled tastes in my brain forever.

My hands shoved down the back of his shorts and squeezed his ass cheeks. All I could think about was burying myself deep inside him and joining us together as closely as we could get.

I scrambled to think of what I could use as lube until I remembered that Hawk had started carrying it in his first aid kit several weeks ago after I'd provoked him at the town meeting. The knowledge that had once made me wild with jealousy was now driving me wild in a whole other way.

After gently pushing him away, I leaned over and grabbed the pack, rifling through it until I found what I was looking for.

"I'm negative, Hawk," I said quickly, knowing his status was most likely the same. "Was tested last month. Can I take you bare?"

His pupils were dark in the moonlight, and his hair was a tangled mess. He'd never been more beautiful to me. "Of course," he breathed. "Yes. God, yes. How can you even —*mmpfh*."

I kissed him hard again, trying to keep our mouths connected while stripping us both out of our shorts until they lay around our booted ankles. I pulled away and turned Hawk until he faced the hood of his car.

"Bend over, sweetheart. Just like that." The pale globes of his ass were easy to see in the dark. I squeezed some lube onto my fingers and reached between his cheeks. "Okay?"

His long, drawn-out groan was answer enough. I leaned forward and pressed a warm kiss between his shoulder blades. "I love you," I said into the now-familiar scent of his skin. "So much."

Hawk brought a hand back to grab me, squeezing my arm as he choked out the same words.

After stretching him as much as I had patience for, I slicked myself up and began to enter him slowly. "More, Jack, *fuck*. More."

Within moments, I was slamming into him, shaking the car and pushing grunts out of him as he begged me to fuck him harder. The freedom of connecting with him wildly like this, outside under the stormy night sky, was unlike anything I'd ever even fantasized about.

"You feel so good, baby. So good. I'll never get enough."

"Show me," he begged.

I clasped his hip with one hand and the top of his shoulder with the other while I fucked him until my brain was about to explode along with my balls. Hawk reached down and gave himself a few firm strokes, crying out as he came with my name on his lips just seconds before I lost the rhythm to my own release.

I shouted into the night and stayed pressed close behind him for several breaths.

I murmured words into the back of his ear, words about how much I loved him… how impressed I was by his loyalty and dedication… how beautiful he was, inside and out… and how I wanted to share moments like this with him for the rest of our lives.

I told him that I wanted the fairy tale.

When I finally pulled out of him, he turned around and held me, burying his face in my neck and pressing small kisses to the sensitive skin there.

"I want to go to your house and open all the windows to the breeze," he whispered. "I want to sleep in your arms and make love to you before breakfast. That's what happily ever after looks like today."

I ran my nose along his jaw. "Today?" I repeated, amused and utterly besotted.

"Mmhmm. You know, in books they make it seem like happily ever after is a single moment frozen in time. They never tell you what happens after the story ends. In real life, people grow. Dreams change. So maybe every day you get to write a new happily ever after. I just know I want all of them to be with you." He pulled back to look in my eyes. "Take me home, Jack."

So I did.

CHAPTER EIGHTEEN

HAWK

*"Follies and nonsense, whims and inconsistencies do divert me, I
own, and I laugh at them whenever I can."*
~ Elizabeth Bennet

HIDING in plain sight had always been my superpower.

"Where's Hawk? We're going to be late for the vote!"
Uncle Drew turned in place and nearly knocked over the
enormous planter of autumn flowers beside the back steps.
"Hawk!"

Em shrugged on her denim jacket over a white dress as
she clattered down the steps to the driveway. "Dunno. Maybe
he's riding with Jack."

Marco nudged her out of the way to claim the front
passenger seat of Drew's SUV. "We're in charge of bringing
Hawk! Jack's already there. *Remember?*" The look he gave her
was pointed, and it made me feel like I was missing
something.

I cleared my throat from the driver's seat, making Marco
jump and grab his chest. "Jesus, Hawk. Warn a guy."

Webb came flying out of the house, pulling Luke along by
the hand like a recalcitrant child. "Coming! Coming! Oh shit.

Aiden…" He turned to look behind him while Aiden's sigh came from the third-row seat behind me. He and I exchanged an eye roll in the rearview mirror.

"Seriously, Dad?" he muttered. The kid was acting more and more like an adult every day, and it was safe to say that I enjoyed this far more than Webb did.

"He's here," I called out the open window. "And so am I, FYI. If you'll recall, I'm the one who said 'load up' fifteen full minutes ago. And Knox and Gage are going in Knox's car. And Porter's already there. The dogs are fed, and the stove is off, and *can you all get in the car, please*?"

Marco patted my leg. "Doesn't matter if we're a few minutes late. You know Ernie York always needs to start with his 'call to order' nonsense. It'll be like skipping the coming attractions at the movie theater." He dug a half-eaten package of Thin Mints out of his glove box and thrust them at me. "Have a cookie. Don't let Drew see."

I jammed a cookie in my mouth as nerves jittered under my skin. I hated being late, and of all nights to leave my arrival up to my scattered family, this wasn't the one. Jack was waiting for me at town hall.

"Everybody ready?" I demanded when Webb and Luke had climbed into the back seat. "You coming, Uncle Drew?"

Drew swallowed. "Maybe you should let me drive."

That definitely wasn't happening. He drove like a drunken elderly snail on his best day. "Oooh, how about *no*? I bet you don't even know where your keys are," I said pointedly.

Drew's eyes widened in panic, and he glanced back toward the house again.

This time, I sighed. "*I* have your keys, Uncle Drew. *Get in.*"

Drew opened the back door and froze. "Wait, where's Reed?"

"Jesus Christ," I muttered.

The third-oldest Sunday brother had driven all the way up

from DC a few days ago since he was somehow technically still registered to vote in the Hollow. It was a very sweet gesture of support from my absentee brother, and it meant a lot to me, especially since I hadn't had a chance to talk to him much about the Save Fogg Peak campaign...

But if Reed was the one who made us late, I was going to disown him entirely and erase him from our family tree.

Half a minute later, Reed came racing out of the house with his dark curls ruthlessly slicked down, pulling a strange jacket that looked like an old-fashioned tuxedo coat over his broad shoulders. I opened my mouth and shut it again. For all I knew, this was how people dressed in DC. In any case, I didn't have time to question his fashion choices.

"*Now* are we ready?" I demanded. "Any other brothers, nephews, uncles, or in-laws I might have forgotten? No? Good." I pulled carefully out of the drive and pointed us toward town.

"Hawklet's gotten sassy since last time I was home," Reed remarked to no one in particular. "I like it."

So did I.

It had been two months since the confrontation with Simon on Fogg Peak. Two months of watching Evola meet our every demand. Two months of outdoor enthusiasts streaming into town to help raise money to rebuild the bridge, thanks to Gracie's work on the social media accounts. And two months of dating bliss with Jack Wyatt, spending every night in his arms and every day working alongside him in the diner, creating our happily ever after over and over again.

Tonight was the rescheduled vote to see whether or not Evola's revised plan, the one in which they kept the development off the high-mountain recreation areas, passed approval by the citizens of Little Pippin Hollow. With a stamp of approval from the Environmental Committee, Mayor York, and all of the other major players in town, I felt confident the resort plans would sail through tonight's vote.

"Slow down," Drew warned. "My brakes aren't all that great."

I opened my mouth to argue with him since he'd just gotten new brakes a month ago, but then I closed my mouth. If he said his brakes weren't great, who was I to argue? I drove more carefully down the road.

Luke shifted in his seat and met my eyes in the rearview mirror. "I still don't get why Evola would have canceled the original vote. I know everyone said they were worried after the bad PR from the social media campaign, but why not take their chances and *then* come back with an alternate plan if the original plan was voted down?"

Gracie, Jack, and I had agreed not to tell anyone the details of what happened on the mountain that night until after the new plans were approved and set in stone. We didn't dare risk our agreement failing because of loose lips.

Presumably, after tonight, we could at least tell our closest family members.

Em spoke up. "Gracie heard that Evola realized if the town rebuilt the historic footbridge and added an education piece about our local connection to a famous artist, the social media exposure alone could help make the mountain an even more popular destination for visitors, which would help the resort. I guess they decided to leave the wilderness as part of the attraction." She shrugged.

I bit my tongue against the instinct to disallow Evola even that much benign interest in our wilderness area.

"Pull over," Drew said suddenly.

"What?" I asked, glancing back at him in the middle row with a frown. "Why?"

"Because… because I said so," he said firmly. "And old folks don't need reasons. It's the only silver lining to this aging business."

"Smooth," Webb murmured, shaking his head.

My phone buzzed, but Marco grabbed it from the cup holder before I could. "Ah, ah, ah. No texting and driving, Hawk Sunday."

I pulled the SUV onto a small side road, tested the brakes carefully before coming to a complete stop, and threw it into Park.

"Now what?" I demanded.

"I... I left my glasses at the house," Drew said after a minute. "We need to go back."

I glanced in the rearview mirror. "They're on your head, Uncle Drew."

He reached up and felt the glasses in surprise. "Not *this* pair. This is my everyday pair. I need my lucky ones."

"I'm not missing this vote. Marco can read anything you—"

"Dammit, Hawk. Stop arguing with me and go back to the house. We could have gotten them faster than it's taking you to argue with me right now. There's such a thing as *too* sassy, you know."

I clenched my teeth and turned us around to head back to the house.

Once we got there, Drew took his sweet time finding his keys to unlock the door and an additional ten thousand years inside the house looking for his glasses. Meanwhile, everyone in the car waited in perfect silence, apart from the squeaking of my teeth as they ground together. Eventually, Em, Webb, Luke, and Marco's phones all buzzed at the same time.

Something was up.

"If we missed the vote, I will literally murder all of you in your beds tonight," I said between clenched teeth.

"I'm sure it's fine!" Em called. "Gracie said we're fine."

Drew came racing out of the house, waving his phone in the air. "They're preparing to vote! Let's get going."

I stared at him, my heart suddenly racing with the fear of

missing it. Several deep breaths didn't help. "If we miss this…" I snapped. Deep breaths be damned.

"Gracie said everyone's already saying it's going to pass without a problem. Stop stressing." Em said, reading from her phone.

I reached for my phone to see if I'd gotten a similar message from Jack, but Marco slapped my hand away. "What did I say? Eyes on the road, Hawklet."

Once we turned onto the road again, Drew reached up and plucked his lucky glasses from Marco's shirt pocket.

"What the fuck?" I asked. "You had them this whole time?"

Marco simply shrugged.

By the time we got to town, I was annoyed as hell and selfishly grateful last night had been my official final night living at the farmhouse. Starting tonight, Jack and I were officially living together, meaning change of address forms for me and all-new hiding places for my Girl Scout cookies. I couldn't wait. And I hoped he'd be willing to cut out from the post-vote party early so we could have our own little celebration because I knew just how I wanted to celebrate.

Jack and I had made good on our plan to have sex in every room and closet of his (*our!*) big yellow Victorian, save one— the little room he'd added onto the back of the house last spring, the one we'd jokingly called the "ravishing room."

Somehow, in a feat of carpentry only die-hard DIYers like my beloved and I could accomplish, when Jack had installed the door, he'd done it so the knob only opened from the inside, panic-room style. It had been stuck firmly shut ever since. But earlier today, Jack had texted that in a burst of nervous, pre-vote energy, he'd finally replaced the whole doorframe, and we could finally get inside, which felt symbolic somehow.

I couldn't wait to decorate the space. But first… there would be ravishing.

"Park here," Drew barked, shocking me out of my sultry daydream. "There won't be room any closer now that we're late."

Instead of reminding him whose fault it was we were late, I did as he asked and took the first spot I saw. When I hopped out and followed my family down the sidewalk toward town hall, there wasn't a single soul to be seen on the street or even loitering outside. We were very definitely late. I tried to suck in a calming breath…

And then we stepped through the foyer and into the assembly hall… and my breathing simply stopped.

The room no longer contained a motley collection of old, mismatched folding chairs from seventy years of potlucks and banners from centuries-old spelling bees. It had been transformed into a velvet-draped, candlelit *ballroom* filled with… Regency-era actors?

I blinked. This couldn't be heatstroke, right? It was September and decidedly chilly. But I couldn't come up with any other explanation for what I was seeing.

A woman in a coral-colored empire-waist dress with matching turban and feathers strolled by and gave me a polite curtsy, and I gasped. "*Ms. Fortnum*? What is happening right now?"

I stepped further into the room and turned in a circle. A woman in a deep blue dress and a sapphire necklace that set off her eyes—Jack's eyes—winked at me. "Melanie?" I whispered. Across the room, a gaggle of girls in white dresses with artfully arranged curls smiled, and one of them waved with way too much energy. "Gracie?" A man in a top hat and long sideburns nodded at me. "Holy… Mr. *Avery*?"

Not actors, I realized. None of them were. This was my town—my friends and family—all dressed up in costumes like something out of…

Em grabbed my hand. She'd shucked her denim jacket, and now I could see that she, too, was dressed in costume.

"Isn't this amazing? The whole town came together... They love you, Hawk."

Webb leaned in and whispered, "By the way, they already did the vote half an hour ago. It passed, thanks to you."

That was great, and later tonight or maybe tomorrow, I'd care very much about that, but for the moment, the vote was the last thing on my mind. My neck twisted around like an owl's, taking in the details of the room's decorations, the orchestra music coming from one end of the room, the chaotic mess of modern-day Hollowans crowding the dance floor, trying to do the Boulanger.

I pressed a hand to my mouth to hold back my laughter even as my eyes filled with tears.

This was the Netherfield ballroom.

This was *Pride and Prejudice.*

This was... magic.

This was someone not caring that they were doing something a little foolish, as long as it made the person they loved smile.

And I knew exactly who had made it happen.

As I approached the dance floor, the music stopped, and a tall man with broad shoulders I would recognize anywhere, anytime, even when dressed in formal Regency attire, made his way through the dancing pairs.

Jack Wyatt was stunning *always*, but dressed in a formal black tailcoat and buff-colored knee-breeches, with a crisp, white silk cravat tied in an elaborate knot at his throat and a dark beaver top hat over his sunshine hair, he made my knees turn to jelly.

He approached me formally, removed the hat, and made a deep bow. "Mr. Sunday," he said, his gravelly voice loud in the sudden pin-drop silence of the room. "In vain I have struggled. It will not do. My feelings will not be repressed. You must allow me to tell you how ardently I admire and love you."

I stared at him, my throat thick with emotion. I swallowed and tried to ignore all of our friends and family watching us.

Jack Wyatt had done this for me. Given me the over-the-top romantic fairy tale I'd wanted for years.

"You're tolerable, I suppose..." I sniffed, when I really wanted to scream, *"Did you just quote Darcy at me?"*

Jack's breathtaking smile broke through his attempts at formality as if he knew exactly what I was thinking—because he probably did—and his blue eyes sparkled with adoration and mischief. My heart nearly hurled itself out of the cage of my body and into his own.

"You are too generous to trifle with me," he whispered.

I stepped forward, reaching up to feel the intricate knot at his throat and the luxurious wool of his tailcoat lapels. "Baby," I said, keeping my voice soft enough to stay between the two of us. "I can't believe... You are..." I shook my head, unable to find the words to describe how happy he made me. How *understood* I felt when I was with him. "But you know you don't need to prove anything to me, right? I don't need *this*... when every single minute with you is—"

"I know." He brushed a finger over my forehead. "Of course I know. How could I not when you show me how much you love me every day? But I'm not always great with words." He gave me a rueful half smile. "I'm never gonna be Mr. Darcy, with the longing looks and the poetic language. And I never want you to doubt how important you are to me. You make the bad days better and the good days amazing, and... and you're my heart, Hawk Sunday," he said simply.

Seriously, if the man were any *better* with words, I'd melt into a puddle of goo right there on the floor.

I cupped his jaw. "I don't need you to be Mr. Darcy for me," I whispered. "I never did. I only ever needed you to be Jack. *My* Jack."

"Always and forever. That's a given." He brushed his lips across mine and winked. "Dance with me, Bird?"

When we kissed, the crowd of friends and family around us whooped with joy—as well as a few semi-lewd puns. We joined the awkward dancers attempting a cross between square dancing, the waltz, and the Macarena.

The orchestra earned their keep for two straight hours, playing killer sets of the most danceable instrumental music in history. Refreshment tables were filled with pitchers of punch, platters of cold meats and finger sandwiches, and fruit-flavored ices for the kids.

And when the room began to overheat from all the dancing and candlelight, Jack led me outside to the cool night air of the parking lot, which had been hung with fairy lights and dotted with chairs, flower topiaries, and enormous tree cutouts I recognized from the town theater group's production of *The Lion, The Witch, and The Wardrobe*.

"Much better," I said, fanning my face with my hand. Jack had removed his tailcoat at least an hour ago and stood in his shirtsleeves and waistcoat. I reached up to untie the knot at his neck. "You must be suffocating."

Jack gasped in mock outrage. "Hawkins Sunday! Are you *taking liberties*? Attempting to *steal my virtue*, right here in this..." He looked around at the paved ground, and his eyes landed on a potted chrysanthemum. "...garden?"

I laughed out loud. "Is it working?"

"Of course not," he lied, leaning closer so I could wrestle with the complex folds of cloth. "What would my mother say?"

I laughed harder. "She'd say, 'Good job, Hawk! Peony and I approve!'"

Jack pursed his lips, knowing this was true. "Still. This reminds me of that scandalous *Pride and Prejudice* variation you told me about last month, remember? The one where Darcy and Lizzy get it on in the garden while she's visiting Pemberley, and she's compromised, and there's the whole blackmail plot..."

"That was hardly *compromising*," I reminded him. "Darcy had already vowed his eternal love. 'Trust me with your body as I trust you with my heart, Elizabeth, and I will keep you safe always.' Remember? She already knew the marriage proposal was coming and they'd be together forever."

Jack covered my hands with his, trapping them against his chest. "Did she?" he said gruffly, but it sounded like he was saying something else.

Startled, I glanced up at him, my heart beating hard. "Yeah," I said softly. "Yeah, she did."

"Good." He grinned and dropped his hands to my waist. "Then, by all means—" he began.

But I should have known better than to expect a man to be left to his own devices in the town of Little Pippin Hollow because a chorus of male laughter sounded from the other side of the plywood tree to my right.

"Oooh! That's strong stuff, Norm," a voice that sounded an awful lot like Ernie York's said delightedly. He made a lip-smacking sound. "But it's good."

"We gotta rejoice that this vote is over and done," Norm Avery said, grumpy as ever. "Now the Hollow can find something new to get its knickers in a twist over."

"Nonsense. There's still the construction left to be done. Plenty to complain about there!" Conrad Pilkner sounded positively delighted at this prospect.

Jack caught my eye and bit his lip to stifle his laughter.

"I just hope they bring in better surveyors this time," O'Henry Brush said. "Last batch was downright incompetent. D'you know, they brought one of their off-roaders into Chuck's garage a couple months back? Engine flooded, whole front end smashed in, and—get this—every single one of those heavy tires was flat as a pancake and stuck through with long steel spikes. Looked like it had gone six rounds with a giant metal porcupine and lost. Weirdest thing I ever saw."

"My Bethy said those steel spikes were some kinda knitting needles. Dee-Pee-Enns, she called 'em," Norm Avery volunteered. "Said she saw 'em herself on Chuck's toolbox."

The others laughed out loud.

"Knitting needles?" Ernie exclaimed. "Nonsense! No disrespect to your Bethy, Norm, but I don't s'pose the ground is littered with knitting needles up on Fogg Peak."

They all laughed again at the impossibility of such an idea.

I stared at Jack in shock, and both of us darted a look inside the hall, where Helena Fortnum was holding court with a group of Hookers. She raised an eyebrow at me and lifted her glass of punch as if in a toast, coral feathers bobbing around her face.

"No," I breathed. "Or… maybe?"

"I think *probably*." Jack shrugged. "Stranger things have happened."

Around here? Stranger things happened all the damn time.

My brother Reed came outside to join us. "Getting too warm in there," he said, yanking at the collar of his button-down shirt. He, too, had taken off his tailcoat earlier.

"Thanks for coming," I said with a smile. "Even though none of us got to vote in the end."

"I hope you're not stressing about that," Reed said. He clapped Jack on the shoulder. "Your man here made very sure it was going to pass before he let them hold the vote early."

I looked up at Jack. "I know. I trust him."

"Good." Reed grinned. "Anyway, I'm glad I came. I wouldn't have wanted to miss tonight. And I needed to be in the area anyway for a work thing, so it was kinda… fate. It's been good to catch up with everyone. To eat Sunday Sundaes with the fam. To wake up in the same bed five days in a row."

"Getting tired of traveling for work?" Jack wondered. "Maybe you're ready to quit the consulting game and take on something more… permanent." He squeezed me tighter, and I leaned against him. "I highly recommend it."

Reed laughed hollowly and ran a hand over his hair, freeing his curls. "Yeah. Maybe," he agreed, though he didn't sound too enthusiastic about it. "Got at least one more project I need to finish before I can think about that." He darted a look around the parking lot courtyard. "Probably gonna have to get back to it real soon."

"You're planning on leaving already?" I frowned. "You know, we'd love you to move back here if you ever felt the urge, right? There are no Washington think tanks in the Hollow, but if you're ready for a change, maybe you could find something new to do. And you could spend more time with us."

"*More* time?" he teased. "That implies we've spent *some* time together. You've hardly been home this week, little brother! You're either moving shit to Jack's love nest, or saving literal mountains, or working all hours."

I felt my face heat, mostly at the pride in his voice. "So, let's hang out tomorrow. I'll take you knife throwing."

Reed's brows rose. "Knife throwing? That doesn't sound like my Hawklet. Surely that goes against some kind of *Pride and Prejudice* lovers' code."

"People change," Jack said, smiling down at me. "Grow. Mature. Horizons get broadened."

I laughed. "My friend Crys is into it. Along with jiujitsu, and casually quoting *The Art of War*, and figuring out which people in the Hollow are on a terror watchlist. You two might get along," I teased. "Since Porter's still, like, half-convinced you're a super spy."

Reed snorted dismissively. "Yeah, right. Don't I wish? But, uh… I might be interested in meeting your friend. Wait… Crys, did you say?" He glanced back into the hall, like he was searching her out.

"Yeah! But Crys volunteered to work at the Bugle tonight

so Ernie and Van could vote," I said. "Apparently, people aren't eligible to vote unless they're permanent residents, and Crys only moved here a few months ago."

Reed's eyes narrowed. "Interesting."

I shrugged. I still wasn't convinced the voting eligibility rules of Little Pippin Hollow were at all fair, but that was another battle for another time. I was just glad it had all worked out in my favor in this case. "Anyway, come knife throwing tomorrow and I'll introduce you."

"We'll see. I, ah… I might have to jump on that work thing I mentioned sooner than later," he said apologetically. "Besides, I'm not sure how I feel about knife throwing with you. I still have flashbacks from the time you tried pitching softball…"

I reached out and smacked him for bringing up such a bad memory of gargantuan failure on my part.

"Hey, hey," Jack said with a laugh, grabbing me around the waist to keep me from attacking Reed again. "He's improved." He lowered his voice to a whisper. "There was even a moment where he threw a rock at a local villain earlier this summer. Hit him right in the calf so the guy couldn't escape."

I barked out a laugh and tried to hide it a beat too late. Jack lifted an eyebrow in question.

"I may have been aiming for his back," I admitted.

Jack's smile widened. "Even if it's not perfect, it still works," he said, his face filled with warmth and affection.

I let out a happy breath.

He was right. This unpredictable life wasn't perfect. Neither of us was perfect.

But it worked.

And I couldn't wait for a lifetime of imperfection with the perfect man…

For me.

EPILOGUE
JACK

*"I declare after all there is no enjoyment like reading! How much
sooner one tires of anything than of a book! When I have a house of
my own, I shall be miserable if I have not an excellent library."*
~ Caroline Bingley

FOR THE FIRST time in a long time, I was nervous around
Hawk.

"No peeking," I warned him again as I pulled him
through my house—now, finally, as of last night, *our* house—
toward the locked room all the way at the back, overlooking
the spot where Hawk planned to start an herb garden next
spring.

The sound of his warm laugh took the edge off my nerves.
"How can I peek with a shirt over my face? And really,
couldn't this have waited until after breakfast? Or at least
coffee?"

"Hush. No. I'm a little bit excited," I explained before
reaching out to keep him from bumping the edge of the table
in the hallway. "Almost there."

"I get the feeling this isn't about the room. If it was about
the room, you would have shown me when we got home last

night, like you promised." Hawk's teasing grin was clear in his voice, even though I couldn't see his face. "And why would you blindfold me to show me an empty space?"

"Oh, it's about the room," I corrected, stopping him in front of the door. "It's definitely about the room. But what you didn't know—and really *should* have known—is that I am actually a *master* of DIY." A little smugness crept through in my voice. "I had the door installed properly all along."

"You what?" he demanded, voice muffled by the fabric. "You mean you could have been ravishing me in the ravishing room for weeks and weeks? Jack Wyatt, is our whole relationship a lie?"

"Not even a little bit," I said seriously. "And, in fact, when you think about it, this kinda proves that we were in a relationship even before I knew we were in a relationship."

Hawk turned to look at me, and though his face was hidden, I knew the exact expression he'd be wearing, the precise level of confusion in those honey-brown eyes. "Huh?"

"I've been taking the doorknob off every night for the sole purpose of keeping you out. I, uh… I did a thing," I admitted.

"A thing?" His voice rose on the last syllable. "Like the thing last night, where you got my brothers to wear top hats and Macarena to the *Sussex Waltz*? That thing? Because really, *Pride and Prejudice* fanaticism aside, I'm a simple man, Jack. I don't know how many more things I can han—*oh*."

I whipped off the shirt, and he stared at the still-locked door, taking in the hand-carved sign hanging on the wall beside it.

Hawk's Nest.

"Remy Fortnum carved it for you," I murmured against his curly hair before pressing a kiss there and inhaling the familiar scent of his shampoo.

"For us," he said, turning his head to look at me.

"For us," I agreed. I reached over his shoulder and

dangled a large, intricately carved brass key I'd ordered online back in May. "Go on. Open it."

After another questioning look up at me, Hawk took the key and turned it in the lock with a soft *snick*. He turned the knob, and before the door even opened all the way, the sound of his gasp filled the room.

Sunlight streamed in through the open curtains on two sides of the corner room, nestled between wall-to-wall built-in bookcases made from a rich dark cherrywood. Remy's carpentry skills and a lot of hours of work by both of us had turned my dream library plan for Hawk into a reality that exceeded all of my expectations.

Hawk took a step inside the room and then another. "What... what did you do?" He turned in a circle, taking in the books shoved cover to cover on the shelves. It was an eclectic mix of his own collection, the few books I owned, and as many *Pride and Prejudice* variations as I could scramble together from resellers and online auctions all over the country.

"It's not the library at Pemberley," I admitted. "But I made sure it at least had a rolling ladder."

Hawk spun around to meet my eyes, bringing his hands up to cover his mouth. Unshed tears filled his eyes as he gaped at me. "You built this for me?" The hushed reverence in his voice dispelled all of the remaining nerves in my gut.

"'If I could, I would have a library of my own,'" I whispered, quoting back some of the first words I'd ever heard him say. "'A whole room filled with books and a sofa and cookies... Hawk is in his reading room, you'd say, and you'd say it respectfully because when a whole room is dedicated to a task, suddenly, we realize it's important.'"

I saw his face change when he placed the origin of my words, and then his tears fell.

"Jack," he said, the single syllable filled with enough

shock and accusation and desire and promise to fill every volume in the room…

And love. Always, always love.

I pulled him toward me, wrapping my arms around him and kissing him deeply before pulling back to answer him in a rough voice. "The day we met, I committed those words to memory because there was something about you, even then, that was special. You were so unapologetically passionate. You reminded me that it was okay for me to be passionate about things, too."

"Baby…"

"Last fall, I started thinking… I wanted to build this for you. So that you'd know this house you helped me turn into a home was yours, too." I snorted a little at my own obliviousness. "So my *friend* Hawk would always have a reason to be near me. I built the addition in the spring because none of the other rooms caught the sunlight quite right and started building up a collection of books. Mr. Yetzer helped—he let me know which books you'd checked out more than once—"

"Oh, god, and I was so judgy about his lack of respect for privacy…" Hawk sniffled.

"This isn't about proving anything to you, baby," I said, remembering his concern from last night. "It's about wanting you to have everything you ever dreamed of. *Everything.*"

"If I have you, I have everything," he said in a voice wavering with emotion. "I love you so much. You don't need to do things like this for me. You're enough. I promise."

I smiled at him, running my fingers through his unruly hair. "I want to spoil you. Let me spoil you, Bird."

A tear escaped his eye, and I leaned forward to kiss it away. We hugged and kissed lazily before he finally pulled away with a sniffly laugh. "I want to see my new library! Show me everything. This is amazing."

I gave him a small tour, pointing out the books and explaining what they all were, showing him the sentimental objects placed here and there on the shelves between the books and indicating a few hidden storage cabinets at the base of some of the shelves.

"You did say you wanted a ravishing room," I teased. "You might need some space to store your... other collections."

He swatted at me before gesturing to the overstuffed leather sofa. "That's perfect, especially for—*ohmygod!*"

Hawk froze in front of the stacked stone fireplace that had been hidden on the right when he'd turned left upon entering the room.

"Is that a working fireplace?"

I nodded. "Real wood, just like the one in the living room on the other side of this wall. They share a chimney stack."

He walked over and ran a finger over one of the several picture frames on the deep wooden mantelpiece. "My dad and me on Glassy Ridge," he murmured. "And Webb with Aiden when he was just born... and here's the one of you and me at the diner when I first started working there in high school... oh my god, I remember this. Your mom made me squeeze a million lemons for Pye Day that year. Look at her laughing at me when I made a face at her... I love this." He turned to me with the emotion clear on his face. "I love you so much for this. I still can't believe it."

I pointed to the other side of the mantel, to a stack of empty frames. "Those are for the memories we haven't made yet."

Hawk threw himself into my arms again and shook with breathy sobs. I hadn't meant for this to turn into a crying fest, but I'd known it was something he'd needed. He needed to know how loved he was, how rich his life was, how much a part of my life he'd already been... and always would be.

He needed to know beyond a shadow of a doubt this was his forever home, here with me.

I moved us over to the sofa and pulled him down in my lap to hold him while he cried.

When he finally caught his breath, I pushed the hair off his forehead and kissed the warm skin there. "I want you to know I'm in this with you, Bird," I said softly. "I'm not going anywhere. This... you and me... we're as permanent and impenetrable as Fogg Peak. Do you understand?"

He nodded, but I could tell deep down he still didn't believe me.

"Do you still have that key?" I asked.

He fumbled in his pocket and pulled out the key ring.

"Look at it more closely," I murmured before kissing him again.

He inspected the key ring until he realized it had three smaller keys on it, as well as the key to the room itself. "What are these for?"

"There are three secure hiding places in this room. Each of those three keys unlocks a different hiding place."

His eyes lit up. "Where are they?"

I shrugged. "See if you can find them."

He scrambled off my lap and began inspecting the books carefully, going straight to the special leather-bound set that I'd specifically placed there as a fake lure. When they turned out to be simple Jane Austen collectible editions, I laughed. "Did you ever think you'd pout at a leather-bound copy of *Pride and Prejudice*?"

He flashed a rude gesture at me and kept looking. Finally, he found one of the hidden spots deep in the corner of one of the shelves. Thankfully, that cubby only held Thin Mints.

"Ah ha! Oh... *ohhhh*. It came prefilled with goodies," he said, ripping into the box and tossing two cookies in his mouth. "Mm."

He renewed his search for the next hiding spot. In the meantime, I walked over to the shelf next to one of the window seats and turned on the speaker system, showing him how to connect his phone to the system to play music. One of our favorite singers filled the room with his deep voice while Hawk continued his search.

He finally found the next hiding spot when he tested out the rolling ladder. It was behind a group of my own sci-fi thriller novels. After using one of the keys to open the hidden compartment, he pulled out a wrapped package.

"What's this?"

My face heated. "Open it up. To be honest, it's more for me than you. You, ah… might have inspired me with that story you mentioned a few weeks ago."

He climbed down off the ladder and unwrapped the box, revealing a Popsicle-shaped dildo.

"Oh my God," he breathed, his voice going a full 12,500 on the Scoville scale. "Will you… that is… can we…?"

"Oh yeah." I grinned. "Whenever you want."

When he continued his search, he found the hidden minifridge behind the door and the phone charging station I'd disguised in an antique cigar box.

"Where's the final hiding place?" he asked. "I've looked everywhere."

I knew he'd never find it if I didn't show him, so I pointed to the far end of the fireplace mantel. "Look under the edge of the mantelpiece for the keyhole."

I followed him to that side of the room. When the turn of the key triggered the nearby built-in to pop away from the wall, Hawk's eyes widened comically. "There's a hidden room?"

I gestured for him to precede me into the small space. It was about the size of a walk-in closet, sandwiched between the living room and the library and hidden between the main level powder room on one side and the large living room fire-place on the other.

It had an overstuffed chair with one of his favorite blan-kets on it, a reading lamp, and an ottoman. The warm red of exposed brick on one side was set off by the fresh coat of navy blue paint on the other. Fairy lights twinkled from the low ceiling. I nudged him further into the space before pulling the shelf-door closed behind us.

"It's a panic room," he said with a grin.

"It's a reading nook," I said, rolling my eyes. "You read too many books if you think you need a panic room in Little Pippin Hollow."

His eyes met mine, shooting a strange intense energy between us. "It's a sex dungeon," he said, nostrils flaring.

"Maybe. But first… it's something else."

I pulled out the small gold ring from my pocket and lowered myself to one knee. I hadn't practiced the speech, and for a single panicked moment, I wondered if maybe I should have come up with something polished.

But then I remembered Hawk didn't want polished. He wanted my heart… and he had it.

"Hawk Sunday, my best friend, my first and only love… will you marry me? Will you be my partner in work, in love, and in… whatever random environmental protests come our way? Will you be my family and build a life with me?"

Hawk fell onto the ottoman and stared at me in disbelief. "You… do you really mean it? You're not… this is real?"

"Of course it's real," I said. "But only if it's what you want. I was ready to elope with you the day I realized I'd been in love with you for years. But if it's too soon for you, we can wait. You can wear this as a promise ring or—"

I didn't get to finish the sentence. Hawk lunged for me, knocking me back onto the soft carpet and kissing my face off. We kissed for a long time, murmuring our love for each other, our promises and plans for the future, and our joy at finally knowing the hardest part, the time of insecurity about how the other felt, was behind us. Whatever troubles came our way from now on, we'd handle them together.

"I love you so much, Jack," he said when I finally slid the ring onto his hand.

"As I love you."

"Thank you for our reading room."

I grinned. "Oh, it's ours now, is it?"

"Of course. It is a truth universally acknowledged that a Sunday brother in possession of a good hiding place must be in want of someone special to hide in it with him... and I've found mine."

Psst! Wanna know what happens when Hawk and Jack finally get busy in the ravishing room? Go to https://readerlinks.com/l/4239478 to get a sexy bonus scene!

Want to see how Hawk's brother Reed gets his own HEA? Grab his mistaken identity, bodyguard, grumpy/sunshine, fake husbands romance here → https://readerlinks.com/l/4239087

And if you want more of the Sunday Brothers, check out the complete series here → https://readerlinks.com/l/3027689

A LETTER FROM MAY

Dear Reader,

This book is a love letter to friendship in all its many forms.

The kind of friendship that turns into passionate Hawk-and-Jack love, obvs, but also…

The kind that rushes in to help when life goes pear-shaped, and reminds you that you're strong and capable when you feel anything but.

The kind that says "talk to me" and doesn't get scared off when your emotions are a volatile whirlwind that could level cities.

The kind that brings you dinner when you didn't know you wanted it, and makes time to help you even when they're busy.

The kind that distracts you with pics of their cute babies, and cat memes, and in-depth discussions of the latest Pride and

Prejudice variations on their Kindle, just long enough for you to remember that things will get better.

I am a fortunate person in many ways, but the greatest blessings of my life are the people in it, and I am endlessly thankful for them.

And that includes YOU, Reader. Thanks for your patience in waiting for Hawk's book, and for spending your precious reading time with me. <3

Love,
May

ABOUT MAY ARCHER

May is an M/M author who lives in Boston. She spends her days planning vacations, mainlining diet soda, avoiding the gym, reading M/M romance, and when all other forms of procrastination fail, writing it.

Visit her website at <u>mayarcher.com</u> to sign up for her <u>newsletter</u> to hear about sales and upcoming releases, freebies and behind the scenes info and more! Or join her Facebook group, <u>Club May</u>!

facebook.com/may.archer.author

instagram.com/mayarcherauthor

amazon.com/May-Archer/e/B075JQVGLX

patreon.com/MayArcherRomance

bookbub.com/authors/may-archer

9 781964 685106